Return of the Mary Celeste

RETURN OF THE
MARY CELESTE

A Novel

STEPHEN HAYES

London · New Delhi · New York

Sūtra House
Independent publisher.
Uncompromising standards.

www.sutrahouse.com

London · New Delhi
New York

Cover Design: slideFactory + Sūtra House Creative
Book Design & Typesetting: Sūtra House Creative

Printed in the United States of America

First Edition

1 3 5 7 9 10 8 6 4 2

Publisher's Cataloging-in-Publication Data

Names: Hayes, Stephen, author.
Title: Return of the Mary Celeste :
   a novel / Stephen Hayes.
Description: First edition. |
   New York : Sūtra House, 2026.
Identifiers:
   ISBN 979-8-9853707-8-2 (hardcover)
   ISBN 979-8-9853707-6-8 (paperback)
   ISBN 979-8-9853707-9-9 (ebook)
Subjects: LCSH: Mary Celeste
   (Brigantine)—Fiction. |
   Suspense fiction. | Mystery fiction. |
   Historical fiction. | Mysteries.
Classification: LCC PS3608.A94

R48 2026

For my mother Alice, who first taught me to love books.

"In order to be a realist, you must believe in miracles."

— David Ben-Gurion

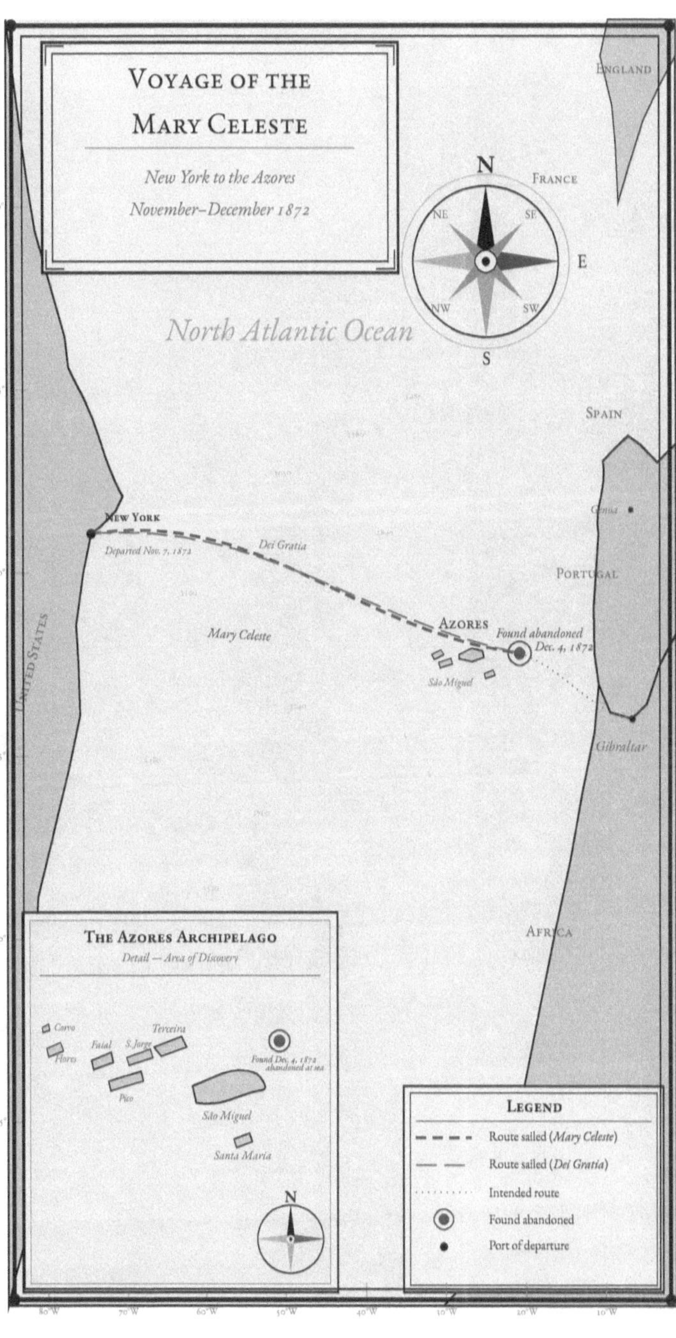

VOYAGE OF THE MARY CELESTE
New York to the Azores
November–December 1872
North Atlantic Ocean
N
NE
SE
NW
SW
E
S
ENGLAND
FRANCE
SPAIN
Genoa
PORTUGAL
Gibraltar
AFRICA
NEW YORK
Departed Nov. 7, 1872
Dei Gratia
Mary Celeste
AZORES
São Miguel
Found abandoned
Dec. 4, 1872
UNITED STATES
THE AZORES ARCHIPELAGO
Detail — Area of Discovery
Corvo
Flores
Faial
Terceira
S. Jorge
Pico
São Miguel
Santa Maria
Found Dec. 4, 1872
abandoned at sea
N
LEGEND
Route sailed (Mary Celeste)
Route sailed (Dei Gratia)
Intended route
Found abandoned
Port of departure
50°
45°
40°
35°
30°
25°
80°W
70°W
60°W
50°W
40°W
20°W
10°W
10°E

PART ONE

The facts:

Tragedy struck the brigantine *Mary Celeste* on the morning of November 25, 1872. The hourly log was later recovered from the deserted vessel. At 8 a.m. the last notation was made. By 9 a.m. no one remained aboard to chalk the next entry.

Something had terrified Captain Benjamin Briggs and his crew, prompting the seasoned skipper to make a decision certain to affect not only himself, his ship and crew, but his family as well—his wife and two-year-old daughter were aboard *Mary Celeste*. Much ink has been spilled in fanciful and scientific attempts to explain the calamity that engulfed this perfectly seaworthy ship, yet all that is known for certain is this: in a matter of minutes, Captain Briggs became convinced that the only way to save their lives was to order everyone into a hastily launched lifeboat. By giving the order to abandon ship, he also launched the greatest of all maritime mysteries.

* * *

On December 5, 1872, a month after leaving New York Harbor, *Mary Celeste* was found drifting on a calm and empty sea. The ship was in fine condition, perfectly intact with valuable cargo safely stored in her hold, but the crew and passengers had vanished. None were ever seen again.

Until now . . .

―――――――

Chapter One

Saturday: 11:30 p.m.

Lights and sirens approaching from behind caught Anderson Owens's attention. He'd been deep in thought and cruising to WCRX, where he hosted a syndicated radio program airing at midnight. When the lights and sirens of several squad cars and unmarked vehicles sped past, he sighed with relief; he'd been going well over the speed limit, and his unpaid tickets were accumulating. His thoughts had returned to his diabetic mother and her struggle to raise his late sister's headstrong daughter. A breeze was blowing the salty scent of the Gulf in his direction, and an April shower had appeared from nowhere just as a front tire blew.

Owens had driven this road hundreds of times in his best friend's borrowed Land Cruiser, and no amount of distraction, not even rain or an occasional blown tire, had compromised his driving, but today was different. It seemed the Land Cruiser suddenly had a mind of its own, refusing to respond to his pressure on the brakes. The vehicle slid off the wet coastal highway and plowed through a gravel embankment. Sarasota was mostly at sea level, but this section of the highway was elevated. Owens struggled for control, relying on rabbit-quick reflexes to steer around rocks and pine trees as he descended through underbrush, a bone-jarring ride to a drop-off where jagged rocks rose from the sea.

A branch tore away the wiper on the driver's side, making it difficult to see through the rain. When he burst into a clearing fifty yards from the sea, the headlights blinked off. The gloom made him question what he saw—the blurry image of a female in a white uniform. She sat on a boulder, her arms crossed over a satchel on her lap. The woman made no effort to move out of the way as the Land Cruiser raced toward her.

Adrenaline shot through Owens as his foot pounded the brake pedal in vain. It wasn't cold, but he was shivering, not that he noticed. He was trained to ignore such distractions and focused on controlling the vehicle, made difficult by the blown tire and steep descent. If he turned the wheel to the right or left, he'd shoot out into empty space and plunge down to the sea. His only hope was surviving a collision with the boulder. Surely the woman would jump out of the way.

She didn't.

Instead, she lifted a hand in his direction, a motion resembling a benediction. The Land Cruiser's engine suddenly died. Rather than stopping, the vehicle rattled and shook, and he felt himself held in place by the seatbelt, which most of the time he failed to engage. Momentum continued to propel him in her direction.

He steeled himself for the collision and was surprised when the vehicle abruptly lost speed and rattled to a halt a few feet from the boulder. He hadn't realized he'd been holding his breath until a hot burst of air exploded from his lungs, his ragged breath now accompanying the *plink-plink* of the Land Cruiser's cooling engine. He jumped out into the rain and pulled tangled dreadlocks from his eyes. "You scared the bejesus out of me. You okay?"

She didn't respond.

The Land Cruiser's lights were out, but the moon emerged from behind rain clouds and he could read the plastic tag above her right breast. Printed in black letters over the image of a cruise ship was a name: Sophia. "I could have killed you, Sophia. Why didn't you try to get out of the way?"

Without answering, she stood, set the satchel on the boulder and smoothed the white pants of her uniform. A gold locket dangling from a chain around her neck glinted in the moonlight.

"What are you doing out here all by yourself in the middle of the night?" he asked, wiping rain from his eyes with a wet shirtsleeve.

It seemed like an eternity before she whispered. "I was waiting for you."

He felt rather than heard the words; her lips didn't seem to move.

"I knew you'd come." She reached out and fondled his wet dreads before brushing them from his face.

Her fingers felt cool on his skin. "How could you possibly know *that*?" he asked.

She offered no explanation.

Before he could launch another question, she reached out and circled him with her arms. Her eyes closed and she slumped against him. "Time is running out, but I need sleep. I..."

She'd passed out.

Owens lifted her chin and studied her slack face. She radiated wholesomeness, hardly his type, so he was startled when he noticed his chest constricting and his scalp tingling, particularly where she'd touched him. At first, he'd believed her to be middle aged, probably because her hair was pulled into an old-fashioned bun, but up close he could see she was in her early twenties, twenty-five tops. She was slender with curves in all the right places, her hair was chestnut-colored, and she had the smooth skin of a porcelain angel. What wasn't angelic was the bitter smell on her breath. He suspected drug use, although she didn't look the type. She'd probably sleep a long time.

He carried her to the back of the Land Cruiser, transferring her weight to one arm to free a hand so he could open the back door, noticing she felt lighter than he would have imagined, not much heavier than a child. Her satchel was retrieved from the boulder and used as a pillow. A quick examination didn't reveal any obvious injuries, and the hospital was in the opposite direction. He made her as comfortable as possible in the back of the Land Cruiser.

He glanced at his watch; it, too, had stopped. The last time he'd checked he had thirty minutes until his show started, after which his listeners would be tuning in to dead airtime. His senses had quickened during the raucous ride to this spot, but now time seemed to have paused, the clouds overhead parting to reveal strips of celestial infinity in the firmament above.

He needed to get the Land Cruiser running and back on the road. After replacing the blown tire with the spare, he checked the muddy undercarriage; no broken driveshaft or blown seal. Everything looked fine. Popping the hood, he observed that the brake fluid reservoir remained full.

The fuel gauge also registered full. Nevertheless, he pulled the gas can from under the jump seat and tried to funnel fuel into a tank too full to hold more. Back behind the wheel, he once again turned the ignition key. This time the lights blinked on and the engine started right away, rumbling to life with a snappy *vroom*. Fortunately, the rain had departed as swiftly as it had appeared so driving without a windshield wiper would be a minor inconvenience.

His dreads were wet, and icy water was dripping down his neck. Owens stepped out and shook away the rain before engaging the Land Cruiser's winch, looping the chain around the trunk of a tree and pulling the vehicle up to the road. He stowed the gas can back under the jump seat. This took time, certainly more than thirty minutes. His cellphone wasn't picking up service, but Vicki, his producer, was smart enough to air a prerecorded episode of his show. His arm brushed against the sleeping girl. Before, he'd been too preoccupied to notice, but he did so now—she was bone dry.

*   *   *

Gravel sprayed the air as he raced into the parking lot of WCRX Talk Radio.

He thrived on tales of the bizarre and supernatural, as did his listeners; *The Anderson Owens Show* was picked up by more than forty affiliates. He usually rolled up to the station around 11:30, giving him time to settle in and read his emails.

Tonight, he was in a rush, but concern for the girl made him hesitate before dashing inside. He checked again, tapping her cheek lightly with his hand. She didn't respond. *She'll wake up and wander off to the bus stop down the road,* he told himself. *But what if she doesn't have any money?* He reached for his wallet and plucked out two twenties, stashing them in the breast pocket of her uniform. He checked his watch—now running again—but the time displayed was wrong; it suggested only a few minutes had passed. He'd reset it later, he thought, dashing inside.

He burst into the studio. "Sorry I'm late," he said to Vicki.

"Late?" Vicki glanced at the clock on the wall, showing twenty minutes to twelve. "You've cut it closer than this before. What happened to you? What's with all the mud?"

"Car trouble."

"Didn't know it was raining. You're on in twenty."

He couldn't explain how—he should have been late—but now there was no need to hurry. He went to the restroom to clean up. Not much could be done about his dirty clothes, but this was radio, not television. He washed mud from his face and hands while thinking about the girl sleeping in the back of the Land Cruiser. What had she said: *She'd been waiting for me, knew I'd come?* And what about *Time is running out?*

For who? For what? Crazy drug talk.

In the sound booth, he adjusted his headphones and tapped his Nikes on the rubber mat. This was the part of his day he enjoyed most, connecting with his fan family. Vicki pointed at the On-The-Air light.

> "Anderson Owens here. Welcome to WCRX Live Talk Radio's Anderson Owens Show. For the next three hours we'll discuss anything and everything, but our Holy Trinity consists of extraterrestrial events, supernatural occurrences and conspiracy theories. We're broadcasting to you on more than forty affiliates across the United States. Tonight, we're discussing Artificial Intelligence—pathway to a brighter future or a surrender to godless overlords?"

An hour later during a prerecorded commercial he dashed to the parking lot with a blanket from the hurricane cupboard near the lobby. The girl was where he'd left her in the back of the Land Cruiser. She didn't awaken when he opened the back door and covered her with the blanket before returning to his microphone.

By 2:50 a.m. he and Vicki were winding down for the night.

> "Time for one last caller. We have Damian, one of our frequent flyers, calling from right here in Sarasota, Florida. What's on your mind, Damian?"

> "Thanks for taking my call, Anderson. Say, something's going down here. Do you know why the CIA is hunting for a woman who disappeared from a cruise ship after it docked in Tampa yesterday?"

He thought about the unconscious girl in the parking lot. Minutes before the blowout, he'd seen police lights in the rearview mirror. He'd been concerned, but they'd sped past without pulling him over.

"Don't know anything about it. Tell me more."

"My cousin's a cop here. He just told me the police have put out an APB on a young girl in a white cruise ship uniform. He tells me they work with feds all the time, but here's the interesting part—always the FBI, never the CIA. The area is swarming with CIA agents. The cops have been ordered to hand her over to them if they find her."

Vicki cued in their theme music. He wrapped up the call and signed off for the night.

*　*　*

The woman was where he'd left her, still dead to the world. He pulled out his cell phone but paused. Was his curiosity enough to warrant a call? He decided in the affirmative and punched in a code known to only a handful of people. After two short beeps followed by a long one, he pressed a few numbers.

A computer-generated voice responded. "Authorization, please."

"*Sotto Voce* #Z902R0R8O. This is Nike. Anything unusual happening in Sarasota that I should know about?"

Another voice came on the line. "Good evening, Nike."

Much better. This voice—very real and sexy. "Yes, CIA operatives are hunting for a woman employed aboard *Island Empress*, docked in Tampa at 1500 hours yesterday. The target is known to have boarded a bus for Sarasota and is in the vicinity."

"Why do they want her?"

"Unknown currently."

"Can you keep me updated?"

"Yes." The usual economy of words.

"Thanks."

Owens hung up. His radio gig served as cover for another job— intelligence-gathering operative for an organization known by only a precious few. His callers usually stretched the truth but often provided useful information. This last caller was evidently on to something; here was a female in a cruise ship uniform, and the closest cruise port was Tampa, forty-three miles from Sarasota. She must be the target the CIA was zeroing in on. But why did they want her?

The hairs tingling on the back of his neck were working like a GPS, revealing an on-ramp to mystery.

Chapter Two

Sunday: 4:10 a.m.

The red and green sign above the 7-Eleven glowed against the night. Owens pulled into the empty parking lot, noticing the police cruiser pulling away from the bus station across the street. He circled to the back of the 7-Eleven and parked behind the overloaded Dumpster.

Along with the police, Feds were undoubtedly prowling about. He didn't want anyone spotting the girl in the back of the Land Cruiser. Until he found out why the authorities wanted her, he wouldn't turn her over. His career was built on sticking his nose where it didn't belong, and he'd had bad experiences with authority before. When confronted, he usually went out of his way to be as uncooperative as possible.

After checking once more to see that she was okay, Owens dashed inside and grabbed a cold Mountain Dew for himself and a hot chocolate for the young woman. She was still out cold when he returned with the beverages. He drove to the harbor and walked the short distance to the dock.

The sky showed little signs of the recent rain, and stars were bright overhead.

Isabella, a cypress-hulled schooner with square topsail named after a beloved Chesapeake Bay retriever, slipped across the glassy surface of Sarasota Bay just as the sun spilled its light over the eastern horizon. The eighty-five-foot ship, built in 1926, was captained by marine biologist Preston Sanders, his best friend. Sanders was sailing home after examining a new oxygen-deprived dead zone a mile off the Yucatán coast.

A lone seagull glided across the sky. Owens sipped his Mountain Dew and waited, thinking about that last caller and the unconscious girl he'd picked up. *Does she have friends and family who care about her? A lover? She doesn't look like a loner; why then was she sitting on that rock in the middle of the night—all alone?* His desire to help people had bitten him on the ass more times than he cared to remember, but he couldn't resist thinking that she needed help and maybe he could provide it, like the Sanders had helped him when he needed it.

Owens was eight, his younger sister still in diapers when their old man abandoned the family, leaving their mother to raise them on a teacher's salary. He'd rewarded her struggle to feed them and keep a roof over their heads by becoming a gangbanger, petty thief, and pothead. He landed in Juvy several times and would have ended up in the slammer sharing a cell with Chester the Molester if Sanders's dad hadn't taken him under his wing. He'd gotten arrested burglarizing the Sanders' residence and Preston's dad had taken an interest in him and turned Owens's addiction to books instead of drugs, kicking him in the ass when he needed it.

The Sanders were remarkable people, as accepting as they were wealthy, ever tolerant of the gawky kid hanging out with their son and haunting their private library.

They were generous as well. When disaster claimed them, Owens learned he'd been left a legacy—enough money to go to the college of his choice. He surprised everyone, including himself, by being accepted to several Ivy League universities, surprised everyone again by deciding on the University of Alabama at Tuscaloosa, known more for hulky football players than gangly scholars.

His best friend, Preston Sanders, had recently become engaged. Owens couldn't have been happier, but an all-too-human part of him worried this would expand the gaping emptiness he'd recently come to experience. He was pushing forty and beginning to wonder if he'd ever find that special someone.

Isabella glided toward the dock. Sanders cast a bowline at him, and before long *Isabella* was securely moored.

"Lookin' fine, bro. Giving up that director's desk has put the spring back in your step, wiped a few lines from your ugly face."

Sanders was two years older than Owens and had recently given up his position as head of the Sarasota Marine Research Institute. With his athletic build and effortless good looks, he was hardly ugly and ladies treated him like sirloin. Owens wasn't exactly stew meat, but women usually considered him a cheaper cut. Before his best friend became engaged, Owens spent far too much time serving as his wingman.

"What happened to you?" Sanders asked, his voice a rich baritone. "Why are your clothes covered in mud?"

"Car trouble during that wet spell, but everything's fine now. You must have hit rain on the way in?"

Sanders shook his head. "Clear skies all the way."

"Freaky. I figured you would've encountered it, considering the direction of the wind. Say, where's Jackie? I thought she was sailing home with you."

Sanders's face clouded over. "Change of plans—again. After her last assignment, she flew all the way to Mérida to meet me for a leisurely cruise back from Yucatán. We hadn't made much headway when her network called and assigned her to investigate a neo-Nazi cell with Hamas connections in Albuquerque. I dropped her off in Cancún where she caught a flight."

Sounded dangerous, but all Owens said was, "Interesting."

Sanders shrugged, but when he brushed unruly hair from his eyes it was easy to spot the concern spreading over his tanned face. It wasn't always smooth sailing for Sanders and Jackie. Both were fiercely independent, and their relationship had more hiccups than most, but Owens could see he was worried about her.

Their footsteps echoed on the dock planks as they walked toward the Land Cruiser, but the sound ended when Sanders came to an abrupt halt. "What the hell did you do to my ride while I was away?" The crease between his eyes deepened. "What are all of these scratches, why is a wiper missing?"

"I had a...close encounter when a tire blew."

Sanders frowned. "I replaced the tires a few months ago, so they're practically new." He pulled open the back door to stow his gear on the floor near the jump seats. A twitch of annoyance passed over his face at the sight of a sleeping female slumped on a seat. "What gives?" he whispered.

"You know me," Owens said, "Always picking up strays. Last night while gunning down the highway on my way to WCRX I nearly ran her down."

"Homeless?"

"Haven't learned anything yet, passed out right after I found her. But check her out; she doesn't look like the homeless type."

"Why do you keep doing this, Anderson? She's not some lost kitten for you to bring home. Let the police decide what to do with her."

"She told me she'd been waiting for me."

Sanders gave a derisive snort, but he did take a longer look at her as he grabbed the untouched hot chocolate and took a gulp. "What's with the uniform?"

Owens ignored the question. "She looks like an angel."

"Well, she's NOT. Don't you remember what happened the last time one of us brought home a stranger?"

"If memory serves, *one* of us ended up with a beautiful fiancée named Jackie Donovan."

"True, but this is different. And stop looking at me like that. I'm right and you know it. Someone must be beating the bushes for her."

"Okay. But let's take her home and let her sleep a few more hours. When she wakes, she can have some breakfast and tell us her story. She looks like she could use a good meal and bath before I drop her off at the police station."

Sanders sighed. "You don't have a bathtub. If you hadn't invested in a swamp—"

"It's a wetland. Besides, most of the property is a trailer park, and you know it. Some of my loyal fans live there."

"Yes, I know. I've met Peggy and her menagerie down by the water. Still, if your tenants paid what they owe, you could afford a place with a tub."

Home was a restored '62 Airstream where Owens holed up amid stacks of books and magazines. "Like I've said before, most of my tenants are seniors on a fixed income. I refuse to force them to choose between medicine and rent."

Sanders's expression softened, as Owens knew it would.

"I seem to recall that *your* place has a tub," he said.

"Stop grinning at me like that," Sanders growled. "You're about to involve me in one of your stunts, and last time we nearly got killed."

*   *   *

Sanders owned a '30s bungalow on Fiesta Key and the canal behind his property was too shallow to permit mooring for a vintage eighty-five-foot schooner. He wasn't fond of keeping *Isabella* at Sarasota Harbor and often talked about purchasing property with a suitably large private dock. So far, he hadn't found time to house hunt.

They placed the unconscious woman and her satchel in the spare bedroom. By late afternoon she was still in Lala land. When Sanders went outside to inspect his damaged Land Cruiser, Owens gave her a closer inspection. She didn't look like a user, but he inspected her arms for needle marks. None. She had to be snowed on something or she'd be awake by now. He again considered taking her to the hospital, but it was likely the authorities had posted someone there as part of their manhunt.

He took the opportunity to pull out his cell and punch #1 on speed dial. He knew she was up; she was an early riser.

"Mama, how's it going?"

"Sweetie! It's good to hear your voice. You haven't called in a while, and I was beginning to worry you'd crashed that Italian deathtrap of yours."

When he wasn't borrowing his best friend's Land Cruiser, he was tearing up the pavement on his 2010 Moto Guzzi V7 Classic. "Mama, I called just last week. Besides, my motorcycle isn't a deathtrap."

"It is as far as I'm concerned. Tell me you wear a helmet when you're on that thing."

"I do."

"Nice try, Pinocchio." His mother was hundreds of miles away, but he could feel her finger jabbing him. "How are you going to provide me with grandbabies if you're dead or your brains are scrambled?"

They'd had this conversation many times before. "You have Keisha."

"True, and she's been a blessing since cancer took your sister, but who do *you* have? You need a wife, and God's greatest gift—children."

"I don't remember you saying that when I was a child."

"Maybe that's because you were such a handful. Living with you wasn't easy back then."

"Yes, Mama." Her mind was still sharp, even though she was slipping more and more into the past, and her religion.

"You must have driven those professors batty at Tuscaloosa."

"Some, but not all. One took a shine to me." He changed the subject, keeping Mama in the dark about Pomeroy and *Sotto Voce*. "Have you been listening to the program?"

"Yes, I'm sorry to say. Making fun of people of faith isn't the path to redemption, Anderson. You must accept the Lord as your personal savior. Remember what Jesus says in John 14:6: *I am the way, the truth, and the life: no man cometh unto the Father, but by me.*"

Studying the Bible had not provided Owens with the spiritual certainty that was the cornerstone of his mother's existence. He trudged on. "Let's talk about something else. How's your blood sugar?"

"Same as always. Good days and bad."

"That's what you say every time I call. How's Keisha?"

"She's fine, starting to get a teenager's mouth on her—complains constantly about pimples and boys—but we get along fine."

"How's she adjusting to the braces?"

"About what you'd expect. Rolling her eyes and complaining about them to anyone who'll listen. About that four thousand dollars you sent—you didn't borrow it from Preston, did you?"

"Mama, I'm syndicated now, and I have investment property. I can afford braces for my niece."

"Don't be foolish with your money, son. I have my teacher's pension and can afford the basics. You don't know how long this radio thing is goin' to last. Hold on to your money. And consider selling that rundown trailer park."

"Yes, Mama. Let me say hi to Keisha. You didn't tell her I'm responsible for the braces, did you?"

"You made me promise I wouldn't, remember?"

"Yeah, thanks."

He waited for his niece to pick up the phone.

"Uncle Anderson? You should see these ugly braces Nanna made me get. I look h-i-d-e-o-u-s..."

*   *   *

It took twenty minutes to reassure his niece she was the most beautiful teenager on the planet. After hanging up, he went to the spare bedroom to check on the girl. Still crashed. As he was about to leave, her hand shot to her mouth, muffling a whimper.

"Mama? Poppa?" she mumbled. "I feel so hot..."

Owens bent down and felt a faint tingling when he placed a hand on her forehead. No fever. Maybe the drugs she'd taken would act like a truth serum. *Maybe I can learn where she came from*, he rationalized. This wouldn't be the first time he'd wormed information from someone without their knowledge, yet this woman's winsome face gave him a stab of guilt.

The bed creaked when he settled beside her. She whimpered again, the sound of a frightened child. "Sophia, how old are you?" he asked.

No answer.

She'd sounded like a little girl when she called out for her Mama and Poppa. "Are you remembering a time when you were a little girl?"

Her eyes remained closed, but she gave a barely perceptible nod.

"Where are you; can you tell me?"

She took so long to respond that he nearly gave up hope for a reply. To his surprise, she slid her balled fist away from her mouth and mumbled, "The ship. I'm on the ship."

"A cruise ship?"

Sophia shook her head. "It's made of wood. With big sails."

"Are you alone?"

"No. Mama's here. She's tired because I cried all night and kept her up. Now she's crying, too."

"Why is she crying?"

"Poppa has returned. His face looks...strange. Poppa is in charge of the ship. He is mostly calm, but he isn't calm now. He just returned to the cabin, so upset he almost knocked over Mama's machine."

"What kind of machine is it, Sophia?"

"Mama sits at it, makes pretty music. Sometimes Poppa sings along with her while she plays. I feel warm and safe while they sing about Jesus. But no one is singing now."

"Do you know why Poppa is upset?"

Sophia bunched her brows. After a few moments she continued. "Something bad has happened! Mama must wrap me in a blanket. I'm crying out for Dolly. At first Mama is too busy, too upset to hear me, but she finally reaches for Dolly and hands her to me. Now we're racing up the stairs to the deck." She shivered and clasped her hands together. "It's cold up on deck...and Poppa is shouting."

Owens was too engrossed to stop. "What is Poppa shouting?"

Sophia's eyes shot open revealing a remarkable shade of blue flecked with silver. He waved a hand in front of her face, but she didn't notice, was still asleep.

Sanders appeared in the doorway, wiping his greasy hands on a rag. "It's easy to lose control if a tire blows while on gravel, but I can't imagine why the clutch and brakes failed. Everything appears in order."

Owens pressed a finger to his lips to silence him.

"I heard you talking and assumed she was awake," he whispered.

"She's still out but responding to questions." Owens turned his attention back to her. "Sophia, what is Poppa shouting?"

"Orders," she replied. She'd been stretched out on the bed, but now she closed her eyes again and curled into a fetal position.

Owens repeated, "What does he want all of you to do?"

"He's screaming two words over and over. One word I've never heard before. It must be a bad word because everyone turns for a moment to stare at him."

"What is this word?"

Again, he thought she wouldn't answer. Then...

"Abandon. Poppa is shouting 'abandon ship!'"

Chapter Three

Sunday: 11:45 a.m.

Twenty-four hours earlier, Air Force One sliced through Saturday's afternoon drizzle to follow the Columbia River toward Portland where the media had gathered at the airport. The body of twelve-year-old Miles Burbridge had been flown to Oregon to be laid to rest in the Willamette Valley where the family lived when not in D.C. Few guests had been invited, but the service on Sunday morning would be televised and accompanied with all the solemnity expected for the son of the President of the United States.

The first couple had looked understandably somber as they deplaned. Before slipping into a waiting limo, the President stepped away from the Secret Service to speak with reporters about Miles's passing, tears wiped from multiple eyes as the President spoke of the boy's love for the Northwest's rivers and mountains, even though Miles's weak physical condition had kept him indoors most of his life.

On Sunday morning, flashes and auto advances went off as cameras captured images of the first couple entering and leaving the Presbyterian Church where, twenty-two years earlier, they'd married. Also present, and looking appropriately somber, were the chief executive's eighteen-year-old twin sons, Eric and Aaron, who had arrived from Stanford several hours earlier. Their good looks and high spirits often landed them on tabloid covers. In contrast, the boy in the polished mahogany coffin had rarely been seen. Miles had been fiercely protected by parents successful at keeping him out of the public eye.

After the church service, the First Family's motorcade followed the hearse to the place of interment—the future site of the Burbridge Presidential Library. As the casket was lowered into the soggy ground, the forest of umbrellas moved back to afford the grieving family a private moment to say goodbye. Unfortunately, pressing matters dictated a brief stay. By three that afternoon, the twins were being escorted back to Stanford and their parents boarded Air Force One for the return flight to Washington.

* * *

Later that evening, Ralph Cotton, White House Chief of Staff, straightened his tie and checked his watch as he waited for Marine One to set down on the south lawn, a hand protecting his comb-over from the rotor's gusts. Lines etched his face, and he had a good start on jowls.

The chief executive exited the helicopter when the rotors came to a stop, sagging shoulders straightening at the sight of waving tourists, some holding candles, some weeping. The carefully arranged photo op had been staged by one of the staffers. The re-election campaign was revving up and pictures of a grieving president returning to work after burying a child were priceless. One poster read: We miss you, Miles. Another:

We love you, Madame President.

Charlene (Charlie) Burbridge glad-handed the crowd and kissed a baby (who happened to be named Miles) before joining Cotton for the brisk walk to the West Wing.

As mayor of Portland, Burbridge rose to national prominence when the city was devastated by earthquakes, fire, and floods after Oregon's largest mountain, 11,237-foot Mt. Hood, erupted.

In contrast to state and federal fumbling in the aftermath of Hurricane Katrina, the Mt. Hood Eruption was handled with remarkable competence, and Charlene Burbridge's successful management of rescue and rebuilding operations was heralded as a model of government efficiency. Later, from the Governor's office in Salem, her unorthodox opinions on wedge issues like climate warming, illegal immigration, and dependency on foreign oil resonated well with those wanting to believe such problems weren't too big to fix.

"How was the flight back?" Cotton asked.

"Smooth enough. I took the opportunity to read Senator Donnington's op-ed piece in *The Washington Post*. He claims that after three years in the White House I haven't accomplished much, other than vetoing a Congressional pay raise and reducing America's military presence in the Middle East."

"Donnington's a fine public servant," Cotton admitted, "but if he saw a video of you pulling a child out of a burning building, he'd look for a way to use the footage against you. Word on the Hill is that he's going to seek the Republican presidential nomination and challenge you next year."

"He has the ear of right-wing conservatives, but he's about as polarizing as they come. He'll soon discover that moderate senators aren't willing to jeopardize their jobs by voting to eliminate Social Security and Medicare, not with baby boomers filling the ranks of retirees."

"I know the man," Cotton said. "Can't decide what rattles him more, the fact that you're a woman or that Oregon, a state barely visible on the political map, has managed to put someone in the White House." After a moment of silence he added, "I watched the service. Quite moving. Does it ever stop raining in Oregon?"

The President shrugged, running a hand through her auburn hair, even though the helicopter ride had done little damage to her no-nonsense coiffure. "I thought the rain added a nice touch. Besides, Miles always liked the rain."

"Condolence letters and flowers are still streaming in. The Oval looks like a floral shop," Cotton said.

She sighed, her bottom lip quivering briefly. "Have them delivered to one of the local children's hospitals."

"Yes, Madame President. By the way, Senator Laughlin and Congressman Wesley want to speak with you as soon as possible."

"I thought the funeral would put them off for a few weeks. They're anxious to shoot a few more holes in my health care reform proposals before we hit the campaign trail."

"No doubt. Oh...by the way, Everett Lukker called for you again."

Lukker was CEO of corporate giant Lukker Pharmaceuticals and one of her largest contributors.

"Have you heard that Senator Donnington was on MSNBC's *Straight Talk* this morning, criticizing your chumminess with Lukker?"

"He'll be talking out of the other side of his mouth when Lukker Pharmaceuticals saves millions of lives by developing a serum to cure Alzheimer's."

"People are worried about unemployment, the deficit and outrageous gas prices."

"Nearly six million US citizens suffer from Alzheimer's disease. It's the sixth largest killer in the US, now with baby boomers added into the mix. Now is the time to develop a cure. I won't have people saying we took our eyes off the ball."

Ralph Cotton huffed and puffed, trying to match her athletic stride, his forehead beaded with sweat by the time they reached the Oval Office. He glanced at his gnawed fingertips while she checked the stack of urgent memos on her desk. He'd stopped biting his nails in the third grade, but his boss's involvement with Everett Lukker had him revisiting several bad habits.

Chapter Four

———

Sunday: 4:05 p.m.

When Sophia slipped back into deep sleep and stopped responding to questions, Owens picked up her satchel and borrowed the locket, her hand falling away as he tugged it from her fingers and slipped the chain over her head.

Back in the living room, Sanders asked, "What was she talking about?"

"Wish I knew."

Owens set her things on the coffee table before heading to the fridge for drinks. They enjoyed them in silence until Owens said, "Did I mention the CIA is looking for her?"

Sanders choked on his Dos Equis. "No, you didn't," he sputtered.

"I'm sure I did."

He was adamant. "NO! I'd have remembered. So, there's more to this than lending a hand to some lost soul. There's that chip on your shoulder. You're still feuding with the CIA, don't want her handed over because you didn't like the way they treated *you* when you worked for them."

Owens didn't bother denying it.

"Why do they want her?"

Owens tossed back the Mountain Dew and wiped his mouth with the back of his hand. "Dunno. But I intend to find out. She needs help."

"And you can never resist playing the part of a knight in shining armor. I swear, one day that curiosity of yours is going to get us killed."

"No one's pointing a gun at you."

"That usually comes later."

"Feel free to sit this one out."

Sanders glared at him.

He set down the Mountain Dew and reached for the locket. "Expensive. Real gold, no base metal exposed in the scratches. The filigree surrounding the '**B**' etched on the front is skillfully done." He handed it to Sanders, who glanced at it and handed it back.

"Don't suppose this is opened very often," Owens said, digging his thumbnail beneath the clasp, forcing the reluctant hinges to swing open. Inside were two sepia-toned pictures under glass.

On the left, a handsome man sporting a doorknocker moustache gazed at the world with a stiff, uncompromising expression. On the right, a woman with hair parted in the middle and coiled at the back exuded a similar air. The portraits were cropped close to the faces, but hints of nineteenth-century finery were visible. The man appeared to be in his thirties, the woman five or six years younger. Both possessed the unflappable and confident demeanor of Calvinist New England theology.

"Husband and wife?" Sanders wondered, his annoyance giving way to curiosity.

"That'd be my guess," Owens answered. "Ya know, these folks look strangely familiar." He handed the locket back to him.

Sanders scrunched up his nose while examining the faded images more closely.

"Now that you mention it, I do feel like I've seen this couple before."

"What about the '**B**'?"

Sanders shrugged.

Owens examined the satchel. "Looks vintage, handmade; worn leather, scratched brass fittings, and clasps, at least a hundred years old."

Sanders set down the locket and turned his attention to the satchel. "She must've gotten this in a secondhand store." He started to open it but stopped. "This is a bad idea.

Whoever she is, whatever she's done, she deserves her privacy."

"I agree. But what if there's a clue in there to help us find out who she is and why the authorities are looking for her?"

Without waiting for a reply, he took the satchel and dumped the contents onto the coffee table. A doll spilled out, along with a bundle of cloth that separated into three garments of various sizes, all too small to fit the young woman sleeping in the guestroom.

"More antiques," Sanders said.

Owens held up the first, a smock for a child of two or three, drab, cheap, and handmade. He set it aside and shook out the second, cut for a girl of eight or nine and made of homespun, more carefully made, buttons down the back, a form-fitting waist, and needlework on the collar and cuffs. But the third garment, tailored for a thirteen or fourteen-year-old, was a remarkable example of seamstress art. "Very impressive; white silk, embroidered with pearls and lace."

"A dress for a tiny bride," Sanders commented.

Owens set down the clothes and picked up the doll, running a finger over the obliterated features of the papier-mâché face. The discolored paper resembled the dirty bandages of a burn victim. Beneath the cloth dress were wooden limbs and a calfskin body. Stitched across the calfskin in faded multicolored thread was a name:

SOPHIA

"Looks like this doll's been around the block and received some powerful luv'n," Owens said. "Must be over a hundred years old. Quite a coincidence, our mystery girl sharing a name with a hundred-year-old doll, don't you think?" He handed it to Sanders.

"More likely someone bought the doll for her at a second-hand shop *because* it was monogrammed with her name. Or she could have purchased it for herself because she likes vintage things. Look at the way she styles her hair."

Owens placed the doll on the coffee table and pulled out his cell phone—über-slim and the same size as a credit card. He aimed its digital camera at the doll and other items and clicked away. When finished, he tapped the smooth panel with a finger and launched an encoded file into cyberspace.

"Soon we'll know more than we care to about these antiques."

Sanders's eyebrows shot up. "You mean...?"

He nodded.

"*Sotto Voce?*"

Owens made a shushing gesture with his finger. "Remember—if you speak that name I'll have to kill you."

Sanders gave him a don't-give-me-that-crap frown. "I hate it when you say that."

Chapter Five

Seven Hours Later

She was still asleep.

The time had come for Owens to leave for his nightly broadcast, but he was worried about her. Again, he placed a hand on her forehead. No fever, and her breathing was deep and regular.

"Your angel has been asleep a long time," Sanders said.

"Call if she wakes up or her condition changes."

Sanders was a marine biologist, not an MD, but he knew a lot about medicine and was certainly capable of keeping watch on someone sleeping off a bad high.

"Fine," he said sourly, "but if she doesn't come to soon, I'm dropping her off at the ER."

*   *   *

He was halfway through his show when his cell started vibrating.

Sotto Voce was ready to provide the requested information on Sophia's possessions. He downloaded the data onto his desktop, downed a slug of Mountain Dew and began reading.

One child's doll with papier-mâché face: *Made in New York City between 1870/1874, a knockoff of the famous Ludwig Greiner style. Like this sample, most had molded hair painted black, wooden limbs and a calfskin body. Girl's name stitched over the body was commonly done in the store at time of purchase. Study necessary to determine if cloth dress is original, but value of this item is compromised due to poor quality of facial preservation.*

An understatement: the doll had no face left to speak of.

Vicki slipped in a recorded commercial for vinyl home siding and he continued reading.

Garment #1, a toddler's smock: Worn by both boys and girls in Europe around the turn of the last century. Fixing the place of origin isn't possible without analyzing the actual item, but the smocking closely resembles work executed on the island of Terceira.

He pulled off the headphones and stretched his shoulders. Terceira was in the Azores, one of nine Portuguese islands in the North Atlantic.

Garment #2, a girl's smock, not from Terceira but also Portuguese, stitched by a different hand than garment #1, in this instance someone left-handed, at least fifty years after garment #1.

He was curious about the fancy dress, skipping over approximated thread counts and possible dye sources.

Garment #3: Portuguese made decades after garment #2. The first two showed enough wear to assume they were worn often. This fancy dress showed little wear, although slight yellowing indicated it was also at least seventy-five years old. Pearls and beadwork of the highest quality. Too elaborate and too small for a common communion dress, it was possibly commissioned by a wealthy worshipper for a polychrome statue of the young Virgin.

He scrolled down to find information about the locket, curious to learn what he could about the photographs inside.

One locket: gold content cannot be determined without examining the original. Style consistent with late nineteenth-century design. Inside, slight water damage indicates these matching photographs are printed on paper rather than polished silver-plated copper of the Daguerreian Era, which in the United States ended by 1860. The *sitters are Benjamin Spooner Briggs and wife, the former Sarah Elizabeth Cobb.*

Briggs—an explanation for the "**B**." Owens wondered why the name was so familiar.

A memory washed over him.

Flashback: a sunny afternoon awash in humidity and pesky flies, the type of summer day a kid could curl his lips around the hot nozzle of a garden hose and gorge on cold water and limitless well-being. He was sitting under the elm in Preston Sanders's backyard in Newport. They were arguing. Sanders, future marine biologist, was shaking his head, telling him he was full of crap. He was saying something about pirates. Owens, not yet the skeptic he would later become, kept shooting him down, convinced it was space aliens.

They were deep into a discussion about the fate of...Captain Benjamin Briggs.

Chapter Six

———

Sunday: 11:58 p.m.

CIA agent Brian Fulton paced as he waited to be admitted into the Oval Office, not his first time in the Oval, although he'd never been here late at night. He paused in front of the French doors leading to the Rose Garden, glanced at the blooming flowers and stared without expression at the dim stars overhead.

Fulton had the hard-bitten look of most twenty-year veterans of the Agency. He had never failed his superiors or questioned them. He had a reputation as someone who could get his hands dirty and keep his mouth shut, and six months earlier he had been appointed special advisor to President Burbridge.

His fingers tightened on a folder stamped CONFIDENTIAL.

*　*　*

Ralph Cotton wore the appearance of someone carrying the weight of the world on his rounded shoulders as he escorted Fulton into the Oval Office. The President was seated behind the Resolute Desk. She pressed a button on the intercom before rising and moving to one of the two yellow couches separated by a coffee table.

Fulton approached the President, who extended her hand to him.

"Agent Fulton, I'm looking forward to your report. Mr. Burbridge will be here shortly."

The President's secretary poked her head in.

"Claudia, thanks for staying so late. Once Mr. Burbridge arrives feel free to go home. You've put in a long day."

"Yes, Madame President." She disappeared.

Arthur Burbridge, lanky and a head taller than his spouse, entered through one of the curved side doors. He shook Fulton's hand and joined his wife on the couch.

"Sorry about all the flowers, Agent Fulton. I hope you don't have allergies."

"I don't, Madame President." He cleared his throat. "Please accept my deepest sympathy for your loss." His eyes diverted to include Arthur Burbridge. "The whole country is praying for you."

She dredged up a weak smile. "Sit, Agent Fulton, and tell us what you've learned." In quiet settings she was surprisingly soft-spoken, even though her voice was embedded with a measure of steel making it impossible to forget her lofty position.

He sat on the couch opposite the President. After Cotton positioned himself in a nearby chair, Fulton began. "Madame President, I'm sure you're familiar with PIDE?"

She nodded, but her husband looked confused.

For Arthur Burbridge's benefit, Fulton explained. "*Policia Internacional e de Defesa do Estado*, otherwise known as PIDE, was Portugal's secret police. Antonio Salazar, Portuguese dictator from 1932–1968, patterned PIDE after the Gestapo, and it remained one of Europe's most tightly managed organizations following World War II."

"PIDE is no longer operational," she said.

"True; the current leader of Portugal no longer has secret police to do his bidding."

The President's mouth tightened, a quick glance passing between her and her husband.

Fulton continued. "PIDE was disbanded in '74 and replaced with another security agency, this one patterned after Scotland Yard. Obtaining their classified files is still difficult, but not nearly as much as when Salazar's henchmen were running things." He placed the file on the coffee table.

Arthur Burbridge leaned forward but settled back on the couch without picking it up.

Fulton continued. "By 1965, Salazar had been undisputed ruler of Portugal for more than thirty years. In '68 he had an accident, fell off a chair at his country retreat outside of Lisbon and injured his head. The accident, and the brain trauma he no doubt suffered, were completely covered up, although close aides later claimed he'd gone berserk. Apparently, he became fixated with the idea of his own impending death and set out to find the source of eternal life."

Cotton's voice drifted over from the far side of the room. "You mean a Fountain of Youth?"

Fulton nodded.

"So, he took the Ponce de León fable seriously?" the President asked.

"In a manner of speaking. Historically, the Portuguese matched Spain's zeal for exploration, but Salazar wasn't looking for the Fountain of Youth in Florida or a remote corner of the far-flung overseas empire he'd spent his life trying to preserve. He was looking for the secret to eternal youth, and he came to believe it was in his own backyard."

"The Fountain of Youth is in Portugal?" Arthur Burbridge asked.

"He was convinced the secret to eternal youth was hidden in a convent or monastery near Lisbon." Fulton rubbed his jaw and continued. "Salazar never married and had no official children to carry on his name, perhaps another reason why in 1965 he launched a campaign to search the region's monasteries and convents for a mysterious woman rumored to be immune to aging."

The President leaned forward. "Interesting. Is this why Salazar closed most of Portugal's religious institutions, converting many into *pousadas*?"

"*Pousadas?*" her husband asked.

"State-run hotels," Fulton explained. "It's entirely possible. Fourteen years in Seminary had turned the young Salazar away from the Church. The last of eleven children and the only male, he must have thought the priesthood his only escape from poverty."

"But he found another path," Burbridge said.

"Yes. Politics provided another route. He ruled Portugal with an iron fist, but after his injury in '68 he became convinced an angel was hidden on Portuguese soil, a creature who didn't seem to age. I've gained access to PIDE files chronicling the old man's obsession with finding a woman reportedly pulled from the sea in the 1870s and hidden in Portugal for over ninety years."

Cotton moved his chair closer. "The idea that a woman immune to aging was squirreled away in the Portuguese countryside is preposterous enough, but what did he expect would happen if she actually existed and he'd gotten his hands on her?"

Fulton didn't mince words. "Having patterned his secret police on the Gestapo, I'd guess she would have been subjected to what Winston Churchill characterized as Nazi fascination with 'perverted science.' An assortment of experiments would undoubtedly have left her dead."

"Then it's a good thing Salazar never found her," the President said.

Fulton opened the folder on the coffee table and pulled out a photograph of a girl in a grey smock, perhaps fifteen or sixteen, praying in a church.

"Where did this photograph come from?" the President asked. "And when was it taken?"

"It was taken in 1968 at the *Igreja de Jesus* in Setúbal, a small town on the Portuguese coast. PIDE was always on the alert for democratic and left-leaning citizens organizing with the left-leaning segment of the Church to overthrow Salazar's autocratic government in favor of a democracy."

The President squinted at the photograph.

Fulton continued. "Surveillance cameras were installed in many churches and cathedrals. One took this picture, but after decades of suppression Salazar's influence was waning in '68, and the film in these cameras remained uncollected. This image wasn't discovered until three years later."

"A pretty girl with haunting eyes. But what is she wearing?" Cotton wondered.

"It's a smock. PIDE was convinced it was made by nuns at *Convento de Santa Isabel.*"

Fulton pulled another picture from the file. "Madame President, your suggestion that I check cruise ship personnel paid off." He handed her the photograph. "Who provided the tip that she might be located at sea?"

Charlie Burbridge arched her eyebrows and ignored his question. She smiled at the picture before passing it around. "So it's true—the same girl, although slightly older."

The picture was passed around the Oval Office with everyone nodding in agreement.

Fulton cleared his throat. "This picture was taken three years ago on the cruise ship *Island Empress.* She worked in the infirmary, and records show she had for years."

"How can the dates on these pictures be correct?" the President asked. "The first was taken in 1968, while the second was snapped in 2008, forty years later. This woman appears to have aged only slightly."

"She isn't immune to aging as Salazar thought, Madame President, but is doing so extremely slowly," Fulton answered.

She flipped over the picture and read the name penned on the back: Sophia Correia. "Where is she now?" the President asked.

"She arrived in Tampa yesterday when *Island Empress* docked. Agents sent to apprehend her learned she'd been targeted by several Haitian crewmates. Under interrogation, one of them claimed a voodoo god told her the young woman was a demon. She admitted to drugging her and putting her on a bus. The destination was randomly selected—Sarasota. I have agents hunting for the girl, and I expect to have her in custody shortly."

* * *

Everett Lukker's secretary took the call.

"This is the White House. The President would like to speak with Mr. Lukker."

"Mr. Lukker has just left a meeting and is on his way back to his office. One moment, please, and I'll connect you."

A few moments later. "Yes, Madame President?"

"We're closing in on her."

Lukker rubbed at his eyes under his glasses. He had just received bad news from his biochemists on a project he was keeping close to his vest. "Sorry, I'm drawing a blank. Who are we talking about?"

"The girl from Portugal? We've discussed her several times. You said it was a wild goose chase, remember?"

A lengthy silence was broken when Lukker finally mumbled, "Impossible. I don't believe it."

"I was skeptical, too, but it's true. I can't believe... Is something wrong?"

"Moments ago, I received disappointing news."

"Anything I should know about?"

"Are you asking as a friend or as the President of the United States?"

"Both."

"Thank you, but I trust you've other important issues to deal with. About that young woman, you're sure she's the one?"

"Positive. She might be the miracle we've been hoping for."

"Madame President, as an atheist I don't believe in miracles, but she just might provide the missing variable we've been searching for."

Chapter Seven

———————

Monday: 12:48 a.m.

Captain Benjamin Briggs.

Owens silently mouthed the name with near reverence. He sat at his desk, slack-jawed and immobile, as if a massive injection of Novocain coursed through him. The commercial ended, and several seconds of "dead air" reached his nationwide audience. Vicki was about to sneak in the theme music when he donned the headphones and leaned toward the mic.

> "Welcome back to the Anderson Owens Show. Folks, tonight I want to focus on a mystery that has fascinated people for over a hundred and fifty years, the disappearance of the *Mary Celeste*."

In the control room, Vicki looked up from a caller list and noticed his wide-eyed look of disbelief. "Everything okay, Anderson?"

"Yeah, but we're not going to discuss global warming anymore tonight. I'm changing topics. Clear the monitor and begin a new list."

"Why?"

"Just do it." Too hard. He softened it with, "Please."

"You're the boss."

His eyes darted back and forth between his desktop monitor, filled with information detailing Sophia's possessions, and the screen where Vicki began posting the names of waiting callers. He leaned toward the mic.

> "We've got James in Monroe, Georgia. What can you tell us about the *Mary Celeste*, James?"

> "Hey Anderson, I can't believe I got through to you. Say, when

I was a scout on a camping trip back in the '70s our troop leader scared the heebie-jeebies out of us one night with the story of the *Mary Celeste*. I remember lying awake all night thinking up reasons why a crew would abandon a perfectly seaworthy ship on the high seas. Frankly, I think a giant octopus attached itself to the hull and got the crew one at a time when they looked over the side."

Owens snorted dismissively.

"I'm currently skimming several reputable websites, and the ship showed no signs of damage from giant octopi or squid. We've got Clay in Hurley, New York: what have you got for us, Clay?"

"Anderson, how's it hangin'? I've been studying up on our mystery ship since I was a kid.

"For the handful of listeners that might never have heard of the *Mary Celeste*, why don't you enlighten us, Clay."

"Sure. The *Mary Celeste* was a brigantine that set sail from New York in 1872 with a cargo of grain alcohol destined for Genoa. Nine days after leaving New York, the ship was discovered as a derelict, valuable cargo intact, adrift without crew or passengers. The last entry on the log slate, a latitude and a longitude, placed the ship in the Azores between São Miguel and Santa Maria."

Owens had long wondered about the location mentioned in the log. It wasn't the quickest or safest route an experienced captain making for Genoa would choose.
Clay continued.

"The ship had travelled almost four hundred miles on her own. After being boarded and claimed as salvage, she was sailed to Gibraltar for an intensive investigation but a good reason why the captain, his wife, daughter, and crew abandoned a newly refitted ship in rough seas without bothering to grab foul weather gear or food hasn't been found. But the crew must have believed the *Mary Celeste* was sinking, and fast, an assumption that turned out to be incorrect and fatal. The fate of everyone on board has always fascinated folks."

"Thanks, Clay. I'm keeping you on the line so we can all benefit from your expertise."

Callers weighed in with theories: a drunken crew raiding the cargo, a fanatical captain who snapped. Clay shot them down. The alcohol had been inspected intact at Gibraltar, no barrels tampered with. Nothing in Briggs's character suggested violence. The board kept lighting up, but no one had an answer that held.

"Thanks guys. Anderson Owens here at ten minutes after one, a beautiful Monday morning in Sarasota, Florida. Curt in Dallas. You're on the air."

"Yeah, is there any truth to the story that President Burbridge is hiding a tiny extraterrestrial with huge eyes in the White—"

Vicki mouthed S-O-R-R-Y from the engineering room.

"Folks, I'd like to thank Brian in Los Gatos, California, who just emailed the entire transcript of the Gibraltar Proceedings. I'm glancing over it now, and Oliver Deveau, first mate aboard the *Dei Gratia*—the ship claiming *Mary Celeste* as salvage—swore the galley was between meals with everything properly stowed away. The ship's food supplies were not tainted in any way.

"But here's where it gets interesting—a lifeboat was launched in an unusual way—ropes were cut to remove it from the roof of the main hatch where it was stored and a portion of the railing was hacked away so the boat could be quickly launched over the side."

Owens continued to peruse the transcripts from the Gibraltar Proceedings, particularly the description of Captain Briggs's abandoned cabin, which included the impression of a child left on the captain's mattress. Back at the bungalow, Sophia said her poppa was in charge of a sailing ship, and that something horrible had happened. He all but forgot his callers when he came upon the name of Briggs's daughter, lost at sea in 1872 along with the crew.

Sophia.

Chapter Eight

Monday: 1:25 a.m.

Leland Pomeroy lay awake listening to the rhythms of the night; the soughing of the April breeze in the oak sheltering his home, crickets calling to each other from the azaleas near the veranda, the beer-soaked exuberance of revelers staggering home to nearby dorms. At eighty-three, Pomeroy was professor emeritus at the University of Alabama, and blind since macular degeneration had claimed his eyesight twenty years earlier.

Over the years, the big antebellum house on the edge of the Tuscaloosa campus had survived fires and several large robust families, but now it was empty except for the blind old man.

The phone beside his bed began ringing. He called for virtual assistance. "Alexa, what time is it?"

"The time is 1:25 a.m."

He reached for the phone, automatically activating a switch to prevent the call from being monitored. "Yes?"

"Dr. Pomeroy? Leland Pomeroy?"

"Who's calling?"

After a pause. "Roger Vintiger."

Pomeroy stroked his white goatee. "Roger. My...but it's been a long time, twenty years or more, I believe. I haven't heard from you since you transferred to...Duke, wasn't it?"

"Yes, and I doubt I would have been admitted into their graduate program without your letter of recommendation."

"Nonsense. You were a brilliant student, although I suffered a pang when you decided to focus on biochemistry instead of the humanities. I hear you work for Lukker Pharmaceuticals. I imagine they reimburse you more than you could have earned as a history teacher.

Are you happy?"

A long pause.

"Roger, are you still on the line?"

"I'm still here. No, I'm not happy. I've sold my soul to the devil and can't get it back. Now my time is up."

"I don't remember you being this melodramatic, Roger. Surely your situation isn't as dire as you're suggesting. What have you done?"

"First, I want to ask you a personal question."

"All right."

"Twelve years ago, I was considered for membership in a secret organization, one I know you're familiar with."

"Roger, what is that I hear? Are you taking pills?"

"Just Imitrex for migraines. I want to discuss *Sotto Voce*—you were a founding member."

A pause. "Go on."

"You didn't think I was membership material," Vintiger said dourly.

"Do you mind telling me how you know this?"

"You have your ways of gathering information and I have mine. It *is* true, isn't it?"

"Yes, it's true. As for *Sotto Voce*, you might not have heard but I'm retired. I'm eighty-three and blind."

"Pardon me, but bullshit! You still have your finger on the pulse of everything going on. Now, would you care to tell me, why—"

"Roger, I detect bitterness in your tone. Isn't your life too full to waste precious time holding a grudge over something that happened years ago? You're a brilliant scientist, and from what I hear you'll soon be instrumental in developing the Alzheimer's serum the world is waiting for."

"I wouldn't be holding my breath for that serum, if I were you, Professor."

"At my age it's dangerous to hold my breath for any reason."

"I suspect you'll live longer than me. In fact, I'm counting on it."

"Why don't you come for a visit, stay a few days. You've probably been working too hard; you sound tired and stressed."

"You were always an inspiration, Professor. I wish I could see you one last time. I want to give you something while I still can. I trust you have a tamperproof email address?"

Pomeroy, alarmed by the acceleration in Vintiger's breathing, gave it to him.

"You were right, Professor. I was never *Sotto Voce* material. Over the past few years Lukker Pharmaceuticals has been secretly building *two* research labs. It's hush-hush and has something to do with an e-file I wasn't supposed to be aware of. I'm sending you the file."

"What kind of file?"

"One revealing an undertaking I've been working on for several years, one that, until now, has been cloaked in as much secrecy as the Manhattan Project. When you find out what I've been involved with you won't think very highly of me, but I assure you I was kept in the dark and never knew the project's ultimate purpose. It was divided among a half-dozen scientists to prevent any of us from learning too much. The separate parts were collected into an e-file—for Lukker's eyes only—but a technical error copied it to my computer. Professor, innocent lives are at stake. You must find a way to use this information."

"Roger, what's this about? Is Lukker involved in something illegal?"

"Illegal is too mild a word. Like King Herod in the Bible, Lukker has authorized his own massacre of innocents. Listen carefully; our computers are monitored so it's only a matter of time until Lukker sends Trachmann to silence me. Be careful; the cover-up on this leads to the Oval Office."

"Where are you calling from?"

"I'm at work. Wait a minute...I hear footsteps, probably Trachmann's. There isn't time to download. You'll need to send someone for it."

"Who's Trachmann?" Instead of an answer, Pomeroy heard the clattering sound of the phone being dropped.

Vintiger's final words were muffled but he was able to make them out. "The key is in the castle."

A series of zzzaps and shrieks traveled through the line, followed by something a blind person would be aware of; the breathing was coming from someone other than Roger Vintiger.

Confident the call couldn't be traced, Pomeroy kept the receiver pressed to his ear for several moments. When the line finally went dead he hung up, a tremor shaking his fragile body. "Poor Roger, what did you get yourself into?"

Pomeroy made his way to an open bedroom window where he typically enjoyed inhaling the azaleas, but tonight he didn't notice the sweet and spicy scent. He would need help for this one. As if accessing names on a computer, he tapped his index finger on the windowsill, each tap representing the name of a talented individual he could count on.

He was alone but spoke out loud, a recently acquired habit. "I need someone with an insatiable appetite for knowledge, opinions as unconventional as they are brilliant, and an unwillingness to accept simple or easy answers."

He stopped tapping. There was a young man who'd briefly worked for the government before Pomeroy recruited him for work even more secretive than that provided by the CIA.

Anderson Owens.

Outside, the moon broke free from the clouds like a hungry predator slipping from its hiding place.

The night had grown unusually silent.

Chapter Nine

Twenty Minutes Later

The cell in Owens's pocket vibrated.

Personal calls during "on air" hours were usually ignored but he was distracted, his brain working overtime to bridge the gap between plausible and ridiculous. Like Houdini, who'd spent years debunking spiritual charlatans, he'd devoted much of his life researching urban legends, ghost stories, and conspiracy theories.

There had to be a rational explanation. Sophia, Greek for wisdom, wasn't a freakishly uncommon name; the antique doll with her name on it could have been picked up at a garage sale along with the satchel, clothes, and locket. Sharing a name with someone lost at sea ages ago had to be a coincidence. Still, he couldn't erase from his mind the woman's watery voice saying, "something horrible has happened." A notion buzzed in his head. He kept swatting it down. *Impossible.*

Without thinking, he snapped open the cell. "Yes?"

"Anderson. Leland Pomeroy here."

Owens recognized the voice of his old mentor, someone who'd turned out to be far more than a wizened old history professor. Pomeroy was *Sotto Voce's* founding member. He hadn't heard from Pomeroy since last year when he teamed up to decipher recently discovered Napoleonic documents threatening the West's financial security.

He'd been meaning to call the old man but hadn't gotten around to it.

"Dr. Pomeroy. This is unexpected. A coincidence since your name came up in conversation only hours ago. Your ears must be hot."

"A quaint expression, but I assure you my ears are the appropriate temperature." The old man's voice contained tension.

"What can I do for you, sir?"

"You can come to Tuscaloosa. We need to talk as soon as possible."

"Things are hectic here right now, Professor. Maybe in a few weeks..."

"Anderson, what I need to speak with you about is a top priority."

Chapter Ten

Monday: 1:55 a.m.

Vicki's voice drifted down from an overhead speaker. "Anderson, I just got a call from Karen at the front desk. Two men are in the lobby demanding to speak with you."

At this hour? "They can wait till after the show."

"They insist on speaking with you NOW."

"Uniforms?"

"No, coat-and-ties. Claim to be CIA."

Owens sat up, his antenna tweaked. "Did they show their bona fides?"

A pause, then, "Yep. Karen says the IDs look good."

"Tell her to escort them to the studio. We'll give our listeners a treat and put them on the air, find out what they want."

"You don't really want to do that, do you? I mean...well, you're the kind of guy that has things to hide. Right?"

"Send them in."

Another pause while Vicki contacted the front desk. A moment later, "They refuse; insist you join them in the lobby, immediately."

"All right. Run a few spots and PSAs while I check this out."

"Whatever you say, Boss."

After pulling off his headphones, Owens forwarded the info on Sophia's possessions to Sanders's home computer.

It was nearly two in the morning and the lobby was typically deserted at this hour, but even packed he'd have recognized the puffed-up profiles of the two agents, arms crossed like Superman, here to protect, if not truth and justice, at least the American way.

Experience had taught him that the U.S. intelligence community was an alphabet soup of agencies often in conflict with each other, despite Homeland Security's desire that all kids on the intelligence playground share and play nicely together. Recruits were selected for their unique gifts but once indoctrinated they all read from the same playbook like they'd been stamped from the same mold. Or so it seemed to Owens when he tried to fit that mold years ago when he cut his teeth at Langley. *Sotto Voce* had seen to it that all record of his association with the Agency was expunged so it wasn't likely these agents knew he was a former colleague. He made a show of inspecting their badges.

"Agents Wheaton and Petty, I'm Anderson Owens. What brings you here?"

"We're looking for a young woman, a cruise ship employee reported missing yesterday," Petty said.

"Not the sort of thing the CIA usually involves itself with. What gives?"

Wheaton took over. "Why don't you just answer the question—have you seen a woman in her twenties walking around in a white cruise line uniform?"

"No."

"If you know where she is and fail to reveal her whereabouts, you could be charged with kidnapping, or worse. Save yourself a whole lot of hurt and tell us where she is," Wheaton said.

"I don't know where she is."

"Really? I think you're lying." Wheaton handed over a picture of Sophia in uniform aboard *Island Empress*. "Look carefully. Her name is Sophia Correia."

It was the young woman sleeping in Sanders's spare bedroom. He shrugged and handed back the photo. "What's she done?"

"She hasn't done anything. But she walked away from a ship contaminated with the Norwalk virus and we don't want her exposing the citizens of Sarasota to illness."

"Nice try, but I don't buy it. What's the real reason you want her?"

Petty glared down his buckled nose, took a step toward Owens. "Why do you think we aren't telling the truth?"

He refused to be intimidated. "I'm fluent in bullshit, and your explanation doesn't pass my smell test, so I repeat: why do you want her?"

Wheaton ignored the question. "Before you lie again and tell us you've never laid eyes on her, you should know we just spoke with an employee at the 7-Eleven near the bus station. A fan of your show, he remembers seeing you buy a Mountain Dew and cup of hot chocolate early yesterday morning. Claims you come often, usually on a motorcycle, other times in a '76 Land Cruiser. He'd just finished sweeping out the place and was carting trash to a dumpster when he spotted the Land Cruiser. The female we want was copping some z's in the back."

"Land Cruisers are hardly in short supply. Lots of 'em on the road."

"Again, nice try. But the Land Cruiser you've been spotted in is a right-hand drive. Not many of those still on the road. In fact, Sarasota's DMV is aware of only two. One is owned by Lieutenant Mark Lopez currently serving overseas, the other is the property of Preston Sanders. You know Sanders?"

"He's a good friend."

"We've traced where he lives from the vehicle's registration. Does *he* have the young lady?"

He shook his head. "Sanders doesn't have her, but I did pick her up last night."

"Why did you lie?"

"I could ask you the same thing—Norwalk virus my black ass." But he decided to tell the truth, the limited version. "Listen, my heart went out to her. She reminded me of myself when I was younger, flirting with danger before I got my act together. She looked like a troubled young woman in need of a break, not someone deserving to be turned over to the authorities. I gave her a few bucks for a bus ticket."

"What did you give her?"

"A couple of dead presidents."

"Be more specific," Wheaton growled.

"Okay, I gave her two twenties."

Petty's jaw tightened. "Rather generous for someone you say you don't know."

"Excessive generosity is one of my many flaws."

Wheaton looked like he'd enjoy taking a swing at Owens. "Forty bucks could buy a one-way ticket to lots of places."

Owens did his best to look contrite. "Sorry."

"The bus station was the first place we checked. We interviewed the fellow working the ticket counter yesterday when the bus from Tampa pulled in. He saw her get off, toting a leather bag, but he swears she didn't buy another ticket. Care to try again?"

"It's time for me to get back to my listeners."

"I have a feeling we'll be seeing you again, Mr. Owens," Wheaton said sternly.

"Failing to cooperate with a federal agency can land you in deep hot water."

"Next time I'll bring a tea bag."

When they'd gone, Owens walked back to the studio to do battle with his conscience. His curiosity won out, not that it mattered if Sanders had already taken matters into his own hands and dropped her off at the ER or police station. But his gut told him she was still asleep at the bungalow.

He fished the cell from his pocket and then paused to consider what he was doing. Sophia Briggs was lost at sea a hundred and fifty-three years ago. Unlike some folks, he didn't believe in resurrections, and the notion that Sophia Briggs and Sophia Correia were one and the same was preposterous. But he lived to solve mysteries, wallowed in the opportunity to discover the truths hidden in them. He texted an encryption program, scrambling a message the CIA wouldn't be able to trace. Pressed send:

```
Cerfgba, lbh bayl unir n srj zvahgrf hagvy srqf neeivr.
Gnxr Fbcuvn naq qvfnccrne. V'yy pngpu hc jvgu lbh yngre.
```

Preston, you only have a few minutes until feds arrive. Take Sophia and disappear. I'll catch up with you later.

CHAPTER ELEVEN

Two Hours Later

Owens's Moto Guzzi snarled to life when he pushed the ignition and twisted the throttle. He tore out of WCRX's gravel driveway and was soon speeding down deserted roads winding toward Sanders's bungalow, the roar of the engine startling sleeping pelicans. Conflicting loyalties kept him on edge: *Sotto Voce* was summoning him, but if Sanders had failed to heed the warning, he could be having an unpleasant encounter with the CIA.

His choice was clear.

Instead of making a beeline for Tuscaloosa after his show, he drove north on Swift Road and turned left onto South Trail. Roberts Bay was on his left, Siesta Key directly ahead of him. Before long he passed the entrance to the Sarasota Marine Research Institute. Sanders might have brought the girl here until deciding what to do with her. He rolled up to the security kiosk beside the front gate. "Has Dr. Sanders shown up this evening?" he asked the guard who was trying to conceal a Big Mac.

"Not since I came on at midnight but let me check." He wiped ketchup from his mouth and pulled out a clipboard. "No. He hasn't signed in."

"Thanks." Owens continued to the bungalow.

It was fortunate that Sanders's neighbors mostly rented by the week; no one stayed long enough to complain about the cyclone of sound and smoke that showed up at all hours, but tonight he killed the engine when rounding the corner, coasting into the driveway. The Land Cruiser was parked in its usual spot. He pulled off his helmet, hooked it on the mirror and dug out his key to Sanders's house, a key that Sanders had threatened to confiscate on more than one occasion.

The key wasn't necessary. The door had been left ajar, sloppy CIA work; Sanders, even in a hurry, wouldn't have left his place unlocked. He stepped inside, resisting the urge to pluck his Walther automatic from its holster. The bungalow was fastidiously neat as always. The bedrooms were empty, the leather satchel missing. Sanders kept ship-shape quarters on both land and sea; the woman's unmade bed indicated he'd followed Owens's instructions and left immediately.

He ran a hand over the imprint left on the mattress. Hairs on the back of his neck stood up. He blamed his imagination for playing a trick on him, but the impression seemed much too small for the young lady he'd left earlier. His mind jumped to an impression left on another bed, the one mentioned in the Gibraltar Proceedings— that of Captain Briggs's two-year-old daughter.

Clothes were missing from Sanders's closet. He pushed aside the remaining garments, dropped to his knees and tapped his fist around the inside of the closet until he felt loose drywall. In a shallow space between studs, Sanders kept a briefcase containing his dad's Glock 17 semi-automatic. The briefcase was where he'd expected it to be, and when opened he learned Sanders *had* taken him seriously. The Glock was missing.

Back in the living room, Owens looked around one more time and was about to leave when something grabbed his eye, a book on one of the numerous shelves. Someone had replaced it upside down.

He pulled down the book, turned it over—*Famous Mysteries of the Sea*. The Sanders family loved books the way little girls loved ponies, would never damage one, but a page was bent back. He flipped to it— *The Remarkable Story of The Mary Celeste*. His best friend had a nose for mystery as keen as his own, and he wasn't surprised Sanders had done similar research, passing on that information by positioning the book in a way certain to grab Owens's attention.

He thumbed to pictures of Captain Briggs and his wife, along with their two-year-old daughter Sophia. Many toddlers looked alike, but he recognized the large soulful eyes, thought he did, anyway. Still, he couldn't discard all reason and convince himself that the young woman he'd encountered was Sophia Briggs, somehow stretching the confines of time.

Had Sanders shown the pictures of the Briggs to the woman? Did he receive a plausible explanation as to why she wore a locket holding their pictures? Another for the antique items in her possession?

He needed to find Sanders, and it wasn't hard to figure out where he'd gone, where he always went when he needed to hide or distance himself from the world—*Isabella.* He'd placed a tracking device on Sanders's ship back when his best friend was experiencing fits of depression over the loss of his parents and he'd worried Preston would sail into oblivion.

Owens checked the remaining books. One other was turned upside down, a portfolio of nautical charts. A red ribbon indicated the last place someone had looked.

He turned to it: Latitude 38.73° N and Longitude 27.32° W—Terceira, an island in the Azores. If Terceira was the destination, the schooner would need to be provisioned before making an Atlantic crossing. Owens proceeded to the small sunroom at the back of the bungalow, opened the French doors and walked out to the small boat launch. Sanders's 25-foot Sea Ray was gone—the reason the Land Cruiser was still parked in the driveway.

He buried his hands in his pockets and glanced at the stars, thinking about the strange woman he'd so recently encountered. Something about her played on his heartstrings and stirred his imagination. She was lovely, maybe even beautiful without the old-fashioned hairstyle, but he'd had his share of attractive women. *Is it her helplessness? Her certainty that I'd arrive for her?* He remembered the feel of her body as she'd slumped against him before passing out. Even unconscious, she'd managed to captivate him. But he'd been captivated before. It never lasted.

It frustrated him to admit his Mama might be right, about him settling down. *But do people like me ever settle down?* He certainly had all the excitement he could want, but being around his best friend and Jackie—when things were going smoothly for the volatile couple—made him feel like he was missing out on something.

It dawned on him where Sanders was headed, an out-of-the-way port where he often supplied his ship. Depending on conditions, it would take *Isabella* several days to get there.

After locking up the bungalow, he climbed back onto his Moto Guzzi. When he reached home, he threw a few things into a bag and headed for the airport. As he waited for his flight to depart for Tuscaloosa he couldn't help worrying about Sophia, but if anyone could hide her, it was Sanders. He was familiar with countless coves and uncharted bays perfect for hiding *Isabella*.

He sent Sanders a text and quickly received one back: *I can't believe I'm doing this. Another of your bad ideas! Yes, she did finally wake up. By the way, this girl is really...different.*

Chapter Twelve

Monday: 4:12 p.m.

Owens shifted his weight in the chair facing Pomeroy's desk. Late afternoon sunshine flooded the room. Pomeroy was standing at the window, casting a deceptively large shadow across the room.

Over the years, Pomeroy's office in the History Department hadn't changed much. The furniture was positioned the same as when Owens was a student sitting in this very chair. He wasn't surprised; blind people probably didn't rearrange furniture too often. But Franklin, the professor's assistant, was new.

The old man was having difficulty arriving at the reason for summoning him to Tuscaloosa. Owens hadn't seen Pomeroy in a while and wondered if the old man was losing his edge.

While Pomeroy considered his words, Owens's thoughts drifted back to the young woman with the satchel. He was an expert at compartmentalizing his thoughts, categorizing them the way a librarian categorizes books—as a covert operative this had always served him well—but Sophia refused to stay in the cubbyhole he'd allotted her. She spilled into other thoughts. He was haunted by the words she'd spoken in her sleep: "Abandon ship!" What was hidden behind that beautiful sphinx-like face? He was determined to find out. His attention returned to Professor Pomeroy, who'd finally begun to speak.

"A group of scholars, scientists, and engineers, including yours truly, came to believe that governments were incapable of bringing about the changes needed to set humanity on a path that didn't include total destruction."

"*Sotto Voce?*"

"Yes. Our brightest beacon of hope was scientific technology, particularly in the fields of electronics and medicine. Last night a former pupil phoned me with devastating news. We found him this morning, murdered."

Owens sat up in his chair. "Murdered?"

The old man nodded. "I have reason to believe that a scientific breakthrough is being used by unscrupulous people to create a particularly nasty weapon of mass destruction."

Chapter Thirteen

Tuesday: 8:30 a.m.

"I'm here to see Roger Vintiger."

The receptionist behind the front desk at Lukker Pharmaceuticals in Colton, Virginia, looked over the top of her glasses and wrinkled her pointed nose at him and the miniature schnauzer squirming under his arm. "You are?"

"Rashard LeBeque from *Heavy Petting*, where dog grooming is our passion." He could have produced credentials capable of opening the front gate to Camp David, but this time he handed over a bright purple card embossed with a phony name and the profile of a poodle.

"What is this about?"

"There's been a situation—disaster really—down at the salon. I've contacted Mr. Vintiger and I must say I didn't think the man capable of such language. How that man luuuvs Maria-Louisa here. But the poor thing has suffered a tragic grooming accident."

She pushed back in her chair. "I received a memo yesterday; Dr. Vintiger is under the weather and will be out for a few days. And if you ask me, that dog looks fine."

He stamped his foot and shrieked, "Are you insane? Just look at what's happened. A tragedy! An outright catastrophe." He thrust the dog in her face. "Bradley, our new employee, is really sweet even if he doesn't know what he's doing. Well, I could just paddle Bradley. He didn't follow my directions at all, *shaved* the hair on the top of Maria-Louisa's muzzle instead of parting it. Her eyebrows should be combed forward and cut at a sharp angle which, as you can clearly see, is not the case. Mr. Vintiger trusted us to have Maria-Louisa ready for the Nationals and now I must tell him she can't compete."

"Like I said, he won't be in today."

Or any other day. After that unsettling phone call early Monday morning, Pomeroy had sent *Sotto Voce* operatives to Vintiger's home on the chance he'd been taken there and was still alive, but Vintiger was found slumped behind the desk in his study, his computer's hard drive replaced with one filled with child porn. Rigor mortis had already found the body. The police had not.

Owens saw the remains at the house late Monday night after flying in on a *Sotto Voce* jet. The hit was professional, the crime staged to look like suicide. A pistol was lodged in Vintiger's mouth. The top of his head had been blown away and carried off by Maria-Louisa, who'd been guarding it under her master's bed. A few tiny marks hidden among the freckles on Vintiger's speckled back gave away the deception—he'd been tasered in his office and transported home where he was murdered.

Someone wanted the police to investigate the dead man instead of the company he worked for, which might not have been the case had the body been discovered at Lukker Pharmaceuticals.

Since Vintiger's body had yet to be discovered by the authorities, most of Lukker's employees wouldn't know he was dead. This was his only chance to slip into the building and explore the victim's office. He was gambling the files hadn't already been erased.

"I called Mr. Vintiger at home this morning. He's feeling much better and will be arriving shortly. Said I should bring Maria-Louisa and wait for him in his office."

"I'm sorry, but that's out of the question."

"Tell you what, Little Miss Attitude, how 'bout I leave Maria-Louisa with you, and you can tell him all about it. The last way I want to spend my morning is listening to him tell me how he's gonna sue the pants off me." He blinked his eyes slowly.

Her mascara-laden eyes widened when Maria-Louisa wormed free from his grasp and landed on her desk, squatting and leaving a puddle.

"Bad doggie!" Owens scolded.

The receptionist puckered her lips, pushed her glasses snugly against her nose and handed him a visitor's pass. "His office is on the third floor. Turn left when you exit the elevator. Second office on the right."

*   *   *

Owens and Maria-Louisa drew curious looks in the elevator and corridor as they made their way to Vintiger's office. He smiled at the security cameras they passed.

The office was unlocked, the door ajar. Not a good sign. Maria-Louisa wiggled free once they were behind the shut door.

Inside was fastidiously neat, a Danish modern showroom with teak furniture and a leather couch. Behind the couch hung several primitive wall hangings, riots of color depicting purple flowers, jaguars, and stepped pyramids. A window covered one wall, a modular shelf with a few books and an aquarium dominating another. He'd hoped to get to Vintiger's computer before the hard drive was wiped, but someone had already sanitized the office. The computer was gone.

Vintiger must have known his computer would be confiscated or he wouldn't have told Pomeroy the "key" was in *the castle*. But Owens didn't see anything resembling a castle. He went through desk drawers, looked under the sisal rug, shone his penlight into the heating vent to see if anything had been hidden there. Nothing. He was stumped. Then he noticed one of the books on the shelf: Franz Kafka's *The Castle*.

Kafka's description of a labyrinthine bureaucracy where all individuals are guilty until proven innocent was hardly a concept Owens endorsed. He opened the book expecting a clue to drop out. When one didn't, he flipped through pages in search of hastily jotted directions to a hiding place. But this castle, like Kafka's, was a dead end.

The lemony scent of furniture polish lay heavy on the air. Maria-Louisa's nose twitched as he continued searching. He'd never met Roger Vintiger, but he was beginning to think of him as a beetle of a man, stepped on by unfortunate circumstances. Sadness and unease settled on him, a feeling at odds with the serene movements of the two striped angelfish gliding about in their tank.

The aquarium.

Inside, a ceramic castle was partially concealed by water plants.

The glittery sand around the base appeared to have been recently disturbed.

He carefully pulled back the cover and plunged a hand into the water, retrieving the castle. The two fish retreated to separate corners of the tank.

Water drained from a hole in the castle's underside, darkening the carpet. A few shakes and an orange pill container dropped into his hand. The label identified the contents as Imitrex, a prescription for migraines, but the container now held something else. This had to be the item Vintiger had desperately wanted them to find. Inside the pill container was a thumb drive. Too bad Vintiger was denied a few more seconds to properly twist the cap. The wet thumb drive was probably compromised.

He considered linking it to his cell to see if any information was retrievable but decided not to push his luck. He pocketed the device, returned the castle to the tank, and was about to grab Maria-Louisa when Lukker walked in, accompanied by two men, one with a poorly concealed gun under his coat.

Owens recognized the CEO from Internet photos. Behind the wire rims, his deep-set eyes were too opaque to reflect light. His black hair was combed straight back, the hollow-cheeked face upholstered with skin pulled so tight it seemed smiling might tear it. Lukker had the jutting chin and compressed lips of a man about to spit—altogether the look of someone who didn't suffer fools easily yet saw fools wherever he looked.

Lukker looked at the dark spot on the rug.

Owens scooped up the schnauzer. "Bad doggie! Shame on you. Now we'll be thrown out."

Lukker scowled. "I understand you're Roger's dog groomer?"

"So true." He dug into a pocket and handed him one of the purple business cards. "Rashard LeBeque at your service, Mr...?"

"The name's Everett Lukker."

"Lukker...you mean like it says on the building? My, my; I'm glad I didn't know the big honcho was coming, or I'd have piddled on the rug myself."

"This is Arnold Trachmann." Lukker passed the card to his feral-eyed head of security. Trachmann's salt-and-pepper brush cut and concrete body invoked the image of an Army recruiting poster.

"I was told you spoke with Roger this morning," Lukker said.

He sensed a trap about to snap shut. This son-of-a-bitch had probably ordered Vintiger's execution, knew he was incapable of speaking with a dog groomer or anyone else. "Actually, I told your receptionist an itty-bitty fib. You see, I do work at *Heavy Petting* but I wanted to return Maria-Louisa personally because..."

"Get to the point."

"Because I...I think Roger is the most delicious man imaginable. So quiet and sophisticated, and a fabulous dresser, don't you think?"

"I assure you I hadn't noticed."

"Well, you see, I never get much of a chance to interact with him at the salon, but he's such a joy to the other stylists that I began thinking about him in a—dare I say it—a fun spanky sort of way. I thought if I returned Maria-Louisa personally well, just maybe, we could have coffee or something. I mean, it isn't like he's married or anything, right?"

Lukker ignored the question.

Trachmann said, "Mr. Lukker, I suggest we have Saveno escort him off the premises."

"My word; don't get your panties in a bunch. Here, you take the dog and I'll be on my way."

Lukker backed away as if the dog were contaminated with a high dose of polonium-210. "Take her back to the salon. Roger isn't coming in today, or tomorrow. He's on a leave of absence. Someone will get in touch with you about the dog."

Trachmann followed Lukker out of the office.

With Saveno on his heels, Owens headed for the door, where he paused to flutter his eyelashes. He pulled out another purple card and handed it to Saveno. "Maybe you have a pooch that needs grooming."

"I hate dogs," Saveno growled.

*   *   *

Saveno pushed Owens into an elevator. He glared at Maria-Louisa and her groomer with dim little eyes. On the ride down, he wrinkled his nose like Owens was week-old guacamole. When they reached the lobby and stepped out of the elevator, he spat, "Get moving, you whining little fudge-packer." Owens felt a hand between his shoulder blades, propelling him toward the front door.

Outside, he set Maria-Louisa down and was adjusting her leash when Saveno kicked her. She yelped pitifully as she rolled across the concrete, drawing the attention of animal rights activists protesting on the sidewalk.

Had he been blessed with the intimidating proportions of bad-ass Leroy Brown, Owens wouldn't have grown accustomed to being underestimated by opponents, as he was now. Balling his fingers into a fist, he reacted instinctively, punching Saveno in the gut with such force that air hissed from the startled man's windpipe. Owens's second swing struck him in the mouth, splitting open his bottom lip.

Staggering, Saveno reached for his holstered 9mm Browning but Owens palmed it easily, tossed it into a nearby shrub before slamming him against the limestone exterior of the building. For a moment Saveno was perfectly still, disoriented from the suddenness of his situation.

When he began kicking, Owens's fingers closed around his throat. "Consider this a warning: harm another animal, and I'll punch you in the mouth so hard you'll need to shove toothpaste up your ass to brush your teeth."

When Saveno's eyes glazed over and he stopped kicking, Owens loosened his hold and the man collapsed on the pavement.

<h1 style="text-align:center">Chapter Fourteen</h1>

The National Gallery, Washington, D.C.: Tuesday Evening

Everett Lukker watched Arthur Burbridge sip champagne in the West Garden Court of the National Gallery. Burbridge's eyes were on his wife, dazzling in a cobalt blue Oscar de la Renta sleeveless gown. The first couple had kept a low profile since returning from the funeral of their youngest son, but this event required their presence.

The President was charming several hundred guests and a dozen ambassadors whose countries had lent the gallery paintings. This special Rembrandt exhibition included drawings, etchings, and twenty paintings of youngsters. *Rembrandt's Children* would open to the public tomorrow; tonight's gala was by invitation only.

Lukker imagined Burbridge going back to Pennsylvania Avenue and rubbing the aching feet of the leader of the free world; he wondered how Burbridge could live in his wife's shadow. He'd been acquainted with the President for ages, but he'd never bothered to know Arthur.

Some things were common knowledge; the President's husband enjoyed watching sports on TV and played a decent game of basketball for a fifty-seven-year-old in need of a knee replacement. Burbridge kept his opinions to himself while enjoying biographies, tending vines at his Willamette Valley vineyard and providing extra discipline for his often-motherless children. He hated fundraisers and these meet-and-greets, but it was obvious he loved his wife, his family, and his country. Everett Lukker despised him.

But it was time to make pleasant. Lukker sharked up to him. The two camera conscious men were careful to smile at each other, empty billboard grins utterly at odds with the masterpieces of expression they were here to admire.

"My condolences on your loss."

There was no sympathy in the comment and Burbridge brushed it aside.

"How is the First Gentleman this evening? Wishing he was still in Oregon tending his vines?"

"I'm fine. Are you enjoying the Rembrandts?"

Lukker's nostrils flared as he stifled a yawn. "Art appreciation is merely part of every well-bred gentleman's wardrobe. My presence here is an elitist obligation."

Burbridge's face would have twisted into a grimace were it not for the cameras. "I'm no elitist, but I'm enjoying the artwork. I noticed your name attached to one of the paintings."

"Yes, an investment I normally keep in a vault and lend out occasionally for shows like this, when I'm feeling generous. But don't kid yourself. You're as much an elitist as Thomas Jefferson, that other grape-growing man of the people."

Burbridge was too savvy to get into a political discussion, certainly not here, and never with Lukker.

He answered with a question of his own. "Do you have children, Lukker?"

"No."

"A pity. Much like an appreciation of art, children add dimension to life. I suggest you spend some time with these canvases, take yours out of the vault more often and really look at it. You may find the element missing in your humanity."

A vein throbbed in Lukker's forehead. "Tell your wife I have what she's been asking for. It will be delivered to the Residence the day after tomorrow in the usual way, inside a bottle of your shitty wine." Walking away, he grinned like a lizard.

*   *   *

The crowd moved back to allow the First Couple to stroll through rooms paneled to evoke the style of seventeenth-century Dutch homes. The President proceeded on her own when Senator Stanton from Oregon pulled Arthur Burbridge away to discuss yet another fundraiser. It wasn't long before a particular painting caught her eye.

The canvas depicted a solemn-faced boy. She was thinking of Miles. Mercifully, few cameras flashed when she wiped away a tear.

"You look stunning tonight," Lukker said, interrupting her reverie.

"I don't feel stunning. Applying make-up in a limo always makes me feel slapped together. An emergency meeting in the Situation Room didn't leave me with much time to get dolled up. The North Koreans are testing missiles again and can now reach our shores."

"I heard. The media is all over it." He studied the faint lines around her eyes, the parentheses framing her mouth. "I hope the strain of office isn't aging you prematurely."

She glared at him for a moment, then turned back toward the canvas. "The eyes of Rembrandt's son Titus are a wonder, don't you think? I've seen reproductions of this painting, but seeing the original is a remarkable experience. Look at the way Rembrandt builds up layers of paint, each one retaining its integrity without dissolving into the next, the coarse strokes of the brush evoking a softness revealing vulnerability."

Lukker shrugged. "Perhaps you missed your calling; you could have taught art appreciation. But in my opinion, people read too much into these things. If you ask me, it's just paint on a canvas. No need to look for what isn't there."

"I think you're wrong. Rembrandt is speaking to us through the centuries, providing us with an insight into our humanity. The child in this painting has been painted with eyes focused on the infinite."

"The infinite? Titus died before his father, so he probably didn't know much about the infinite."

They stepped over to another canvas, the one owned by Lukker. The President cleared her throat. "Years ago when I was governor on a trade junket, I visited your headquarters in Virginia. I doubt you remember, but I commented on a photograph of a child on your desk."

"Yes, my younger sister," Lukker replied.

"When I inquired after the pretty girl in the photograph, you identified her as your only sibling who died from a brain aneurysm at fourteen. Since then, you haven't mentioned your family; Zoom conferences show no photos of parents in your office, just that one photo. I can't help but notice that the girl in Rembrandt's painting is a dead ringer for your sister. The hairstyle and seventeenth-century clothes are different of course, but the likeness is remarkable. Is that why you purchased this painting?"

"I purchased the painting because it's a good investment, nothing more. I won't bore you with how much this painting has appreciated in value since I bought it, but the amount is considerable."

The President studied Lukker's inscrutable expression. Perhaps the resemblance *was* merely a coincidence, but she somehow doubted it.

He changed the subject. "I have another delivery for you."

Her lips tightened. "I don't know how much longer I can risk my presidency by doing this."

Lukker's smile didn't reach his cold black eyes. "We both know you'll do what you must for as long as it takes."

Chapter Fifteen

Tuesday: 9:41 p.m.

Pomeroy's movements were slow and practiced as he poured Owens a drink from a bottle of Glen Garioch, bottled in '65. Owens took the glass from his blind mentor's hand. The scotch was excellent, even if the news wasn't.

"We've put our best people on it but, as you suspected, Roger's thumb drive was corrupted by water. If only he'd screwed on that cap properly," Pomeroy lamented.

"Have we been able to retrieve anything?"

"Patience. You just brought us the thumb drive a few hours ago. We'll need several days to recover all we can...but one word was repeated often enough to leave distorted ghost images. The word was 'Sacramento,' prompting us to believe we'd learned one of the locations of the two secret labs Roger mentioned."

"From your tone I can guess that *Sotto Voce* hasn't turned up any connection between Sacramento and Lukker Pharmaceuticals?"

"Correct. We haven't."

"Did we get anything else?"

"Not yet. I'm hoping to find an explanation for Roger's reference to King Herod.

His eyebrows shot up. "As in King Herod, from the New Testament?"

"Yes. What do you know about...Herod?"

"The Bible would have us believe he killed a bunch of kids—the so-called 'Massacre of the Innocents.'"

Pomeroy set down his glass. His eyes no longer functioned, but they still shone like beads of mercury whenever he discussed history. "More paranoid than most rulers, Herod did execute anyone who challenged his authority, including several family members."

Owens sipped his scotch. "Can you think of a reason why Vintiger would reference such a nasty dude?" he asked.

"No. But it must have something to do with the secret research labs he spoke of. He told me countless lives were at stake. He willingly sacrificed himself to provide us with information, and we owe it to him to find out what he was willing to die for."

Owens closed his eyes. Purple flooded his mind. *Why purple?* Then he remembered. He opened his eyes. "I'd better get going," he said, standing up.

"Where to?"

"Vintiger had wall hangings in his office, bright tropical weavings showing jaguars, stepped temples...and purple flowers—orchids called *Guaria Morada*."

"The national flower of Costa Rica. Quite beautiful, I'm told. I understand locals revere the flower which, they say, evokes peace, love, and hope for the future."

"I doubt Lukker is making a pill version of *that*." He drained his glass and set it down. "I suspect Vintiger bought the weavings while visiting a Lukker facility in Costa Rica. There's a little-known Sacramento there."

"Excellent! I knew you were right for this assignment. Before you go, I have something for you." Pomeroy reached into his desk drawer and pulled out a gun wrapped in a nylon holster.

"Much as I love presents, I already have a gun. Thanks anyway."

"You don't have one like this." Pomeroy also produced ammunition.

Owens reached for the gun, studying what looked like an unremarkable weapon.

"Don't let this fall into the wrong hands."

"Very lightweight. Plastic?"

"As you undoubtedly know, even plastic guns have metal, some as much as a pound. Try boarding a plane with one of those."

He examined it more closely. "What did you use to solve the problem of a metal-less spring?"

"The moveable components, as well as the bullets, are made of a flexible ceramic alloy, a recent *Sotto Voce* invention. It uses traditional bullets as well, so use the ceramic ones sparingly. This gun will pack as much punch as a traditional weapon, but is invisible to metal detectors. Many would kill for the opportunity to analyze this weapon. Don't lose it."

*   *   *

Before flying to Costa Rica, he snapped open his laptop and interfaced with an expensive piece of hardware orbiting the Earth, an information-gathering Echelon satellite. NSA had commissioned it, but covert *Sotto Voce* engineers had equipped the satellite with electro-optic modulators small enough to fit on a processor chip, creating a nearly invisible supercomputer capable of executing a variety of functions unknown to NSA. Light pulses operated a second global tracking device that was as undetectable as it was untraceable. Owens found the signal revealing *Isabella's* location. He knew where Sanders and Sophia were headed, but he wanted to confirm the time they would reach their destination.

After punching in a narrow range of coordinates, a grid of the earth appeared on the screen. A blinking red light showed the schooner's current position, and the satellite's supercomputer calculated *Isabella's* speed. She would reach Midas Cay in just over forty-eight hours.

Chapter Sixteen

Thursday: 3:34 p.m.

Behind the controls of a Vision SF50, a new breed of very small jets, Owens raced under an azure sky dotted with clouds. He thought about Everett Lukker: The guy reminded him of something that might have escaped from a tomb. He was ashamed to admit it, but the guy made his skin crawl.

The fact that Lukker Pharmaceuticals owned a facility in Costa Rica wasn't surprising. A quarter of the world's medicines came from rain forests. Underdeveloped countries were cutting them down at an alarming rate and it had become "trendy" for drug companies to invest in on-the-spot facilities, hiring local scientists and research assistants to extract and synthesize chemicals from plants and animals, and lab test these chemicals' ability to fight diseases.

He piloted the aircraft toward the northern province of Guanacaste near Liberia, where a lesser-known airport close to his destination didn't service tourists. English would have served him fine anywhere near the capital, but in the provinces he'd need to rely on his Spanish.

Six years earlier he'd traveled to Costa Rica as part of an expedition hunting for ancient crystal skulls. The expedition didn't find any, but the experience did familiarize him with the land and people of Costa Rica.

In his eagerness to depart he'd failed to obtain local currency. A call to *Sotto Voce* was all it took to secure Costa Rican *colones,* along with a jeep. After settling the jet onto the tarmac, he taxied to the far side of the jungle-edged runway and parked in the converted Quonset hut reserved to keep the plane from unfriendly eyes.

A dark-skinned local with a machete tucked into his belt waited for him in a shack that served as the terminal. The man smiled at him with bean-colored teeth as he exchanged *colones* for a wad of U.S. bills. He was handed keys to a Suzuki Samurai capable of navigating rough terrain and unpaved roads. Included in the price were several six-packs of bottled water in a duffel bag on the back seat.

According to his map, Sacramento was up the Tempisque River. From Liberia he headed south, cut through the Palo Verde National Park and continued down an unpaved road to Puerto Hamorro, stopping at a rustic dock beside the Tempisque River to stretch his legs.

Here the river was sinuous and the vegetation took on a jungle-like aspect. The crocodiles sliding down the muddy banks into the shallow water were bigger and looked more threatening than the alligators and caiman in the marsh behind his trailer park. It was hot and humid, and he'd have paid dearly for an ice-cold Mountain Dew.

He reached for the duffel bag of bottled water and was disappointed to discover a mix-up; instead of water the duffel bag contained someone's stack of well-thumbed porn magazines.

Darkness had settled over the rain forest when he arrived in Sacramento, hardly more than a cluster of sheds and cabins beside a river that had nearly dried up. Sacramento had no electricity and few visitors. The only rentable room was above a thatch-roofed tavern.

The dark-skinned proprietor, who probably wasn't much older than thirty, was a tobacco-breathed woman with few teeth. A younger woman shadowed her, probably a daughter. He paid thirty-one hundred *colones* for the room and breakfast, around ten U.S. dollars, but was reduced to breaking the spider webs in the room himself, along with shaking dust from the bedcover. He knew Costa Rica was famous for its remarkable biodiversity—five percent of the world's wildlife could be found within its borders—but the huge spiders inching across the ceiling made it difficult to close his eyes.

With a rolled copy of *Busty Beauties* as his only defense, he finally dozed off, dreaming of the *Mary Celeste*, her lost crew, and the young woman Sanders was hiding from the CIA.

CHAPTER SEVENTEEN

Friday: 7:00 a.m.

A knock rattled the door at 7:00 a.m.

He'd only managed a few hours of sleep; spiders, humidity, and jungle noises had kept him up much of the night. The sheets clung to him as he rose from the bed, scratching itchy welts in hard-to-reach places. He squinted at the bright tropical light flooding over the copper-skinned youth standing outside his door. Thirteen or fourteen, with shiny black hair and large dark eyes, he was handsome but for the yellow teeth clenching a sloppily rolled cigarette.

"Breakfast costs fifteen hundred *colones*. If you want, better come downstairs fast before I feed it to the hogs and chickens." As if on cue, a rooster crowed.

"You are?" Owens asked.

"I am Álvaro, and when my mother is away, I run this place."

Owens had been looking forward to utilizing his Spanish. "You speak English."

"Yes. Missionaries from Chicago. Tell them you love Jesus and they teach you English. I teach myself how to lie."

"I'll be down in a few minutes," he said, his stomach rumbling like an empty cement mixer.

His room didn't include plumbing and he hadn't seen an outhouse last night anywhere near the building, so he urinated into a chipped ceramic pot near a glassless window after evicting the creepy-crawly living inside. He pulled aside an oilcloth blind and dumped his business behind the building.

Downstairs, the tavern was empty except for Álvaro who sat at a long table. He puffed on his cigarette and thumbed through a copy of *National Geographic*. Owens expected the kid to be ogling photographs of topless natives in the Congo and smiled to see Las Vegas showgirls before the magazine was flipped over.

Álvaro disappeared into the kitchen and returned with a wooden plate of black beans and rice, seasoned with onions and peppers, accompanied by fried eggs and corn tortillas. Shrimp were added to the mix, reminding him that no place in Costa Rica was far from the sea.

"Good *arroz*," Owens mumbled between spoonfuls, familiar with a dish the locals eat with fish, chicken, or whatever else is handy. Álvaro produced a cup and clay pitcher containing *guaro*. On his last trip to Costa Rica, Owens had poached his brain with this distilled drink made from sugar cane. He'd learned his lesson and now drank with moderation.

"If you are still here tomorrow there should be a little beer," Álvaro said, ash from his cigarette falling onto the floor.

He had no idea how long he'd be staying since he wasn't certain what he was looking for. As he finished eating, his eyes settled on the purple orchids growing in jars, the *Guaria Moradas* depicted in the hangings in Roger Vintiger's office.

The boy took away the plate, leaving the pitcher.

When he returned Owens asked, "The woman I paid last night, your mother?"

"Yes." Álvaro held out his hand. "Fifteen hundred *colones* for the breakfast."

"Where is she this morning?"

"She and my sister make weavings to sell to tourists."

"Do you get many tourists here?"

He shook his head. "The weavings go to shops at resorts on the coast."

He paid, waiting until the money was pocketed before saying, "She told me the price of the room *included* breakfast."

The huckster shrugged and slapped the money back onto the table.

"Keep it. I want to buy some information. Are there any pharmaceutical companies around here?"

He stared blankly at Owens.

"A place where they make drugs."

The boy's expression brightened. "You want drugs? No problem. Lots of coke around. Other stuff, too."

Including marijuana, judging from the smell of his cigarette. "I'm talking about medicine."

"Yes, there is an American company, maybe ten kilometers from here, where I think they make the medicines. The place is a fortress on high ground surrounded by a river, all concrete with armed guards. No military here in Costa Rica. Very peaceful, but drug lords control many areas and companies outside major cities sometimes hire their own security."

"Have you ever been inside?"

More ash fell from the cigarette as he nodded.

"Why did you go?" he inquired.

"Sometimes I go with my sister. She visits at night, usually on Fridays and Saturdays. Sometimes the men don't want her, want something different," the boy said, matter-of-factly.

He felt like a Neanderthal for asking. Prostitution was legal and profitable for persons over eighteen. Pedophilia was often tolerated.

"Do many Americans work there?"

"Not anymore. Two, maybe three years ago when construction was finished, Americans came several times in a helicopter to take out the drugs. A man with a sad donkey face would wander into town, spend a little money, but I haven't seen him in a long time."

He slapped a photo of Roger Vintiger on the table. "This him?"

"It was long ago, but yes, I think it is him. He bought some weavings from my mother. Friendly, with big sad eyes. My sister offered several times to cheer him up but he wasn't interested."

"Do you think you and your sister could get me into this place?"

"Maybe, but it would be expensive."

"How much?"

"Two hundred thousand *colones*."

"That's a lot."

The cigarette dangled from the boy's mouth. "Something in there must be important for you to pay just to see inside."

The kid had him over a barrel. Owens doubted he'd ever seen that kind of money and couldn't help but admire the little opportunist, within reason. "A hundred and fifty thousand *colones*, but I'll nod when you tell your sister I only paid five hundred."

"Let's shake on it."

He pumped the kid's hand. "Lose the cigarettes; they could give us away. If all goes well, when we return I'll sweeten the deal with a bonus. I have some magazines I think you'll enjoy."

*　*　*

Owens had long ago accepted his line of work often required difficult choices, but he and Álvaro couldn't think of a way to get inside without using his sister Katia as bait. Despite her assertion that the men treated her well, he regretted involving the young woman in a manner that lowered him to the same ethical level as those who also paid for her services.

Álvaro shrugged, ash falling from his cigarette. "You're not asking her to do anything she doesn't already do."

It was small comfort. Besides, if Roger Vintiger was right, many innocent lives were at stake.

Yesterday the sky had been clear. But weather changed quickly in Central America and a thick layer of clouds now blotted out the sunset as he coaxed the jeep through the rain forest. Álvaro sat in the back clutching a canvas sack while Katia rode shotgun and provided directions. The raucous chatter of howler monkeys and macaws accompanied an orchestra of a hundred sounds heralding the night. The rain forest was dry, each leaf and branch an outstretched tongue lifted skyward toward the clouds. Rain was imminent and the humidity was becoming oppressive as they drove on. When Katia gave the word, he pulled the jeep behind a grove of wild nispero trees.

It was Friday night and Katia usually made the trip on a rusty bicycle. Owens pulled the bike from the back of the jeep, set it on the ground and plucked the telltale cigarette from Álvaro's mouth, grinding it into the dirt with his boot. "Katia, your brother and I will go ahead to give the place a look-see. Wait an hour so you can arrive at your usual time. You're sure only one guard will be posted at the entrance?"

"I cannot promise, but this is usually so."

As he brushed at the mosquitoes circling him, Owens couldn't help noticing how her curves filled out her thin cotton dress. The pesky swarms didn't bother her or her brother.

"Three ticos guard the building and I'm friendly with all of them, but the big one at the entrance likes me and should not be a problem. But how will I know when an hour has passed?"

He removed his watch and handed it to her. "You can tell time, can't you?"

She nodded.

"I need you to distract them for, say, half an hour to give me an opportunity to sneak inside and look around."

"No problem."

He reached into the jeep and slipped a backpack over his shoulder. It contained a satellite phone, machete, binocular goggles with night vision, and wire cutters. Also inside was the gun Pomeroy had given him. He snapped in a clip of traditional bullets, holstered the weapon under his arm and grabbed Álvaro's sack. Something moved within it. Inside was a live chicken, its beak impaled in a cork to silence it. "What gives?" he asked, tossing the sack to the boy.

"We can't just walk through the gate and ask to be let inside. We will need to cross the river and cut through the wire fence."

He had no idea how a chicken was going to help them cross the river, but the kid seemed to know what he was doing. He began trekking down the dirt road, with Owens close on his heels.

It didn't take long for them to reach a drawbridge spanning a shallow river approximately thirty-five feet wide and all but dried up. The bridge was down, the wire gate open in anticipation of Katia's arrival. In the distance electric lights were on. He donned the goggles and saw razor-wire surrounding the compound. Small shacks, probably erected to house the workers who'd built the lab, were dark and showed no signs of life.

Near the entrance of the main building a guard watched the road, an AK-47 slung over his shoulder. Katia said only one guard would be outside, but this one was joined by another.

Álvaro whispered, "I do not recognize these guards. These aren't the ones Katia is expecting."

"Will they hurt her?"

The boy shrugged. "Not if they want her to come back."

Hardly reassuring. They silently melted into the underbrush when Álvaro pointed at surveillance cameras in surrounding saragundi trees.

The river circled the compound like a moat, and they needed to cut through the jungle for an undetectable way to cross, twisting vines, Manchineel trees with poison bark, and Acacia trees covered with ants making it slow going. Hacking away at the vegetation with the machete, he was forced to rely on the night vision goggles. Álvaro had no difficulty seeing in the darkness.

The humidity was smothering, gluing his shirt to his chest. When too exhausted to raise his arms, he let the boy commandeer the machete. Álvaro attacked the vegetation with the stamina of the Energizer Bunny. Owens wiped his wet brow with a sleeve and swiped at the ubiquitous mosquitoes, his cheeks burning with embarrassment at not being able to keep up with the kid. Suddenly, Álvaro struck Owens's wrist with the blunt side of the machete. He'd been distracted by thoughts of mysterious Sophia. This was a dangerous place to become distracted; the branch he'd been about to touch hissed before slithering away.

They hadn't gone much farther when Álvaro paused, pointing the machete at an opening leading down to what remained of the river. "Here it is good to cross."

Relieved, Owens paused to catch his breath, but after a closer inspection of the river he was dubious. Through the goggles he saw many pairs of orange eyes glowing like embers. "There's no current here, just scattered puddles of muddy water we can easily walk around, but what about the crocs?"

The boy wasted no time removing the chicken from the sack. He plucked the cork from the bird's beak. It didn't need to be coaxed into clucking angrily. "Get ready to run," he said, releasing the bird.

The chicken flapped its wings, skimmed over a few puddles and landed in the center of the riverbed. It pecked at the ground and ignored the reptiles until one crawled close enough to snap at it. The chicken leapt away at the last instant and ran in circles evading the lunging predators.

"Let's go!" Álvaro bellowed, jumping down the bank and sprinting.

Through the goggles Owens could see the crocodiles scurrying after the chicken— all but one, arguably the largest. Ignoring the chicken, it headed their way faster than he thought possible.

CHAPTER EIGHTEEN

Friday: 8:15 p.m.

The croc was closing in when they scurried up the far bank. Álvaro reached for his arm and pulled him to safety, the pursuing croc snapping at the space he'd occupied only seconds earlier. The beast retreated and Owens collapsed on the ground; he could feel his heart beating in the center of his head as he sucked in ragged gulps of sticky air.

Their destination was fifty yards away. When Owens caught his breath, they quietly scrambled through the underbrush until reaching a mangled wire fence protecting the site from pesky crocs and prying eyes. He spat on a leaf and tossed it against the fence to be certain it wasn't electrified, then reached for the wire cutters and began snipping an opening big enough for him to pass through. Álvaro tried to follow.

"Stay here until I return."

"This is like cops and robbers. I do not want to miss out on the fun."

He was responsible for the boy. "This isn't a game. Are there wild chickens about?"

"Yes, but hard to catch. Why?"

"We'll need to cross the river again when we leave and you only brought one. Nab another while I worm my way inside. Be careful."

"You're the one with the *colones* in your wallet; that makes you the boss."

After closing in on the lights, Owens paused behind a fallen log to wait for Katia, who soon appeared on the bike. The guard at the door smiled at the sight of her. She hesitated when she leapt off the bike and saw the guards at the entrance but recovered enough to throw her arms around the one not holding the AK-47. He scratched the stubble on his chin before worming a hand under her dress, his hands cupping her buttocks. She wasn't wearing panties and Owens was glad the boy wasn't there to see his involuntary appreciation of his sister's physical attributes.

The armed guard disappeared inside while the one Katia selected kissed her roughly on the mouth. She yelped when he bit her on the bottom lip.

Owens's hand reached for his gun.

She broke free and shot a glance in his direction. Was she giving him a green light to proceed? He wasn't sure.

An attempt was made to pull her inside, but she removed the watch he'd lent her—which looked more expensive than it was—and used it to lure him into the bushes beside the building. While she distracted him, Owens inched closer. No attempt to beautify the area had been made and he passed through a landscape infested with waist-high weeds, the only bare spot being a leaf-strewn landing pad for a helicopter, unused for some time by the looks of it. He reached the door and snuck inside.

No air-conditioning. The sweltering interior was more suited to producing mushrooms than drugs. The light inside was dim, but bright enough to make the goggles painful. He pushed them up onto his forehead and used the flashlight to explore the building, his ears cocked for sounds of approaching footsteps.

Quiet as a caterpillar, he inched down a corridor that widened into several dark research labs. The flashlight picked out surveillance cameras festooned with spider webs. They didn't look operational, but he decided to check, grabbing a dust-coated chair from a lab and pulling it up to one of the cameras. He yanked the power cord from the ceiling as quietly as he could. The cord pulled free, much too easily. It wasn't wired to a power source—this camera, and he suspected the others, were merely window dressing. Suspicion grabbed him like a creeper vine. *Am I being set up?*

He stepped down from the chair and made his way toward a lit room. Peeking inside, he saw the other two guards, the one who'd lost first crack at Katia looking at porn on an old computer and the other dozing on a cot. The unpainted concrete walls were damp and moldy. Still no air-conditioning, but a ceiling fan rattled over them.

Owens continued his investigation, his flashlight illuminating more unused laboratories. The lab stations were filled with items one would expect to find, although the microscopes and other equipment looked ill-treated, like objects from high school science classes, understandable were this facility not owned by one of the largest pharmaceutical companies in the world. No personal effects were present to indicate the recent presence of scientists or lab technicians.

The boy had said this facility was only three or four years old and Americans had choppered drugs from it, but the thick layer of dust blanketing everything, except areas where it appeared the roof had leaked, made him doubt scientists had ever worked here.

So why did Vintiger want us to come here? he wondered. *What was I supposed to find?* There was always a black market for stolen drugs, especially illegal ones, but if drugs weren't being manufactured here, why the armed guards? And why these guards?

Had they been professionals he wouldn't have gotten inside so easily.

He continued searching until encountering a locked door. To free his hands, he set the flashlight on the ground, placing it so the beam illuminated the lock. Not one to travel without a tension wrench and lock pick, he inserted the wrench into the cylinder and applied a light amount of torque. With the pick he felt around, lifting all the pins. An easy process, much too easy. Pulling the door open, he reached for the flashlight and stepped inside, closing the door behind him after spotting an inside latch to prevent him from being trapped inside. He flipped a switch on the wall and a light came on, blinding him for a few moments.

When his eyes acclimated to the brightness, he saw that he'd entered a sizable storage room with wooden crates stacked against a wall. Some of the crates had been pried open, exposing packages of medicine. Several packages contained vials labeled as vaccines for diphtheria, tetanus, and pertussis—the standard "cocktail" of baby immunizations referred to as DTP vaccines. They weren't expensive, even in developing countries, and he couldn't imagine Lukker paying anyone to protect them.

The remainder of the room was filled with machines for sealing the vials and packaging them, but like everything else here, nothing appeared to have been touched recently. Labels were scattered about and broken vials crunched beneath his Nikes. Since drugs didn't appear to have been developed or produced here, he could only surmise that vaccines were shipped here for repackaging. Hardly cost effective, so there had to be another explanation. Was something being added to the vials? Something dangerous? If so, why was this place being preserved and guarded instead of destroyed?

Owens pocketed a sample of vials, turned off the light, and had just opened the door when gunshots thundered outside.

Chapter Nineteen

Friday: 8:40 p.m.

The guards inside followed the sound of gunfire where Katia was receiving lessons on how to fire a machine gun. She had little difficulty drawing together all three guards. The men pawed at Katia and vied for his timepiece as they passed around a flask and made a show of firing *their* semi-automatics into the night sky, as well as in the direction of the river.

Owens slipped out the front door, noticed only by Katia who winked at him as he disappeared into the underbrush. She lured the men back inside once he'd gone. He dropped the night-vision goggles back over his eyes and dashed a hundred yards toward the waiting jeep. He stopped dead in his tracks at the alarming sight before him.

Álvaro was lying on his side in the dry riverbed between several puddles. A dozen crocodiles surrounded him, several of the largest snapping at each other. From a distance he couldn't tell if the boy was alive or dead. He must've caught a stray bullet and rolled down the river embankment.

The boy moaned, a welcome sign, but when the crocodiles closed in dread scattered through him like a ball of mercury hit by a hammer. "You're surrounded by crocs," he shouted. "Don't move!"

The reptiles could go a year without eating, and these probably hadn't scarfed down anything in months. He was mystified why they hadn't attacked already. He figured he might be able to distract a few of them, but certainly not all. A sack of chickens would have proved useful.

Owens couldn't stand there and let the boy become a snack. He reached for his gun and girded himself with a firm breath, wishing he was holding an elephant rifle instead of a plastic pistol. Either way, bullets weren't the best way to kill these reptiles. Their prehistoric brains allowed them to snap and bite even when filled with hot lead. But another thought bit into his mind, something he'd learned while studying these crocodiles during his crystal skull search.

He pulled out his satellite phone and connected with a *Sotto Voce* operative in London who'd gotten him out of serious shit before, a fellow techno-guru named Casper, an apt nickname for someone pale as a ghost from spending too much time indoors in front of computers.

Seconds felt like hours, but he finally heard Casper's voice.

"Blimey if it isn't Nike. Doc Pomeroy told me you were in Costa Rica and might be needing a bit o' help. How goes it?"

"Casper, I'm trying to save a friend's life. Can you access Costa Rican crocodile sounds?"

"No problemo. The World Zoological Institute here in London has nearly a quarter of a billion files. I'm hacking into WZI's database as we speak. Finding several dozen files. Can you be more specific?"

"Yeah—Juvenile crocs in distress."

He knew a few facts about these reptiles: it was the crocs' highly developed parental instincts he wanted to tap. Adults of both genders often went to great lengths to protect threatened young, even offspring not their own. One of the men on the crystal skull expedition was nearly killed after plucking a baby croc from a river. Several fifteen-foot adults attacked his skiff in response to the juvenile's cries for help.

"Got it, mate. What else?"

"I need a way to broadcast the sound. I can receive and store the audio file on my satellite phone but I don't think it'll generate enough noise to do much good. Any thoughts?"

"You're in the Guanacaste Province. Surely you didn't slog into the rain forest without a radio."

Time was running out for Álvaro. Owens didn't understand why the crocs hadn't already attacked, but saving the kid required him to remain calm. "There's a radio in my rented Samurai."

"I'm interfacing with a nearby 50-kilowatt repeater near the Nicaraguan border, once operated as a radio propaganda outlet. The station's repeater boosts the signal, but I can't give you its exact AM frequency so you'll need to hunt for it. Your crying croc will be on the air in less than a minute. Remember, the typical human can hear audio frequencies as low as 20 Hz and as high as 20 KHz. Crocs hear differently than you and me so it might sound like static, or nothin' at all. Anything else?"

"That should do. Thanks for the help."

"Easy-peasy. Stop by next time you're in the neighborhood. Bring along Preston. The gang can reminisce and put down a few pints. You two can meet Toaster's new bird. She's quite nice even if she does have a face like a smacked bum."

"I'd like that, Casper. Gotta run." He pocketed the phone and dashed for the jeep parked on the far side of the river, distracting a few crocs who turned to stare at him with luminous eyes.

Back at the Samurai, his hands were shaky as he inserted the key into the ignition and turned on the radio, fumbling with the dial until snaps and hisses—what he assumed were juvenile crocodile-in-distress sounds—issued from the speaker. He set the volume to maximum before leaping out and sprinting back to the boy.

Álvaro wasn't moaning anymore and must have passed out, maybe the reason the crocs hadn't yet attacked. Movement would have drawn them to him more quickly. Seconds felt like hours and he fretted they weren't going to take the bait. He was also concerned that the boy would regain consciousness and start fidgeting.

Owens reached for the plastic gun and aimed at the largest croc. Just as he was about to press the trigger he saw motion; they began inching away from Álvaro. After a slow start, they moved quickly toward the distress sounds. It wasn't long before Owens jumped down from the embankment and dashed toward him.

Álvaro's scalp was matted, the goggles making the blood appear to ooze green. The wound was consistent with a bullet graze to the head. Owens examined the injury; the wound was superficial. The kid was his responsibility, and he'd failed to keep him safe, but the guilt flaming through him receded when Álvaro finally stirred. He lifted the boy and carried him to safety. Álvaro found his legs once they reached the far bank.

"You aren't paying me enough," he mumbled.

"What else do you want?" Owens shouted, the radio still screeching reptilian distress sounds.

"I'll take the jeep."

Rain began to fall as they approached the Samurai, now surrounded by numerous crocodiles of varying sizes. Several crocs had already flattened and shredded the front tires while others attacked the wheels at the rear. Remarkably, one large fellow, its jaws snapping at the air, had raked its claws at the handle, leaving deep scratches in the paint while managing to open the passenger door. The bulk of its body was stretched across both front seats, its head projecting above the wheel as if it were about to drive away.

The radio would continue to attract crocodiles until the battery ran down. Owens was anxious to deliver the vials to Pomeroy and decided not to wait. Before starting the long walk back to town where, hopefully, he could bum a ride to the airport, he handed Álvaro the keys.

"She's all yours, kid!"

* * *

By the time the sun came up he'd already reached his plane and was back in the cockpit, pushing the Vision SF50 to the max while racing back to Tuscaloosa. As the mountains of Costa Rica vanished beneath rain clouds, he reached into his pocket and fingered the vials he'd collected at the compound outside Sacramento. Hopefully, they would prove instrumental in deciphering the mysterious file Vintiger wasn't supposed to see. But another mystery was sinking its teeth into him, a mystery of a more personal nature, one he was determined to solve.

CHAPTER TWENTY

Earlier

Trachmann tapped on the door to Lukker's office.

"Come."

He stepped inside. "Sir, your request that I place surveillance monitors in Vintiger's office paid off, as you suspected it would."

Lukker's smile was nearly a grimace. "We might not have witnessed Vintiger hiding that thumb drive in the fish tank if we hadn't."

"Sir, you instructed me to let you know when there was a security breach at the Costa Rican facility. Someone just entered without authorization."

"Good."

The surface of Lukker's lake-size desk was clear but for a keyboard and a small photograph of a young girl. A bank of computer monitors covered a wall opposite his desk and several blinked to life when he tapped a keyboard, revealing the interior of the lab in Sacramento. They watched in silence until the intruder appeared on a monitor.

Trachmann squinted at the grainy images. "It's that dog groomer, the ass bandit we confronted in Vintiger's office."

"I should have guessed. He gave us a business card, didn't he?"

Trachmann nodded.

"I'm assuming you checked to see if he really worked at a dog grooming salon."

"Of course. I personally drove out to the address on the card and spoke with the owner. I was told Rashard LeBeque was one of *Heavy Petting's* best groomers."

"Interesting: printed business cards, and a fabricated background convincing enough to fool most people. But not you?"

"I only checked to be thorough. Despite the elaborate ruse, I suspected that Rashard LeBeque was merely a cover. I don't know who this fellow is or who he works for, but I admire his inventiveness. What matters most is that we knew Vintiger would be useful spilling the beans for us and would reach out to someone, just as you predicted."

"Do we know who Vintiger phoned?"

"No. I'm looking into it, but I haven't turned up anything so far. A firewall on the call prevented us from listening in or tracing it. Highly professional."

Lukker was reminded of the reason he'd hired Trachmann. He needed someone who would do as he was told without asking questions. Trachmann's impressive physical development came late. He was bullied by older siblings and a drunken father. When growth finally kicked in he'd sought revenge, levelling his rage at everyone he could. A stint in juvenile hall for stabbing his father hardened him, and after committing a few petty crimes he'd enlisted in the Army and was imprisoned for nearly beating a fellow recruit to death.

Lukker had followed the court proceedings and had been impressed by Trachmann's lack of remorse. He had provided a team of lawyers to free Trachmann and harness his rage, and the investment had paid for an all-too-willing lapdog to do his bidding.

"That *was* Roger's dog?" Lukker asked.

"It was," Trachmann responded, running a hand over his salt-and-pepper crew cut. "He's quite capable, a professional based on the way he took down Saveno."

They continued to watch the monitor.

Lukker smiled when the intruder pulled a chair up to one of the surveillance cameras and yanked out the cord.

"Those things should have been hidden better," Trachmann said.

"Those cameras were meant to be found," Lukker explained. "But there are others with minuscule lenses embedded in the concrete walls. It would take hours for him to locate them all."

Lukker followed the stealthy movement of the trespasser, who paused at many of the lab stations to examine the equipment. "This is where we'll find out how good he is. He's approaching the packaging room. Let's see if he's skillful enough to pick the lock."

"What if he can't?"

Lukker entered a code into his keyboard. "Like most reality TV shows, there's a script involved. I'm writing this one, and he *will* get inside. I can silently unlock the door from here. He'll think he opened it himself. But something tells me we shouldn't underestimate this fellow. There he goes: he's got a tension wrench and lock pick, and I bet he knows how to use them."

A hidden camera had been placed at the perfect location to monitor the break-in, and both men nodded with admiration at the speed with which the pins were lifted within the cylinder.

Owens didn't need help. In short order, the door swung open.

Trachmann asked, "When are you going to explain to me why you're going to so much trouble setting up this guy?"

A finger shot up to Lukker's lips. "Silence. I want to see what he does next."

The interloper bent down and pocketed a sample of vials.

"Mission accomplished," Lukker said. "We have our scapegoat."

CHAPTER TWENTY-ONE

Saturday: 1:20 p.m.

Soon after Owens joined Sanders and Sophia aboard *Isabella*, Sophia approached him and said, "Captain Sanders won't say where we're headed. I have a feeling he knows something about me he doesn't want to talk about. I get the same feeling from you."

"We're headed for the Azores," Owens said.

"Why?"

"Guess it's time to come clean."

"You look clean to me."

He stifled a short laugh. "It's an expression for telling the truth."

"I see," she said, not looking like she saw at all. "Why does there need to be an expression for telling the truth?"

"Can't answer that, but listen, Sophia, let's play a game."

Her eyes brightened, and her voice filled with childlike glee. "A game?"

"Yes. Tell me everything you know about yourself, and then I'll tell you what I know. Let's start with your parents. What can you tell me about them?"

Her face clouded over as quickly as it had brightened. "I don't remember my mother and father."

"Are those their pictures inside your locket?"

"I've had the locket for as long as I can remember, but I really don't know who they are. Sometimes when I'm sad I open it and pretend they're my parents, especially the woman because she looks like she might be trying to smile while the man looks a bit frightening."

"Do you remember a voyage on a wooden ship with large sails?"

She bit her bottom lip in concentration. "No. Why do you ask?"

"You just said, 'as long as I can remember,' but how long *can* you remember?"

She was slow to answer, her eyes focused on the horizon. Finally, "I remember working on a cruise ship, more than one, but they all blur together."

"Most people have childhood memories, special events like birthdays and holidays, pets, and favorite foods—a first kiss by a boyfriend. Have you ever had a boyfriend, Sophia?"

"I don't know."

Owens felt uneasy at her doe-like gaze. "Haven't you ever wondered why you don't remember such things?"

The question appeared to trouble her. "No. Until recently, I believed everyone's memories evaporated like mine after a few years. Now you're suggesting this isn't true, and I'm beginning to believe you."

"What's changed your mind?"

"I don't know how to explain it, but things are starting to pop into my head, images of people I can't identify: an old nun, a woman who was kind to me on a ship I once worked on—she wore a white coat."

"A doctor?"

"Yes, at least I think so. She was nice to me. And there are other things I don't understand how I could know: Bible stories I don't remember reading. It makes me wonder what else is buried in my head."

"Go on."

"When I mend sails on this ship, I feel very comfortable with a thread and needle in my hand."

"Captain Sanders says you mend sails like a pro."

"I feel like I've done similar work before, many times."

"Perhaps you have. Is there anything more you can tell me about yourself?"

"No, so now it's time for you to...come clean."

"I'll tell you what I know, which isn't much. Let me start with a question: how old do you think you are?"

"Twenties. Maybe a bit older."

"That's certainly how old you look, but do you feel older than that?"

Her eyebrows pressed together. "I don't know. What does 'old' feel like?"

He didn't have an answer. Obviously, she didn't have age-related aches and pains preventing her from doing chores aboard *Isabella*.

"Do you have any idea where your satchel and the items in it came from?"

"No. Like my locket, I've always had them."

"These items are very old. Research on the doll suggests it was made in New York City in the early 1870s."

She gave him a curious look. "You've researched my doll?"

"I had your possessions analyzed."

She didn't have a poker face and was obviously upset.

He placed a hand over hers, again feeling the spark he'd experienced when he'd rescued her on that rock near the coast. "Sophia, you'd passed out and Captain Sanders and I wanted to help you. You were unconscious for so long we began to worry. I thought the contents of your bag might provide clues about who you were and where you belonged. What we discovered was interesting, to say the least."

"What do you mean?"

"I know the identities of the two people pictured in your locket. We borrowed it while you slept, researched it as well."

Anger drained from her eyes and her bottom lip quivered as she fingered the locket, dime-size tears rolling down her cheeks. "Until now, I've never known it to be off my neck." She wiped her eyes with the back of her hand. "Were they my relatives?"

He'd seen many women cry, but watching her lashes fill with tears paralyzed him for a moment. "The pictures are of Benjamin Briggs and his wife Sarah. I don't suppose those names ring a—sound familiar?"

She shook her head.

"There's a possibility you're related to them."

"I don't see how. My paychecks are—I can't remember the phrase— oh yes, 'automatically deposited' into a special account, and the stubs have always shown the name Sophia Correia." Her eyes, once light blue like the surrounding ocean, had darkened to stormy gray. "What did you learn about my things?"

"The clothes are all Portuguese. The elaborate gown is at least seventy-five years old, created on the mainland near Lisbon. The second smallest garment was stitched seventy or eighty years earlier, while the toddler smock was sewn on Terceira, approximately a hundred and fifty years ago."

"I don't understand. If these clothes were made before I was born, who were they made for?"

"It's possible they *were* made for you. You might be older than you think, much older."

"I still don't believe you have come entirely clean."

He proceeded carefully. She seemed fragile and he didn't want to hurt her.

"Sophia, do you know what a mystery is?"

"Yes, the Mystery of the Eucharist—when bread is transformed into the body of our Savior."

I should have seen that coming, he thought. "Do you know any other mysteries?"

She thought about it. "Yes. Cruise ships have libraries. The Hardy Boys. Sherlock Holmes. Hercule Poirot. When I help hand out books, these are very popular. Sometimes I think I'll read one, but there's never enough free time."

"There are other kinds of mysteries. In fact, you're at the heart of one right now."

She swallowed hard. "I am?"

He nodded. "I'm addicted to mysteries. They're manna from heaven for me."

Her face lit up at the mention of manna. "The Book of Exodus!"

"Sophia, I'm going to tell you a fantastic story about a ship called the *Mary Celeste* and her unfortunate crew, one of the greatest mysteries of the sea."

Chapter Twenty-Two

Sophia didn't flinch when told about the *Mary Celeste,* no flicker of awareness, not even when Owens mentioned the captain's two-year-old daughter Sophia. He'd hoped to receive some clarification from her, an explanation for the enigmatic items in her possession, something he could build a scaffold around to support an acceptable explanation. But she'd merely stared at him with the rapt attention of a child hearing a fairy tale.

"What do you think happened to those poor people?" she asked.

Sanders spared him from speculating. Before heading below he ordered, "Get those sails in. We don't have much time."

With Sophia's help, Owens began furling the sails.

"Why don't we have much time?" she asked.

"We're abandoning ship."

Her eyes filled with concern. "Why would we do such a thing? We aren't sinking, are we?"

He paused from gathering in a sail. *Did the use of the word "abandon" jog her memory?* "No, we aren't sinking. A US warship is racing toward us, and it's you they want."

"Why would they want me?"

"Wish I knew. It's probably a misunderstanding, but you're not being turned over to anyone until I get answers to a few questions. I'll finish up here. Go fetch your satchel."

Sophia was about to head below when something rising from the depths off the starboard bow caught her attention. Her eyes filled with alarm and she crossed herself before pointing at it.

"Our ride is here," Owens said calmly.

For the first time since finding her sitting on that boulder, he saw

Sophia look afraid, her thin body shaking as an object shaped like a giant manta ray rose from the depths.

Chapter Twenty-Three

Saturday: 2:40 p.m.

The USS *Wilcox,* a Ticonderoga-class guided missile launcher, sped toward the schooner at 30.5 knots. Her complement of 33 officers and 327 enlisted personnel had been increased several days earlier by authorization of the CNO, Chief of Naval Operations. The complement now included a team of CIA agents. In charge—Brian Fulton.

Fulton paced on the deck near the bow, salty spray glistening in his hair. The CIA had learned Sanders's ship departed Sarasota Bay several hours before dawn a few days earlier, just as agents appeared at his residence.

The CIA also learned the schooner arrived three days later at Midas Cay, where Anderson Owens, shorn of his trademark dreadlocks, joined them. Owens had filed a false flight plan to throw them off, but he was foolish if he thought the CIA, with eyes and ears everywhere, couldn't hunt him down. A local merchant remembered the men provisioning the ship and purchasing clothes, shoes, and foul-weather gear for a woman.

The CIA, under the guise of the U.S. Coast Guard, had issued a BOLO—Be On the Lookout—for Sanders, whose ship departed Midas Cay before the *Wilcox's* arrival.

As luck would have it, an oil tanker spotted Sanders's ship and provided coordinates.

There was no way the vintage schooner could outrun the *Wilcox.* This would be a short chase.

CHAPTER TWENTY-FOUR

Saturday: 3:50 p.m.

Agent Fulton squinted into the binoculars but didn't see what he was looking for.

The USS *Wilcox's* four General Electric LM2500 gas turbines were propelling the six-hundred-foot vessel across the Atlantic so rapidly that the vessel's wake was lengthy enough to be seen from space.

An hour later, *Isabella* registered as a blip on the *Wilcox's* radar, and before long the ship appeared as a speck on the eastern horizon. With the binoculars, Fulton was able to make out details; the schooner wasn't carrying sail, and no smoke issued from her engine. She appeared to be propelled by current alone. In fact, radar confirmed she was headed in their direction.

"I intend to accompany you," Fulton informed Captain J.P. Kornievsky, in charge of the boarding party.

"Sorry, sir, but request denied," Kornievsky said emphatically. "You haven't trained with our team and will undoubtedly be a liability if we encounter resistance."

"Let me remind you that I am a special advisor to the President of the United States. You will comply with my request."

"I don't care if you work for Santa Claus and come with orders from the North Pole. Unless I'm so directed by the commander of this ship, you'll be sitting this one out."

Fulton decided not to press.

When Kornievsky assembled his team, he allowed Fulton to explain the mission.

"Preston Sanders and Anderson Owens, along with their traveling companion—a young woman—are to be detained and handed over to me. This is a matter of national security."

"Let's not lower our guard, men," Kornievsky added. "This schooner may be old, but she's painted us with radar of her own. Those aboard have known about our pursuit for some time."

*   *   *

A rigid inflatable boat carrying a team of four SEALs, all armed with MP5s, was launched when the *Isabella* was one and a half nautical miles distant. Designed for high buoyancy, the solid hull of the RIB was extremely fast and capable of functioning in weather far more extreme than currently encountered.

Kornievsky and his men were not only SEALs but members of DEVGRU, a Naval counterpart to the Army's Delta Force. He and his men were among the world's premier maritime counterterrorism units.

"She's a beauty," shouted one of the men as the RIB shot over the waves toward *Isabella*.

With his team glued to his heels, Kornievsky was first to scale the sides of the cypress-hulled schooner and set foot on *Isabella's* curved pine deck. Using silent gestures, he sent his men to search below deck to find their hiding targets. Cautiously, he headed toward the forward compartment and the crew's forecastle. He encountered no one and continued aft to the galley, this one filled with sufficient provisions to supply a small crew heading just about anywhere. Plates and utensils were properly stowed away and the stove was cold.

Separated from the galley by a bulkhead, the fish hold was usually the section on vintage ships to receive the most updating. *Isabella's* fish hold had been converted into a highly sophisticated telecommunications center that included radar and ultraviolet sensors capable of seeing in the dark. This vessel might have been built in the 1920s but she carried state-of-the-art technology. The captain of this vessel easily saw the *Wilcox* approaching.

Aft of the telecommunications center was the engine room. When launched, these ships were often equipped with 120/150 horsepower engines turning a single screw in a cutout space in the rudder, but the engine Kornievsky was staring at was capable of considerably more horsepower. Like the stove, the engine was cold.

It didn't take long to search the eighty-five-foot ship, and Kornievsky could hear his team moving toward him through the remaining compartments. They met up in the main cabin, typically home to the captain and crew. Clothes were neatly stored in lockers, along with personal effects, including photographs of a comely blonde. Nothing indicated a hasty departure.

A member of the team lowered his MP5 and slipped the strap over his wetsuit-covered shoulder. "Where's the crew, Captain?" he asked. Kornievsky's jaw was taut. "Everyone—up on deck!" he barked.

They reassembled above near the main hatch.

"Check under the lifeboat," Kornievsky ordered. The yawl was upside down and securely tied to the roof of the main cabin, a possible hiding place for their quarry.

"Lifeboat empty, Captain," came the answer a moment later.

Kornievsky squinted up at the rigging, where the sails were neatly stowed away. No crew members dangled from the rigging.

Isabella's crew was nowhere to be found.

"Did another ship snatch them, sir?"

"The *Wilcox's* SONAR would have alerted us to other vessels in the vicinity."

"A seaplane?"

Kornievsky shook his head. "RADAR would have alerted us." He didn't want to return empty-handed but had no choice. "Back to the boat," he ordered.

*   *   *

When they returned, Fulton was waiting for them beside the boat launch. "Why didn't you bring Sanders and his companions back with you?" he asked, scowling.

Kornievsky wiped sea spray from his face. "No one was on board, sir."

Fulton didn't look happy. "What do you mean—no one was on board? That *is* Sanders's ship, *Isabella*, isn't it?"

"That's the name painted on her stern."

"Then where are they?"

Kornievsky was blunt. "They've vanished."

Chapter Twenty-Five

Seventy-Five Minutes Earlier

Owens tried to calm Sophia, who'd latched onto his arm with one hand while pointing at the mysterious object off *Isabella's* starboard bow with the other. Her voice trembled. "What is it?"

He liked the feel of her hand on his arm. "I'm willing to bet you know the story of Jonah."

Sophia recited, "Now the Lord had prepared a great fish to swallow up Jonah. And Jonah was in the belly of the fish three days and three nights."

"I'll take that as a 'yes.' "

She just blinked at him.

"I keep forgetting that sarcasm doesn't work on you." He chose his words carefully. "According to the Bible, God sent the big fish to save Jonah who had been thrown into the sea during a storm. This is a submarine, a mechanical fish sent to provide for *our* deliverance. But don't worry; instead of three days and nights, we'll only be inside a few hours."

She released his arm, apparently relieved it wasn't a sea monster. "I know about submarines. Tourists buy rides on them for short excursions underwater to take pictures of fish, but I've never seen one that looked like that!"

The craft was half the length of *Isabella*. It bobbed to the surface and looked more like an airplane than a fish. The hatch opened. A bull-necked man with a bald head and red walrus moustache emerged. "Someone need a ride?"

"Burton, good to see you again. Thanks for answering my call."

"Anderson! How could I refuse your request for help. And where is my former SMRI colleague? Ah, there he is. Preston, good to see you again. It's been too long."

Sanders grinned and gave a mock salute. "Always a pleasure, Burton."

Owens made the introduction. "Sophia, this is Burton Mazlow, who'd be one of the world's most renowned engineers and inventors if he weren't such a pain in the ass."

"Hello, young lady. I'm happy to be of service. And Anderson, good buddy, a little respect if you please since I'm the pain in the ass that's come to pull your bacon from the fire."

Mazlow tossed a line and they pulled the vessels together.

Sophia looked confused until Sanders explained, "We're all good friends." Her look of concern vanished when Mazlow joined them on *Isabella's* deck and they pounded each other on the back.

"How long has it been since you decided to quit SMRI to go off and do your Captain Nemo bit?" Sanders asked.

"Nearly five years, but I trust you'll find the time well spent."

"Sophia, why don't you grab your things so we can get on our way," Owens said.

When she returned with her satchel, Mazlow was touting his invention like a proud papa. "*Amelia*, here, is my latest example of a winged submersible, a vehicle flown like an underwater airplane. She can carry three passengers in addition to the pilot, but we should descend as quickly as possible. *Amelia's* RHSI doesn't work unless we're submerged."

"RHSI?" Sanders asked.

"Reverse Hyperspectral Imaging."

Sanders was wide-eyed with curiosity. "Sounds creative."

Owens didn't want to be caught here shooting the shit with Mazlow and made a show of scanning the horizon for signs of an approaching warship.

Unfazed, Mazlow continued. "As you know, hyperspectral techniques detect and identify targets based on spectral signature. But I've devised a way to use this technology in reverse by extending formerly limited Short-Wave Infrared and Long-Wave Infrared bands to ricochet any image I choose, such as empty ocean."

Owens stopped looking at the horizon. "So, you can't be red-lighted by SONAR. You can cloak like a Klingon bird of prey."

"More like a Romulan warbird," Mazlow corrected.

Sanders was intrigued. "What about power?"

"*Amelia* gathers thermal energy from the ocean."

"Remarkable. What about buoyancy?" Sanders asked.

"*Amelia* glides through the ocean by changing her buoyancy to dive and surface, unlike motorized, propeller-driven undersea vehicles. This also cuts down on noise."

"How deep will she go?" Sanders wondered.

"I've taken her down 5000 feet."

"That must be a record for the deepest solo ocean dive."

"If not, it's pretty darn close. But the *Wilcox* is approaching, and we'd be wise to chew the fat later at my workshop on Corvo Island. Don't worry about *Isabella*, Preston; I won't let the Navy claim her as abandoned salvage."

Sanders went below to collect a few things from his cabin, including a digital camera containing pictures he'd snapped of Sophia.

They boarded *Amelia,* strapped themselves into the narrow seats. Their ears popped when Mazlow sealed the hatch. The interior was illuminated by panels of glowing lights and gauges, and for a moment only bubbles could be seen through portholes. Sophia's mouth fell open as they dropped beneath the surface, her nose pressed against the translucent carbon portholes.

The air inside the submersible was rich in oxygen. "We'll feel light-headed for a moment," Mazlow explained.

Sophia held her breath when a pod of sperm whales swam by.

"How long will it take to reach where we're going?" she asked.

"Submerged, we'll reach Corvo in four hours," Mazlow answered. "Tell me, Sophia, do you have a last name?"

She struggled to answer. "Correia, I think."

Mazlow cocked his head. "You think?"

Owens placed a comforting hand on her shoulder. "We're on a quest to confirm her last name."

"Sounds like an interesting story."

*   *   *

Owens and Sanders were enjoying mugs of rum on the deck of a stone windmill Mazlow had converted into a laboratory. Wind-whipped flecks of gold danced on the darkening sea as they admired the sunset with their host. Sophia could be seen nearby, walking on the narrow beach.

"This is quite an isolated spot," Sanders observed.

"True, but the nearby Mid-Atlantic Ridge provides the extreme underwater environments necessary for my work."

A small addition extending from the western side of the windmill provided humble living quarters, while the large circular interior was crammed with equipment: bathymetric data analyzers, hydrographic light tables, and technology that left Sanders impressed and Owens scratching his head.

"Don't you get lonely out here?" he asked.

Mazlow shook his head. "Corvo might be the smallest island in the Azores Archipelago—cows outnumbering people three to one—but the tiny population is so friendly that no one bothers locking doors. São Miguel isn't far and has a sizable population, and nearby Terceira is home to the U.S. 65th Air Base Wing at Lajes Field. I hop over once or twice a year for free rides to Washington."

"You still do business with the Government?" Sanders asked.

Mazlow laughed. "Someone has to pay for my toys."

Sanders had another question. "Does the Azorean government know you're here constructing potential weapons for the U.S. military?"

"No. I'm just an eccentric fellow who likes to tinker on machines and be left alone. Say, contacting me through the VoIP switching platform we worked on together was brilliant. The Navy's reliance on outmoded systems makes it easy to hide communications. Double brilliant of you to remember that Mazlow Switches successfully shield calls without the fuss of encrypting them. Sparks aboard the *Wilcox* couldn't have known you'd contacted someone to fetch you. Must have thought you'd vanished into thin air."

Owens smirked. "Mazlow Switches?"

He beamed and twisted his moustache. "Inventor's prerogative."

"Well, I hope your standing with the Navy hasn't been compromised by helping us," Sanders said.

"Nonsense. If they find out, I'll use the incident as a tool to pitch them the entire system. I think we just demonstrated why the Navy needs to update its ship-to-shore communications capabilities. So, tell me more about Sophia. You both appear quite attached to her, especially you, Anderson."

"We've grown close," he admitted. "We've exchanged confidences over the past few days, I have anyway. She's an excellent listener."

"But there's something more, isn't there?"

Owens struggled for words. "Burton, I don't need to tell *you* that mysteries draw me like a bear to honey. Sophia is at the heart of something I can't explain and can't get out of my mind. She's different from anyone I've known. I can't believe I'm saying this because it doesn't make sense, but there's an ineffable quality about her that makes me not only want to protect her but *need* to."

"Perfectly said," Sanders chimed in, helping himself to more rum.

"I'd be inclined to think you'd both gone off your rockers, yet I, too, sense an oddness about the girl. But there's got to be more you guys aren't telling me. What do you know about her that I don't? Why has the U.S. government sent a warship to fetch her?"

Sanders leaned back in his deck chair and let his best friend do the talking.

"Burton, how old would you say Sophia is?"

"Mid-twenties."

"What would you say if we told you we were investigating the possibility that she's over a hundred and fifty years old?"

Mazlow let out a bark of laughter. "I'd say you've had enough rum."

"Maybe I have, but it's my nature to suspend disbelief and keep an open mind until the last possible minute—even absurd notions contain elements of truth."

A rasping noise escaped from Mazlow. "Imagining that sweet young thing as a modern-day Methuselah really pushes the envelope."

"You've seen that locket she wears?"

"Sure."

"Inside are pictures of a man and woman."

"Her parents?"

"Possibly. The pictures are of Captain Benjamin Briggs and his wife Sarah."

"So, she's Sophia Briggs. Why did you say you were on a quest to confirm her last name?"

"Because…well here's where it gets interesting. Benjamin and Sarah Briggs, along with their daughter Sophia, disappeared along with the crew of the *Mary Celeste* in 1872."

Mazlow raised his tufted eyebrows and leaned forward in his chair. "The *Mary Celeste*?"

"You recognize the name?"

"Of course, the great mystery of the sea. Her crew disappeared after sighting Santa Maria, not far from here. But I'm surprised to hear you jettison reason so easily. If this young lady is pretending to be Sophia Briggs, she's having a bit of fun with you. She could've found the locket at a swap meet or flea market."

"I believe her when she says she doesn't know how she acquired the locket, or any of the items in her satchel—some worth a pretty penny. She's never heard of the *Mary Celeste and* makes no claim to being anything other than what she appears to be. I've known my share of liars, silky-toned bullshit artists capable of convincing me that up was down—some even quoted scripture as well as she does—but this girl is arguably the most guileless individual I've encountered."

"She does have a remarkably earnest quality; I'll give you that. Have you asked her who she thinks she is?"

"She claims to have memory problems, although her fingers provide clues."

"Her fingers?"

"Yes. A tear opened in *Isabella's* jib a few days ago and she offered to repair it, mended that rip like an old sea dog, so well that Preston and I figured she must have repaired sails before. After that, I gave her pencil and paper, told her to draw pictures or write anything she wanted. After filling several pages with scribbles, she wrote a name."

"What name?"

"C-o-r-r-e-i-a. She wrote it repeatedly. When asked about it she claimed she couldn't remember where the name came from, but she used it on cruise ships, for payroll and IDs."

Mazlow played with the ends of his moustache. "A long time ago, before many of the young men left on whaling ships or emigrated to the States, numerous inhabitants of nearby Terceira shared the surname Correia, the Terceira equivalent of 'Smith.' "

"Perhaps she picked it up there."

"I doubt it. The name's become rare."

"Now, but not a hundred and fifty years ago."

"I'm a big fan of science fiction, but I'm not ready to buy into the preposterous notion of her being a hundred and fifty years old."

"Frankly, neither am I. But I can't stop asking myself why..."

"Why?"

"Why is the CIA so determined to locate this girl that they'd deploy a U.S. warship to find her?"

*　*　*

The next day was Sunday and all public offices in the Azores were closed. The afternoon was warm and sunny. They stretched their legs by walking to Vila do Corvo, the only settlement on the island and home to the island's only tavern. Mazlow introduced everyone to the pear-shaped proprietor, Senhor Avila, who brought them mugs of local rum made from distilled passion fruit.

Sophia smiled and refused a mug.

Senhor Avila disappeared again, this time returning with a bottle of Coca Cola, which Sophia happily accepted. "Thank you, Senhor Avila. This is very thoughtful of you."

A broad smile split his face. "You're most welcome, sweet lady. How long will you stay on Corvo?"

"I'm told we leave tomorrow," she said before taking a sip from the bottle.

"I hope your stay here has been a pleasant one, and perhaps you will return in the future."

"It would please me to return to such a beautiful place."

Owens's jaw had dropped in disbelief. He noticed Mazlow and Sanders were similarly surprised. "Sophia?"

"Yes?"

"When did you learn to speak Portuguese?"

She frowned at him. "I don't speak Portuguese."

"What was that you were just saying to Senhor Avila?"

"I thanked him for the cola and told him I'd be happy to return here someday."

"You weren't speaking English."

She took another sip of Coke. "It isn't nice to tease me."

The rum in Owens's mug couldn't keep his mouth from going dry.

CHAPTER TWENTY-SIX

Monday: 9:30 a.m.

Mazlow provided them with a speedy ride to Terceira aboard his prized hydrofoil, modified with turbojet-boosters capable of achieving 60 knots.

"It feels like we're flying," Sophia said, laughing and leaning overboard to see if they'd left the surface of the water. Sea caps churned beneath the foils under the vessel and shot into the air behind them, sparkling like diamonds.

When they reached Terceira, Owens and Sanders thanked Mazlow for all he'd done, and Sophia kissed him on the cheek. Then they entered Angra do Heroismo, the oldest city on the island and the historical capital of the Azores. Owens had been on the island before and led them toward the town center, known as Old Square, a likely place to find the town hall to research the name Correia.

The square was paved in an intricate black and white geometric pattern and lined with trees unique to the island. At the town hall, they were directed next door to the Hall of Records.

Assisting them was Sra. Canário, a humorless matron with tight black curls dangling from gray roots. Sophia looked startled when Owens asked her to tell the woman that she and Captain Sanders were father and daughter, come to Terceira to research her Azorean great-great-grandmother and namesake, born in 1870.

She hesitated. "I'm still unaccustomed to speaking Portuguese, and I don't want to lie."

"Just this once? I won't ask you to do it again."

It took more coaxing, but she finally agreed. She approached the counter, and using her newly discovered Portuguese, explained to Sra. Canário what they were looking for. Owens watched as she searched through shelves for the correct leather-bound book. From her expression, it was plain the one she searched for was missing.

A heated discussion erupted in a backroom. Through the open door, Owens could see Sra. Canário conversing with a gray-haired man, who disappeared for a moment and returned, placing a thick volume in his coworker's hands. When the book was placed on the counter, Owens had Sophia ask, "Why was this book not with the others?"

The answer was disturbing. "Yesterday, even though the Hall of Records be closed on Sundays, our supervisor, she indicated the gray-haired man in the backroom, was summoned by command of the mayor and forced to open for two Americans. They made a sizable donation for the purchase of new computers in exchange for access to our records. The ledger they were studying hadn't been returned to its proper place on the shelf."

Owens pulled out his cell and punched up a photograph he'd been shown by Dr. Pomeroy. The picture was of a somber-faced Agent Fulton. He showed the photograph to Sophia. "Ask Sra. Canário to show this picture to her supervisor. Ask if this is one of the men who came yesterday."

Sra. Canário walked the phone over and returned shaking her head. *If not Fulton, who else would be tailing them*, Owens wondered.

A musty smell hung in the air when the ledger was opened.

Mazlow had been correct; at the end of the nineteenth century, "Correia" had been quite common. Numerous pages listed Correia births, deaths, and dates of departures for emigrants.

"Do you see the name Sophia anywhere?" Owens asked Sra. Canário.

"How are you spelling Sophia?" she asked.

"S-o-p-h-i-a," he answered, "but in the old days it might have been spelled differently."

"Actually, Sophia, spelled with a 'ph,' *is* the older version. Today it is commonly shortened to Sofia with an 'f.'"

"It's the older spelling we're looking for."

Sra. Canário studied the pages. "There are no S-o-f-i-a-s, which, as I said, would be the newer Portuguese spelling, but there are two S-o-p-h-i-a-s." A crease deepened in her wide forehead. "Strange, but one of these Sophias has the word *adoptada* written beneath it, and the year 1875."

"Which would mean?" Owens asked.

"This Sophia was adopted."

She turned the large leather-bound book so they could read:

SOPHIA DE SILVA CORREIA

ADOPTADA AOS ---- TRÊS ANOS 1875

"Why is this strange, and why did someone try to erase most of the entry?" Sanders asked.

"Historically, formal adoptions were rare in the islands. Few had money to pay for the fee and paperwork. Many people were related, and children were often shared without the fact being recorded. It's possible the adoptive parents changed their minds."

She took back the book and scanned the remaining pages. "There is nothing else here relating to Sophia de Silva Correia, no record of a marriage, births of children, death, no indication she emigrated from Terceira as so many did."

"You said there was another Sophia listed around this time," Owens said.

"Not exactly, but another Sophia, also a child of three, left the islands years later. No last name is recorded. Aside from the fact that she was born long after 1870, it's unlikely she is the one you seek."

"Why is that?" Sanders asked.

"Because it's doubtful she had any progeny. It's written in the book that she was sent to a convent on the coast near Setúbal and Sesimbra in 1895."

"You've been extremely helpful," Owens said.

As they turned to go, Sra. Canário suggested, "You might check with the Correia family about that first entry. The family was quite prominent in the 1870s. Their ancestral home is near São Mateus, a village on the coast only one and a half kilometers from here. A pleasant walk."

*   *   *

"Why did you tell that woman I was Captain Sanders's daughter, and why are we looking for my great-great-grandmother?"

Sanders didn't want to be included in any part of this conversation and wandered off when Owens pulled Sophia over to a stone bench shaded by a large palm tree. Exotic flowers were blooming everywhere, and he stared at them for a while before saying, "I'm trying to learn more about you, and I didn't want that woman asking unnecessary questions."

"It's wrong to lie."

He scratched his cheek, and for a moment considered what his life as a secret operative would be like if he never lied.

"Why do you want to know more about me?"

"Because you're special."

"Special...how?"

"Well, take this lying thing. Most people tell fibs every now and then and don't think much about it. It takes a very special person not to lie—ever."

*　*　*

They headed out of the city, west on the coastal road toward São Mateus. The afternoon sun warmed them as they passed fields of slow-blinking cows grazing in verdant fields, the vivid hues of green washing down from nearby mountains to the azure sea. He took her satchel when she began struggling with it.

"It's beautiful here," Sophia said. "Beautiful, and familiar."

They reached São Mateus an hour later. Fishing boats were returning from the sea and displaying their catch on planks set over the sand. The boats were motorized but it wasn't difficult to imagine the billowing sails of bygone whalers and fishing boats.

"I've explored these waters for SMRI," Sanders said. "They're a treasure trove of marine life."

Sra. Canário had given them a description of the Correia estate—a two-story white stucco manor house with red window sashes and an orange tile roof. The house, set back from the water's edge and facing the small natural harbor, needed repair. They followed a stone path leading to the entrance and Owens pounded the rusty iron knocker on the front door.

A short old woman with white hair parted down the middle came to the door, wiping her hands on her apron. "*Olá.*"

Sophia answered. "*Boa tarde. Pode ajudar-nos?*"

"*Depende. Que é que você quer?*"

"*Nós gostaríamos de fazer-lhe algumas perguntas.*"

The woman said something in rapid fire Portuguese, possibly too fast even for Sophia.

"*Você fala inglês?*" Sophia asked.

"My grandson, Miguel, speak the good English. I speak *um bocadinho*—a little bit. Why questions for me? You MP? Miguel again in trouble with girls on base?"she asked, her eyes dark as she glared at them.

Owens pulled Sophia aside. "Tell her we aren't here because of her grandson. Tell her your family came from here and we're trying to locate them."

"I will not lie to this woman."

"We aren't lying. Just tell her."

Sophia bit her bottom lip and looked like she was going to refuse but finally did as he asked. After a brief exchange with the woman in Portuguese, she said, "Her name is Sra Correia. She says we aren't the first to ask about the Correias. She says we can stay for dinner."

"But first I work you. Fisherman son and grandsons home soon." She rubbed her stomach. "They be hungry from day of fishing."

Sra. Correia led them through several rooms filled with furniture shrouded with lace doilies. Faded ancestral photographs covered the walls and Sanders examined them for images of Sophia. He didn't spot her.

In the kitchen, the old woman handed out aprons and put them to work chopping onions, debearding mussels, and cleaning littleneck clams. She added slices of linguiça sausage to an enormous iron pot simmering with stock, wine, olive oil, and a dozen other ingredients. Owens donned the birth control glasses to help keep his eyes from watering while dicing the onions.

Four men smelling of sweat and fish burst into the kitchen, one carrying a canvas sack. The oldest, perhaps fifty, gave the old woman a peck on the cheek. None looked surprised to see three strangers working like sous-chefs.

"More Correias from America.," said the youngest to no one in particular. He nodded at the male strangers but saved most of his attention for Sophia.

Sra. Correia opened the sack and dumped the contents into a metal pan large enough to bathe a toddler. *Isto é tudo que você trouxe do resto?"* she said, scowling.

"Ó Avó, tudo mais foi vendido aos restaurantes," the youngest answered.

"Terá que chegar. Vai lavar-te. Sirvo daqui a vinte minutos."

Sophia explained, "Sra. Correia is upset the men sold most of their catch and didn't bring more home for dinner."

"It isn't polite to take food from their mouths," Sanders said. "Perhaps we should come back after dinner."

When Sophia suggested this, Sra. Correia shook her head and pointed her knife at them. "All welcome here. Add more water to stew is all." Her hands were a blur as she gutted several small cod, stripped the flesh from the bones and created fillets, which she added to the pot, along with chopped tomatoes and a small pinch of saffron.

While waiting for the mussels and clams to open, Sra. Correia winked at Sophia and said, "Nice to have another woman in house of so many men." She pointed at the oldest man. "Only son remain, but his wife..." she pretended to slash the missing wife's throat with the knife, "...run away to São Miguel and leave me to raise boys. Maybe you take an eye for one of my grandsons."

* * *

Wine flowed freely and there was more than enough food. When they'd all pushed away from the table Owens tried to press money into the old woman's hand, but she refused. When offered a second time, she reached for the bills and buried them in her apron pocket. The women did the dishes and tidied the kitchen. Owens and Sanders offered to help but joined the men in the front room when they were shooed away.

Curly-haired Miguel, the English-speaking grandson, handed them each a cigar and matches. "For outside only, or you will feel Grandma's broom on your head. I invested in the company that rolls them here in the Azores. Maybe I be rich one day, like the Elon Musk."

Sophia finished in the kitchen and joined them in the front room.

Guitars and violas appeared. The grandsons circled Sophia and began serenading with music and soulful songs, each competing for her attention. Owens and Sanders listened in, noting that she seemed to enjoy the music and male attention. After a while they stepped outside to breathe in the night air.

Owens lit his cigar. The breeze was warm and the sky free of clouds. His gaze lifted to the infinite specks of light overhead. Many of the stars shining down on them had burned out ages ago, their dying light traveling billions of miles to reach the earth only now. Memories were like that, he thought, flickering long after the events that inspired them.

"When are you going to fill me in on what we're doing here?" Sanders said. "And take off those damn glasses!"

He pretended to look hurt, returned the specs to his pocket.

"I know you enjoy toying with intelligence agencies, but this is serious business. You may have friends in high places to pull your butt from the fire, but I don't."

He'd wondered when his best friend was going to blow, had expected an outburst on Midas Cay. "Don't you want to find out if the notion tapdancing in our heads is true?"

Sanders's cheek muscles hardened. "Nothing is tapdancing in my head, except regret for the foolishness of again allowing you to turn my life upside down." His voice was loud enough to draw attention; Miguel appeared in the doorway and observed them for a moment before returning inside.

"Where's your curiosity? This girl just might be the oldest living human, yet she doesn't look a day over twenty-five. Where's she been for the past hundred and fifty years—Shangri-La? This is mind-boggling stuff and I, for one, gotta follow every clue to unravel this mystery."

His best friend gave him the silent treatment.

"Haven't you done the math? Sophia Briggs was lost at sea when two years old, yet our Sophia appears to be in her twenties. If they are one and the same, then she is aging, but too slowly for people to observe—one year to six or seven of ours."

Sanders didn't look convinced.

Owens rubbed his forehead. "I know it's preposterous but think about it; when she looks seventy-five, she'll actually be over five hundred years old. And if that isn't enough to punch your ticket for a ride on the Im-Fucking-Possible Express, we've also reason to believe she might have been present during one of the most mind-boggling occurrences aboard a ship at sea."

Sanders took a long pull on the cigar and avoided eye contact, a prickly silence settling over them. A few minutes later he asked, "Why did you need *me* to hide Sophia? You're the one spinning fanciful notions about her—which I'm sure you'll come to regret—but what was so important you couldn't deal with her yourself?"

"I needed to make a quick trip to Costa Rica."

"What was so important in Costa Rica?"

"*Sotto Voce* business. While I was there, I contacted an old friend in London who said to say hello."

"Who?"

"Casper. He said Toaster has a great new girl, but I gather she isn't much of a looker. We've been invited to drop by, meet her, and throw down a few pints with the gang."

"Reminds me of another time you landed me in hot water."

"As I recall, you turned the heat up on that water yourself. Oh, here's another reason I didn't show up right away." He pulled two items from his pocket, handed them over. "Sophia won't be able to fly off this island without one of these." They were U.S. passports. Sophia's cruise ship picture was inside one, but the name was different. "There's also one for you, since we can assume yours has been flagged."

Sanders checked out his new name: Sidney Klumperstein. "These look real."

"They *are* real, Sidney."

"We're going to Portugal, right?"

"That's where two of the garments in Sophia's satchel were made."

"Listen, since you decided to involve me in this escapade, you can at least tell me if you've learned why the CIA is pursuing Sophia."

"I don't have the whole picture, but Pomeroy told me the CIA operatives who came for the girl at WCRX report to Agent Fulton, special advisor to the president."

"Go on. There must be more to it than that."

"I've learned that the President ordered Fulton to do whatever it takes to find Sophia."

Sanders finally looked surprised. "Why would she do that?"

Owens shrugged. "It might have something to do with what I uncovered in Costa Rica."

Sanders waited to hear more. When nothing followed, he said, "This cigar tastes like feet."

Owens exhaled a cloud of smoke. "So true."

*　*　*

Sra. Correia's hospitality included lodging for the night. The old woman had just ambled out of the kitchen to join them when Sophia announced she was ready for bed.

"You share my room," the mistress of the house said. "This way no grandson ends up in your bed."

When Sophia had gone, Sra. Correia reached for one of the cigar butts in a nearby ashtray, lit it and inhaled deeply. The silvery smoke wafted on the light breeze along with strands of her hair. "For years I not smoke from fear of the early grave, but now I be eighty-five it too late to die young." She took another puff. "These cigars no good—*sabe a merda*—but Miguel the only one left with dreams, and without dreams there be no future." She looked tired as she stared at the boats rocking in the harbor, the cigar butt glowing in her hand. "You come to ask questions. Now good time."

"Sophia thinks her last name is Correia," Owens began.

"She grown enough to know own last name."

A gull passed overhead, its shape barely visible against the sequined sky. When the moment felt right Owens asked, "Are there any stories you can recall about the Correias that might have been...a bit strange?"

Her face wrinkled like an old apple as she thought about it. "All *famílias* have share of strangeness. Is not true with your *família*?"

He could tell a few stories about the Owenses and nodded.

"Years ago, a nephew born with, how you say, *um terceiro testículo.*" She pointed the cigar at his crotch and held up three fingers. "Then there be my mother's sister who dressed like the boys, run off to sea and pulled nets like the men. Even pray to growing the beard."

Owens asked, "What about a girl who might have been rescued at sea and adopted a long time ago, say in the mid 1870s."

She closed her eyes for a few moments. They thought she'd dozed off, but she finally said, "I was small girl when hear strange story that takes place before I born, a story not told for years but once the big whisper on Terceira." She twirled a finger near her head. "Grandsons maybe lock me up if I tell crazy story about little mermaid who live in this house after taken from the sea."

Owens was all ears and leaned forward on the bench. "Go on."

"Many fishermen see and hear strangeness when land is far and sun is hot. *Lenda da família* say that when grandfather on mother's side still a young man, he fishing and find mermaid *menininha.*"

"*Menininha?*"

"Hmm...small child."

"Tell me more," Owens blurted.

"He say he find her holding on to boat that be..." She held out a hand, palm up, and flipped it over.

"Capsized?"

"Yes; capsized. Little mermaid make the magic and turn into real child.

Grandfather give to grandmother but keep magic a secret. Grandmother, like me, have only the sons and be happy to finally have daughter to teach cooking and mending of sails and nets."

"Do you believe this little girl was a mermaid?" Owens asked.

"Yes, when I small girl. But Grandpa says he also find dolly and picture of *menininha* floating nearby." She tapped her wrinkled forehead with a crooked finger. "When older I not think mermaids have such things."

"I don't suppose so," Owens said.

"Years later when Grandpa oldest person on island and soon to leave this world, he changes story. He says he made up part where *menininha* found in capsized boat. Also part about mermaid magic. He tells me he does this because truth even more hard to believe."

What could be harder to believe than a mermaid transforming into a human child? Owens asked himself. He didn't have to wait long for an answer.

"Before dying he whispers that after finding floating picture and dolly, not far away is *menininha*—small child—walking on the water."

Owens suppressed a smile. "Like you said, fishermen see and hear strange things when land is far away and the sun is hot."

She continued. "As years pass, my grandmother believes this child cursed by God." She crossed herself.

Sanders beat him to the question. "Do you remember why?"

"Terceira deep with religion, and Grandmother more deep than most. She become scared and believe girl a demon, refusing to share island with her. *Família* spend much to send adoption daughter to convent not far from Setúbal and Sesimbra, far from erceira. My grandmother forbid any speaking of her again."

Portugal was studded with religious institutions. "I don't suppose you remember the name of the convent?" Owens asked.

Without a word, she disappeared inside and was gone long enough for them to think she'd gone to bed. She finally returned, with a heavy book. "Correia *família* Bible." She turned to the end page where something was written in faded ink.

Convento de Santa Isabel

"My mother tell me Grandfather write. I always think this where mermaid baby sent."

"So, it was more than just a family legend?", Owens mumbled.

He turned to Sanders. "Sophia said the name Isabella brought her comfort. Could this be the reason? Isabel and Isabella are pretty darn close."

Sanders's lips tightened.

Sra. Correia stood to go. "I never speak this thing and not know why should do so now."

"One last question," Owens promised. "Did you ever learn what frightened your grandmother so much?"

"It be said the child *nunca envelhecia*—never aged."

CHAPTER TWENTY-SEVEN

Tuesday: 4:00 a.m.

"What time is it?" Sanders rasped from the far side of the large bed, his hair in sleep-spikes.

"Four o'clock."

Sounds rose from the kitchen below—it was hard to sleep late in a household of fishermen.

Owens rose from the creaky bed and looked out the window, seeing the dim glow of cigarettes dangling in the mouths of Correia men as they ambled down to their boats.

He returned to bed. Sanders was back asleep, and he decided to catch a few more zzzs.

He drifted off to sleep and dreamt about a little girl walking on waves only to be adopted and then abandoned. The dream went from fantasy to nightmare when the father who'd forsaken him and his sister inexplicably appeared in a rowboat, abandoning him again by setting him adrift on the water. Only he couldn't walk on water and sank beneath the waves. He tossed and turned, damp with sweat with his heart pounding. Hours later, while recalling his nightmare, Owens didn't need a psychoanalyst to interpret his dream.

After washing sleep from their eyes in water from a pitcher near the bed, Owens and Sanders dressed and headed downstairs. The kitchen door was open. A rooster outside was crowing and he followed a path to the side of the house where Sra. Correia was collecting eggs from a chicken coop. She gummed a smile at them and continued gathering speckled eggs in her apron.

Owens walked down to the beach. To his surprise, Sophia was not asleep upstairs but was sitting on a wooden box mending a sail. She was concentrating on her work, didn't notice him approaching. He admired her skillful use of needle and thread until she glanced up and smiled. She blushed at the sight of him.

An hour later, Sra. Correia called the three of them to the kitchen for a breakfast of scrambled eggs with local sausage, shapeless donuts rolled in sugar, and hot coffee. When he couldn't eat another bite, Owens pushed away from the table and again pressed bills into her hand. This time she gladly accepted. He helped carry the dishes to the sink. When they were alone, she said, "Sophia say a trouble thing this morning."

"What did she say?"

"I no think she speaking to me, the faraway look in her eyes, like she talk to someone not here. She say, 'Time running out,' but gives no answer when I ask what she means. What she talk about?"

"I wish I knew."

"You see that she have the eyes for you? Cheeks turn red like cherries when you come near."

He'd wondered if he was seeing something in her eyes that wasn't there. Now he had his answer. "I don't think she's had many boyfriends. She's sweet, but there are too many years between us."

"Men be so much silly. The heart knows no age."

*   *   *

They took a local bus to Lajes Airfield. In addition to being the strategic home of the 65th Air Base Wing, the largest U.S. military organization for well over a thousand miles, the base serviced NATO planes and functioned as an international airport with daily flights to Boston, Toronto, and Lisbon. He was determined to follow every clue leading to Sophia's past, and that path now led to Portugal and *Convento de Santa Isabel*.

It was hard to believe that slow-paced São Mateus and bustling Lajes were part of the same small island. Lajes Airfield was heavily trafficked, the small terminal swarming with military families and tourists catching connecting flights. While approaching the ticket counter, Owens recognized a face in the crowd.

"Shee-*it*!" he muttered under his breath.

He pulled his companions into a gift shop, handed Sophia money and suggested she grab a few magazines and candy bars for the flight.

When she was too far away to hear he warned Sanders, "Doctor Pomeroy showed me a photo of Fulton and he's out there in the terminal. I doubt he's alone."

"He was probably on board the *Wilcox* and flew in on one of her Seahawks."

"By the way, did I mention the CIA has a BOLO out on Sophia? And you?"

Sanders's mouth twitched. "No, you didn't. What are we going to do now?"

"No doubt he has pictures of us so it's time for disguises." His eyes darted around the gift shop. He grabbed an inflated beach ball with *Swim the Azores* written on it, along with a bulky sweatshirt and two baseball caps, all emblazoned with the Air Force logo.

"Let's transform her into just another pregnant Air Force wife, here for a little R&R with hubby stationed on Terceira."

"How are you going to convince her to pretend to be pregnant?"

"We could say we were playing a game called Immaculate Concept—"

"Don't go there, Anderson. This girl takes her religion extremely seriously."

"I'll think of something. As for you, there must be a way to hide that ugly face of yours."

An injured airman rolled by the front of the gift shop in a wheelchair, an arm and leg in casts. Hmmm.... Owens made his way to the checkout counter, where he purchased everything with a credit card.

"Won't that leave a paper trail?" Sanders asked.

"Nope. The card taps into an untraceable *Sotto Voce* account."

"Handy. Filling out your tax return must be...interesting."

The image of a rented Samurai jeep filled with snapping crocodiles, a vehicle he'd given away, sprang to mind. "Let's just say I don't go to H&R Block."

Peeking out of the gift shop, he saw a door stenciled **First Aid** on the far side of the terminal. A medical assistant was locking the door on her way out. Fulton had returned to the front entrance and was separated from them by the crowd. Crossing the terminal was risky since Fulton probably wasn't alone, but they'd have to chance it.

He hustled Sanders and Sophia to the first aid station and jimmied the lock. Inside, they were confronted with the strong smells of bleach and antiseptic.

"Why are we here?" Sophia asked. "Is someone hurt?"

"Okay, hot shot. Time for you to think of something," Sanders said to Owens.

He thought quickly. "Sophia, you know the story of King Herod?"

"Yes."

"Then you know that an angel appeared to St. Joseph and told him to take his family and flee into Egypt and not return until wicked Herod was dead."

She nodded. "King Herod wanted to kill our Savior and murdered boy babies in Bethlehem."

"That's right. Well, another bad man is out there in the terminal, and he's looking for us. Think of this as a game, our own flight into Egypt. Captain Sanders will play St. Joseph and you get to be Mary. We don't want the bad man to find us, so we're going to disguise ourselves so he won't know who we are. If anyone stops you and asks questions, just smile and pretend you don't understand."

"I don't remember reading that the Holy Family disguised themselves or refused to answer questions," she commented.

"Well, don't you think St. Joseph would have done anything he could think of to carry out that angel's command to save his family?"

"I suppose. Are you an angel?"

Sanders answered for him—a stifled laugh.

As usual, Owens searched her face for sarcasm but didn't spot any. He noticed her resistance to going against her conscience remained strong. It took more coaxing than when they were at the Hall of Records, but it wasn't long before she was unrecognizable, her hair tucked under a cap hiding her features and the partially deflated beach ball beneath the baggy sweatshirt suggesting she was in a family way. Owens plucked the BCG's from his pocket and reached over Sophia's protruding tummy to set them on her nose. "Perfect."

"So much for birth control glasses," Sanders said.

He ignored him. "Now when you walk to the ticket counter, waddle a bit."

"Waddle?"

"Yeah, like a penguin." He demonstrated.

She pressed a hand over her mouth to keep from laughing.

Next, Owens ordered Sanders into a wheelchair and began wrapping his head with spools of gauze taken from a supply shelf. When finished, only Sanders's eyes and mouth were visible. Owens started to place a baseball cap over the bandaged head.

"Don't put it on backwards, like I'm some sort of gangbanger."

"Dude, can't imagine what gang would have you."

"Very funny. Remind me later to kick your butt."

Chapter Twenty-Eight

Tuesday: 3:12 p.m.

Fulton walked past the injured airman being wheeled toward the ticket counter of SATA, the main airline of the Azores. He was looking for a slim young woman with long dark hair and gave little thought to the pregnant woman trailing the wounded airman pushed by a buddy. Many pregnant women were waddling about, joyfully hugging servicemen or making tearful goodbyes.

The crowd thinned when the Lisbon flight departed. Fulton joined up with his backup. "Any sign of them?"

"No, Boss."

Fulton rubbed his eyes. "We've got forty minutes until the next flight leaves. I'm going to grab some aspirin in the gift shop. Meet you in the coffee bar."

"Score some Visine while you're at it, Boss. You look like a heroin addict."

Fulton entered the gift shop, made his way to the medicine shelf and grabbed a bottle of aspirin. He hunted for eye drops, asked for help when he couldn't find any.

"All sold out. Check at the first aid station across the terminal," suggested the woman behind the counter.

He paid for the aspirin and wandered over to the first aid station. Inside, he said to the medical assistant, "The gift shop sold out of Visine. I was told I might be able to get some here."

Her eyes darted around as she handed him a container of eye drops.

"How much?" he asked, reaching for his wallet.

She shook her head, deep in thought.

"Anything wrong?"

She hesitated to answer, but finally blurted out, "Something odd is going on. I left for a coffee break, locking the door as always. When I returned the door was still locked, but items were missing."

"What items?"

"A wheelchair and a half-dozen packages of gauze."

Fulton's hand shot up to his throbbing head.

CHAPTER TWENTY-NINE

Tuesday: 4:20 p.m.

They abandoned the wheelchair in a bathroom stall near their departure gate and buried the disguises in a garbage container. Sophia was ghostly white as they boarded the plane.

"It's only a two-and-a-half-hour flight to Lisbon. Is this your first time on a plane?" Owens asked.

"I'm not sure, maybe."

He offered her his seat. "Here, sit by the window so you can see better."

She shook her head. "I prefer sitting between you and Captain Sanders."

When they took off, she twined her fingers through Owens's and scrunched her eyes shut.

A mild jolt passed over him when her fingers wove into his. He'd experienced this on previous occasions, but it was getting harder to dismiss the sensation as static electricity. It didn't help that Preston didn't seem to be experiencing anything extraordinary from her touch.

Ten minutes later when the plane finished its ascent and leveled off, she opened her eyes.

Sanders had been studying her. "For years I hated flying."

"Because of what happened to your parents."

"You know about that?"

"Anderson mentioned it. I'm a good listener if you want to talk about it."

Owens couldn't help overhearing and was impressed that during her own fear she was trying to comfort someone else.

"Perhaps another time," Sanders said.

Eventually color returned to Sophia's cheeks and the vibration of the plane made her drowsy enough to fall asleep. She leaned against Owens, her soft breathing like the purring of a kitten.

He enjoyed the feel of her beside him, the warmth of her body pressed against him. Two and a half hours to Lisbon; he wished it were longer.

* * *

Darkness had fallen when they arrived at the Lisbon airport. Before renting a car they paused at an information kiosk but failed to score directions to *Convento de Santa Isabel.* They did receive a recommendation for a nearby hotel where they could spend the night.

In the morning they gobbled down a continental breakfast of sweet breads and syrupy coffee before setting their sights on the Almada, a town south of Lisbon where the *Museu Nacional de Trabalhos Religiosos* (National Museum of Religious Works) was located, according to the clerk at the front desk. They were told the institution kept records of monasteries and convents closed during the Salazar years and housed much of the confiscated art.

Owens drove the rented Audi onto the Ponte 25 de Abril spanning the Tagus River. He and Sanders had been to Lisbon on several occasions, but Sophia seemed unfamiliar with the city, giving Owens an opportunity to play tour guide. "Formerly known as the Ponte Salazar, this was once the longest suspension bridge in Europe." He pointed to the east. "Now it's dwarfed by the newer and much larger Vasco da Gama Bridge."

Sophia glanced upward at dangling men scraping rust from the bridge as they sped beneath the two massive towers.

A shadow passed over her face.

Sanders asked, "Are you all right?"

"Yes. But I feel like I've seen this bridge before, only it was different."

"I have feelings like that all the time," Sanders said. "Déjà vu, they call it."

Owens wasn't so sure and considered another explanation. A brain-freezing one.

A plaque near the southernmost end of the bridge stated the inauguration date: 1966. *Could the bridge have been incomplete when she saw it? Almost sixty years ago?*

She lowered her eyes to the cruise ships in the harbor, a wistful smile on her lips...

After living for years in a convent, had Sophia made her way to Lisbon, found work on one of the many cruise ships in the harbor? It would have been a perfect way to disappear, and with new crews and passengers rotating frequently her prolonged youth and periodic memory loss wouldn't have been easily detected.

*   *   *

The museum was in a former monastery, the white stone facade shimmering in morning light. No tourist buses jammed the entrance, no trouble parking. They climbed the stone steps to the booth beside the entrance, bought tickets and checked Sophia's satchel at the information desk, where they asked to see the curator. They were told Vincente d' Oliveira would be with them shortly.

But for their footsteps the place was as quiet as it must have been when still a monastery. Sophia ambled away and Sanders whispered, "These paintings are second-rate, but a few of these painted statues look amazingly lifelike."

On the far side of the room, Sophia paused at a scene of Christ being whipped, blood dripping from His back, glee animating His tormentors' eyes. *The Flagellation.*

She mumbled something.

Owens walked over to her. "What did you say?"

" 'Then as now, the world was filled with evil people, and like our Savior, you, too, will be tested by them.' Someone said these words to me; I don't know who. But I know I've seen this painting before."

She was trembling and he put an arm around her. "Are you sure? Many of these pictures look alike."

"Of course she's sure," Sanders said. "Just look at her; white as a ghost."

Owens studied the sign beside the painting, recognized the name *Convento de Santa Isabel.* "Does anything else look familiar?" he asked her.

She didn't answer until several rooms later when confronted with another artifact from *Convento de Santa Isabel*. The museum was crowded with many statues of the young Virgin, but one caught her eye, exhibit #629. "I've seen this statue before, too."

Her eyes glistened with tears. The statue wore a fancy dress like the one in Sophia's satchel, but it was torn in places and discolored with age.

"I'm no seamstress," Sanders whispered to him, "but Sophia's dress would fit this statue perfectly."

A dapper man approached, his polished shoes clattering on the glazed floor tiles. "*Olá*. Welcome to our museum. I am Vincente d' Oliveira."

He shook hands with Owens and Sanders, gently brushing Sophia's with his lips. "Much of this art can move an old man like me to tears," he said expansively. "I see it is the same with you, *senhorita*."

She eked out a smile.

"We don't receive nearly as many visitors as the illustrious Gulbenkian Foundation, but we are proud of our modest collection."

Owens whispered. "He must have heard you call this stuff second-rate."

Sanders scowled at him.

"I understand you need assistance locating a *convento*?"

"Yes, Sr. Oliveira. Can you give us directions to *Convento de Santa Isabel*?" Owens asked.

"Saint Queen Isabel is an extremely popular figure in Portuguese history. Her name is associated with many buildings, including several conventos."

"We're looking for the one on the coast not far from Setúbal and Sesimbra," he said.

"Let me think. Hmm...yes I believe I know the place, now a *pousada*—state-managed hotel—like so many of our religious buildings. Pardon me for saying this, but there are far more interesting *pousadas* in the region than this *Convento de Santa Isabel*, including a few in former castles. Is there something special about this one that interests you?"

"We're looking for someone who might have once lived there," he said.

"Such a person would be quite old. Only a few elderly nuns still served God there when *Convento de Santa Isabel* was closed in the late sixties."

Sr. Oliveira escorted them back to the information desk where he hunted through a rack of brochures for a map. He inked a circle around the location. They thanked him and Sophia reclaimed her satchel. She stopped as they headed for the front door.

"Sr. Oliveira, does your museum accept donations?"

"We've been known to," he said.

"I have something I believe belongs here." She opened her satchel and pulled out the lace dress.

"Beautiful, indeed," Sr. Oliveira said.

"This belongs on one of your Madonnas, exhibit #629. I believe it was sewn for her a long time ago at *Convento de Santa Isabel.*"

Owens popped in, "The dress has been authenticated by a foremost authority."

"A thing of beauty. I can't imagine how this dress got separated from its Madonna, but it would please me greatly to reunite them. How did you come by it?"

"I've had it for a long time."

"You are most generous, *senhorita.*" Once again, he kissed her hand. "Twelve kilometers from here is *Hospital Sagrado do Coração* for aging nuns and priests—what you Americans call a nursing home. Many residents from closed *conventos* ended up there."

*   *   *

Before Owens could steer the Audi in the direction of the highway, Sophia said, "I want to visit that hospital."

She seldom made requests. He altered their direction.

Located on a bluff overlooking the Tagus River, *Hospital Sagrado do Coração* was a shabby institution. Sophia walked briskly into the gloomy labyrinth, a hand covering her nose to block the smell of urine and bleach. A nun clutching a clipboard floated their way and offered assistance. Sophia exchanged words with her in Portuguese.

The nun led them to a cramped office where Mother Sílvia, according to the name on the door, looked up from the stack of papers on her desk. There were no other chairs.

"How may I help you?" she said brusquely in English.

Sophia's expression was momentarily blank. Owens was about to apologize for wasting the woman's time when Sophia said, "I think I'm looking for someone."

The nun peered over her spectacles. "You think you're looking for someone? Either you are or you aren't. Which is it?"

Outside, someone began shrieking. Soon the sound was accompanied by distant moans.

"Dementia," Mother Sílvia said matter-of-factly. "Are you going to stand there, or are you going to tell me who you are looking for?"

Sophia bit her bottom lip, struggled to remember. "Mother Lucy... no, Mother Lúcia. I don't suppose there's anyone here by that name?"

"Perhaps a dozen. A common name."

"She came from *Convento de Santa Isabel* on the coast not far from Setúbal and Sesimbra," Sanders added.

Mother Sílvia set down her pen and crossed her spotted hands in front of her. "I'm inclined to send you on your way, but..."

"But what?" Owens wasn't enjoying the old prune.

"Young lady, what is your name?"

"Sophia. Sophia Correia."

The old woman froze for a moment and then crossed herself. "Wait." She rose from her chair slowly and shuffled away, leaving them in her office. When she returned, a yellowed envelope was clenched in her hand. After settling back into her chair she explained, "This unopened letter was sitting in our safe when I arrived thirty years ago, and I understand it to have been here twenty years before that. It was written by Mother Lúcia from *Convento de Santa Isabel*, summoned by our Lord in 1974. She also wrote the note attached to it." She handed Sophia the envelope.

"What does the note say?" Sanders blurted.

Sophia took several deep breaths, her voice wavering as she read: "If a young woman called Sophia Correia comes asking for me, please deliver this to her."

Sophia abruptly thanked Mother Sílvia and, instead of opening the envelope and reading the letter to them, left the office on shaking legs.

*   *   *

They found her in the car. Owens glanced around to see if Fulton had picked up their trail. But for them, the parking lot was empty.

"Let's give her some privacy," Sanders suggested. "Receiving that letter must be unnerving."

They hiked to the far side of the bluff and killed a few minutes staring at the massive Sanctuary of Christ the King with its outstretched arms projecting towards Lisbon, visible in the distance.

Sanders closed his eyes for a moment and turned his face toward the warm sun.

"Sophia seemed...different in there. Did you notice?"

"Yeah. Most of the time she acts like a shadow, but not this time. She was determined to visit this place, marched in assertively."

"Who do you suppose this person is who wrote Sophia a letter decades ago? And how did Sophia know to ask for her?"

"It seems our angel's memory is improving," he said.

"What do you suppose is in the letter?"

"Dunno. Can't wait to find out."

When they returned to the car, she was staring out the open window gazing up at the downy clouds like they were lost souls. The unopened letter was on her lap.

<hr>

CHAPTER THIRTY

Wednesday: 1:20 p.m.

Owens drove the Audi down the four-lane highway heading to Setúbal, Portugal's third largest port. At Setúbal he turned west toward Sesimbra, where the highway narrowed as it cut through former swampland, now rice fields and golf courses.

Sophia was quieter than usual, her new assertiveness retreating while they tried to coax her into reading the letter.

"Maybe it's a mistake to open it," she said, "only…"

"Only what?" Owens asked.

"I remember words, words that I feel were spoken by the woman who wrote this letter."

"What words?"

She cleared her throat. "Then as now, the world was filled with evil people, and like our Savior, you, too, will be tested by them." They were the words she'd mumbled in front of *The Flagellation* in the museum.

"Aren't you busting a gut to discover what this Mother Lúcia wanted you to know fifty years ago?" Owens asked.

"Just because I asked for her doesn't mean I know who she is. Besides…"

"Besides what?"

"Let her take a few breaths, Anderson," Sanders admonished. "Can't you see she's upset?"

They sat in uncomfortable silence, until she said, "If I am the Sophia Correia this letter is addressed to, a letter that under normal circumstances would have been written long before I was born, then it's possible the preposterous story you've been telling me is true—I am Sophia Briggs, lost at sea long ago. Do you know what that means?"

"Tell us," Owens said.

Her voice quavered. "It means I'm a...a freak."

If he hadn't been driving, Owens would have hugged her tight. It was wrong to press her, but this was the reason they'd come, to discover the unknown, and the unknown was waiting in that envelope on her lap. "You don't have to read it if you don't want to, sweetheart."

She looked at him, her weak smile not reaching her eyes. "I do have to read it. If I don't, Mr. Owens—"

"For the last time, please call me Anderson."

"All right, Anderson. If I don't open it, I think you will—what's the expression? —bust a gut."

Owens and Sanders eyed each other and dissolved into laughter.

"Did I say it wrong?" she asked.

"You got it perfect," Sanders answered.

*　*　*

Several kilometers down the road Sophia opened the letter. She read it a few times before translating:

MY DEAREST SOPHIA:

SINCE I HAVE NO WAY OF FINDING YOU, I'VE ENTRUSTED THIS LETTER TO THE CAREGIVERS HERE AT THE HOSPITAL OF THE SACRED HEART, WHERE I AM LIVING OUT THE REMAINDER OF MY DAYS. OVER THE YEARS I HAVE PRAYED FOR ONLY ONE THING BESIDES GOD'S GRACE---THAT I MIGHT SEE YOUR FACE ONE LAST TIME BEFORE I'M CALLED HOME TO HIM. I HAVE NO REASON TO BELIEVE YOU REMEMBER ME OR THE DECADES WE SHARED, BUT I'VE READ THE BIBLE TOO MANY TIMES TO GIVE UP ON MIRACLES. IF YOU ARE READING THIS, EITHER YOUR MEMORY HAS RETURNED OR GOD HAS BROUGHT YOU HERE, A MIRACLE EITHER WAY.

LONG AGO I TOLD YOU I BELIEVED YOU ALSO WERE ONE OF GOD'S MIRACLES. I BELIEVED THEN, AS I DO NOW,

THAT HE IS GUIDING YOUR STEPS WHILE SUMMONING YOU TO DO HIS WORK. YOUR PATH IS UNDOUBTEDLY DIFFICULT, AND I HAVE LEFT SOMETHING FOR YOU AT THE CONVENT THAT WAS OUR HOME FOR SO MANY YEARS. LOOK BEHIND THE PINK STONE MORTARED INTO THE WALL BEHIND THE ALTAR IN THE CHAPEL. IT WILL REVEAL SOMETHING YOU MAY NOT KNOW, AND I PRAY IT WILL GIVE YOU STRENGTH TO CARRY ON GOD'S MISSION.

I NOW REALIZE THAT OUR FATHER ABOVE HAS DECIDED WE WILL NOT MEET AGAIN IN THIS LIFE, AND I MUST BE CONTENT TO WAIT FOR YOU IN HEAVEN. MAY OUR LORD JESUS CHRIST FOLLOW YOU ON YOUR JOURNEY EVERY STEP OF THE WAY.

WITH MANY BLESSINGS, PRECIOUS ONE,
MOTHER LÚCIA
JUNE 29, 1974

*　*　*

Owens steered the Audi off the highway and negotiated the gravel path leading to the hotel. Sanders studied the *Convento de Santa Isabel* brochure. A golf course spread around them. The spot was serene except for a lonely golfer struggling in a distant sand trap.

Wisps of Sophia's hair lifted on the breeze. After staring at the landscape for a few moments she said, "I've come to a realization." She spun around and headed back to the car, saying over her shoulder, "I don't like mysteries."

*　*　*

The once solemn exterior of *Convento de Santa Isabel* was enlivened by a fresh coat of whitewash. Owens handed the keys to the valet. A doorman came for the luggage, and they made their way to the massive front doors. Sophia couldn't resist pressing a hand against the weathered oak, smoothed by centuries of touching.

Aside from the addition of a front desk, plush lobby furniture and flowers in large vases, the interior still exuded the sanctity of a convent, provided one didn't look too closely at the fully stocked bar separating the lobby from the dining room, formerly the refectory.

"Does any of this look familiar?" Sanders asked her.

"No, but I'm certain I've been here before."

At the front desk, Owens, with Sophia's help, requested two rooms, a double for him and Sanders, a single for her. "Find out if either was once the chapel," he said to her.

The young man behind the pencil moustache at the counter overheard them and switched to English. "The former chapel is now our honeymoon suite. Fortunately, it is available—for fifteen hundred euros a night."

This was going to be easier than he thought. "We'll take it," Owens answered.

Sanders reached into his back pocket.

"Best give your credit card a rest," Owens said, plucking his from his wallet. "Yours has undoubtedly been flagged and mine can't be compromised."

The porter grabbed their few belongings and showed them to their rooms.

It wasn't difficult to imagine generations of orphans and unwanted girls, maybe even Sophia, hurrying through these corridors like so many church mice. Owens recalled watching Sophia mopping *Isabella's* deck, as if repetition of movement was a way of seeking grace. He could easily envision her on her knees, scrubbing and polishing these smooth stones.

They stopped at a wooden door different from the others. Sophia ran her hand over the intricate carving of the Annunciation. "*Muito Bonito.*"

"The honeymoon suite, our finest accommodation," the porter explained.

Sophia pulled them aside while the porter unlocked the door. "The painting we saw in Sr. Oliveira's museum, the one where Jesus was being whipped, this is where I saw it, here in this hallway, opposite that statue of the Virgin."

"Are you sure?" Preston asked.

She closed her eyes as if doing so would enable her to see more clearly. "Yes, I'm sure."

Understandable, Owens thought, since this was once the entrance to the chapel. He couldn't wait to see what fifteen hundred euros had bought them.

Chapter Thirty-One

Wednesday: 3:35 p.m.

Ralph Cotton tapped on the door to the Oval Office.

"Come in." The President was leaning back in her chair, studying proposals for healthcare reforms. "Ralph, have we heard from Agent Fulton yet?"

"He's in Lisbon. No word since his arrival."

"Let him know our patience is limited. It's urgent we find that young woman."

"I'll see to it."

Cotton placed a stack of medical journals on the edge of her desk. "You might want to glance at these." The journals were advance copies yet to reach newsstands.

"What is so important? Another outbreak of avian flu? Obesity still on the rise?"

"No. Normally I wouldn't trouble you, but..."

"But what?"

"I thought you might want to get behind the wheel of this bus before it runs over us."

"Which bus are you referring to?"

"Madame President, as we already know, stories about a strange medical occurrence have been showing up on TV and radio. Bloggers are going wild. These journals document a new epidemic that has affected people in at least thirty states."

"I'm aware of it, but I've been more focused on Alzheimer's. Thirty states! How many people are we talking about?"

"The number is small but growing."

Her face knotted up. "A terrorist attack?"

"No, at least it doesn't appear so. This epidemic is targeting children."

"Is this illness fatal?"

"More than likely. Toddlers around the country are showing alarming signs of physical deterioration."

Her eyes narrowed. "Go on."

Cotton pushed his glasses to the top of his pudgy nose. "I'm no doctor or scientist so much of this is beyond me, but—according to these journals—children are experiencing a mutation in the gene referred to as Lamin A."

"I know something about this. You're saying that children are suddenly contracting muscular dystrophy."

"Not exactly. These children are showing a wide range of aging-like changes, more closely associated with progeria."

On top of the journals he'd placed on her desk was a document. He picked it up and handed it to her. "CDC has begun issuing these daily bulletins."

SPECIAL ALERT

Category C — Bioterrorism Warning

- From January 3 to April 28 of this year approximately 314 illnesses were reported that are likely to be associated with progeria.

- Progeria is an extremely rare genetic disorder usually affecting fewer than forty individuals worldwide. The cause for this sudden increase is unknown at this time.

- Victims, usually under five years of age, suffer characteristics such as baldness, aged-looking skin, stiffness of joints, hip dislocations, cardiovascular problems, arteriosclerosis, and a premature cessation of growth—all the ailments of aging.

  Please contact CDC if you are aware of individuals with these symptoms.

The President appeared to look past him. "Madame President?"

"Yes. Sorry. A preposterous thought came to mind. You must have a reason for bringing this information to me instead of sending it through channels. There's more bad news. Let's have it."

"Evidence suggests these children were infected with contaminated doses of vaccines for diphtheria, tetanus, and pertussis."

"It's been a while since my children were small, but I believe you're referring to baby immunizations, the DTP vaccines?"

"Yes. And here's where the shit hits the fan, Madame President. These vaccines were all made by Lukker Pharmaceuticals."

She pushed back in her chair. "You're concerned because Everett Lukker is one of our largest donors."

"Yes. Most politicos know he is smiled on by this administration, considered a member of your inner circle. I advise you to distance yourself from him, starting now."

"Ralph, I know there's no love lost between you and Everett Lukker, but I don't set my friends adrift just because they're in trouble."

"It has always troubled me that you consider him a friend."

"I find it presumptuous for you to suggest who should and shouldn't be my friend," she said sharply.

"I don't think you understand how serious this is. If Lukker goes down the tubes he could take you with him. This has the capability of mushrooming into a major political scandal, one capable of derailing your bid for a second term and tarnishing your legacy."

The President turned her body away from him, ever so slightly, her tone softening when she said, "Calm down, Ralph. I've already spoken to Everett. He's scheduled a press conference, hasn't he?"

"Yes, for 1:00 p.m. tomorrow. But—"

"He has an explanation for what is happening."

"It had better be a good one. Wall Street isn't waiting. Shares of LUK are tumbling to a record low. At this time tomorrow, who knows? It's hard to imagine what he could say to stop the hemorrhaging. Your healthcare reforms could be relegated to a back burner if this develops into a major scandal and sucks us in."

"Thank you, Ralph. Please make sure I receive all CDC daily bulletins."

"Yes, Madame President." He reached for the journals.

She stared at the stack as if they were a basket of cobras. "No. Leave them."

When her Chief of Staff had gone, she began mumbling repeatedly,

"…preposterous…"

She pressed a button on her intercom and her secretary appeared.

"Yes, Madame President?"

"Janet, cancel my appointments for the rest of the day."

*   *   *

Cotton drummed his fingers on his desk. He grabbed a pencil and fiddled with it, snapping it in two. Finally, he picked up his phone and dialed a number. All lines leaving the West Wing were secure, but when dialing *this* number, he was more cautious than usual.

"Yes?"

"We just had a conversation about Everett Lukker. She claims she spoke with him and he has an explanation for all this. I've always thought of her as a straight shooter, but for the first time since I've known her, I don't believe she's being straight with me."

As he listened, he pulled out a handkerchief and mopped his damp brow. When the conversation ended, he hung up and began chewing his nails.

Chapter Thirty-Two

Wednesday: 3:54 p.m.

The porter's eyes darted between Owens and Sanders, probably wondering which one of them was going to carry Sophia across the threshold of the honeymoon suite. "Mr. Klumperstein and I will take the suite," Owens said. The porter kept a straight face when Owens winked at him and handed over a generous tip. "Please escort our companion to her room so she can rest until we take her to dinner."

Inside the honeymoon suite, the altar was gone. The polished stone floor gave no indication where it had been located.

"The stone walls must be twenty-five feet high, and all painted white," Sanders complained. "There are thousands of rocks. How will we find a 'pink' one?"

He didn't have an answer.

An opening had been cut into the wall adjacent to the chapel so a cell could be converted into a sumptuous master bathroom. The Estremoz white marble tub was large enough to baptize an entire family.

Sanders rubbed his chin. "I suppose we could tell the truth and let hotel maintenance tear open the walls for us."

"Geez—what would that sound like? Excuse us, but our traveling companion, who just might be a hundred and fifty years old even though she doesn't look a day over twenty-five, needs to tear open walls in your most expensive suite to find a mysterious item hidden fifty years ago by an old nun who our companion doesn't remember. Oh, and sorry if the wall we need to demolish is now located in the suite's luxurious new shower, in which case we'll need to destroy that as well."

"We could be far less generous with the truth, but I see your point."

Owens pushed the king-size bed away from a wall and stared at the space behind it.

Randomly tapping the stones was getting Sanders nowhere. "In the letter, the old nun said it was hidden by a rock mortared into the wall behind the altar. Every wall from floor to ceiling is whitewashed stone and mortar. There's no pink stone, and no way to tell where the altar once was."

*   *   *

An hour later their door received a soft knock. "Anderson? Captain Sanders?"

Sanders cracked open the door. Trickles of sweat cut through the white powder covering him.

"I thought you gentlemen were going to take me to dinner," Sophia said. "The refectory is filling up quickly and—why is white powder spilling under the door into the hallway?" She stared at the marks on the walls, a tire iron in Owens's hand. "What are you doing?"

Owens wiped sweat from his eyes. "We're trying to find out if that nun really hid something for you, but I'm beginning to have doubts. She said it was in the wall behind the altar, hidden behind a pink stone, but we can't find it. Don't suppose you remember being in this room or can provide a clue where the altar was?"

She pushed her way into the room. Red crept up her throat to her face. "Is anything of mine sacred to either of you? You both treat me like a child, prowl through my belongings, keep secrets from me and ask that I lie to people. Now you're damaging what was once a house of God to take something else that belongs to me. Maybe it was foolish of me to share the information in my letter. I'm beginning to wonder if you two really do have my best interests at heart."

A puff of white dust and paint lifted into the air when Owens sank onto the bed, now in the middle of the room. "You're right. We've been treating you like a child, yet in our defense you act like one much of the time. But we're beginning to see that you're changing, asserting yourself more."

When she went to the supply closet to search for a broom to sweep up all the dust, Preston turned toward Owens. "I've been keeping it to myself, but I've noticed the way she looks at you, like a schoolgirl having her first crush. Surely, you've noticed."

Owens *had* noticed but said nothing. He'd done his best to discourage her fixation on him, with minimal success. The spark he'd felt on the flight from Terceira was but one of the times her touch had ignited something in him.

When Sophia returned with a broom, Owens took it from her and patted the spot beside him on the bed. "I'm not so old that I can't remember when *I* was younger, wanting to be taken seriously, stretching boundaries."

They all sat in silence. After a few minutes Sophia said, "Captain Sanders, do you remember your parents?"

"Yes, I remember them."

"I wish I could remember mine. Tell me, what sort of boundaries did you stretch when you were a teenager?"

A glance passed between Sanders and Owens. The marine biologist rarely mentioned his parents, but sharing now could ease the tension.

"I was pushing boundaries the last time I saw my parents alive," he began. "We were headed to Boston where my father had a business meeting, and then we were heading to Los Angeles to visit my ailing grandmother. We were booked on Flight #11 out of Logan International Airport. I was nearly eighteen, had met a girl and decided to hang around a few more days, catch a later flight. My parents were unhappy about it, but I was stubborn, forced them to continue to LA without me. Their flight departed at 7:59 a.m. and at 8:46 the plane deliberately crashed into the World Trade Center's North Tower, killing everyone aboard."

"Anderson told me that a disaster took your parents." She placed a hand over his. "You would have been killed along with your parents if you hadn't been...stretching boundaries."

Sanders ran his free hand over his face. "I've thought about their deaths every day since the disaster, wondered why I'd survived when so many hadn't, but you're right; I wouldn't be here today if I hadn't been acting like a typical teenager."

She gave his hand a pat, then opened her locket and studied the photographs of the Briggs. "You think these were my real parents, don't you?"

"It doesn't seem possible, but Anderson and I have been unable to prove otherwise."

"The tale Anderson told me about *Mary Celeste* and her crew is incredible. If he's right, then you and I have something in common."

"What's that?"

"The two of us have parents who both died together."

Sanders was spared saying more when she turned toward Owens and pointed to one of the few patches of wall unmarred by the tire iron. "What we're looking for is there."

"If you don't remember being here, and the pink stone is now painted white like all the others, how can you be certain?" Owens asked.

"You're looking too closely. It's like a puzzle; ignore the individual pieces and look for a large image." She rose from the bed and approached the wall, pointing a finger at a group of stones, a triangle-shaped one in the center. "See how these stones come together, loosely forming a cross?"

Owens had only focused on the shape of individual stones and didn't see anything resembling a cross, but she seemed certain.

"What we're looking for is behind the one in the middle."

She took the tire iron from Owens and scraped at the mortar, which crumbled easily. The rock remained firmly in place when she tugged at it, but muscle provided by the men loosened it. Just as it was about to fall from its resting place, Owens and Sanders grabbed the stone and lowered it to the floor.

She reached into the opening and retrieved a small metal box, carried it to the bed where she sat with it on her lap. Once again, she was in no hurry to dive into her past.

Sanders may have started out as a reluctant participant in this adventure, but now he was fully engaged. They joined her on the edge of the bed; sandwiched between them, she looked even smaller.

Owens stared at the box like a squirrel eying an acorn. "There's a saying in the Bible that my Mama quotes all the time, " '...the truth will set you free.' Maybe the truth inside this box, good or bad, will free you from the fog that's clouded your memory. Mother Lúcia must have thought so to have preserved for you whatever's inside."

After staring at the box for several moments, she tugged open the latch and lifted the lid.

Inside were three photographs, the largest rolled like a diploma. A yellowed piece of lace tied around it matched that on the fancy dress Sophia had given to Sr. Oliveira for his museum. The two novices probably spent months sewing the dress for that statue of the Virgin.

Sophia removed the ribbon and unrolled a group portrait, nuns and three rows of children posing in front of the oak doors of *Convento de Santa Isabel*. Stiff faces, no smiling in a sepia-colored world devoid of laughter.

She was about to roll it up when Owens pointed at a small girl, four or five, standing in the front row. "Notice that her dress doesn't match the other girls. She must have just arrived from the Azores and still wears a Terceira smock—garment #1 in your satchel. And if you look carefully, you can see the gold locket."

Her voice was a pensive whisper. "Is it really me?"

"I think so," he said, his arm over her trembling shoulder. "Does this picture trigger any memories?"

She squinted at the photograph, shook her head. On the reverse was an inscription. She translated: "The Orphans of *Convento de Santa Isabel* and Their Teachers—1885."

"So, that small girl wasn't four or five," Sanders speculated. "More like fourteen or fifteen."

Two additional pictures had also been preserved. In a double portrait, Sophia still wore her locket, and a tailored smock with a form-fitting waist, the needlework on the collar and cuffs identical to that on garment #2 in her satchel. In this close-up, Sophia appeared only a few years older than in the first picture. She flipped it over and read,

"Sophia Correia and Lucia Soares—1918."

"I guess Mother Lúcia wasn't exaggerating when she wrote that you two had spent decades together," Owens said.

The third photograph, a dry plate printed on a thin sheet of metal, was older than the others. Scratched into the metal on the reverse was a date: 1872—the year *Mary Celeste* sailed from New York's harbor. Beneath the fancy clothes Sophia was probably still in diapers. Much of the image was corroded but it was still possible to see her standing in front of a carousel, her eyes glancing to the left where a mule appeared to be laughing at her. The beast's mouth was open but curiously had no tongue.

Sanders owned a modest collection of antique photographs. "A gelatin-bromide dry plate," he observed. "These were popular before the development of photographic techniques that could capture squirming children or animals without strapping them down. Animals and toddlers had difficulty sitting still for the time it took to register their images."

"This must be the picture Sra. Correia's grandfather found floating in the ocean," Owens said.

"It's possible," Sanders said. "In New York there's a museum dedicated to the history of Central Park. I've wandered through it several times. I recognize the carousel in the background, a famous Central Park landmark that opened in 1871. It was powered by a blind mule. If Sophia's parents took her there days before the *Mary Celeste* sailed, then this is quite possibly the last picture taken of anyone on that fateful voyage."

Owens and Sanders were startled when Sophia burst out laughing, a screechy sound laced with hysteria. When she could speak again her question was surprising.

"Why do you suppose the mule in the picture doesn't have a tongue?"

"I'm sure it *did* have a tongue," Sanders explained, "but movement in early photography rendered images invisible. The mule's tongue must have been moving too quickly for it to leave an image. Judging from your sideways glance in the picture, I'd say that mule had just licked your face."

Her hand sprang to her cheek, as though feeling the sticky tongue of a beast that had died before the last century began.

"Why don't you go back to your room and study those pictures; see if anything triggers a memory," Owens suggested. "We'll clean up and join you for dinner."

She left, taking the photographs and metal box with her.

Alone, Owens said to Sanders, "I'm at the crossroads of a place I've never visited before. I've been able to debunk every outlandish notion that's come my way, but here I am, confronted with unequivocal proof that Sophia is, in fact, who we think she is. She's an anomaly of nature—the world's oldest human. It's possible she's something I've denied my entire life. A miracle."

*   *   *

Steamy water flowed over Owens, the pounding shower jets doing little to wash away the notion that his concept of reality needed to be realigned, restructured to accept what moments earlier had seemed unacceptable.

Thirty minutes later he was dressed and tapping on Sophia's door. Sanders had gone ahead to the refectory to grab a table.

"You must be starving," he said when she answered his knock.

"I am, but there's something I want to discuss. Please come in."

Her room was smaller than the one he shared with Sanders. She sat on the bed, pushed aside the box of photographs and patted the spot beside her.

"What's up?" he asked, sitting down.

"This is new for me, rather embarrassing, but..."

"But what?"

"Time is running out, and there is something I've wondered about. You are the nicest man I've ever met, and...well..."

"Go on."

"I see people all the time, holding hands, looking into each other's eyes. They look so...so..."

"Happy? In love?"

"Yes. But there's something else. Will you...I want to..." She leaned forward, smelling of lemons and incense, and gave him a clumsy kiss. A look of confusion as she pulled back.

She has a crush, he thought. *The oldest female on the planet has a schoolgirl crush on me.*

Her antique comb was missing, and her hair was down to her shoulders.

Had she ever been with a man? "What you're feeling is natural," he said, assuming a parental tone while concealing the fact that nothing involving her was natural.

"I believe God wants us to be together," she said.

This wasn't the time to share his religious doubts. "And we *are* together, but the timing isn't right." He gave her a light kiss on the forehead.

"Why not?" she asked, her breathing ragged.

Why not? Minutes ago, he'd learned she was four times older than the oldest woman he'd ever slept with, three times as old as his own mother...but at this moment, gazing into her open and inviting face while she offered herself to him, such considerations were hard to focus on. He couldn't deny the attraction he had for her since the day he'd encountered her sitting on that rock.

Her flesh was a magnet pulling him toward her, hard to escape even if he wanted to, which at that moment was far from his mind. He studied her eyes for a signal convincing him to proceed, a checkered flag to start things off, tell him it was okay to press the pedal to the metal. In her blue eyes he saw more than a pellucid and fathomless ocean, he saw the promise of something he'd been looking for his entire life. Their mouths fused together.

But guilt gnawed the corners of his conscience. He hit the brakes and pulled away. "I think we need to slow down." In truth, *he* needed to slow down. He didn't want to say what he was thinking, that intoxicating though she was, only days earlier he'd wondered if she were batty. Now everything was helter-skelter. Willing or not, whatever age she was, he wasn't about to take advantage of her.

"You don't understand," she exclaimed. "This is the way it is supposed to be. God sent you."

"Maybe yes, maybe no, but so far God hasn't given *me* the message. I think you need to give yourself time. Be sure it's what you really want. If you feel the same way in a few weeks, then I'm your guy."

He could only imagine what emotions were swirling through her. Most women he'd known would have pouted over such a rejection, turned churlish, but she gave him a wan smile and patted his hand. She sighed deeply, returned her hair to its previous appearance. After brushing wrinkles from her pants she said, "Let's go eat. I'm famished."

Owens knew he'd done the right thing, but he deeply regretted his decision. If she asked again, he wondered if he'd be able to resist.

Chapter Thirty-Three

The Next Morning

No one answered when Owens and Sanders knocked on Sophia's door the next morning to escort her to breakfast. Last night at dinner she had bubbled with conversation and consumed her meal enthusiastically, saying or doing nothing to indicate displeasure or disappointment over what might have been. Owens might have convinced himself it had never happened were it not for the lingering feelings of arousal that had kept him up much of the night.

From a distance they saw her in the dining room chatting at a large table with two men. Owens didn't recognize the burly one, but the other had made a lasting impression when they'd met a few weeks ago.

Saveno.

*   *   *

"You're certain it's him?" Sanders asked.

"Positive."

"Why would Lukker send men to Portugal?"

"Wish I knew." Owens peered from behind a column and saw a waiter arrive at the table with mimosas.

Saveno opened his wallet and handed over a 100-euro note.

"Keep your eyes open," he said to Sanders. "I'll be back in a few minutes. Don't let them leave."

"What am I supposed to do if they—"

No time. Owens hurried back to the honeymoon suite and grabbed his laptop.

*   *   *

"Nice to see you again," Owens said to Saveno when he returned to the dining room.

Sophia was quite jovial. "These two gentlemen offered to share the last table with us."

Owens and Sanders dropped onto the empty chairs. "Kick any puppies lately?" Owens asked.

Saveno grinned. "What a coincidence—Anderson Owens, a.k.a. Rashard LeBeque. Dog grooming must be very profitable for you to be traveling in Portugal."

Owens had no idea what Saveno was doing here, but doubted it was a coincidence. The man seated beside him, a typical goon from central casting, had a poorly hidden gun holstered under his coat.

"Who's your friend?" Owens inquired.

"Just a travel companion. We've been having a pleasant conversation with Sophia. We've been telling her about the corporate jet we flew in on, promised her a ride back to the States."

So, it was Sophia they wanted. "We already have return tickets." A lie. "Thanks anyway."

Saveno and the goon stood up. "We're leaving now." The refectory was packed with diners. "I wouldn't make a scene if I were you. Someone could get shot in the confusion." He reached for Sophia's arm, pulled her to her feet.

"I don't understand," she said, alarm rising in her voice. "I thought we were going to have breakfast."

Owens glanced in the direction of the front desk where stone-faced hotel personnel were gathering. His tone was firm and commanding. "Go with them, Sophia. Trust me. Everything will be fine."

She didn't look convinced but let Saveno guide her out of the refectory. Owens reached for the metal box she'd left, and he and Sanders tailed them to the entrance.

As they were about to leave, a blue-and-white police car pulled in front of the massive oak doors and two uniforms stepped out. They were joined by two coat and ties who leaped out of an unmarked sedan.

"Mr. Saveno, please come with us," one of the policemen ordered.

Before Saveno or his companion could reach into their holsters, guns were aimed at them.

Owens grabbed Sophia and pulled her away as Lukker's two henchmen were cuffed and hauled off.

"I don't understand what just happened," Sophia said.

"It seems that Saveno and his friend match the descriptions of two men passing bogus euros."

"Who were those men with the police?"

"They work for Europol," Owens answered. "They hunt down counterfeiters."

He was thankful she didn't ask how he knew this. He handed her the metal box and walked her back to their table. "Let's have breakfast."

His cell rang along the way. "Yes?"

"Pomeroy here. We have a situation on our hands and I need you back here immediately. Do you have the girl?"

"I do."

"It seems we've been working at cross-purposes. You've been trying to learn the identity of a young woman with a mysterious past, while I've been trying to stop Lukker before he can do more harm. I've just learned that she is at the core of *both* endeavors. I now know why Lukker and the authorities are looking for her, why they'll do anything to lay their hands on her."

"How long have you known Lukker was also after Sophia?" he asked.

Pomeroy didn't answer.

Owens felt a tightening in his chest as he returned the cell to his pocket.

Sanders and Sophia both eyed him curiously.

"What are you both waiting for?" Owens said. "Time to grab our luggage and check out. We're off to the airport."

CHAPTER THIRTY-FOUR

Thursday: 10:30 a.m.

CDC PROGERIA BULLETIN #7

Current number of documented infections:

824

The reporters circling Everett Lukker didn't wait for him to read his prepared statement. They peppered him with questions as he approached the podium, a tight-faced bodyguard at his side.

After touting the successes of Lukker Pharmaceuticals despite this recent setback, he pointed at a reporter whose over-Botoxed face appeared regularly on one of the major news broadcasts. "Has the Food and Drug Administration pulled any of your products, and if so, do you think this will signal the collapse of Lukker Pharmaceuticals?"

Lukker's face registered no emotion. "The answer to the first part of your question is no; none of our products have been pulled by the FDA. In a few days the Food and Drug Administration will issue its own report, but Lukker Pharmaceuticals is not waiting. We have voluntarily pulled from the market *all* our pediatric vaccines—not just those produced and packaged in Costa Rica—and unused samples should be returned for a full refund."

A cacophony of questions erupted and Lukker brushed them aside. "As for the second part of that question; this is NOT the end of Lukker Pharmaceuticals. We aren't responsible for the terrorist act that has compromised our products. Our company has worked in partnership with several governments, including that of Costa Rica, to research and develop medicines that have saved countless lives."

The tank-sized reporter from the *Washington Globe* pushed to the front of the crowd. "Why Costa Rica?"

"A quarter of the world's medicines come from rain forests, such as those in Costa Rica. Perhaps we failed to take into consideration the Costa Rican government's limited ability to protect our facility to the extent promised."

"Are you blaming the Costa Rican government for what happened?" someone yelled.

"I'm merely sharing what I know: I've been informed that security at our facility in Sacramento, Costa Rica, was compromised. A preliminary inspection revealed that packages of our products, inoculations to immunize newborns for diphtheria, tetanus, and pertussis, were opened and a dangerous contaminant added. Since we were guaranteed protection by the Costa Rican government, I've asked the State Department to demand an investigation to determine how this could have taken place."

"When was this break-in?" bellowed someone over the crowd.

Lukker was intentionally vague. "Sometime within the past three years."

"Do you have any idea how many babies have been infected?" asked blond and statuesque Jackie Donovan. With credentials stretching back less than two years, she might have been considered wet behind the ears had she not already proven she was willing to brawl with media heavyweights to land a big story. Her face was beginning to appear on cable news shows.

"We are one of the world's largest producers of DTP vaccines. About 4.5 million doses of Lukker vaccine have been distributed in the U.S. alone over the past three years, though not all have been used."

"I've heard the number of infected is as high as half a million. Is that possible?" Donovan pressed.

Lukker paused before answering. "The exact number is not known, but *that* number is absurdly high."

The husky-voiced host of Court TV's most-watched show shouted from the back of the room. "You stated these children were infected sometime within the last three years; why is this coming to light only now?"

"We had no reason to believe our products had been tampered with and this contaminant doesn't induce symptoms until a child reaches two or three. Complicating matters, no single test can confirm the diagnosis of this affliction." Lukker cleared his throat, his eyes narrowing. "I want to say something now that I hope you'll all include in your reports: as soon as Lukker Pharmaceuticals was made aware of this...crime, we began working on a serum to counter the effects. In fact, we're on the edge of a breakthrough and expect to have a cure within a matter of months if not weeks, provided the parents of the infected cooperate by providing us with the necessary blood and tissuesamples."

"When did you find out about the Costa Rican break-in?" someone shouted.

Lukker remained unruffled, having anticipated the question. "After building the Sacramento facility, we were disappointed to learn that the Costa Rican government was unwilling to honor its commitment to provide protection from roaming drug dealers who occasionally crossed over from Nicaragua. We only learned recently that someone had infiltrated our operation to add dangerous elements to our vaccines."

"Who do you think is responsible for this?" yelled Jackie Donovan.

"Not many laboratories are sophisticated enough to create progeria, and we intend to cooperate with the State Department to find out who is responsible. It's possible that this is part of a terrorist attack on the USA using a new WMD."

"About these samples of children's blood you expect parents to hand over, why would they do so if you were even marginally responsible for infecting their kids?" asked someone holding a CNN microphone.

"The responsibility for this development rests with the terrorists who perpetrated this attack on our nation's greatest treasure—our children."

Lukker stared into the cameras. "For our part, Lukker Pharmaceuticals is halting research of all non-lifesaving products to focus on this illness. Warehouses have been purchased and will soon be equipped with refrigeration units to store this vast reservoir of contaminated blood for our scientists to study."

More than one reporter hollered, "How many warehouses and where are they located?"

Lukker proceeded without answering. "It will require massive co-operation to collect thousands of samples—several from each child—but if this is achieved in a timely fashion, a cure can be found for these children. And when we arrive at an antidote, Lukker Pharmaceuticals will provide it free to all the infected."

The *Wall Street Journal* reporter shouted, "The CDC bulletin says 824—how many do you expect? How much is 'vast?' "

Rather than answer, he produced a picture and held it up. "This photograph was recently retrieved from storage. We had no reason to look through old surveillance footage, but as you can see it clearly shows the break-in. My hope is that your news feeds can distribute this picture so an arrest can be made."

The photograph Lukker held up was only a few weeks old. It showed Anderson Owens picking the lock to the storage room in Costa Rica.

*   *   *

Jackie was shocked to see Anderson in the photograph, but she pulled herself together enough to approach one of Lukker's bodyguards who'd lingered behind. Her cheeks dimpled when she smiled. The stiff expression melted from his face and his smile broadened when he glanced at her bare wedding finger. No one noticed when she passed him a business card as he turned to follow his boss inside. "Give me a call if you want to talk. I'll make it worth your while."

CHAPTER THIRTY-FIVE

Thursday: 3:05 p.m.

A cab dropped them at the bungalow on Siesta Key. The front door was closed but unlocked. Sanders instinctively reached for the Glock, even though he'd left it on board _Isabella_.

Owens pulled his gun from the holster under his coat. He pushed the door open. Jackie Donovan was sitting in Sanders's favorite chair. "Hi boys. Miss me?"

Sanders dropped his rucksack and pulled Jackie into his arms. Their long kiss ended when Jackie noticed Sophia and pulled away. "I don't know who you are, but I hope you haven't stolen my man."

Sophia's cheeks turned red.

Sanders introduced the two women. "Sophia, this is Jackie Donovan, my fiancée. Jackie, this is Sophia Correia Briggs."

"Glad to meet you, Sophia."

The two women exchanged smiles.

"How long have you been here?" Sanders asked.

"I flew in from Virginia a few hours ago. This morning, I was at Everett Lukker's dog and pony show."

"We were flying home from Portugal and missed it."

"Anderson, you'd better keep those ugly glasses on and wear a cap. The world is looking for you."

"Thanks for the warning."

"Where have you boys been hiding?"

"Portugal," answered Sanders.

"Something hush-hush?"

"Not something we want to discuss with a reporter, not even one as drop-dead gorgeous as you," Owens answered.

Jackie ran a hand through her fiancé's unruly hair. She grazed his lips with hers and asked, "Am I too beautiful to learn why the CIA is looking for you and Miss Sophia Correia Briggs? I already know why everyone else is hunting for Anderson."

Owens had been heading to the fridge for a cold Mountain Dew but froze. "How do you know about the CIA?"

Jackie looked pleased to have all eyes on her. "They know I'm Preston's fiancée and I was questioned when I arrived at the airport— you'll have to share your secret for evading authorities. I hadn't been here longer than a few minutes when two boys from the Agency pounded on the door. They grilled me as to your whereabouts, then left. I think they were headed to SMRI to see if you were holed up there."

"We had the cab circle the neighborhood to be sure the coast was clear," Owens said.

Sanders peeked at the street through the blind covering his front window. "Well, it isn't clear now."

Across the street, two men were exiting an unmarked car, and heading their way.

Owens dashed to the sunroom at the back of the bungalow. Sanders's Sea Ray had been docked at Sarasota Harbor since he'd fled with Sophia, but he was hoping someone else's boat was nearby, close enough for them to borrow. No such luck. He rejoined Sanders at the front window.

The agents were wearing earpieces, and that gave him an idea. He pulled out his cell, dialed a pre-set number and gave a few terse orders.

The men crossed the street and continued up the driveway, but stopped in their tracks before reaching the front porch. They spun around, raced back to their car and sped away.

"We were just spotted at the Sarasota Mall," Owens explained. "It's a very big mall."

*   *   *

Owens climbed into the Land Cruiser, followed by Sanders and Sophia.

Before hopping in, Jackie demanded to know, "What's going on here? Why are CIA agents prowling around?" She spotted the damages on the Land Cruiser. "And what happened here?"

"It's an interesting story," Sanders acknowledged. "Quite a scoop for you when this wraps up."

"When what wraps up?"

"Trust us. We haven't led you astray before, have we?" Owens said.

"As a matter of fact—"

"Just get in," Sanders ordered.

*　*　*

Another unmarked car guarded the entrance to Owens's trailer park. Fortunately, the property backed up to wetlands. Peggy Pruitt watched them cross the marshy expanse and greeted them at the edge of her rental space, a lemon-yellow boa constrictor wrapped around an immense arm, a paper hat covered in blue glitter perched rakishly on her grey head. When he bought the property a few years back Peggy was already a tenant, had lived on this remote corner of the park for decades. The Land Cruiser came to a halt in front of her aqua and pink trailer.

Peggy was as kind as she was large, her massive figure covered in a pastel muumuu, her surprisingly small feet in neon orange flip-flops. She offered sanctuary to the injured creatures that made their way to her door. Soon after he bought the place, she gave him a tour of the marsh, pointing her walking stick at the dry, hard to spot grassy patches where he could safely drive without sinking. Peggy was a close friend and the self-proclaimed #1 fan of the Anderson Owens Show.

"Anderson! I knew you wouldn't forget my birthday. But why did you cut through the—wait a minute, this has to do with that car staked out near the entrance. What gives? Terrorists? Martians? I'll get my shotgun."

He usually spent a few hours with her on her special day, but this time he'd completely forgotten. "Let's hold off on weapons...for the time being. Nice boa. Not from around here."

"Probably a pet someone set loose in the marsh. Pulled it out of an alligator's mouth last Sunday."

Owens made the introductions. "Peggy, you know Preston, but I don't believe you've met his fiancée, Jackie."

Peggy made a tsk, tsk, tsk sound. "Preston, you should have told me you were in the market for a wife. I'd let you park your shoes under my bed anytime."

Sanders grinned. "Don't think I haven't thought about it, Peggy, but you're more woman than I can handle."

"Pity. And who are you?"

Sophia smiled at the yellow snake licking the air with its tongue and said nothing.

"She's Sophia," Owens said. "I brought her here to meet you and help celebrate your birthday. Can she stay a day or two?"

"Of course she can. You know I adore company, even the two-legged kind. But tell me the truth, Anderson, did you really bring her here to celebrate my birthday, or are you hiding her from that guy parked out front?"

He gave her a peck on a fleshy cheek. "I need you to keep Sophia away from him, or anyone else who might come looking for her."

Peggy's eyes shone brightly in her large pink face. "Is this a matter of national security?"

"If I tell you, I'll have to kill you."

She beamed. "You know I luuuv it when you say that."

Chapter Thirty-Six

Two Hours Later

Owens turned onto Boulevard of the Arts in downtown Sarasota, parked at the Hyatt Regency in a shady corner of the parking lot where the Land Cruiser wasn't likely to draw attention—the authorities would be looking for it. Sanders and Jackie hurried with him to the Ritz-Carlton next door. If the authorities spotted the Land Cruiser, it was unlikely they'd search thousands of hotel rooms.

"If there's a BOLO out on me with a trace on my credit cards, how will I pay a hotel bill?" Sanders asked.

"No problem. Use the documents I've provided and register as Mr. and Mrs. Sidney Klumperstein—honeymooners. When you get to your room, call for a car rental. Order me something as maneuverable as the Land Cruiser but less conspicuous." Owens handed him his credit card. "Have a good time on *Sotto Voce*. You deserve it..."

* * *

After ordering Owens a Jeep Wrangler, Sanders and Jackie frolicked like teenagers in the large shower, wrapped themselves in hotel robes and ordered room service. Jackie sat on the bed and took a sip of champagne. "You promised me a scoop."

He settled beside her on the bed. "Yes, when this wraps up."

She wrinkled her nose. "When what wraps up? Why was there a CIA stakeout at Anderson's place? Why is Everett Lukker broadcasting Anderson's picture to the world? C'mon, you know I can keep a secret, Mr. Klumperstein."

Sanders laughed. "Reporters make their living by exposing secrets, not keeping them."

She brushed her lips against his. "You have my word—I won't reveal anything until you or Anderson flash me a green light. So, tell me about Sophia."

She set the glass of champagne on the nightstand and slipped a hand inside his robe.

Chapter Thirty-Seven

Friday: 2:45 p.m.

Pomeroy waited for Owens on the expansive front porch. His bushy eyebrows lifted at the sound of his approach. "Good afternoon, Anderson. Thank you for coming so quickly."

"Some weather, huh?" He sat in the empty rocker beside Pomeroy. Thunder cracked and fat silver raindrops began to fall.

"Yes. This shower is going to make it muggy. You've come alone. I'd hoped you would bring the girl."

"She's rather...delicate, and likely to be traumatized when she learns she's part of a hellish plot."

"I was looking forward to meeting her. Perhaps another time."

Franklin, Dr. Pomeroy's assistant, approached and handed Owens the latest copy of *Journal of the American Medical Association.* "Do you need anything else, Professor?"

"No, thank you, Franklin."

When they were alone Pomeroy said, "Reports like the one in this copy of JAMA are circulating strange results from medical tests on toddlers around the country. What do you know about progeria?"

"It's been discussed on my radio show a few times. I know it's a syndrome that turns kids into senior citizens."

"Very true. Victims suffer characteristics such as baldness, aged-looking skin, stiffness of joints, hip dislocations, cardiovascular problems, arteriosclerosis, and a premature cessation of growth—all the ailments of aging." Pomeroy's tone was grim. "Were I not in my eighties I could be a poster boy for progeria. What else do you know?"

"There isn't a cure. The disease usually appears when the victim reaches two or three, with death resulting before the thirteenth year. Fortunately, it's extremely rare. Until recently, only a hundred cases had been reported since the condition was identified in the late nine-teenth century. Before that, afflicted children were shunned as imps and demons."

Pomeroy's lips tightened into a grimace. "Our lab discovered some-thing interesting in the samples you brought back from Costa Rica."

"Let me guess—progeria."

"More precisely, a compound that triggers cell mutations that de-velop into progeria. I take it you have seen Lukker's press conference on TV?"

"I'm aware of it. I guess my trip to Costa Rica was counterpro-ductive. Lukker isn't trying to hide what we uncovered—he's gone public about the break-in and accused *me* with contaminating his vac-cines."

"I'm not so sure your trip was a waste of time, even though it did get you slapped with a warrant for your arrest. What can you tell me about that facility in Costa Rica? Did you notice anything peculiar?"

Owens thought about it. "I remember thinking how easy it was to breach security.

The guards were not professional, and once inside I was under-whelmed by the labs, hardly state-of-the-art equipment."

"Did the facility appear to be operational?"

"No. The place didn't look like it had been used for product re-search in a while, even though the building was relatively new. Dust everywhere and water damage from a leaky roof. Frankly, I saw little value in having a facility there."

"Why?"

"Lukker told reporters that his company was interested in preserv-ing the environment, yet Costa Rica has a tremendous record of pro-tecting its rainforests, perhaps the best in Latin America. A quarter of the country has been placed under federal protection, and the num-bers of national parks, forest reserves, and wildlife refuges are remark-able. So why Costa Rica?"

Pomeroy tapped his short fingers on the arms of his rocker. "Could it be because Costa Rica is the only country in Central America that doesn't have a military? The government could make any number of promises offering protection, but without an army to provide that protection..."

Owens caught the old man's inference. "The promises are worthless. Are you saying Lukker wanted that facility broken into?"

"I doubt it was ever a legitimate research lab. I suspect Lukker created the semblance of one to fool authorities. After you left for the Azores, we continued working on Roger's thumb drive. We already knew that he was upset by his involvement. He told me that Lukker, like King Herod, had authorized his own massacre of innocents."

Owens couldn't believe what he was hearing. "Was Vintiger suggesting that Lukker contaminated his own products, allowed innocent babies to be infected?"

"I'm afraid so. We've been able to retrieve quite a bit of the information buried in that damaged thumb drive. Roger sacrificed his life to provide us with detailed documentation of Lukker's experiments on animals as well as humans—proof of unthinkable crimes."

One of the rare moments in Owens's life when he was speechless.

Pomeroy continued. "The question we need to ask: why would Lukker do this?"

Owens found his voice. "He must be insane, like Hitler, Stalin or Pol Pot."

"I agree with you, but if murder was his goal, he could have targeted any sector of the population, but he picked young children. I believe I know why."

Shaking his head, Owens said, "I can't imagine an acceptable answer, but go on."

"Many drug companies and biotech firms realize that the quest for youth is our aging population's Holy Grail. For years Lukker has been promising an Alzheimer's vaccine, but secretly he's been manipulating human growth hormones to develop age-management medicines."

"Fountain of Youth drugs?"

"Yes. According to the file, Lukker has come closer than anyone to creating a formula for retarding age, and he's done so by studying the cause of progeria," Pomeroy explained.

"The key to eternal youth lies in kids dying from old age?"

"I believe Lukker is convinced this is so."

"Then Lukker isn't really interested in finding a cure for progeria?"

"Hardly. People who have rare diseases don't get much research attention because their numbers are modest and the potential market for new drugs to treat them is also small. Until recently. Now the number of progeria victims is skyrocketing.

"I'm no scientist," Owens admitted, "but it follows that he needs more patients to experiment with."

"You're probably correct. Not that I'm keen on giving monsters like Lukker the benefit of the doubt, but he might have thought he could cure these infected children. He's collecting their blood and tissue samples, countless variations of cells with defective Lamin A. Why would he do this? To cure progeria? Unlikely. He's promised to give away the cure once he obtains one, so where's the profit?"

"And what does this have to do with Sophia?"

Pomeroy stroked his goatee. "I can only say she's an integral part in all this."

"I don't understand."

"I suppose you've observed that this young lady is—different?"

"I've never met anyone quite like her."

Pomeroy smiled. "No, I don't suppose you have. Do you know where she comes from and how old she is?"

He sensed something in Pomeroy's tone, wanted to know what the old man knew about her, how he'd learned it. He didn't have long to wait.

"Didn't you travel to the Azores and Portugal to answer those questions?" Pomeroy's smile was replaced by a look of concern. "I suspect you and Dr. Sanders have grown fond of the young lady, but there's something about Sophia Correia you might not know."

"I'm listening."

Pomeroy cleared his throat. "The Oval Office has evidence that the late Portuguese dictator António Salazar spent years hunting for her because he believed she possessed the secret of eternal life. The evidence must be quite convincing because President Burbridge has dispatched agents to locate her and turn her over to Lukker."

Owens's rage turned to confusion. "I wondered why the CIA was looking for her, but I don't understand. I thought the President had enlisted Lukker to find a cure for Alzheimer's. Most anti-aging drugs, including human growth hormones, are illegal. So why the interest in Sophia?"

"Here's a possible answer," Pomeroy said. "Lukker has poisoned thousands of kids to develop a fountain of youth drug. Now he no longer believes they're going to provide him with his formula, and he's convinced himself that Sophia is the missing variable."

Owens's mouth had gone dry. "The question is—why is the President still helping him?"

"I wish I knew. Someone close to the President is trying to dig up answers for us."

Who, Owens wondered, but he knew better than to ask. "I'm beginning to wish I hadn't voted for her."

Pomeroy rubbed his spotted forehead. "Me, too. I'm still waiting for an answer to my question; have you learned Sophia's age?"

"Before I answer, I think we each need a shot of your Glen Garioch, probably several."

As if reading his mind, Franklin returned with the scotch, two glasses and an ice bucket. He added cubes to his drink, but Pomeroy took his straight.

"Professor Pomeroy, let me begin by asking who was president when you were born."

"Warren G. Harding."

"When Sophia Correia was born, Ulysses S. Grant was in the White House."

Pomeroy's glass hovered in front of his mouth. Finally, he downed the scotch.

"What you're suggesting is extraordinary, mind-boggling."

"I didn't believe it at first myself, crossed the Atlantic to find proof."

"Not much surprises me anymore, but this does," Pomeroy muttered. "I knew she was old, but not that old. What more have you learned about her?"

"First off, her last name isn't Correia; it's Briggs. Sophia Briggs." He refilled the old man's glass.

Pomeroy's hand shook as he took a sip. "Briggs isn't that unusual a name."

"True, but her parents were Benjamin and Sarah Briggs. Her father was a sea captain. You know the name of his ship, but you might have forgotten it; the *Mary Celeste*."

"The *Mary Celeste*. The ship that became a legend after its crew disappeared?"

"Yes. Sophia Briggs was two years old in 1872 when she accompanied her mother and father on that ill-starred voyage. The fate of those aboard has long remained a mystery. Dr. Sanders and I believe Sophia was aboard the *Mary Celeste* on that baffling day, and I can fill you in on what we've learned about her, but much remains unexplainable."

He spent the next few hours detailing all that had happened since his first encounter with Sophia. When he finished, the level of scotch in the bottle was significantly lower.

Pomeroy invited him to spend the night, but he declined.

"I need to get back to WCRX before the station owners realize just how expendable I am."

"Before you go, I have something for you." He tapped a case near his feet with his cane. "You might have need of this."

"What is it?"

"A disguise kit. With Lukker broadcasting your photograph and fingering you as the culprit responsible for the break-in, I figured this might come in handy."

*   *   *

Another unmarked car was parked in front of his trailer park when he returned.

He circled around and made another swamp crossing. Peggy was waiting for him in front of her trailer. "Anderson! Just in time. Come inside."

They entered her trailer. Sophia was seated on the davenport. She looked different. Her hair had been cut. Gone was the long old-fashioned style that, at first, had made him think she was older than she was, even though she'd turned out to be older than he could have imagined.

"What do you think, Anderson?" Sophia exclaimed, turning her head back and forth to show off her new shoulder-length cut. "I asked Peggy for a new style. Didn't she do a wonderful job?"

"She certainly did," he admitted.

Peggy pulled Owens to the kitchen and whispered, "The feds have been knocking on doors looking for you and Sophia; they were here an hour ago demanding to search my trailer. I told them this was America and showed them the business end of my shotgun. They went to get a warrant, so you'd better find another place to hide her."

"Thanks, Peggy, you've been a doll." To Sophia, "Grab your bag, we're heading out."

Sophia disappeared into the bedroom to gather up her things.

Peggy's mouth was a tight little bow. "Before you go, I have a quick question or two, beginning with, 'Where did Sophia come from?'"

"Why do you ask?"

"Because she's so...so different."

"How so?"

"Well, most young ladies are skittish around snakes, but not her. I watched from a window as she went down to the marsh. A water moccasin, maybe forty inches long, slithered out of the water and headed toward her. She could have easily outrun it, but she remained still, held out a hand so the snake could lick it before returning to the marsh.

"I didn't know there were poisonous snakes in the area."

"The snakes around here can deliver a nasty bite but aren't deadly. I've never seen a water moccasin in these parts. If I'd known one was nearby, I'd have kept her inside. I didn't want to startle the snake into biting, so I waited until it had gone to tell her that, unlike my new pet boa, water moccasins are poisonous. She just smiled; said she knew it wouldn't bite."

Owens was becoming accustomed to Sophia's specialness and played it down. "So, she's good with animals. What else is strange?"

"Well, she's as sweet as she could be but...heck, Anderson, she doesn't even know her own birthday. After the snake incident I kept her inside. She was helping me bake a cake and I asked what she liked to do on *her* birthday. She said she'd never celebrated one, didn't know when it was. What gives? Was she adopted?"

"Something like that."

Peggy shook her head. "She can't remember birthday presents. Or playing pin the tail on the donkey with friends." Her eyes welled up. "You need to take her to Chuck E. Cheese so she can let her hair down, what's left of it anyway, and loosen up, play Whack-A-Mole and have a good time."

"Can't right now, but maybe there's something else I can do." He pulled out his cell and texted a request for the birth date of Sophia Briggs.

The answer came in a few minutes. He smiled. Too perfect. Sophia Briggs was born in 1870 on October 31—Halloween.

Chapter Thirty-Eight

Sunday: 6:40 a.m.

Owens now knew why the authorities had thrown out a dragnet for Sophia, but there were plenty of unanswered questions and he had no intention of handing her over to anyone. After kicking around several locations, a safe house popped into his mind, one he'd resisted using until now.

Sunday was dawning warmer than usual. They were north of Atlanta and had just crossed the Chattahoochee River twenty miles south of Paxton. His mother had been born here, returned to raise her granddaughter after years of living up north.

Owens called her on his cell.

"Yes?"

"Mama, I didn't wake you, did I?"

"Son, you know I rise with the chickens."

"You live in a row house in the middle of town; what chickens are you talkin' about?"

"Just an expression. I listened to your show last night. What's with all the repeats?"

"I've been out of town."

"You're going to lose your listeners if you don't treat them better."

"Yes, Mama."

"Listen to what I say, son, there's a lot of competition out there and radio shows get pulled all the time, shows better than yours."

"Yes, Mama. Listen—I'm calling for a reason."

"You need a reason to call me?"

"I'm a half hour away."

"Don't speed. You drive too fast."

"I'm bringing someone for you to meet."

"A girl?"

"Yes, a girl."

"Praise Jezzus! It's about time you settled down. She isn't pregnant, is she?"

"No."

"Where do her people come from?"

"You wouldn't believe me if I told you."

*　*　*

His mama beamed when she saw his new haircut, but her smile dropped lower than her support hose when she saw the young lady beside him.

"Mama, this is Sophia."

The silence was long enough to make Sophia blush and stare down at her shoes.

"I hope we haven't come at a bad time."

"I'm forgetting my manners," Mama apologized. "Come in and sit. Are you hungry, dear? Let me rustle up some pancakes."

"Can I help, Mrs. Owens?"

"No, thank you...Sophia. Make yourself at home."

He followed Mama into the kitchen where she pulled a large bowl from a cupboard.

"Anderson—"

"Yes, Mama?"

"This girl isn't right for you."

He was enjoying this. "Because she isn't black?"

"Don't make me smack you."

"What is it then?"

"Gawd Almighty, Anderson, what are you thinking? That girl's much too young for you."

He turned to look at Sophia; she did look significantly younger than him. "She's older than she looks."

Mama set down the eggs and milk she'd collected from the fridge, pulled a chair away from the table and sat down. "Son, we need to talk. I'm worried about you."

He sat down, reached for her hands and squeezed them. "Mama, I'm just having fun with you. Sophia isn't my girlfriend, but I was hoping she could stay with you for a few days."

His mother's sigh of relief was palpable. "Of course she can." She rose and went to the pantry for a bag of flour.

Keisha walked into the kitchen, rubbing her eyes. "Nanna, who's that in the living—" Her face lit up when she spotted him. "Uncle Anderson!" she squealed. "You cut your hair."

"Yep." He ran a hand over his head. "Hey, smile for me."

She flashed her braces at him.

"Beyoncé, step aside. Keisha's prettier and can sing circles around you."

"Uncle Anderson, Beyoncé's so over. She must be past forty by now. Besides, when have you heard me sing?"

"I've heard you in church."

"Are you lying to me? I don't remember seeing you in church."

"Of course you don't see me. Didn't I tell you I have an invisibility cloak just like Harry Potter?"

Keisha punched him in the arm. He hugged her and planted a kiss on her forehead.

Out of the corner of his eye he saw Sophia standing in the kitchen doorway, a wistful smile on her face.

Mama also spotted her. "Come join us, dear. We're going to have pancakes and then get ready for church."

"Can't stay, Mama. I've got work that can't wait."

"There's no work so important that it can't be put off until you've honored our Heavenly Father on His Sabbath. You can leave after service."

In the course of his work for *Sotto Voce* he'd stared down the barrel of guns and been tortured, but his mother's tight lips and unflinching expression often turned his resolve to mush, made him feel ten years old again. "Fine, I'll leave after church. But if God strikes me dead it'll be your fault."

"*You* don't have a problem going to church, do you, child?" Mama asked Sophia.

Sophia smiled. "No problem. But I'm not used to eating before service."

"At our church you'll be needing a lot of energy."

Owens kissed his mama on the cheek and made for the front door. "I've got a clean shirt in the car. When I get back, I'm going to check the label on your pancake syrup. If it isn't sugar-free, I'm gonna pour it out."

"You do that, then we'll check the sugar content in those Mountain Dews of yours."

CHAPTER THIRTY-NINE

Sunday: 8:25 a.m.

CDC PROGERIA BULLETIN #11

Current number of documented infections:

17,002

Paxton was coming to life. At the end of the street where Anderson Owens's mother and niece lived, Agent Fulton waited for a bakery to open for business. When the closed sign was flipped over, he entered and ordered a bran muffin and a cup of black coffee.

At 9:00 a.m. he punched Ralph Cotton's private number into his cell. "Fulton here. I'm in Paxton. Found the girl. She's with that radio talk show host."

"The talk show is a cover. Anderson Owens is a trained operative as dangerous as they come. It would be a mistake to underestimate him."

"What do you want me to do with the girl?"

"It's time she was brought to the White House, ASAP."

"It might get messy. She isn't alone."

"Do I need to remind you of what's at stake?"

*　*　*

Fulton stepped out of the bakery and climbed into his car. He adjusted the holster under his left arm before driving around the block and parking several doors past the Owens's townhouse. He watched as Anderson opened the back of the Wrangler, removed clothing, and returned inside. Three women: one old, one teenager, and his target, along with one male—but he'd have surprise as well as a gun on his side. Just as he was about to climb out of the car and make his way up the stairs, a door across the street opened and a brawny young man smoking a cigarette and carrying a mug of coffee appeared with a Rottweiler on a leash. Fulton sank down in the front seat and tried to make himself as inconspicuous as possible.

The dog pulled the young man to a nearby tree, lifted a leg and lacquered the trunk with pee before crouching down to do his business.

"You'd better be picking up after that beast, Deshawn."

Deshawn grinned at Mama Owens standing on her front steps, spatula in hand. He pulled a plastic bag from the back pocket of his jeans. "No problem, Miz Owens."

He bent down, scooped up his dog's waste and deposited it in a nearby garbage can.

"How's your mama doin' this mornin'?"

He shrugged. "Too early to tell if it's a good day or bad."

"You better not be smokin' near her oxygen tank."

"Wouldn't dare."

"Good. Now get over here and help us eat this mountain of pancakes I'm cooking."

"Miz Owens, you don't gotta be feedin' me all the time."

"I don't *gotta* do anything, but I can't seem to cut back my recipe. Do me a favor and help me get rid of a stack or two. You can tie Burgie to the railing here."

Deshawn loped across the street, tied Burgie to the rail beside the stairs and disappeared inside.

Fulton cracked his knuckles. Now there were three females and *two* men inside. And a Rottweiler at the door. Even if the dog didn't raise an alarm by barking, it was getting crowded in there. Anything could happen. He settled down, his eyes riveted on the front door.

An hour later Deshawn reappeared. He untied Burgie, returned to his own front porch and began reading the morning paper, the large dog curled around his feet.

*　*　*

"Church is four blocks away. I'll drive," Owens said. "It'll be easier on your legs, Mama."

"Thanks, Anderson, but Jesus sacrificed himself for us, was nailed to a cross to save our souls. I can endure a bit of discomfort to honor His sacrifice."

He noticed that Sophia had brightened at the prospect of going to church, even if she did appear uncomfortable in one of Keisha's dresses. They strode down the sidewalk, following in Mama's wake. Morning clouds were breaking up, and the sun was warm on their skin, the fruity scent of blossoms heavy on the air.

Gospel of the Redeemer Church dominated the intersection where several of Paxton's historic neighborhoods converged at Main Street. The steps leading to the entrance of the brick and limestone church were packed with people dressed in their finest. They were engulfed by chatter and a garden of brightly colored hats. Owens was slapped on the back and welcomed back to the fold. Four years had passed since he'd attended service.

Mama introduced Sophia to Pastor Jasperson, who smiled at her warmly.

"Welcome to our church, Sophia. God brightens our congregation with your presence. And Anderson, it's been a long time. Welcome home."

He shook the pastor's hand. From the corner of his eye, he saw the pleased look on his mother's face.

The crowd began surging up the steps. Inside, light filtered through stained glass windows, the bright colors spilling over the altar.

"Where are the paintings and statues?" Sophia whispered as they made their way down the crowded pews.

"This isn't *that* type of church. But check out the enormous organ on the back wall."

Sophia turned and looked at the source of the organ music swelling around them. "It's a fine organ," she said, her eyes shining as they sat down.

Keisha left them. Before long, she filed onto the stage with choir members dressed in royal blue and gold gowns. The choir sat in chairs behind the altar, facing the congregation.

A processional hymn started the service, followed by several readings from the Bible, more choir singing.

Pastor Jasperson made his way to the pulpit, cleared his throat and began with, "Welcome brothers and sisters of Jesus. I want to start this morning by asking how many of you brought a child with you today. Show God just how many children are with us here this morning."

Squirming children were raised into the air for all to see.

"Beautiful they are. And doesn't our Lord tell us what He thinks of children in Luke 18:15-17? Luke describes another beautiful day, a day when Jesus was preaching. Children were present, and they ran up to Jesus. But the crowd began holding them back, preventing them from approaching our Lord. Yet Jesus ordered: *Let the little children come to me, for it is to such as these that the kingdom of God belongs. Truly I tell you, whoever does not receive the kingdom of God as a little child will never enter it.*"

Sophia jumped like she'd been shot when Mama Owens, seated beside her, sprang up and shouted, "Great is the Word of God!"

Owens patted Sophia's hand.

The choir clapped their hands and pounded tambourines, shaking the air with shouts of "Hallelujah."

* * *

Twenty minutes later Pastor Jasperson wrapped up his sermon. The choir filled the church with energetic versions of *Jesus Lift Me* and *Bless the Word, O My Soul*. When Sophia stood and left the pew, Owens assumed she was stepping outside for fresh air.

Mama, eyes closed, was praying softly, and he took the opportunity to reach for his cell to text Dr. Pomeroy he was delayed. He didn't see Keisha stepping forward to begin her solo, and he didn't notice that most eyes had turned to the far right, where a young woman was climbing the steps toward the pulpit. When Owens finished texting and looked up, he saw Sophia approaching his visibly upset niece. The organ music stopped. Keisha stepped away from her fellow choir members and whispered to Sophia. "What are you doing up here? Go back to your pew."

Sophia didn't answer.

"Nanna! Uncle Anderson!" Keisha was no longer whispering.

Pale as porcelain, Sophia didn't move, her eyes glazed over.

Owens bolted up the steps and hurried over to her. "What's wrong? Are you sick?"

The church went silent as Pastor Jasperson joined them, asking, "Child, are you feeling God inside? Is there something you want to say?"

Sophia's voice was brittle, and the congregation struggled to hear. "God wants everyone to go home."

The pastor beamed. "Yes, He does. Of course, He does. God wants all His children to find their way to His heavenly home."

She shook her head and appeared to be struggling for words. She finally spoke out, this time loud and clear. "God wants everyone to leave this building. Immediately!"

Owens put an arm on Sophia's shoulder to steer her back down the stairs but winced when his fingers touched her. Static electricity.

The church couldn't have been quieter had it been empty. Pastor Jasperson laid his hands on her, one on a shoulder and the other on her head. His body jumped as though receiving an electric shock. With his hands still touching her, Jasperson's head flew back, and his spine arched like a strung bow. When he finally pulled away, his glasses had fogged up and his face was slick with sweat. He mumbled something under his breath, lifted his hands toward heaven and shouted. "Everyone, we will now leave this church in an orderly fashion. Go quickly!"

The congregation filed out onto the lawn in front of the church, blinking as they charged out into the noon sun. Ignoring the risk of another shock, Owens pulled Sophia down the stairs to the exit. Outside, Mama joined them on the grass. She shook Sophia hard, breaking her trance-like state.

Sophia started blinking and blushed at the sight of everyone staring at her. "What happened? Why are we outside? Is service over?"

"It most certainly is," Mama said, her hands shaking. "Don't you remember anything?"

Before Sophia could answer the air around them quivered like heat over a desert.

Hair on the back of Owens's neck stood up as Gospel of the Redeemer Church rose from its foundation and burst into a massive orange fireball. Bricks and large chunks of mortar spewed from the conflagration and rained down on the congregation. Thousands of smaller projectiles whizzed overhead like swarms of angry hornets, many embedding in the parked cars people were sheltering behind. Others ran onto Main Street to avoid the flaming debris raining down. In an instant it was over, with only a large crater left where the church had stood. Approaching sirens could be heard, and in a matter of minutes ambulances, police cars and fire trucks arrived.

Mama started shrieking, "Where's Keisha! Keisha! Where are you, child?"

"I'm over here, Nanna." Keisha, still in her choir robes, was crying under a blooming dogwood tree. Other than her bleeding lip, she looked uninjured.

Owens rushed to assist the paramedics with the wounded. Like Keisha, many had been struck by projectiles and were bleeding, but no one appeared seriously hurt.

Police closed off Main Street and worked crowd control. Firemen uncapped hydrants, connected hoses and began dousing the crater with powerful jets of water.

"Must have been a gas leak!" shouted a fireman.

When he looked up after helping the injured choirmaster into an ambulance his stomach dropped like a trapdoor under a noose.

Sophia was nowhere in sight.

Chapter Forty

Sunday: 12:02 p.m.

Fulton was parked across the street from Gospel of the Redeemer Church when the congregation stormed out the front doors. The girl and Owens were the last to exit the building before it exploded. Chunks of debris struck his car.

In the excitement and confusion that followed, he saw Owens release his grip on the girl to help the injured. In the melee, no one saw him pull her into the car and press a needle into her neck. She barely struggled.

Outside of town he made the call. "Seized her in Paxton. We'll be there in about eight hours."

"Paxton? We're receiving word of an explosion there today. Tell me you didn't blow up an entire church to get her," Ralph Cotton demanded. "On second thought, I'd rather not know."

* * *

"Where are you taking me?" Sophia asked, rubbing the needle mark on her neck when the Propofol rendering her unconscious wore off.

Fulton didn't answer.

"Will you pull over so I can go to the restroom?" she asked, urgency seeping into her voice.

Clouds were gathering in the distance, and the acrid scent of rain was heavy in the air. A sign indicated a gas station/rest stop at the next exit. Fulton pulled off the freeway and drove up to one of the pumps. The rest of the station was separated from the pumps by about twenty yards of asphalt. The place looked deserted until a lanky young man with freckles and a buzz cut left the garage and trotted over to them, wiping his hands on a rag. "Fill 'er up?"

Fulton wondered if he'd driven into a time warp, couldn't remember the last time an attendant pumped gas for him. He nodded as he reached for the lever to open the gas latch. "Regular unleaded."

"Cash or card?"

"Cash. Is the ladies' room unlocked?"

"Yep." He pointed back at the garage, where the restroom doors were in plain sight. He unscrewed the gas cap, dropped in the hose and tended to the windows while the tank filled.

The dress Sophia borrowed from Keisha was lightweight with short sleeves. It wasn't cold but she couldn't stop shivering as she left the car and raced to the restroom.

The attendant blinked at the gathering clouds, his nostrils flaring as he pumped the gas. "Rain's coming. You can smell it."

A few minutes later the tank was full and Fulton handed over the money. He circled around and pulled up in front of the restrooms, stepped out and looked at his watch. He was about to pound on the door when she emerged.

"Where are you taking me?"

"You'll know soon enough. Until then, don't ask questions." He pushed past her into the restroom, leaving the door open so he could keep an eye on her.

"Did you write 'HELP' on the mirror with lipstick?"

"I don't have any lipstick."

"Let's see." A quick search of the restroom: nothing was written on the mirror. He overturned the wastebasket and checked the paper towels that spilled out. She hadn't left a message to alert anyone to her abduction.

His back was turned for only a few moments, but when he spun around he was startled by the sight of another car parked beside his and a man holding the girl with a gloved hand over her mouth. He reached for his gun and burst from the restroom.

Someone was hiding behind the open door. A strike to Fulton's wrist sent his gun clattering over the rain-speckled asphalt. His nose collapsed when a fist collided with it. Fulton remained on his feet long enough to receive a blow to his jaw that landed him on the ground. Several kicks to the head sent him spiraling into darkness.

A sign promoting discounted lube jobs prevented a full view of the pumps, but when Sophia glanced in that direction Trachmann said, "That attendant looks like a nice guy, maybe a baby at home. Try and signal him and I'll have Saveno blow his brains out. Wouldn't want his death on *my* conscience."

Saveno pulled back his coat to give her a quick glimpse of his gun.

Trachmann plucked Fulton's weapon from the wet pavement, pocketed it and shoved Sophia into his car. He jerked his chin in the direction of the unconscious man lying on the pavement. "Grab his keys and put him in the trunk of his car. Follow behind. We'll find a good place to ventilate his head and ditch the car where stink from the trunk won't be noticed for a while."

"Gotcha, boss." Saveno did what he was told, but not before stomping on Fulton's right leg until the fibula and tibia snapped.

Trachmann slid behind the wheel and blocked his face from the watchful attendant as the two cars swung around the front of the station and passed by the pumps. A dozen miles down the highway he set his windshield wipers to a higher speed and pulled out his cell. "I have her. She was in Paxton, Georgia."

"I'm not surprised, knowing how much you like to torch things. The news is saturated with reports of that church explosion. I've been temporarily replaced as the lead story on every news broadcast. Any complications?"

"I've got a smashed-up agent in the trunk of a car."

"Fulton?"

"Yeah. He led us to the girl."

Lukker's voice was hard. "Then he's served his purpose. You know what to do. He works for the President, and his disappearance will not go unnoticed, so there had better not be any witnesses."

*   *   *

As the car sped along, Sophia closed her eyes and took deep breaths until her heartbeat returned to normal. She turned and studied her driver. "I've seen your friend before."

Trachmann glared at her. "Where?"

"At *Convento de Santa Isabel.* I thought he was nice, but he was passing around bad money. Who is the man in the trunk? Why did you beat him?"

Trachmann lifted a hand to cuff her but changed his mind when confronted with her enormous blue eyes. "His name is Fulton. We've been tailing him for days, followed him to Paxton. I would never have guessed he would be willing to blow up a church to get you."

"He didn't blow up the church," she said calmly.

"Yeah, like you'd know. A brilliant idea, really. In the mayhem, snatch the girl. I'm surprised Fulton had the nerve to pull it off."

* * *

Trachmann pulled the car to the shoulder of the rural road they were traveling to avoid the freeway. When Saveno pulled up behind, Trachmann stepped out of his car but left the engine running. He opened the passenger door, reached for a wrist and pulled Sophia into the rain. "Get into the other car," he ordered.

She did as she was told.

"What gives?" Saveno asked.

"I want you to continue toward Colton, but there's something I've got to do. I can't get Doogie Howser back at the station out of my mind. Lukker will have our nuts in a vise if we leave witnesses linking us to Fulton's disappearance. I should have popped the kid. A mistake I can fix. Stay on this road and I'll catch up with you in a few hours."

* * *

Trachmann sped back to the gas station. No cars were at the pumps, and the kid was gone. He plucked out his wallet and waved it in front of the elderly black man in worn gabardines who hurried out of the garage to greet him. "I was here an hour ago for a fill-up and didn't get my credit card back. There was a young guy here at the time. I'm sure he'll remember me."

"That would be Bobby Klesper. His shift ended. He didn't say anything about a card left behind."

"When will he be back?"

"Hard to say. Bobby is on leave from the Army having just finished basic training. Tomorrow he's off to Fort Benning to be deployed someplace. He's a good kid and was just helping out here, which is why he probably forgot to give back your card. He must have put it in the register. Lemme take a look. How 'bout I top off your tank for the inconvenience?"

Trachmann smiled. He opened his wallet and pretended to forage around. "Would you look at this! Gosh, am I an idiot or what?" Trachmann pulled out a credit card. "I just misplaced it in my wallet."

The old man shook his head. "Too bad you didn't check better before retracing all those miles."

"Yes, and too bad I didn't have an opportunity to thank Bobby for his service. The fine young men and women in uniform defending our freedoms are making this world a much safer place."

Chapter Forty-One

Sunday: 7:28 p.m.

CDC Progeria Bulletin #16

Current number of documented infections:

31,777

The cell in his pocket started ringing. "Yeah?"

"Anderson, have you heard from your mom in the last few hours? There's been an explosion at Gospel of the Redeemer Church in Paxton." Sanders's voice was filled with alarm.

"I know."

"Isn't that your mother's church?"

"She's fine. Keisha, too."

The relief in Sanders's voice was palpable. "It's all over the news. Anderson, are you still there? Can you hear me?"

"Sophia's missing."

"What do you mean—missing?"

"I was helping paramedics with the injured and when I looked up, she was gone."

"But why is Dr. Pomeroy sending a jet—"

Owens had already hung up. Exhaustion made his vision blur, but he refused to quit searching. The day had dawned sunny and bright with a hint of impending showers; now an evening rain was soaking him to the skin. He shivered as he returned to his mother's townhouse to dry out and consider what to do next.

*   *   *

"Stop squeezing so hard," Mama cried out, but she hugged Owens just as tightly.

He held her hand as they walked to the kitchen where a large pot of coffee perked on the stove. His eyes darted about. "Where's Keisha? She's all right, isn't she?"

"She's across the street at a friend's house. Other than a chipped tooth, she's fine." She handed him a towel. "You're dripping all over my floor."

He toweled off as best he could while she poured him a mug of steaming coffee. "I've been combing the city looking for Sophia, but no luck."

She wagged a finger at him. "Anderson, you haven't been up front with me about that young lady."

"Why do you say that?"

"Don't look at me all innocent-like and tell me you don't know what I'm talking about. She isn't normal."

"Maybe it was a mistake bringing her here."

"Listen son, you've made many mistakes in your life—and one of these days I'd like to sit down and discuss them at length—but bringing Sophia here wasn't one of them. Much of this town, including your niece and me, would be dead if it weren't for her. Sometimes the fabric of Heaven rips open and a being drops down. I believe. Sophia is one of these special beings. I believe God speaks to her."

He was too bushed for a theological debate. "There might be a more logical explanation. Maybe she smelled the gas wafting up from the basement. That's what the authorities are saying caused the explosion, right?"

She frowned at him. "Several hundred worshippers filled that church, and no one else smelled gas." She shook her head. "I know you love God even if you occasionally break His commandments and don't keep holy the Sabbath, but you're a good son and a good man. I believe He chose you to bring Sophia here to save His people."

He wasn't ready to throw overboard the old Anderson by admitting she might be right.

"You believe in mysteries, and what is a miracle if not a mystery?"

To him, the difference was huge, but this wasn't a time for debate.

"Anderson, you're one of the smartest people I know, even though you think miracles are only for the foolish and deluded. But one day when my prayers are answered I trust you'll accept the truth—miracles do happen, but only for those smart enough to believe in them."

Keisha burst through the front door, soaked to the skin. "Nanna, I was on TV!"

"Child, haven't you sense enough to come in out of the rain? Besides, it's getting dark. Time to stay inside."

"I showed them my tooth. Uncle Anderson! You're back. Isn't it all just too cool?"

He squeezed her until she elbowed him. "How's the tooth?"

"A flying chunk of cement hit me in the mouth when I was on the lawn in front of the church. See where it cut me?" She pulled out her lower lip. "It hit me in my front tooth and chipped it. One of the nice paramedics said I might have lost a few teeth if not for my braces. A reporter overheard and asked me a few questions on camera."

Keisha shook her head when he pressed her with, "Did you smell gas inside the church before the explosion?"

"No," she answered. "The reporter asked the same thing. It was smart of you to bring Sophia here to save us."

"Yeah, I guess it was..."

Part Two

CHAPTER FORTY-TWO

Two Days Later

Finding Sophia was Owens's overriding concern. He worried she'd been struck by flying debris. She already suffered from memory loss, and now she could be experiencing a concussion, maybe total memory loss. Another thought crossed his mind. Could she have been abducted? Unlikely; no one other than Preston knew Sophia was in Paxton so he had no reason to believe she'd been taken, but after lengthy searches he fretted over the possibility he was wrong.

He renewed his search, with each fruitless hour adding weight to the beating lump in his chest. As he dashed through the rain searching abandoned cars, litter-strewn creeks, and collapsing sheds, he pondered how quickly she'd woven herself into the fabric of his well-being, someone whose absence could leave such a gaping hole at his core. He'd initially responded to her like an older brother or protective parent, but now, in her absence, he was forced to conclude she was more than a project or stray soul in need of help.

He felt bound to her in a manner he'd never experienced, as if her essence had been braided into his, and it frightened him. She represented everything he'd fought against his entire life—a world where fantasy and emotion overruled logic.

And it wasn't just the way she looked at him, which stirred something inside he'd never felt before, something deeper than passion. There was more; he couldn't deny she was attractive and apparently capable of performing inexplicable feats, although he still struggled to wrap his head around the notion of miracles.

As he searched for Sophia, pausing to wipe drizzle from his eyes, he reflected on the night he'd first encountered her; he was beginning to question the malfunctioning of the Land Cruiser delivering him to the very spot where she claimed to have been waiting for him. What had she called him—the answer to her prayers? And what was to be made of the church explosion here in Paxton? Was it the result of a random gas leak, and equally important: why was she aging so slowly?

He had questions in need of answers. Were there rules governing her supernatural activities? Living for over a hundred and fifty years was the stuff of science fiction, and many people would call it miraculous, but beyond her extended youth, did the power to control a Land Cruiser, tame snakes, and sense imminent disasters come from within? Or was it given to her, and if so by whom, or what? These were questions he hoped, in time, she might be able to answer.

Through a veil of deep-rooted doubt, he glimpsed the possibility of a guiding hand. *What had others called it? Intelligent design? God?* Doubt had been his companion far too long for him to jettison logic and replace it with religious mysticism. Unlike Mama, he wasn't ready to splash about in a pool of spirituality, but he couldn't deny that he was coming closer to dipping in a toe to test the temperature of the water.

*　*　*

Several weeks passed, but without clues he'd run out of places to search for her.

Sotto Voce was uncharacteristically silent on the matter. He buried himself in the physical task of helping clear away rubble and prepare the site for construction of a new Gospel of the Redeemer Church, a project that would take months if not years to complete. He'd hoped physical labor would distract him from thinking about Sophia, but the missing young woman had taken up permanent residency in his head.

He was in a dark mood when Pomeroy finally called. "Anderson, I need you in D.C. as soon as you can get here."

He wasn't in the habit of refusing the old man. "I'm staying here until I find someone."

"I know about the explosion. I understand your mother and niece are all right?"

He sagged against a light pole damaged in the explosion. "Yeah, they're fine."

"Any suspicion of foul play?"

"No. Investigators blame the explosion on a crack in an underground main. They suspect the gas followed a sewer line or traveled through the ground. They figure it took less than two hours for the gas to collect in the basement before it ignited, causing the explosion. Everyone managed to get out in time."

"Remarkable. Anderson, pieces of this puzzle are coming together. You and Dr. Sanders have earned the right to be in on what's about to happen, so I've sent a jet to pick you up. Dr. Sanders is already aboard."

Owens's affection for his old mentor ran deep, but he wasn't about to be pulled away from his search. "Like I said—can't leave. Need to find someone."

"Sophia Correia? I know she was with you in that Paxton church before it exploded."

His insides felt like they were curdling. He hadn't informed Pomeroy that he was hiding Sophia with his mother, but the old man always knew more than he let on.

"I was trying to protect her. Didn't do a very good job."

Dr. Pomeroy's voice was calm. "Anderson, I know where she is. Come to D.C. and all will be explained."

His head began spinning. How could Pomeroy know where Sophia was? "Where should we meet?"

"Go to the Hard Rock Café next to Ford's Theatre. Someone will call and arrange a pickup."

* * *

He and Sanders landed at Reagan National just before 10:00 p.m. Drizzle was hardening into rain, and the white buildings of the Capitol reflected on the wet pavement as they taxied toward their destination. At the Hard Rock, loudspeakers were shaking with Shakira's *Hips Don't Lie* while bureaucrats, reporters, and lobbyists stood shoulder to shoulder at the bar, blowing off steam. He nabbed a booth.

They'd just ordered drinks when the call came. "Yes?"

"Mr. Owens?"

"I've been expecting your call."

"Then you know what I want to hear."

"*Sotto Voce* #Z902R0R8O"

"I trust Dr. Sanders is with you?"

"He is."

"Grab a cab and head over to the George Washington Memorial Parkway. In ten minutes you'll be picked up in front of the Iwo Jima Memorial."

The connection ended. They made for the door just as their drinks arrived.

* * *

The giant bronze soldiers recreating a famous moment on Iwo Jima seemed to ignore the rain while raising the stars and stripes, an endless task that would engage them for as long as the Republic endured. Owens and Sanders were gazing up at the illuminated flag when a black sedan pulled up and a door opened.

They climbed inside.

The driver didn't turn around. "I'll be dropping you off. You're expected and will be ushered inside immediately."

They rode in silence.

The car stopped in front of a concrete barrier and the doors automatically opened.

"This can't be right," Owens said. "There must be a mistake. Are you sure this is the right place?"

The driver's answer was succinct. "Get out!"

They did as they were told and the sedan drove off, leaving them standing in the rain. It wasn't cold, but they shivered anyway.

Sanders shook his head. "Hanging with you is never dull. This is promising to be an interesting evening."

Looming in front of them was the White House.

* * *

After clearing security at the side gate, they were met by Ralph Cotton at the entrance to the West Wing, but it soon became clear that the West Wing was not their destination. Cotton led them in the direction of the Residence.

They walked briskly beneath the vaulted ceiling of the Center Hall, bypassing the kitchen on their left, entering an elevator that brought them to the second floor and another central hall.

"Where are all the guards?" Sanders asked.

"President Burbridge likes security to be as inconspicuous as possible in the Residence. But rest assured, if you spit security will be here before it hits the carpet."

They passed through the stair landing and turned right into a room filled with antiques.

"Please wait here." Cotton closed the door behind him.

"This is the Treaty Room. I've seen pictures of it," Owens said.

Sanders looked a bit pale. "Aren't you wondering why we're here?"

Before he could answer, Cotton returned. "Gentlemen, please follow me."

They turned to the right after leaving the Treaty Room and walked to a sitting hall. Cotton paused. "I was against allowing the two of you to participate in this meeting. Obviously, I was overruled. My primary job is to protect the President, and I'll use whatever means necessary to accomplish that task."

"How Haldeman and Ehrlichman of you," Owens shot back. "I trust you meant whatever *legal* means?"

Sanders placed an arm on his best friend's shoulder. "Mr. Owens isn't as intimidated by this setting as I am. Believe me, it isn't our intention to harm the President."

Cotton opened a door and they followed him into a sitting room adjacent to the Lincoln bedroom. Lights were off. The small room was dimly lit by a blazing fire. In a corner, a middle-aged woman sat straight-backed and expressionless, a stethoscope around her neck and an empty wheelchair at her side. Two large wingback chairs faced the fire and gave no indication of anyone occupying them, until Owens recognized a familiar voice.

"Ah, here at last. Come in, boys."

He gasped, "Dr. Pomeroy?"

"Yes. Come make yourselves comfortable."

"I'm surprised to see you here, Professor. I thought *Sotto Voce* worked outside official circles."

"Getting an invitation here wasn't all that difficult. President Burbridge and I have many friends in common, including Ralph Cotton, who I've known for years. Ralph's concern for his boss prompted him to bring Sophia Correia to my attention. But let's not be rude. I want you to meet someone."

Beside him sat another wizened old man with a narrow face, pinched nose and small jaw. Short as Pomeroy, he was bald, lacking eyebrows and eyelashes, and his crêpe-like skin was spotted with age.

"Permit me the introduction," Pomeroy said. "Anderson Owens and Preston Sanders, I'd like you to meet Miles Burbridge."

Sitting next to Pomeroy was the President's twelve-year-old son.

CHAPTER FORTY-THREE

Sunday: 11:40 p.m.

CDC PROGERIA BULLETIN #25

Current number of documented infections:

42,408

Owens and Sanders rose from their chairs when the President and her husband entered the room, a classified folder in the President's hand. She set it on an end table near a pitcher of water and glasses. Pomeroy remained seated.

"Mr. Owens and Dr. Sanders, Arthur and I welcome you to the White House. Please sit down. Professor Pomeroy you both know, and I trust you've already met Miles." She waved her hand toward the corner of the room. "Back there is Miles's physician, Dr. Pamela Simons. Pardon the cramped quarters, but this room is one of the easiest in the Mansion to keep heated."

Arthur Burbridge shook their hands and explained, "Miles is sensitive to bright light and cold. The White House's twenty-eight fireplaces are functional but provide inefficient heating; the building is mostly gas heated, which stirs up dust and makes it difficult for Miles to breathe. He spends most of his time upstairs on the third floor where his small room, installed with a dust-free heating system, is easy to keep warm."

The President walked over to Miles and crouched down. "Honey, how are you doing? Is it warm enough in here for you?"

Miles spoke slowly, his voice nearly a croak. "Yes, Mom. Thanks."

She placed a hand on his withered cheek and smiled at him, grey shadows of fatigue on her face. "Let me know if you get tired and I'll have Dr. Simons help you back upstairs."

Miles attempted a smile but only managed a grimace.

The President rearranged the thick blankets covering him. "Please, everyone sit down." After joining her husband on a settee adjacent to their son, the President leveled a harsh glance at her Chief of Staff. "Ralph, please let us have the room."

Red-faced, Cotton stood and left without a word.

When he'd gone, Pomeroy said, "He has your back more than you know, Madame President."

"We aren't here to discuss Mr. Cotton's loyalty. You are a man with influential friends, Dr. Pomeroy. How is it I haven't heard of you before today?"

"Much like the underappreciated earthworm, my work is mostly done in the dark." He smiled and tapped his white cane. "Speaking metaphorically, of course."

The President leveled a hard look at Owens. "I saw that photograph of you on TV, along with the rest of the world. I imagine it's causing you to be more cautious than normal. I'm looking forward to hearing why you were breaking into private property."

Before launching into an explanation, Owens turned his attention to Miles.

"Your funeral was...touching."

"Yeah, I guess most folks don't get to watch their own funeral the way I did, but at least people no longer try to steal pictures of me by pointing zoom lenses at the windows." His words were slow and spoken with difficulty.

"How long have you known Miles's funeral was a ruse?" the President asked Pomeroy.

"Not long. It occurred to me that the only way for someone like Lukker to have a Rasputin-like hold over a sitting president was to control the well-being of a loved one. I thought about those close to you and began ruling people out."

"But not everyone," the President piped in.

"No, not everyone." Pomeroy continued. "Miles, supposedly deceased, kept springing to mind. Quite an accomplishment hiding him in the most public house on earth. It must be difficult keeping Miles away from the White House Medical Staff."

Arthur Burbridge nodded. "It certainly is."

The President turned toward Owens. "Before we go any further, I have a question I'd like answered. Mr. Owens, CIA agents came to your workplace and informed you that they were searching for a young woman missing from a cruise ship, did they not?"

He shot a challenging glance at her. "They did."

"They had reason to believe you knew the whereabouts of this woman, yet you lied to them. You'd left her with Dr. Sanders. You later enlisted him to hide her aboard his ship. Intentionally thwarting a federal investigation is a criminal offense. What prompted the two of you to conceal the subject of a CIA search, a search that *I* authorized? Why shouldn't I have the two of you turned over to the Justice Department?"

Sweat dampened Owens's armpits. He didn't take well to threats, but he chose his words carefully. He'd been dressed down before, but this was the President of the United States. "You're assuming I told Dr. Sanders the CIA was looking for her," he said. "I doubt you'll be able to prove it."

"I don't think I need to. I'll simply ask. How about it, Dr. Sanders?"

Sanders was straightforward, as usual. "I knew."

Owens's exasperation flared. He was well aware of his best friend's penchant for honesty, but hoped, in this case, he'd make an exception.

"So, gentlemen, I'm waiting for an answer. Why did you set yourselves against the CIA?"

Instead of sharing his disdain for the CIA, Owens shot from the hip. "Has this girl been indicted or accused of a crime? I don't think so. Just because you're president doesn't mean you can arrest citizens without due process."

The President's brows knitted together. "Agent Fulton told me she'd resided in Portugal before working on cruise ships. Isn't she Portuguese?"

Owens smiled and shook his head. "She was born in Marion, Boston." For the moment, he kept the date of her birth to himself.

The President sighed. "Her being an American would have provided a stronger cover for bringing her home."

Owens continued. "I felt a special connection to this girl, and they lied to me about their reason for wanting her."

Sanders shot his best friend a look cautioning him to be careful, a look Owens ignored.

"I'm curious, President Burbridge. You couldn't have told the CIA you believed the girl could cure your son of a fatal disease because that would be an abuse of public resources. Besides, Miles was already supposed to be dead, so what lie did *you* give for instigating their search? Did you pull that old chestnut out of the fire—national security—to cover up the fact that you were using taxpayer money for personal reasons?"

The President's face knotted with anger, and the atmosphere in the room suddenly grew as tight as a drum.

Owens continued, his fists clenched. "With all due respect, Madame President, your administration was responsible for this young woman being hunted like an animal. She means a lot to me and you're the reason she's now been abducted."

"Let's all take a deep breath and calm down," Pomeroy said. After a few moments of listening to the crackling fire Pomeroy changed the subject. "When did Miles first show symptoms of progeria?"

"Our twins developed normally, but two years after Miles was born he started showing signs of premature aging," the First Gentleman explained.

The President picked up where her husband left off. "Few doctors knew how to treat progeria. No one wanted to help; door after door was slammed in our faces until we contacted Lukker Pharmaceuticals. Everett Lukker was extremely interested in Miles. He flew to Portland to meet with us. After so much rejection it was a relief to find someone willing to help."

"Did Lukker offer an explanation as to why he was willing to help Miles when all others refused?" Pomeroy asked.

"We didn't press him, which in hindsight I'm beginning to realize might have been a mistake," the President admitted. "We provided Lukker with Miles's blood and tissue samples for experimentation. With the medicines he provided, Miles's progeria went into remission. We thought our son had been cured."

"It must have come as a relief," Preston said.

"Yes. We enjoyed several years of normalcy as a family." The President's expression brightened for a moment but quickly faded. "I entered politics and ran for mayor of Portland, and later governor of Oregon. It wasn't until after I secured the nomination for president that Miles's symptoms returned—with a vengeance. Had I known Miles wasn't cured I would never have run in the first place."

"Why was Miles's death faked?" Dr. Pomeroy asked.

Arthur Burbridge spoke up. "Miles wasn't seen publicly after the inauguration and rumors were rampant. The paparazzi went into a frenzy. At first it was just the tabloids claiming there was something peculiar going on, but soon the administration was being pummeled with questions about Miles; the press corps wanted to know what we were hiding."

"I guess it was only a matter of time before the truth came out," Sanders said.

The First Gentleman altered his position on his chair. "Yes, Dr. Sanders, so Miles's funeral was arranged as a red herring," "Would it really have been so bad, the public learning of Miles's heroic struggle?" Owens piped in.

The President explained. "We had a family discussion about it, and we considered going public. Miles was interested in spearheading a campaign to draw public awareness to childhood diseases, but in the past few years something changed to alter our decision to let nature take its course."

Owens frowned and asked, "What changed?"

"We learned that it was unlikely Everett would ever cure Miles and had only managed to arrest the disease and spare Miles from further aging," she explained. "We were ecstatic until an unexpected side effect appeared." She paused, her voice thickening.

A weak smile from Miles seemed to give her strength.

"Progeria is a devastating illness, but not particularly painful, until recently. In the past year Miles has begun experiencing uncontrollable spasms that have transformed his life of limitations into one of chronic agony. Dr. Simons tried various types of pain management. Nothing worked."

"Is the pain getting worse?" Sanders asked Miles.

The boy nodded. "And now that I'm not aging anymore there's no telling how long I'll have to live with this—"

Miles stopped mid-sentence, air hissing from his lungs. His thin lips turned blue as he clenched the arms of his chair with all his might. Veins stood out in vivid relief on his neck and forehead as pain rattled his fragile body. The spasm passed quickly but left him struggling for breath.

Pamela Simons and the President were at his side instantly, a stethoscope pressed to the caved-in chest. "Son, let's have you go back upstairs. This is exhausting you."

He shook his head. "I'd rather stay...if it's okay."

The President gave her son an unconvincing smile. "Sure it is. We just want what's best for you."

When Miles's breathing returned to normal Dr. Pomeroy said. "I think I know why Miles has already been buried. Your parents have given you a tremendous gift, haven't they, Miles?"

This time the nod was barely perceptible.

"And I'm certain you're aware of the legal and political risks they've taken by giving it to you?"

Before Miles could respond, Sanders asked, "What are we talking about?"

Anderson beat Pomeroy to the punch. "Terri Schiavo."

"That woman in a vegetative state in Florida back in '05?"

It was Owens's turn to nod. "Remember the political and religious circus that situation set off?"

Sanders's bottom lip dropped as he turned to the Burbridges, now seeming more like ordinary parents than the nation's First Family. "You've given Miles the power to end his life, haven't you?"

"Yes," the President admitted. "Much as I love my son and can't imagine a world without him, his father and I have decided that Miles should decide when he has had enough."

"I'm sure I don't need to remind you that the law in most jurisdictions doesn't support euthanasia," Pomeroy said.

"True, but Oregon's Death with Dignity Act has been in effect since 1997, permitting assisted suicide. Miles may spend time here in the District of Columbia, but officially he is a resident of Oregon."

"Still, you would need two doctors to certify that the illness is terminal, and the patient has no more than six months to live." Although blind, Pomeroy appeared to be studying the President's face. "The outcry from the public would be brutal. Miles may be in pain, but he isn't in a vegetative state."

The President's face tightened. "To avoid controversy, we've rendered the issue moot by convincing the media that Miles has already died. What happened in the Schiavo case was a political circus and Congress would have been well advised to stay out of such a painful and complicated family matter. I'm willing to debate just about anything in a public forum, but this cuts too close to the bone."

Pomeroy cleared his throat and changed the subject. "Let's return to Everett Lukker, shall we?"

Arthur Burbridge fidgeted uneasily on his seat. "What about him?"

"For starters, he's a murderer."

The President scowled. "The Oval Office is a bubble, but I'm not as isolated as you might think, Professor. I'm aware of the unflattering things said about him, but you go too far. What proof do you have he's a murderer?"

"For starters, he killed one of his employees, Roger Vintiger, who happened to be a former student of mine. Roger was murdered trying to reveal information about Lukker's crimes." Pomeroy reached for the cell in his pocket. "You'll recognize my voice on this recording; the other is Roger's." He pressed a button. The anxious voice of Roger Vintiger became audible:

"I'm sending you an e-file I wasn't supposed to be aware of.
(Difficult to hear)

"Listen carefully—my time is limited. Our computers are monitored so it's only a matter of time until Lukker sends Trachmann to silence me. Be careful; the cover-up on this leads to the Oval Office."

"Where are you calling from?"

"I'm at work. Wait a minute...I hear approaching footsteps, probably Trachmann. No time to download. You'll need to send someone for it."

"Who's Trachmann?"

"The key is in the castle."

Pomeroy hit stop when the lengthy series of zzzaps and shrieks ended. "Vintiger was later found with his head blown off. Why would a man risking death indicate the cover-up on this leads to the Oval Office, Madame President?"

All eyes were riveted on the chief executive.

"It's true that I cut through red tape for Everett. Loyalty? Yes. But I also believed his company was best suited to develop a serum to fight Alzheimer's. But over the years," her composure faltered, "his willingness to help Miles seemed to become…"

"Conditional?" Owens asked.

"Yes. I was told that the pattern of cell deterioration between Alzheimer's disease and progeria was so similar that a serum capable of curing one would likely eradicate the other."

"Did you ask for documentation, evidence that Lukker was being straightforward with you, Madame President?"

She shook her head. "I shouldn't have accepted his word for it, but I convinced myself that I could protect millions from a terrible illness while promoting a cure for my son. But now I suspect Everett hasn't been honest with me. All these babies infected with progeria! How can this be? I agreed to this meeting because my Chief of Staff has assured me that Professor Pomeroy can shed light on Everett's true motives."

Pomeroy leaned forward in his chair. "Lukker wanted that lab in Costa Rica found and used Vintiger to divulge its location. He intentionally contaminated his own products and hid his actions by blaming Owens. Madame President, you should order an immediate investigation."

The President's mouth was a hard line. "Everett already requested one from the Costa Rican government, but our State Department has received word that Nicaraguan terrorists have crossed into Costa Rica and napalmed the facility. Nothing remains. I suppose you're about to tell me that Everett is responsible?"

Pomeroy side-stepped the question. "Anderson, tell the President what you discovered in Costa Rica."

Owens described the unused lab, poor security, and samples of infant inoculants contaminated with synthetic progeria.

Pomeroy continued. "Thanks to Roger, we now know Lukker wasn't interested in finding a cure for Alzheimer's *or* progeria. The goal was to corner the market on HGH drugs and turn a fountain of youth cocktail into a trillion-dollar industry."

"You know quite a bit, Dr. Pomeroy." the President remarked. "I have access to nine intelligence-gathering agencies, yet you know more than I do. What is the source of your information?"

Owens wondered if Pomeroy would share the existence of *Sotto Voce* but the old man ignored the question as he continued. "Lukker believed the answer to human longevity was linked to a disease that caused premature aging, but he needed a vast reservoir of blood and tissue samples for his experiments."

"My guess: much more than could be provided by Miles and a handful of other progeria victims," Owens blurted out.

"Lukker created the samples he needed, but he wasn't as close as he thought," Pomeroy explained. "He was forced to look elsewhere."

The President clenched her hands tight enough to turn her fingers white. "Vintiger must have discovered I'd quietly authorized the use of government resources, not only to fund Everett but to find a mysterious young woman who might provide a cure for progeria and lead Everett to another for Alzheimer's."

"She has a name," Owens added, "It's Sophia Correia Briggs."

Miles hadn't said anything in a while. Now he struggled to speak. "I've been dreaming about her. I knew she was real!"

Chapter Forty-Four

Monday: 12:05 a.m.

High winds buffeted the low rolling hills of Walker County, North Carolina, creating a galloping motion with power lines hugging a road separated from the freeway by a large field of mud and grass. Aside from distant freeway lights, the landscape was blanketed in darkness relieved every few minutes by bursts of lightning. This was dairy country and the cows were in their barns for the night, all but a stubborn black-and-white Holstein who, unnoticed, managed to step over a fence pulled down by a falling tree branch.

The cow chewed its cud and mooed plaintively at the loud claps of thunder as it ambled down the center of the wet road, passing the spot where, last year, seventeen-year-old Derek Wormdahl had steered his pickup into a power pole when his girlfriend steered her hand into the front of his pants. The damaged utility pole had managed to hold together for another year but gave way now, splitting and pulling the power lines down onto the road, where they sizzled and sparked on the wet asphalt for a few moments.

Waddling up to them, the cow paused to moo, sniff the electrically charged air and stare blankly at the downed power lines before placing a hoof on one. The Holstein froze mid-moo, tongue dangling from her mouth, her eyes bulging in their sockets as she dropped to the asphalt and pitched over on her side, smoke rising from her twitching wet hide.

* * *

The wet road needed repair: potholes filled with water were hard to spot and made for a bumpy ride. The nearby freeway would have been faster, but Saveno followed orders and avoided the freeway. Every few minutes he looked for Trachmann in the rearview mirror.

Saveno slowed down when his high beams fell on the downed utility pole and black-and-white mound blocking the road in front of them. He braked ten yards back, leaving his lights on but killing the engine. "Stay where you are," he ordered, jumping out of the car.

Saveno stared in the direction of the fallen wires and pole fragments before crouching down to study the motionless Holstein. But before he could shuffle back to the car the cow's tail twitched, shifted position, and glanced against one of his wet oxfords. In a matter of seconds, it was over: Sophia's hand flew to her face as her captor shook violently, his jaws locking, his eyeballs rupturing. The current lifted Saveno and threw him into a muddy ditch on the left side of the road.

She hopped out of the car and made her way to the edge of the road, looked down. Burns discolored Saveno's face, along with parts of his body where electricity had scorched away clothing. Smoke rose from the melted keys in his blackened right hand.

Sophia turned her head and vomited, although she hadn't eaten since that morning. Wiping her mouth with the back of a shaky hand, she spotted one of Saveno's oxfords lying on the road. She reached for it, changed her mind.

She remained standing in the road, rain slithering down the collar of her dress, but when Trachmann drove up she was no longer shivering.

Chapter Forty-Five

Monday: 12:06 a.m.

The President turned her head in the direction of Dr. Simons, who'd returned to her seat at the back of the room. "Pamela," she snapped, "we agreed we weren't going to tell Miles about this girl and let him get his hopes up."

"Forgive me, Madame President, but I did so in a moment of weakness on one of Miles's bad days. He was so desperate for hope that I gave in."

The President sighed and said, "It seems we've all been having lapses in judgment."

Owens considered his questionable decision to hide Sophia with his mother and niece and couldn't disagree. But he was curious and a question spilled out. "You say you learned about Sophia after Salazar's government fell, but the dictator died in 1970 and information concerning his regime is old news. U.S. Intelligence didn't just happen to uncover this information now. There's more here than you're letting on. My guess—you had the CIA searching through Portuguese documents _looking_ for her. What tipped you off?"

"You're very astute, Mr. Owens," said Pamela Simons from the back of the room. Her steps were absorbed by the thick rug as she left her corner to stand before the fire. Her face was flushed as she pushed her glasses snugly against the bridge of her nose. "I was the one who tipped off the President about a girl who seemed to possess the key to longevity."

Owens had more questions but remained silent as he scratched the stubble on his chin.

After a nervous pause, Dr. Simons cleared her throat and explained. "After leaving medical school, I was hired by Royal Atlantis Cruise

Line. As a ship physician, I worked various vessels for over ten years before leaving to start my private practice."

She hesitated, with all eyes on her. "Talk spreads quickly at sea and word had spread throughout the Line that there was a young woman working for Royal Atlantis thought by superstitious crewmembers to be a demon. When I was transferred to *Island Empress*, I learned this so-called 'demon girl' was a member of the crew."

"What did you do?" Sanders asked.

"Well, cruise ships carry thousands of passengers and crewmembers, and it took a few months for our paths to cross, and when they did I saw that this soft-spoken young lady, shunned as a pariah, didn't live up to her reputation."

"Why is that?" Owens asked.

"She didn't strike me as demonic, although as a trained physician I don't believe in demons. But she had a quality, a vulnerability and innocence that made me reach out to her. I arranged for her transfer to sick bay where for the next decade she assisted me with dispensing Dramamine and sunscreen."

"When did you notice she was different?" asked Sanders.

"It took a while, but eventually I began to realize that, despite passing years, she didn't appear to be aging. But that wasn't all that concerned me." Again, she hesitated.

Pomeroy transferred his cane to the other hand and reached out. She appeared reluctant to clasp his hand, but Pomeroy's sympathetic expression prompted her to grab and squeeze it, his gesture encouraging her to continue.

"Well, along with her arrested development, she had memory lapses. It took a while before I noticed but her memory would blank out after two or three years. She wouldn't forget everything, and I doubt anyone else noticed—she was good at hiding it—but every few years she would forget things."

Owens had risen from his chair and had begun pacing. He couldn't remain silent. "What sort of things?"

"She'd forget my name, along with the name of fellow crew members, even the name of our ship. Occasionally I'd have to...to..."

"Reboot her?" Owens suggested.

Pamela Simons managed a watery smile. "Yes. That's a good way of putting it, although I could never retrieve any childhood memories. However, she did occasionally mumble, and I shared my belief with the President that she was probably Portuguese. I was curious and took a sample of her blood for analysis. Something interesting turned up."

A hot knot tightened in Owens's gut. He took a deep breath to brace himself.

Dr. Simons paused to pour herself a glass of water from the pitcher. After a few sips she continued. "Sophia Correia's blood contained mutations in the gene called LMNA, commonly known as Lamin A, the structural scaffolding that holds cell nuclei together. Like Miles, she had the genetic mutation that codes for progeria."

Chapter Forty-Six

Monday: 12:10 a.m.

Trachmann pulled out his cell and dialed Saveno several times as he sped over the undulating hills, his car buffeted by high winds. His calls went unanswered.

Traveling at ninety miles an hour, he hit the brakes when a motionless car appeared in his headlights. A puzzled look cut into his hard features when he saw the girl standing in the road. He killed the engine, stepped out of the car and into the wind, and looked about for Saveno. He eyed the oxford lying on the wet asphalt. Close by, downed power lines and a dead cow blocked the road. In a nearby ditch he found Saveno.

Trachmann didn't waste time staring at the charred remains. Carefully, he approached Sophia. "Saveno was a moron, but he had his uses, even if he was too stupid to avoid being electrocuted."

She said nothing.

"You must be a moron as well. Too stupid to escape."

Again, she said nothing.

He grabbed her by the shoulders, shook her. "Did you hear what I said?"

Her lips moved slowly, her voice barely audible. "I didn't want to leave him."

"Saveno? He's dead."

Her eyes settled on the trunk of the car.

He reached for his gun.

She surprised Trachmann by positioning herself between him and the car. "I won't let you kill him," she said.

"Get in the car," he ordered.

She refused to move.

"Have you forgotten that he kidnapped you first? Do you even know who he is?"

"It doesn't matter."

"It matters to me," Trachmann said, brushing her aside.

In the distance, lights indicated a large vehicle heading their way.

"Fuck!" He aimed his gun at the trunk and squeezed the trigger. The gun jammed.

The voice behind him was soft but commanding. "You will not kill him."

He turned his head and scowled at her, then fired several more times, his gun useless.

Rage shook him. He pushed her into his car and carefully navigated around Saveno's vehicle and the dead cow. When they were a few miles away he asked, "Why didn't you cross the field and flag down someone on the freeway?" He repeated the question when she didn't respond.

She finally answered. "I didn't want to escape."

"Why not?"

"I was waiting for you."

CHAPTER FORTY-SEVEN

Monday: 1:30 a.m.

Conversation halted when Miles began shaking with another seizure. This time his mother ignored his protests and ordered Dr. Simons to wheel him back upstairs.

When they'd gone, Arthur Burbridge rose and headed over to a nearby thermostat. "For security purposes, these bulletproof windows don't open, but with Miles back upstairs we'll all be more comfortable if I turn up the air-conditioning to cool us down."

"A brave young man," Pomeroy said solemnly, mopping his brow with a handkerchief. "Does Lukker know Miles is still with us or was he duped along with everyone else?"

Arthur Burbridge answered, "He knows Miles is alive, but he'll keep the secret for the time being, if only to hold on to federal funding."

"Let's wrap this up," the President said when Pamela returned. "There isn't much left to tell. Arthur and I met Pamela after she returned to private practice. When Miles became ill, we hired her to care for him on a permanent basis."

Pamela took a deep breath. "I lived with the Burbridges in the Governor's Mansion in Salem. Accompanied them to Washington. When Miles's immunity system finally rejected Mr. Lukker's treatments, I remembered this 'special' young woman who also carried the code for progeria, which in her case appeared to be retarding aging instead of accelerating it."

"At first, Everett joined us in thinking this girl couldn't be real, much less useful," the President admitted.

"He's managed to become a believer," Owens shot back. "Two of his thugs tailed Sophia, Dr. Sanders, and me to Portugal where they tried to grab her. Fortunately, they failed."

"Everett said something about receiving disappointing news," the President added. "The secret he was looking for must not have been as close as he thought. Everett referred to this young woman...Sophia...as the 'missing variable.' But she isn't missing anymore."

Pomeroy's phone rang. "Yes, Franklin. I see. Keep me informed." He returned the cell to his pocket, a frown shadowing his face.

Ralph Cotton poked his head into the room. "A word Madame President?"

She still looked irritated with her Chief of Staff but didn't brush him off when he whispered something in her ear, something that appeared to disturb her. "Before this meeting, Special Agent Fulton located Sophia Correia. He had a hunch that you, Mr. Owens, might bring the girl to stay with your mother in Paxton. His hunch paid off. I ordered him to bring her here as soon as possible. They were expected to arrive any minute, but Ralph is informing me otherwise."

The tidal wave of relief that washed over Owens quickly retreated when Cotton announced, "Madame President, I've received word that Agent Fulton was just discovered beaten and locked in the trunk of a car. He's unconscious in intensive care in Durham."

"Is he expected to recover?" she asked.

"Yes. He has a concussion, but doctors are optimistic they can reduce brain swelling. Bones in his leg are broken but I'm told he'll pull through."

"And the g—" she glanced at Owens, "Sophia?"

"She wasn't with him."

The President leveled a gaze at Pomeroy. "I'll wager that call you just received filled you in on this disappointing turn of events."

"Yes," Pomeroy said grimly. "Lukker is obviously behind this."

"Then we'll just have to order him to turn her over," the President declared.

Pomeroy scoffed, "I doubt he'll admit to a charge of kidnapping. We can also assume that, if he has her, he isn't bringing her to his headquarters in Colton—surrounded by press and protesters since his press conference."

The silence that had settled over them broke when Pomeroy said,

"Anderson, I promised the President the whole story. This would be a good time for you to fill her in on what we've discovered about Sophia."

Mixed feelings about the President's role in this made Owens hesitate, but he complied. "Madame President, Sophia Correia is more unique than you know. Dr. Sanders and I have researched her past and discovered that her birthname is Sophia Briggs. She is not a citizen of Portugal; in fact, she was born in Massachusetts, on October 31, 1870."

The President was momentarily speechless.

"You have proof of this?" Arthur Burbridge asked.

"Yes." Due to the heat, Pomeroy had removed his overcoat but now he reached for it and removed an envelope, handing it to the President.

She took it, removing copies of the photographs Owens and Sanders had retrieved from *Convento de Santa Isabel*. She studied them carefully, managing a stiff smile at the comic image of a tongue-less mule that seemed to be talking to little Sophia. Before passing the images to the First Gentleman, she reached for the classified folder and produced another photograph which she added to the stack, saying, "The CIA dug this up. It was taken in 1968 at a church on the Portuguese coast."

Sophia could be seen praying.

Sanders added more photos of Sophia. "I snapped these a few weeks ago on our run to the Azores."

The President gathered up all the pictures and studied them chronologically. "Where did these older ones come from?"

Sanders chimed in, telling her about their trip to *Hospital Sagrado do Coração*. He added, "A letter written by a long-dead nun, someone who knew Sophia when both were children, led us to *Convento de Santa Isabel*, now a state-run *pousada*, where these photographs had been hidden in a wall."

The President listened attentively before turning her attention to the image of Sophia praying in '68. "Here she looks to be around sixteen or seventeen. In your pictures fifty plus years later, Dr. Sanders, she looks only slightly older. So, it's true—this individual is remarkably old—but how do you know she was born in 1870, and in Massachusetts?"

"We know, Madame President, because Sophia Briggs was involved in a famous mystery. She vanished at sea along with her parents and the crew of the *Mary Celeste* in 1872."

"The ship she sailed on sank?"

"No, the *Mary Celeste* survived the voyage."

The President's expression went blank. "Arthur, are you aware of this ship?"

A thin grin lined Burbridge's face. "Of course I am! Read about it as a boy: seaworthy ship found adrift on the high seas, no sign of crew or passengers, provisions all accounted for, cargo intact, log slate left on board—the perfect incident for spooky speculation. But I recall that no one aboard that voyage was ever heard from again."

"Until now," Owens said. "Sophia Briggs was the daughter of Benjamin Briggs, captain of the *Mary Celeste*, and two years old when she and everyone else aboard disappeared."

"If true, and it's a big 'if,' this individual hasn't stopped aging, but is doing so extremely slowly," Arthur Burbridge said.

"We believe that to be true, sir," Owens added.

"What proof do you have that this is *that* Sophia Briggs?" Burbridge asked.

Owens explained, "There's too much evidence to ignore. The locket Sophia wears has the Briggs's pictures inside and it's clearly visible in two of the photographs retrieved from *Convento de Santa Isabel.*"

He described the items in her satchel. "The doll was made and sold in New York at the time of the *Mary Celeste's* departure. Her satchel contained three garments that led us to Terceira where we learned a fisherman had pulled Sophia from the sea, his family adopting her only to ship her off to a convent near Lisbon years later when it became evident she wasn't aging normally. "

Against his better judgment Owens added, "In the spirit of full disclosure, there's something I need to get off my chest."

The President looked at him curiously. "Well?"

He cleared his throat and struggled to begin. "I was raised in a religious household, but I've developed into a skeptic. I host a radio show that pokes holes into ideas both sacred and profane, and I've witnessed the evil men can do, especially in the name of religion, but..."

"Go on."

"I can't believe I'm about to say this, but there's a possibility that a...a force is protecting Sophia."

"You wouldn't by any chance be referring to God, would you, Mr. Owens?" asked Arthur Burbridge, "because I'm aware of your program, have listened in several times and what you're suggesting is the last thing I'd expect from you. Care to explain?"

He hesitated, sensing the thin ice he was stepping onto. "I'm sure everyone here has heard about the church that blew up in Paxton."

The President and her husband nodded.

"Sophia Briggs was attending service at Gospel of the Redeemer Church when it exploded. I know this for certain because she was a guest at my mother's house. We took her to Sunday service."

"I understand that, aside from minor cuts and scrapes, no one was seriously injured," Burbridge said softly. "People are calling it 'the Paxton miracle.' "

"My point exactly, and usually I'd be leading the charge to debunk such a notion," Owens exclaimed. "Nearly two hundred and fifty worshippers, and a young woman shows up and convinces the congregation to leave minutes before va-voom—the church goes nova! And no serious injuries? There are those who believe God sent Sophia to save the folks in that church—my mother is one of them—and maybe even save all these kids infected with progeria."

"Are you one of them, Mr. Owens?" asked the President, her eyes cutting into him like a laser.

He'd been asking himself that very question for days. He still wasn't sure how to answer and chose his words carefully. "We have entered a great mystery, no doubt about it, but as far as miracles go, I remain in the *Doubting Thomas* category."

The President stood up. "Divine plan or not, I hope we find her soon. I've a gut feeling that, despite Everett's claims that his cure is near, Sophia Briggs, agent of the Almighty or science fiction heroine, might be the only hope these children have. And we can't determine what causes Ms. Briggs's progeria to work in reverse until scientists examine her.

"Mr. Owens, you and Dr. Sanders have a leg up on the *Mary Celeste* incident, and we need to learn if something happened to her on that voyage that altered her progeria, enabling her to resist aging."

The President might as well have asked them to juggle chainsaws. "You want us to do what no one has been able to do for a hundred and fifty-three years—solve the mystery of the *Mary Celeste*."

Burbridge answered for his wife. "Mr. Owens. I've heard you say on your program more than once that your Holy Trinity consisted of extraterrestrial events, supernatural occurrences, and conspiracy theories. I believe this is right up your alley."

Chapter Forty-Eight

Wednesday: 1:35 p.m.

Thirty-six hours later Sophia was still missing. Owens couldn't push worrying about her onto a back burner long enough to rack up more than a few hours of sleep.

President Burbridge had authorized the creation of a blue-ribbon think tank—*The Mary Celeste Committee*—to solve the mystery of the *Mary Celeste* and find possible explanations for Sophia's longevity, with the goal of acquiring knowledge to cure, or at least arrest, the symptoms of progeria now affecting thousands of children.

She put Professor Pomeroy in charge of coordinating everyone's efforts and asked Owens and Sanders to collaborate. The committee taxed itself to unravel the ship's secrets, focusing on fanciful possibilities that might have protected Sophia against the undesirable effects of the progeria gene. But the worm in the *Mary Celeste* apple remained elusive.

* * *

Sanders burst through the front door and caught Owens pacing in his cramped living room. "I've discovered a theory on the internet," he said, "a speculation that the crew of *Mary Celeste* fell victim to a seaquake, one that rattled the ship and loosened the stays on several barrels of alcohol, releasing fumes that disoriented all aboard."

They were debating the possibility when Peggy softly knocked on the door. She carried a platter of brownies. "Any word on Sophia?"

Owens shook his head.

She handed him the platter and left.

"I've heard that seaquake theory, yet the loss of a few barrels of grain alcohol was too little to be commented on by the cargo's new owners in Genoa when the barrels were finally delivered, and opening hatches or pumping out the bilge would have reduced the threat brought on by explosive fumes."

Sanders reached for one of the brownies.

Owens continued. "Besides, a quake would have left more signs of damage than were reported by the crew who found the *Mary Celeste* drifting on the high seas. And there was a vial of oil for a sewing machine found standing upright in the captain's quarters, making it unlikely the ship had encountered violent seas or seaquakes."

Sanders divided the brownie and popped half into his mouth. "Seaquakes aren't uncommon near the Azores. A large one was recorded in December of 1872 only weeks after the *Mary Celeste* was found abandoned. But I can't imagine why a captain in the middle of a seaquake, experiencing vibrations and churning seas, would abandon the safety of a large ship and order his family and crew into a small lifeboat." He finished the brownie. "I've been thinking..."

"About what?"

"Methane. I've encountered methane vents during my underwater explorations and can't help but wonder if a burst of methane venting from the sea floor might have interacted in some way with Sophia's system, perhaps *after* the family and crew were in the lifeboat. I've contacted colleagues to delve into the possibility that exposure to large amounts of methane might have affected her. They're exploring the possibility, although no one thinks such a thing probable."

They were grasping at straws. "I've been thinking about something, too," Owens said. "The captain's log was missing, but the hourly log slate was left behind in the first mate's quarters. Do you remember the last documented location of the ship?"

Sanders brushed crumbs from his shirt. "Yes. A curious entry was made at 5:00 on the morning of the crew's disappearance. According to these notes, Captain Briggs had sailed his ship to the northeast, steering a course that would take him between São Miguel and Santa Maria."

"Anything unusual about that?"

"Hmmm...now that you mention it—yes. He was guiding his ship close to the Dollabarat Shoal, avoiding a southeast course which would have set the ship on a safer and more direct path toward the Strait of Gibraltar and into the Mediterranean to reach Genoa."

"You're an experienced sailor; can you think of a reason he would have navigated his ship into dangerous water?"

Sanders scratched his chin. "No. Except..."

"What?"

"According to the Gibraltar inquest, the captain's bed was discovered wet and unmade. Remember Oliver Deveau?"

"Yeah, first mate aboard the *Dei Gratia*—the ship that discovered the abandoned *Mary Celeste*. He was first to set foot on the deserted ship."

"True," said Sanders. "He testified that the impression of a child's body was clearly visible on the bed in the captain's quarters."

"So what?"

"Life aboard ship in 1872 would have been difficult, even if you were the captain or a member of his family, in which case one would be expected to toe the line as much as the crew. Briggs's dad, a sea captain himself, was known to employ his sons and work them harder than the rest of the crew."

"So, it wouldn't be a Carnival Cruise to Jamaica."

"Hardly. The routine would have been rigorous, no sleeping in, bunks and beds made at dawn and breakfast served in the mess at sunrise. We know from the last entry made on the log slate that all was well at eight a.m., but no one was aboard at nine a.m. when the next entry would have been made. Yet the galley was clean, everything properly stowed away. Rain coming through the open hatch above the captain's quarters could explain why the bed was wet, but for it to be left unmade—unusual. Unless..."

"Go on."

"This is pure conjecture," Owens admitted, "but I can think of one reason why Captain Briggs might have sailed between the two islands instead of heading southeast, a reason other members of *The Mary Celeste Committee* overlooked. Try this on: the *Mary Celeste* had been experiencing rough weather approaching the Azores, nearly gale conditions, and the sea between the two islands would have been calmer."

Sanders was confused. "Captain Briggs was an experienced sea-man and quite capable of handling rough conditions."

"True, but calmer water may have been just what he needed right about then."

"I'm not following you."

Owens jumped up. "Don't you see? Captain Briggs was trying to slow down the erratic motion of his ship because it was disturbing someone, and my guess—he was trying to comfort a person who'd probably been up crying all night, the person whose impression was left on the unmade bed for that first mate to find, someone who must have been sick."

"You mean?"

"Sophia!"

Owens pulled open his laptop and opened the file he'd created on the *Mary Celeste*. It consisted of hundreds of pages, and it took a while for him to find what he was looking for. "Here it is, in a letter Captain Briggs sent to his mother on Sunday, November 3, 1872, two days before the ship sailed from New York Harbor. '...The work of preparing *Mary Celeste* for the voyage is tedious and very tiresome, yet my spirits soared on October 27 when I was joined by Sarah and Sophia, although Sophia soon came down with a bad cold and is now suffering miserably.' "

"Back at the bungalow before you two sailed to Midas Cay, Sophia was mumbling in her sleep. Said she felt hot. Maybe she was reliving events on *Mary Celeste*, events that occurred when she was two years old."

Sanders stretched and cracked his knuckles. "Since it's reasonable to assume many progeria victims have suffered common colds with-out being cured or living to extreme old age, it isn't likely this is the answer we're looking for."

Owens wasn't so sure. "What if her father was wrong? What if she wasn't sick with a cold, but had contracted something else?"

"I can't imagine what that something might be," Sanders admitted. "I don't recall any disease affecting the Eastern seaboard at that..." He stopped mid-sentence. "Wait a minute."

Owens leaned forward, seeing the cogs turn in his friend's mind.

"A massive epidemic affecting most of the Eastern seaboard claimed nearly four million lives in November of 1872."

"I don't remember reading about the deaths of four million people," Owens said.

"Who said anything about people?"

Chapter Forty-Nine

———

Wednesday: 1:40 p.m.

Paint would have gone a long way toward softening the room's appearance, the bare concrete walls, floor, and ceiling evoking the feel of a bunker. Tungsten bulbs in the overhead gantry provided the windowless space with hard white light, illuminating the unconscious woman in the hospital bed in the center of the room.

Straps held her slender arms in place while an IV drip delivered fluids. A bank of machines surrounded her, monitoring her vital statistics: heart and blood pressure, oxygen and carbon dioxide levels in her blood, and many other readings, each adding to the chorus of clicks and beeps providing the only indication that she was alive.

Lukker and Trachmann approached the bed. "You're gambling a great deal on this girl," Trachmann said. "She hardly looks like a fountain of youth. Are you sure you know what you're doing?"

Lukker scowled. "Just be handy when I require muscle. You aren't paid to question me, but since you ask, I know far more than Salk did when he set out to discover a cure for polio. And speaking of muscle, how well defended is this facility?"

"It would take a small army to breach the security I've put in place. I've recruited two dozen battle-hardened mercenaries and equipped them with M16 A4s and M203s, along with shoulder-held missile launchers in the unlikely event of a chopper invasion."

When Lukker turned his attention back to the girl, he saw that her eyes were open. He looked down his sharp nose at her. "So, you're the goose who will lay my golden eggs."

She mumbled something.

"Speak up. What did you say?"

"I said I don't know of any geese that lay golden eggs."

"A common children's fable. You aren't very informed, are you?"

She tried to sit up, but the restraints held her down. "Who are you?"

"My name is Everett Lukker, CEO of Lukker Pharmaceuticals."

"Why was I brought here?" she asked.

"To save mankind."

She struggled to look directly at him. "You're too late; someone has already been sent to save mankind."

"So, you take your faith as a Christian seriously."

"I do. You intend to keep me captive here?"

"Yes. You, like everyone in this facility, serve me. Your body contains the secret I need to bring my work to fruition."

She glanced at him without a hint of fear in her eyes. "I am not your servant."

"If it makes you feel better, consider yourself my guest. You'll be here for the foreseeable future."

"Like the monkeys in those cages I saw when they brought me in here. They looked like they were being tortured."

"Those monkeys are here to serve the cause of science. But don't worry. You're more precious to me than they are; any pain you experience will be minimal."

"But the pain I'm feeling *isn't* minimal."

Lukker frowned. "I see from the monitors that your heartbeat is regular and you aren't exhibiting any signs of stress. I see no indication that you're experiencing pain."

"Maybe your machines don't show it, but I'm feeling pain. I share the pain of those poor animals."

"Trachmann suggested there was something odd about you. I see now that he was right."

She ignored the insult. "If you're afraid I'll run away, I doubt that's possible. Besides, I could have run away but didn't. I'm here because I choose to be. Please remove these straps."

Trachmann smiled, bent down and adjusted a strap, tightening it. The rhythmic beat of the blood pressure monitor altered to register her discomfort, again when he tightened the other strap.

Instead of crying out she responded, "I know a secret."

"Really?" Lukker grinned. "What secret?"

She hesitated but continued when Lukker turned to leave. "You are afraid of God."

A brittle laugh. "You couldn't be more wrong. I'm not interested in spiritual hokum. I'm focused on diminishing time's dominance over man."

"Why?"

"So everyone can live as long as you. Don't you think it selfish that you're able to live so long while the rest of us are reduced to only a handful of years?"

"In truth, I don't know what to think. If I'm as old as my friends think, it is by God's choice, not mine. I bow to His will, as should you. It isn't too late for you to seek His forgiveness."

Lukker laughed. "Is that what you think I need, forgiveness?"

"We all need God's forgiveness."

"Rest assured, people will forgive me when I start delivering the miracle of extreme longevity." He turned and walked away with Trachmann in tow, leaving her to the company of the machines.

When they were a dozen yards from her room Trachmann said, "A BOLO has been issued on her and we can't be sure someone in our operation won't betray us and alert U.S. authorities that she's here. We're compromised by her presence. In fact, a reporter named Jackie Donovan has already learned our location. She's arrived asking for an interview. Says she wants to discuss a secret file she's acquired outlining a project to infect children with tainted vaccines."

"How did she find out where we are?"

"We've intercepted a cell call between her and one of your bodyguards."

"You assured me this facility was secure. Drop the ball again and there will be serious consequences."

A widening red patch appeared on Trachmann's neck. "I'll see to it that the informant is silenced and made an example of."

"I'm not ready for the public to learn what we're working on, but I'm curious to find out what this reporter knows."

"What about the girl? When will you be finished with her?"

"Soon. I've ordered every conceivable test to be run on her, and as quickly as possible. When our computers are filled with this data her usefulness will be over, and I'll turn her and the reporter over to you for disposal."

Chapter Fifty

Wednesday: 1:50 p.m.

Owens was confused. "If not people, who...or what?"

"They call it the Great Epizootic," Sanders explained. "An epizootic is a disease prevalent in one kind of animal, and in this case, we now suspect that an unknown equine virus had been imported from Canada."

"Like avian flu, but affecting horses?"

"Yes. About four million animals died in the Great Epizootic of 1872, nearly a quarter of the nation's horses. Doctors were powerless against a deadly virus which, strangely enough, seemed to strike hardest at horses stabled in urban areas."

"Now that you mention it, this does sound familiar. I think I once saw an exhibit about this in Boston. Didn't this epidemic play a part in the great Boston fire of 1872?"

"Yes. In early November a fire broke out in the downtown section and there weren't enough horses available to move firefighting equipment to the scene, most being dead or incapacitated by the disease. The fire raged for days."

"And this epidemic spread to New York?"

"You've got it backwards. It reached New York several months *before* the Boston fire, as early as September of 1872. Several hundred horses a day were dying in New York City; transportation and deliveries were at a standstill."

Owens grabbed his laptop and again scrolled through his *Mary Celeste* file. "The *Mary Celeste* would have been tied up at a pier in New York Harbor at the time." He stopped scrolling when he found what he was looking for, the downloaded pictures they'd retrieved from *Convento de Santa Isabel.* "Would this equine flu have affected mules?" He handed over the laptop.

Sanders thought about it for a few moments and then smiled. "Yes. Of course it would." He studied the dry plate showing Sophia at the age of two, standing in front of a famous Central Park landmark that opened in 1871—a carousel pulled by a blind mule.

Owens remembered the discussion they'd had about the anomaly: the mule had no tongue in the dry plate because the tongue was moving too quickly to register. "The mule appears to be laughing, but in reality, it's merely been caught in the act of licking the child in the picture—Sophia."

"Possibly infecting her with a virus known to be deadly to horses and mules." Sanders said.

Owens's throat went dry. "Could this virus alter progeria, mutate the disease into a fountain of youth?"

"Sounds fantastic, but I've heard you say it many times on your show; *anything is possible*. And as improbable as this seems, it's the only lead we have. But..."

"But what?"

"The cause of the Great Epizootic is still being debated, and the infected animals are long gone. I don't see how this helps us."

"Aren't there current strains of equine viruses continuing to affect horses around the globe?" he asked.

"Yes. Today most horses are given a vaccine for West Nile and several other viruses, but I don't think that mule could have been infected with WNV."

"Why not?"

"Several reasons. First, WNV also affects birds, and I don't recall hearing about a massive bird die-off. Also, WNV only appeared in North America in the 1990s, and the virus is passed by mosquitoes— not passed from horse to horse. During the Great Epizootic, horses were known to infect one another."

"Still, the West Nile Virus might be close enough to the outbreak in 1872 to affect progeria," Owens said, a spark of hope fanning through him. "Wasn't smallpox cured with a similar disease?"

Sanders's left eyebrow cocked. "Yes, people were immunized for smallpox by being intentionally infected with cowpox, a less virulent disease. We may be on to something."

Owens reached for his cell to share their thoughts with Pomeroy, who listened without interruption before saying, "We can't assume current strains are the same as those rampant on the East Coast in 1872. The differences in viruses, even those affecting similar animals, can be remarkable. Still, with over fifty thousand children now infected we have little choice but to explore every possibility, no matter how farfetched."

*   *   *

Pomeroy shared this information with the committee, and tissue samples from progeria victims were injected with West Nile Virus and a host of other equine diseases, including Eastern, Western, and Venezuelan Equine Encephalomyelitis. It only took a few days for the bad news to arrive. Progeria tissue samples remained unaffected when injected with WNV or similar viruses.

"Without examining blood or DNA samples from an actual victim, there's no way to examine, or even narrow down, the exact strain of virus responsible for the Great Epizootic," Sanders explained.

After receiving the disappointing news, Owens turned to Sanders, smacking his forehead with an open palm. "I just remembered where I saw an exhibit on the Great Epizootic. It's time to make tracks."

"Where are we headed?" Sanders said.

"To find the samples we need."

"How do you expect to find blood or DNA samples from horses dead for more than a hundred and fifty years?"

Owens grinned. "I have an idea."

CHAPTER FIFTY-ONE

Wednesday: 5:50 p.m.

CDC PROGERIA BULLETIN #34

Current number of documented infections:

50,006

The Boston Firefighters Museum closed in ten minutes, leaving little time for them to admire the granite, brick, and red tile facade. Owens had wandered through the building several years earlier during a break from a media conference. He and Sanders made their way to the back of the museum where he found what he was looking for.

A museum docent noticed their interest and filled them in. "Old Scipio here was too beloved by the residents of Boston to end up in glue bottles or the local landfill. He now resides in this massive display case, a reminder of the gentle animal that once pulled water pumps to fires and nibbled carrots and sugar cubes from generations of children."

Among the first of Boston's horses to succumb to the Great Epizootic of 1872, Old Scipio was displayed near an enlarged photograph taken in 1870. The horse was pictured harnessed to a steam pump and surrounded by adoring children—several blurred from an inability to stand still.

Sanders looked dubious. "A stuffed horse?"

"Why not? Scientists are extracting DNA from blood and tissue samples from Egyptian mummies, and mummies are a lot older than Old Scipio here."

Sanders shook his head. "Nineteenth-century taxidermy didn't preserve much of the original animal. Back then, bones were cleaned in arsenic and acids and used to build a framework stuffed with straw and sawdust. Hides were then attached after being stripped and cured, with little done to prevent the growth of corpse-eating microbes and bugs."

Owens refused to be discouraged. "Still, it's possible."

"I suppose so."

"Good. Now we need to convince the curator of this museum to let us take his prize exhibit."

Owens snapped open his cell and dialed a private number. After several more transfers he was connected to the Secretary of Homeland Security. Before long, he and Sanders had removed Old Scipio from the display case and were wrestling him into the back of a rented truck, the task made more difficult by the overwhelming stench.

When finished, Sanders asked, "Where are we headed?"

"Hanscom Air Force Base," Owens shot back. "Pomeroy has arranged a military cargo plane to transport us to CDC in Atlanta, where forensic experts will try to extract DNA samples from Old Scipio. Finding blood, even degraded blood, will be unlikely, but some viruses have been known to mix with old DNA."

It was a long shot. Old Scipio had loved children, but could he save them?

Chapter Fifty-Two

Thursday: 11:05 a.m.

CDC Progeria Bulletin #41

Current number of documented infections:

61,339

Forty-eight hours later Owens received a call from Ralph Cotton, summoning him back to Washington.

"Has Sophia been found?" he asked.

"No."

"So, what's this about?"

"A plane will be waiting for you at Sarasota Bradenton International at 7 p.m. Come alone and please don't be late." Cotton hung up before Owens could ask more questions.

That evening he was once again escorted to the Residence. "Why does the President want to see me?" he inquired.

"She doesn't."

A crease appeared on Owens's forehead.

"Miles has asked for you," Cotton said.

"I'm surprised. What does he want?"

"He won't say."

"How's he holding up?"

"Not well," Cotton answered. "Dr. Simons doesn't think he has much time left."

"Are his seizures getting worse?"

Cotton nodded.

The President, her husband, and Dr. Simons were huddled outside Miles's door. They acknowledged Owens without saying anything. He noticed the dark circles around the President's red-rimmed eyes. When she and her husband followed him into the dimly lit room Miles greeted them with a slight tilt of his head, his thin nostrils fluttering like moth wings. His jaw moved slowly, and it took several moments for audible words to emerge. "Mom, Dad; would you both wait outside? I'd like to talk with Mr. Owens, alone."

The President's mouth opened, but no words came out. She blew him a kiss and exited the room, followed by her husband, who closed the door behind them.

*   *   *

The room was stiflingly hot yet Miles was swaddled in blankets, his face, head, and hands nearly translucent. His skull appeared ready to burst through the parchment-thin skin.

"Hello, Miles." Owens reached for his hand but stopped short of squeezing it for fear he'd tear the skin. "Good to see you again."

"Thanks for coming."

"The call that you wanted to see me came as a surprise. I'd think you'd want to spend as much time as possible with your family."

"Family and Dr. Simons are all I ever get to see." Miles again struggled to find his voice, several rasps and wheezes passing his lips before words emerged. "Dad says you're the go-to guy for things that can't be explained, so I asked you to come."

Owens was curious, but Miles appeared so unwell that he hesitated to continue. "Are you sure this isn't tiring? Are you experiencing much pain?"

To his amazement, Miles smiled, his withered lips stretching farther than Owens would have thought possible. "I don't feel pain anymore, probably a bad sign, and the reason Mom is outside that door crying. I'm falling apart, except for my ears which are working better than ever. She doesn't know I can hear her." Tears gleamed in the corner of his eyes. He went to brush them away, but the effort proved too much and his hands fell back to his side.

Miles's eyes darted in the direction of the laptop on the nightstand beside the bed. "A few nights ago, I couldn't sleep and Dad kept me company. Dad likes card tricks and showed me a few to pass the time—he isn't very good—and when we got bored we decided to check out the website for the Anderson Owens Show. I learned that you're a big fan of Harry Houdini."

Owens brushed sweat from his brow with a sleeve. "That's right."

"I Googled Houdini. After he became rich and famous as a magician and escape artist, he devoted his life to exposing spiritualists as quacks, while at the same time trying repeatedly to contact his own dead mom."

He nodded. "You must have found out that Houdini, by his own admission, never managed to contact the dead. When he died, his wife held séances for ten years on the anniversary of his death. Houdini was a perpetual no-show."

"So I read. But after Houdini died, why do you suppose he *didn't* contact his wife? Or mother? Do you think it was because there's no such thing as an afterlife?"

If the kid was expecting a guarantee that heaven existed and a roadmap to the pearly gates, he was talking to the wrong guy. "I just can't say."

Miles looked less than pleased with Owens's answer. "Dad and I listened to a few of your podcasts." He tried to imitate the intro: "Welcome to the Anderson Owens Show, where we discuss anything and everything, but our Holy Trinity consists of extraterrestrial events, supernatural occurrences, and conspiracy theories."

Owens grinned. "Maybe you should have your own show."

"We both know that will never happen," Miles said soberly. "But the reason you're here—I want to know more about that pretty lady being discussed."

"Sophia?"

"Yes. I keep having dreams about her. I want you to tell me everything you know about her."

"It's a long story."

"I'm not going anywhere."

"Okay, I'll tell you everything I know." Owens undid the top button of his shirt. "Last week during our meeting with Professor Pomeroy, before a seizure sent you upstairs, you heard quite a bit. But there's more."

"Professor Pomeroy—the old blind guy who looks like the dude on the KFC carton?"

"Yes. Anyway, after you left, the discussion continued."

Owens filled him in on the woeful tale of the *Mary Celeste*, how evidence suggested Sophia had been on board, only to vanish for decades before reappearing a month ago. Miles listened attentively.

When Owens finished, Miles took several deep breaths and said, "Two nights ago, Sophia came to see me. I was dozing off when the door swung open and she walked into this room. I recognized her from the photos everyone had been gawking at that night, except Professor Pomeroy of course. I thought I was dreaming."

Owens rubbed the stubble on his damp cheek. He didn't want to burst the kid's balloon, but he'd always pursued truth with the determination of a terrier latched onto a pant cuff, and the truth here was not difficult to understand; Miles had experienced a dream. He wasn't prepared to lie, even if the boy was dying.

"Miles, it isn't possible. You probably *were* dreaming, or hallucinating. We don't know where she is, and it would be impossible for her to break into the White House without anyone else seeing her. Why are you so sure it was Sophia?"

"It was her," the boy said with certainty.

"No one else saw her, right?"

"Just me."

"You're a smart kid. Did you ask anyone to check surveillance tapes?"

"My dad had the cameras checked."

"You told him you saw Sophia?"

"Heck no. He's worrying about me enough as it is. Didn't want him to think that, in addition to everything else wrong with me, I'd come down with a case of the crazies. I just told him I saw someone I'd never seen before sitting beside my bed. It was his idea to have the tapes checked."

Owens smiled. "Well, there you have it. You see; it isn't possible. No one could get in here without permission. Listen, don't feel embarrassed; it's totally understandable. Sometimes meds make people see and feel strange things, vision blurs and words get mixed up."

Miles didn't look embarrassed. "I stopped taking meds weeks ago.

Besides, when she appeared, I saw her more clearly than anyone I've ever laid eyes on, like it was possible to count every strand of hair on her head."

"Miles, if you invited me here to ask if I believe it possible for someone to materialize in this room, I'd have to say 'no.'"

"Because such a belief would be...irrational?"

"Yes."

Miles pressed on. "But you just told me that you believe she was two years old when she vanished while traveling on a ship in—what year did you say it was?"

"1872."

"Heck, I can do the math. That would make her at least a hundred and fifty years old. Doesn't sound reasonable to me. How do you explain this?"

"I can't," Owens admitted.

"Then here's something else for you to chew on, something that falls under the category of 'supernatural occurrences.' You asked if I was sure it was her? Check this out." With great effort, Miles pulled back the thick blanket wrapped around him. Something was tightly pressed against his withered body. Owens recognized it immediately.

"You asked how I knew it was Sophia? Here's how I knew." Cradled beside Miles was a child's doll with papier-mâché face. Most of the painted face was missing, and a hint of black paint was all that remained of the hair. Owens reached for the doll and lifted the tattered dress to observe what was written on the calfskin body—Sophia.

Owens struggled to contain his surprise. "The last time I saw this doll it was in a satchel back at my trailer."

"Well, as you can see, it's here now. Sophia sat right where you're sitting, pulled the doll from under her sweatshirt and handed it to me. She said it had seen her through a lot of hard times, figured it would help me."

Owens didn't know if he was humoring Miles or himself. He took a deep steadying breath. "What did you say to her?"

"I reminded her that I was a guy, didn't much take to dolls. She laughed and said it would be our little secret."

"What else did she say?"

"At first, she didn't say much, but when I asked why she'd come, she said to comfort me. Claimed she got the idea from *you*."

"From me?" His head was spinning. Years as radio's "guru of the unusual" hadn't prepared him for this.

"It pains her that you're worried about her. She came to offer me comfort, and to ask me to let you know she's okay. She said time was running out and she'd be going home soon."

"Did she say anything else, like where she was being held captive?"

"No."

The boy's next question was one he'd been asking himself for as long as he could remember. "Mr. Owens, do you believe in God?"

He took a deep breath, his heart pounding while he assessed the situation. He was in the White House talking with the dying son of the President, discussing the improbable appearance of a woman over a hundred and fifty years old and apparently able to breach the most extensive security on the planet. Now he was being asked if he believed in God.

"Miles, you should ask a theologian, a priest or minister, someone like my mother. She's a firm believer, lives by her faith. She swears God is present in our daily lives, watching over us, guiding us toward salvation."

The kid wouldn't let him off the hook. "I can imagine what they'd say, but I'm not asking them; I'm asking *you*."

He deserved an answer and Owens desperately wanted to provide one. But what to say? The President had asked a similar question, and he'd referred to himself as a professional "Doubting Thomas." *Has my opinion changed?* he wondered. *Am I ready to believe in something greater than myself?*

The boy's eyes were on him. Owens cleared his throat and answered as best he could. "God enters many equations as a default factor."

"A default factor?"

"Yes. When all rational explanations fall short, many people find an answer by turning to God. Is that what you're doing, Miles, turning to God?"

"I'm trying to. Is there any other way to explain the existence of a hundred-and-fifty-year-old lady capable of avoiding White House security, or for the appearance of this doll?"

"Not that I'm aware of."

"There's so much suffering in the world, so much evil. I need to believe these serve a purpose, even though I don't know what it is."

They chatted until Owens sensed him tiring. "I wish I could be more helpful."

The shadow of a smile flickered over Miles's face. "You've been more helpful than you know. God may only win by default, but He does *win*. Thanks for coming. I knew you'd be honest with me." One hand continued to clutch the doll, but the other lifted toward Owens.

This time he carefully shook it.

The door opened and light spilled into the dim room. The lanky figure of Arthur Burbridge was silhouetted in the door frame. "How are you guys getting along?" he asked like a dad monitoring a slumber party.

"Fine, Dad, but it's time for me to rest." Miles tilted his head toward his guest. "It's been great talking with you. Goodbye, Mr. Owens."

———

CHAPTER FIFTY-THREE

Thursday: 10:25 p.m.

Owens returned home. After paying for the cab and dashing into his Airstream, he flicked on the lights, dropped his duffel bag, and hustled to the bedroom where Sophia's satchel was stashed under his bed. He reached for it and dumped the contents onto his mattress. The doll was missing, or so he thought until finding it concealed within one of two remaining smocks. *My imagination, or is the barely visible smile mocking me?*

As usual, he hunted for a rational explanation: someone borrowed the doll after he left for D.C., flew it to the White House and, before he arrived, slipped it into Miles's bed when the kid was asleep. But how did the doll find its way back to the satchel under his bed? Not many knew Miles was alive, and those who did had no reason to pull such a stunt.

Still, he pulled out his laptop and punched the keyboard, accessing the three concealed cameras placed around his trailer. He downloaded the digital stream of surveillance for the entire time he was gone. Yesterday at 2:34 p.m., Peggy appeared at his door, another plate of goodies in hand, but she left when no one answered her knock.

That was all. No break in. No doll-stealing.

When his head started pounding, he returned the doll and other items to the satchel and stowed it back under his bed.

* * *

Another day without state or federal agencies discovering Sophia's whereabouts. He couldn't remember being in such a funk, couldn't focus on his program and had Vicki airing reruns and scrambling for guest hosts while he and Sanders struggled to solve the mystery of the

Mary Celeste.

Frustration gnawed at him. He felt responsible for Sophia's disappearance, chastised himself for bringing her to Paxton even though she had saved many lives by emptying the church before it exploded.

*   *   *

Sanders left for Norfolk to retrieve *Isabella* from the Navy, and Owens returned to Paxton to help rebuild Gospel of the Redeemer Church. He was manning a bulldozer and dumping rock and concrete onto an old flatbed truck when he noticed the motorcade heading up Main Street in his direction. A few minutes later the limos stopped in front of a group of volunteers that included his mother. A door opened and Arthur Burbridge, accompanied by sons Eric and Aaron, stepped into the afternoon heat. They were swarmed by volunteers and greeted by Reverend Jasperson. Hands were shaken for photographers.

Burbridge made a speech about volunteerism being the backbone of American communities, praising those who'd come together in this time of need. "The President wishes she could be here to offer support, but urgent business has called her away." After concluding his remarks, he headed Owens's way while the twins pitched in, loading debris into waiting trucks.

Mama had been passing out bottled water, but stopped to watch her son chat with the President's husband.

A photo frenzy occurred when the athletic twins removed their shirts to cool off. While the photographers were distracted with the twins, Arthur Burbridge delivered the sad news. "Miles died a few hours after your visit. He was telling me how much he'd enjoyed talking with you when his eyes closed and he slipped away." Burbridge's voice thickened. "My son's life was extremely difficult, but whatever you said gave him a measure of peace. His mother and I thank you."

Owens's eyes stung. Fortunately, the day was hot and onlooking photographers only saw him swiping the sheen of sweat from his face. "Miles was quite an inspiration. How's the President holding up?"

"She's doing her best to hide her grief. You might have heard that earlier this week we flew home to Oregon. Miles died just shy of his thirteenth birthday and it was easy to let folks believe our family was gathering back home at his gravesite to celebrate his life, which was true, even though we were also burying him for the second time."

Owens could only imagine how they'd moved the body without raising suspicion.

The First Gentleman's voice quivered. "We interred our son at the edge of our vineyard, near the site selected for the presidential library, where most people believe he was buried a month ago. The area was sealed off in the middle of the night to keep out prying eyes."

Following a pause he continued. "Afterward, I tried to convince the President to stay a few days so she could have privacy to fall apart, but she was determined to keep busy and flew back to Washington."

He changed the subject. "I assume you and Dr. Sanders haven't solved the mystery of the *Mary Celeste* or come up with a theory to explain why Sophia is aging so slowly."

"We've digested everything written on the subject, but still don't have any answers."

Burbridge squinted at the hot sun before saying, "The President and I have long been at odds over allowing Lukker into our lives, even for Miles's sake. I never trusted the man, not even when his medicines seemed to help our son. I've long suspected that Lukker had an agenda beyond helping Miles, and it's my belief he has infected over fifty thousand children with progeria intentionally.

"Miles is gone now, but we must prevent others from sharing his fate. Something else; if the President's enemies find out about this, her close association with Lukker would undoubtedly compromise her proposed healthcare reforms, and possibly her ability to govern."

Owens had remained silent but finally spoke up. "I'm sorry sir, but politics leaves a bad taste in my mouth, but I do care about thousands of children facing a death sentence."

"You're right, of course, and the President would be the first to agree with you. She's crushed by the realization that her support for Lukker might have put him in a position to do such harm. She's questioning her judgment and may rule out a bid for a second term."

Owens had definite thoughts on the matter but kept them to himself.

"I think it would be a mistake if she chose not to run again. True, she made a deal with the devil to save our child—most mothers would—but otherwise she's been a good president and, given a second term, could end up being a great one."

"Why are you here, sir?" he asked. "Has the search for Sophia turned up something?"

Burbridge cleared his throat. "I'm here to do what most husbands would in a similar situation."

Owens attempted a grin. "There aren't other men in your situation."

"True. But most husbands would help their wives, if they could."

"You have an idea where Sophia is?"

"I believe Lukker's hiding her in the Bahamas. At a fundraiser a few days ago I bumped into a college chum who's done very well for himself as a broker for the used seaplanes he buys and refurbishes. His clients are well-heeled CEOs and venture capitalists in need of small carriers capable of flying to locations too small for landing strips. Seaplanes are in big demand lately but currently out of production. Potential buyers must wait months if not years for quality restorations."

Owens was all ears.

"My friend was recently contacted by a representative for someone in a hurry to acquire a plane. This 'someone' was willing to pay handsomely." Burbridge reached into his pocket and handed over a copy of the check.

Owens read the amount and let out a whistle. "I don't recognize the name of the company."

"Neither did I. The company is an investment group located in the Grand Caymans, and the check is drawn on a local bank there. I've been informed that the company is a subsidiary of Lukker Pharmaceuticals."

Owens rubbed the back of his neck. He'd allowed his hope to rise and now felt deflated. "With a seaplane there are thousands of destinations within Lukker's reach. Is it possible he took Sophia to the Grand Caymans?"

Burbridge shook his head. "Before the plane was delivered, it was tagged with a tracking device."

"Where did it go?"

Arthur Burbridge answered, "To the land of myth and legend."

Chapter Fifty-Four

Saturday: 1:15 p.m.

When Owens made the call, Sanders had retrieved *Isabella* and was sailing past Palm Beach at 20 knots.

"Arthur Burbridge has provided a clue as to where Lukker might have taken Sophia," he said excitedly.

"Where?" Sanders asked.

"The land of myth and legend."

The radio signal was compromised by static and crackling.

"I'm not sure I heard correctly. Please repeat."

"Be careful," Owens advised. "I'm sure you already know there's a hurricane headed your way. The National Hurricane Center has clocked sustained winds at 98 mph. They're calling this one Hurricane *Marlene*."

"I'm already feeling her punch."

"Pomeroy believes Sophia is in the Bahamas, in the Bimini chain to be exact. The government of the Bahamas expects *Marlene* to get worse and is anticipating serious damage. *Marlene* is moving at 20 mph, but if she stays on course she'll come ashore within 24 hours. I'm monitoring your position and see that you'll reach Fort Lauderdale in two or three hours. I'll meet you there. Preston...Preston? Are you still there?"

A few moments of static passed before: "Yes, I'm still here. By the way, one of these days I'm going to put *Isabella* in dry dock and take her apart to find that blasted telemetry chip you planted."

"Sounds like fun. I'll help."

The line went dead.

* * *

Serious wind was kicking up in Fort Lauderdale when Sanders arrived.

"Let's find a watering hole," Owens said, "slam a drink or two while I fill you in on my conversations with Burbridge and Pomeroy."

After hiking past several closed bars, they found one bracing for the storm but still open.

* * *

"Bimini?" Sanders scoffed. "You've got to be kidding. You can't possibly think Lukker believes the nonsense associated with that place, do you?"

"No, I don't," Owens admitted. "But many do. You know the story better than most."

Sanders took a large gulp from his bottle. "You're going to recite the legend no matter what I say."

Owens plowed ahead. "According to the tale told by the Arawaks of Hispaniola, Bimini was an island where the inhabitants lived a life of luxury and longevity, gifts of a magic fountain. Legend has it that Sequene, an Arawak chief from Cuba, went in search of the island with some of his tribesmen and never returned. Rumors spread that they found what they were looking for. Ponce de León is thought to have heard these tales, and while failing to discover Bimini or the Fountain of Youth, he did manage to trip over Florida."

Sanders rolled his eyes. "I know these fables as well as you. The lure of the Fountain of Youth is surpassed only by the quest for the Holy Grail. I've explored Bimini on several occasions. But if Lukker doesn't believe the legend, why Bimini?"

"Aside from the fact that Bimini is outside the jurisdiction of the FDA and the laws of the United States, it's a great place to develop a potion of everlasting youth, on an island long associated with miracles. He could invent a catchy name, like Biminex, and he could export and market age-defying products without being pestered by the FDA or the IRS."

Sanders drained his bottle and waited for his friend to pause for air.

"You're a marine scientist, Preston. When do you think *Marlene* will strike Bimini?"

"I'm not a meteorologist, but she's veering northeast of Bimini at the moment. Tropical storms and hurricanes are notoriously erratic, but Bimini will probably receive most, if not all, of *Marlene's* wrath. What else did Burbridge say?"

"He told me Miles passed away."

Sanders pushed aside his empty Dos Equis. "Can't say I'm surprised, but it's a damn shame. Living like a bird in a gilded cage couldn't have been easy. Life can be so unfair."

Their somber mood lifted when Pomeroy called with good news. "Scientists at CDC have managed to isolate blood traces from that stuffed horse."

"It's about time," Owens exclaimed. "What took them so long?"

"Keep in mind, much of the display was contaminated by human preservation techniques over the years, and tissues infected with this virus would have been the first in a dead animal to decompose. The best places to hunt for DNA are hair follicles, inside teeth, bones and hooves. It took a while because Old Scipio was actually five or six horses assembled as one, with the various parts deriving from animals that died before the Great Epizootic began.

"The pelt covering the skeleton was not Scipio's, so hair samples yielded nothing.

Horses typically have 205 bones, nearly the same as humans, and these had to be microscopically examined, like looking for a particular grain of sand on a beach. Corpse- eating microbes and bugs had devoured most of the DNA, but our scientists found what they needed when a fibular tarsal bone yielded several usable DNA samples.

"Sounds promising," Owens replied.

"Scientists can now differentiate between the virus that caused the Great Epizootic and modern West Nile Virus. Serums based on these extractions are spurring regrowth of damaged progeria cells. It's still a long way to finding a cure, but scientists are cautiously optimistic they're on the path to finding one."

"That's great news," Owens said flatly.

"You don't sound pleased," Pomeroy commented. "It may take a month or two, but now at least there's hope for these children."

He rubbed his forehead. "I *am* pleased, but I can't help thinking about what would have happened to all of those kids if Sophia hadn't appeared, prompting Preston and me to travel to Portugal to find that picture of a mule licking her face."

"Quite a coincidence," Pomeroy said.

"Maybe, maybe not. I've never been a big believer in coincidences, but it's unlikely that Preston and I would have hunted for a victim of the Great Epizootic—the key to unlocking the cure for thousands of children infected with progeria—had we not seen that picture."

After a few moments of silence, Pomeroy added, "The rest of the news isn't so good. If the two of you are alone, press speaker."

The bar was deserted, the proprietor nowhere in sight. He pressed speaker.

"We've located the second secret research facility Vintiger mentioned. Lukker has established himself southeast of the North Bimini chain on Sequene Cay, at a failed luxury resort. He's the new owner, controls the entire island. His computers are protected by an extremely sophisticated firewall, and we've been unsuccessful at hacking our way into them. Are the two of you familiar with the Human Genome Project?"

They both answered "Yes."

"We believe Lukker is mapping each of Sophia's genes and matching them with chromosomes, using the Human Genome Project as a checklist. Most labs would take years to complete this, but Lukker has the resources to do this far more rapidly. In fact, he could be finished in a matter of days."

"What's the rush?" Owens asked.

Pomeroy's voice wavered. "My guess, they're extracting all the information they can before disposing of her."

Owens's stomach went into freefall. "Maybe it's time to send in the Marines."

"We can't. Bimini is part of the independent Bahamas and a member of the Commonwealth of Nations. The Brits may be our allies, but they'd squawk like we'd landed Marines down a chimney at Buckingham Palace."

"Another reason for Lukker settling on Bimini," Owens said. "Only forty-eight nautical miles from the United States, yet he can bask in the protection of the British government and ignore U.S. laws and regulations."

"So how do we break her out of there?" Sanders asked. "They've no doubt set up security operations and can spot anyone approaching the island."

Owens wasn't deterred. "*Marlene* will provide us with cover," he replied. "Those on the Cay will be focused on the storm, giving us a chance to slip inside and rescue Sophia."

Sanders looked skeptical but didn't say anything.

"Just a moment, gentlemen," Pomeroy said, "I'm receiving additional information."

Franklin, Pomeroy's assistant, could be heard in the background.

A few moments passed before Pomeroy was back on the line. "Most of the researchers and lab technicians have left Sequene Cay. I doubt Lukker would be concerned enough for their safety to send them out of the danger zone; it's more likely he's concluded his work. We believe Lukker and Trachmann are still on the island, along with a handful of mercenaries hired to guard the facility.

"There's something else," said Pomeroy, "and I know this will be of great concern to you, Dr. Sanders. I've just received news that someone else has learned of Lukker's whereabouts. Your fiancée is Jackie Donovan, a reporter?"

"Yes."

"She flew to Bimini several days ago to interview Lukker and hasn't been heard from since."

* * *

Pomeroy was firm. "I'm authorizing a rescue team to invade the island. Anderson, I know you've had CIA training, but this is not your wheelhouse. You and Dr. Sanders will be sitting this one out. I'll let you know who's in charge when the team is ready to deploy."

"Bullshit! There isn't time to wait," Owens spat. He had no intention of sitting back and twiddling his thumbs while others risked their lives. He hung up on Pomeroy.

Sanders had overheard the conversation and wasn't having it. "I'm going with you."

"No you're not."

"You can't expect me to stand around with my thumb up my ass while others rescue my fiancée. I'm going, and I'll do whatever it takes to bring Jackie home safely."

Owens leveled a steely glare at his best friend. "I'm taking charge, have already made arrangements. You can come, but you'll do as *I* say. You've never shot and killed anyone, have you?"

"No, but there's a first time for everything."

"Listen, I'm pulling rank on you because I can't handle the possibility of losing you or Jackie, but Sophia must be our primary concern if all those infected kids are to be saved."

Sanders looked like he was about to say something, but his best friend's unflinching expression, a look he'd rarely witnessed before, prompted him to keep quiet.

*   *   *

"No, Jackie didn't say anything to me about chasing after Lukker or discovering his whereabouts," Sanders said. "If she had, I'd have told her she was nuts and tied her up to keep her safe, if necessary."

Owens was curious how she'd located Lukker when everyone else was in the dark, but if Owens knew anything it was that Jackie Donovan was not to be underestimated. She could charm the skin off a snake, and she was bullheaded enough to take risks as she built a high-profile journalistic presence, both to satisfy her ego and pay for a grandmother in an assisted living facility without help from her rich boyfriend. Owens was aware of the friction between the couple whenever Preston felt Jackie was taking unnecessary chances.

Sanders's voice was thick with emotion. "The wind will rip apart *Isabella's* sails if they come unfurled, so we'll need to lash them down with extra care. We'll rely on motor power."

"You can't be serious," Owens exclaimed. "You could be facing 125 mph winds and 50-foot waves, suicidal even if you had a full accompaniment of experienced hands, which you don't."

"She *will* withstand it, and I'll sail her myself if I have to."

"Even if we navigate *Isabella* to the Cay without sinking or running aground, she'll be spotted and we'll lose the element of surprise."

Sanders's jaw muscles tightened. "Seaplanes aren't designed to land in hurricanes, so unless we decide to swim fifty miles in hundred-mile winds we're out of alternatives."

Owens placed an arm on his shoulder. "Not really. There *is* another way. We need transportation with a lower profile, much lower, something that can handle a hurricane."

Sanders stared at him for a few moments. "Of course; when did you make the call?"

"Hours ago."

* * *

Owens and Sanders stood at the end of the dock, gazing past the vacant mooring spots. Their view of the horizon would normally have been blocked by cruise ships, but they had sailed away to safety, allowing them to see the strange airplane landing on the choppy water.

"What the hell?" Sanders shielded his eyes from the growing wind and squinted at the hybrid seaplane landing in the distance.

Closer to shore, a yellow pilot boat flying a red and white flag approached the dock. Quick and durable, it easily withstood being slammed against the dock by the agitated water. "The Navy has asked me to pick up two fellows named Owens and Sanders.," shouted the grizzled skipper, his weathered baseball cap pressed low on his head.

"That's us," Owens answered.

"Then come aboard and be quick about it. I just picked up a mayday."

They dropped down to the lurching boat and quickly donned lifejackets. The skipper pulled away from the dock and headed into rough water.

* * *

The amphibious cargo plane bobbed about on the roiling water like a toy in a bathtub. The pilot boat approached and cut its engine. The waves hurled them against the side of the bouncing plane. Owens and Sanders grabbed rungs on the fuselage. As the boat sped away, they scrambled across the exterior of the plane toward the clamshell doors in the rear. Wind whistled as it passed over the opening, located high enough to prevent most waves from entering. They were soaked by the time they entered the interior.

The cargo floor was converted into a rollerized conveyor system, and Burton Mazlow was bellowing at the Navy personnel struggling to align *Amelia* on the rollers. His beloved submersible swung precariously on cables about four feet over the cargo floor. She struck the interior walls of the fuselage like a clapper in a bell as the plane pitched back and forth. Mazlow was red in the face as he barked, "Be gentle with her! She's filled with sensitive equipment."

Owens could see that Amelia had come loose while being flown over the Atlantic and an attempt was being made to secure the submersible, but it didn't appear to be going well. "Burton, what's the problem?" he shouted.

"I wondered when you two were going to show up. The winch isn't working properly. Both cleats needed to maintain tension have failed. No time to fetch replacements, so we need to repair what we've got and launch before our window of opportunity closes."

"This conveyor can be turned over, can't it?" Owens asked.

Mazlow rubbed his temples with his fingertips. "Yes. It can be turned over to leave a smooth, flat surface to accommodate wheeled or tracked vehicles."

"Great. Order the men to flip it over. We'll coat the floor in fire-retardant foam, set *Amelia* on the cargo floor and, at the right moment, release the cables. If this plane lifts off swiftly at a steep enough angle, gravity will cause *Amelia* to slide down the cargo floor and pass through the clamshell doors, dropping into the water. It won't be pretty, but it might be the only option we have. Can *Amelia* handle being dropped fifty to a hundred feet into the ocean?"

"She's designed to withstand tremendous pressure," Mazlow yelled.

"It's too wet for foam to do much good, but the ocean has already made it pretty slick in here," Sanders announced.

"Then we go without foam," Mazlow decided.

Airmen flipped the rolling conveyor and prepared for takeoff. Owens and Sanders removed their lifejackets to fit through *Amelia's* narrow hatch. Mazlow followed them inside, leaving the hatch open for now. They scrambled into thin neoprene wetsuits, and strapped themselves in. Owens tucked Pomeroy's plastic gun into his waistband. "We're going to need more firepower."

Mazlow twisted his walrus mustache and smiled, unlatching the door of a metal locker located close to the piloting console. Inside were rounds of ammunition and a rack filled with an assortment of rifles. "Put your peashooter away and check these out."

Owens was impressed. "These M4s appear to be standard army issue, but the others look like prototypes."

Mazlow explained. "Many of these weapons aren't on the market yet. All, except the M4s, are equipped with silencers and can be fully submerged. We're going to get wet leaving *Amelia*, although water will drain out of these weapons in less than eight seconds."

A voice from the cockpit crackled over the radio. "Weather window deteriorating. *Marlene* is slamming us 50 degrees to the west with every cresting wave, and our anemometer shows winds approaching 90 knots. We can't hold this position any longer. I hope you guys are strapped in. It'll be a short ride, but exciting."

Owens felt the cargo plane fighting the rotating sweep of *Marlene's* great winds as he tugged at his seatbelt and harness. Had he strapped himself in any tighter he wouldn't have been able to breathe. The others did the same, and moments later he felt the plane picking up speed until it began skimming the troughs.

Waves striking the bottom of the fuselage pummeled the plane like artillery fire as they bounded over the water, and not even *Amelia's* thick hull could block out the sound of wind shrieking about them like an angry banshee as the plane struggled to break the ocean's grip.

When airborne, Mazlow contacted the cockpit. "Be sure you drop us in the Gulf Stream, and not too close to Bimini. Otherwise, our mission could be over before it begins."

For Owens's benefit, Sanders clarified. "Bimini lies at the northwestern edge of the Great Bahama Bank, a vast area of warm, shallow water. Since we're about to plummet from this plane like a meteor, we need deep water to avoid crashing on the bottom and becoming mired in a sandy crater on the sea floor. The Gulf Stream separates Bimini and the bank it rests on from the mainland. Here the waters swiftly flow north through a cavernous undersea trench. The deep water will protect us from *Marlene* while we approach the island."

Turbulence rocked the plane. Mazlow shouted, "Bimini is already experiencing *Marlene*, but her eye is still fifty miles away and won't pass over the island for a few hours. The current will propel us to the area quickly, but we'll want to circle around so we can sneak up on the compound from the rear."

"If this storm grows into a Category Three, will this flying bucket hold together?" Owens asked.

Mazlow smiled. "You've flown into hurricanes before, haven't you?"

"Once, but it wasn't intentional, and I certainly didn't enjoy it."

"Don't worry," Mazlow said. "Planes are designed to go very fast through the air, and they don't care if the winds are 5 knots or 150 knots. This 'bucket' can handle a lot of abuse but prepare yourself for some rough bumps along the way. Fortunately, we'll fly down into the eye without the need to punch through hurricane walls."

"That's a relief."

Sanders muttered, "This will still be one helluva ride."

Twenty minutes later Owens felt the pilot fighting intense updrafts and downdrafts. Rain and hail pelted the plane as it descended toward the bubbling cauldron below. When the plane leveled off, he could feel waves ricocheting off the bottom of the fuselage. Static electricity began building around *Amelia*, discharging with a flash and loud bang. Owens ran a hand over his shorn head and grinned at Sanders, whose hair was literally standing on end.

"Seal the hatch!" Mazlow ordered. "We're nearing the drop."

Sanders unbuckled himself and rotated the water hatch, doing the same with the airlock beneath it. He barely had time to strap himself back into his seat when the rear doors opened.

"Good luck, gentlemen," the cockpit radioed. The cables preventing *Amelia* from sliding back and forth were released. The plane began a steep climb, and the submersible slid down the length of the slick cargo floor.

The drop was mercifully brief, no sustained G-force but Owens felt his stomach in his mouth. *Amelia's* stabilizers were designed to work only when the craft was submerged, and the wind caught her wings, temporarily preventing a straight descent. She yawed considerably to the right, but a gust straightened her before she pitched into the sea in a graceless belly flop.

─────────

CHAPTER FIFTY-FIVE

Sunday: 1:25 p.m.

The steel latch was drawn back allowing the door to swing open. Jackie had been sitting on a cot in the dark for nearly two days and had been let out only for brief bathroom trips, the light spilling into the storage space where she was confined. After several moments her eyes adjusted. A man stood in the doorway, a tray in his hand, a machine gun slung over his shoulder.

"I've brought you something to eat," he said.

He appeared less seasoned than others she'd seen before being locked up. He couldn't hide the lust in his eyes when he looked at her. "Thanks," she said, accepting a tray loaded with mangled vending machine treats and a small carton of milk. The carton had been opened.

"The hurricane knocked out the generators; refrigeration units are out until the backup ones come on. Most of our supplies are spoiled. I checked the milk myself. Smells okay."

She set the tray on the cot, reached for the warm milk and gulped it down, wiping her mouth with the back of her hand.

He leered at her. "Everyone is preoccupied with the hurricane, but I was worried about *you*, all alone down here in the dark."

She chewed her bottom lip for a moment. "Aren't you nice." Rising from the cot, she went and stood beside him. "Can't you take me someplace where I can splash cool water on my face, where we can get to know each other?"

"Nice try, Blondie. But you aren't going anywhere."

"Do you know why I'm being held here?"

"I heard something about you being an industrial spy."

"I'm no spy. I'm a reporter in pursuit of a story. I've been kidnapped, along with another woman. She's being tortured. Lukker's insane, in case you didn't know."

"So what? His checks don't bounce. That's all I care about."

"The girl's named Sophia; do you know where she is?"

"Can't say."

"Oh, I should have guessed. You probably aren't important enough to have access to the entire facility."

His jaw tightened and a vein at his temple bulged. "Yeah, I've seen her. She's in one of the medical labs."

"This may not be America, but I'm a U.S. citizen. People are looking for us. Important people. If you keep us locked up in here, you'll end up in as much trouble as Lukker. So far, you've been real nice to me, and if you turn your back and let me walk out of here I'll put in a good word for you when this is over."

His face remained immobile. "What's your name?"

"Jackie."

"Okay, Jackie. Here's what I think. I think you're a lying bitch. I don't believe anyone's looking or they'd probably have come for you by now."

"There's a hurricane raging outside, remember? They'll be here as soon as it's over. Make a deal with me and I'll have my network write you a fat check. You're a mercenary, right?"

"Mercenary is an ugly word. I prefer soldier of fortune."

"Okay, soldier of fortune. I'm willing to pay more than Lukker."

He shook his head. "Trachmann caught one of Lukker's bodyguards on a cell phone spilling information and planning to leave, ordered him hanged from a soffit by piano wire. You say you're a reporter, so I'd be willing to bet you're the one he called. Maybe you're the reason they sliced him up and fed him to the monkeys."

Semi-darkness made the guilt registering in her eyes difficult to see.

"As for me, I won't be able to spend money if I'm dead, and if I betray Lukker I might as well put a pistol in my mouth. But I don't see any reason why we can't have fun passing the time."

Her feet dangled in the air when he locked an arm around her waist and lifted her up, pulled her close until her breasts pressed against his chest. She struggled as he sealed his lips over hers, stopped when something poked her from the pocket of his shirt. Pulling her face from his, she wormed her fingers into the pocket, removing a pencil stub and small book of crossword puzzles. "I'm horrible at these," she admitted before being silenced by another slobbery kiss.

Coming up for air, his breath hot and ragged, he said, "It gets boring standing around all the time with nothing much happening. It helps to have something to pass the time."

"The eraser on this pencil has hardly been used. You must be smart." She opened the book.

He pulled it from her hands and jammed it back in his pocket. "Like I said, it helps to have something to pass the time." He pressed his body against her, this kiss more urgent than the others.

"Slow down. What's the rush? Why don't you set down that heavy rifle so we can get acquainted?"

He hesitated, then removed the rifle from his shoulder and propped it against a wall. Grabbing her by a wrist, he dragged her back to the cot, pushed her down and dropped onto her like a skydiver whose parachute had failed. She was ready for him, jerking her knee upward with enough force to make him howl in pain when it collided with his erection. The tray bounced off the cot and clattered on the concrete floor. She reached for it, repeatedly striking him on the head until he toppled from the cot.

She jumped up and dashed for the rifle. It wasn't where he'd left it. The weapon was in the hand of another mercenary standing in the doorway, laughing at the figure sprawled on the floor. "I had a hunch I'd find you down here, Palfrey."

"Just checking to make sure she's all right," he spat between clenched teeth.

"She'll be all right, so long as you keep your dick in your pants and leave her alone."

The injured sentry staggered to his feet and managed to grab the rifle thrust at him.

"Trachmann wants everyone at their station, so get your ass back outside with the other knuckle draggers."

"Yessir. Whatever you say. But what's the point? Nobody could get to this island in a hurricane."

"My orders come from Trachmann. Maybe you'd like to discuss them with him personally. He's in his office tuning his piano."

The man rubbed his crotch, grumbled and limped away.

"Palfrey's got pussy fever. You wouldn't have stopped him for long."

"I guess I should thank you...." He didn't volunteer his name. She looked up at his scarred face. "I have the feeling I'm out of the fire and into the frying pan; either way I have a feeling this isn't my lucky day."

He smiled. "Palfrey had the right idea, but that little ass wipe needs to go to the end of the line. You're gonna get the Holiday Inn treatment; we picked straws to see who gets to check in first." He plucked the tray from her hands, bent it in half and flung it into a corner. "Turns out it's *my* lucky day. Hope your nails are sharp, 'cause I like it rough."

He pulled the rifle from his shoulder and set it down out of her reach, unbuttoned his shirt and let it drop to the floor. Built like a professional wrestler, his body was a menagerie of tattoos that included a crouching hyena on his right bicep.

A siren went off. "Shit, perimeter alert."

With shirt and rifle in hand, he hurried out the door, pulling it closed behind him.

Jackie dashed across the room, plucked the pencil stub from her bra and jammed it into the latch just as the door slammed shut. Pressure was exerted on the stub, causing it to explode into a shower of splinters. She waited until sure he'd gone before tugging on the door handle. A sigh of relief. Enough of the pencil had remained intact to prevent the latch from locking. The door swung open.

The concrete hallway outside the room where she had been confined was filled with red light but was otherwise empty. She passed elevator doors and made her way into a cavernous space that included stairs. She encountered no one as she climbed to another level, this one filled with medical equipment, computers, and cages where the red eyes of monkeys stared back at her.

Footsteps approached. She barely had time to duck under a desk before a man with broad shoulders and a brush cut approached, a rifle in one hand. He paused when his cell beeped. "Trachmann here. Yes, Mr. Lukker, but I can hardly hear you. I agree; it's time to eliminate the reporter. The girl, too? I'll dump their bodies in the monkey vats. A few hours in the acid and there won't be anything to prove they were ever here. Mr. Lukker...are you there? You're breaking up."

Jackie heard crackle and static.

"Our cellular links must be taking a hit from the weather. Yes, good idea. I'll dispose of our guests after I make the broadcast."

Trachmann hurried away, and Jackie continued searching for Sophia. Before long a voice blared on a PA system. "Attention: Trachmann here. The hurricane is interfering with our cell phones. Switch them off and turn on your transceivers. Tune in to frequency 460.671 MHz for updates." A siren went off. "Our perimeter alarms are going off. Be alert for updates and further instructions."

Jackie knew it wouldn't take long for her escape to be discovered. She left her hiding place and entered another room filled with cages, a few empty but most occupied by monkeys. She stared at the creatures for a few moments...and then began opening doors. There were scores of cages in several rooms. She worked quickly, pressing herself against a wall when someone approached.

One of the guards raced past, too much in a hurry to notice her or the open cage doors. She continued, creeping into all the rooms with cages, making sure each was unlocked and opened. The monkeys were surprisingly quiet, holding their tails and remaining in their cages until one of the largest, eying her curiously, bared its fangs and hissed at her.

"Get going," she whispered. "This is where you guys provide me with a distraction."

A large specimen cocked its head as if understanding her and dropped to the floor. Many of the others followed, leaping to the ground and scurrying away.

Not long after releasing the monkeys, she heard shots.

CHAPTER FIFTY-SIX

Sunday: 1:40 p.m.

They approached Bimini two hours after the drop.

Mazlow slowed their approach to Sequene Cay, stopping a hundred yards from shore and settling *Amelia* on the ocean floor, thirty-five feet beneath the surface.

They each selected a rifle, inserting it into the quick-release holster on their backs. Mazlow provided underwater breathing apparatuses of his own design, UBAs that strapped to the chest and were smaller and lighter than those currently used by Navy SEALs.

After passing through the air and water locks, they swam away from the submersible in the direction of the shore. Owens's CIA training was a distant memory, but he'd been instructed in amphibious insertions, spending two months at the Naval Special Warfare Training Center in Coronado. Still, he couldn't suppress the feeling that he was swimming inside a giant washing machine.

More than once, he became disoriented, rolling about until he couldn't tell up from down. He was grateful to finally feel sand beneath his feet, but when he tried to stand and work his way toward land the seabed eroded beneath his feet.

He'd never experienced current like this and struggled to regain his footing. Despite disorientation, he reached shore before the others, pausing to help pull Mazlow and Sanders from the wild surf. They tore off the dive masks limiting their field of vision but kept the goggles protecting their eyes from blowing sand. They reached for their rifles and craned their necks for signs they were being observed. All was clear.

Suddenly...the gale stopped, not a dissipating storm blowing itself out, more like the unplugging of a wind machine on a Hollywood set as compressed thunderheads gave way to an eerie oasis of calm.

The eye was passing over the island.

The sky kaleidoscoped from gunmetal gray to cerulean as sunshine spilled over the Cay from the aperture in the swirling clouds.

"Follow my lead," Owens commanded.

With rifles in hand, they began their trek.

Mangrove swamps forced them to wade through water up to their chests, baby lemon sharks darting through their legs. Once on dry land, their progress was hampered by downed palm trees. The neoprene gear bottled in body heat and they were panting by the time they reached the far side of the Cay, where the terrain became rockier.

Half of the island was little more than a sandbar, but here on a slight elevation was a three-story building, its height and concrete construction unusual for the region. Closed metal storm shutters on all windows and doors gave the impression of a bunker, but lying amid debris on the circular driveway was an architectural rendering of a fabulous vacation destination.

The sign announced the site as the future home of the Grand Bimini Casino and Resort. Owens could see that the building was designed to withstand hurricanes; had the original owners not gone bankrupt they'd probably have added tropical touches to make it more appealing.

"It's fitting that Lukker, who's risking his personal and financial reputation, would hole up in a place designed for gambling," Sanders said, his voice partially muffled by the wind. "I hope luck is on our side."

Until now, Owens hadn't placed much stock in luck, but recent events had him thinking about changing his mind.

CHAPTER FIFTY-SEVEN

Sunday: 2:55 p.m.

Footsteps echoed on the concrete floors, alerting Jackie to sentries converging on her position. She dodged into a utility closet filled with circuit boxes and electrical wiring and hid behind the door, leaving it partially open to give the impression that the closet was unoccupied. Holding her breath, she listened as two sentries nearly collided with each other. "Palfrey, why aren't you at your station?"

"Didn't you hear the news? That blond reporter managed to worm her way out of the supply room."

"Yeah, I heard. What does that have to do with us?"

"I came inside to hunt her down. That bitch kneed me in the nuts, and I'm thinking she's responsible for opening the cages. The goddamn monkeys are everywhere."

"Trachmann hasn't given permission to shoot them."

"Don't give a fuck about permission."

From her hiding place, Jackie could see the guard who'd tried to entice her with milk. He held two limp monkeys by their tails, and when he lifted a pant cuff a nasty bite was visible near his ankle. "Vicious critters. I was standing just inside the entrance when these two came toward me. The drugs they get must make 'em insane because instead of escaping through the open door they came after me. I shot one, but the other sank its teeth in my leg. The little fucker wouldn't let go, not even after I shot it in the head. Pried it off with my rifle."

"Better get back to your station. Now that the hurricane has temporarily died down Trachmann thinks Blondie might try to escape."

"There isn't any place for her to go."

"Did you get a close look at her?"

"As a matter of fact, I did."

"Then you saw she's in great shape. South Bimini is less than two miles away. She could swim the distance while the eye passes over us. Lukker and Trachmann have authorized extreme measures to prevent her escape. Do you know what that means?"

"Yeah. It means that I can put a bullet in *her* head."

The sentry hurried away.

The space outside the utility closet was vast, probably designed for hundreds of slot machines and gaming tables that never arrived. Jackie smiled at the sight of her would-be attacker limping away, but the smile evaporated when she accidentally knocked over a spool of cable. The sound echoed, drawing Palfrey's attention.

He dropped the dead monkeys and approached the closet. Jackie was trapped inside. With his rifle aimed to fire, he entered and grinned when he saw her. "Hey, Blondie! How's it going?"

Cramped in the corner behind the door, she couldn't maneuver well, but she lifted a leg and tried to kick him where she'd already done damage.

He was quick to respond, smacking her in the forehead with the butt of his rifle. She went limp and collapsed to the floor.

CHAPTER FIFTY-EIGHT

Sunday: 3:00 p.m.

The more Owens thought about it, the more it made sense: Lukker had located his facility on a site long associated with the Fountain of Youth, but the chosen spot was repeatedly struck by hurricanes. Why waste time and money building from scratch when a nearly complete structure was already here and could be picked up for a song, one designed to withstand whatever nature could throw at it?

The screechy sound of a metal gate being raised prompted him to dive for cover. A sentry was hightailing it out of the building, a limp body slung over his shoulder. A blond woman. Jackie.

"Drop your weapon," Owens ordered, rising from his hiding place so the fellow could see the semi-automatic pointed at him. Hopefully the guy wasn't stupid enough to raise his rifle. Owens didn't want to risk hitting Jackie.

The sentry hesitated, his eyes dropping to three dead guards lying face down in the sand, one with a tattoo of a crouching hyena on his bicep.

"Your compadres didn't obey. Maybe you'd like to join them."

The rifle fell to the sand.

Sanders dashed forward and pulled Jackie from the sentry's shoulder. He looked relieved when she moaned and he could see she was breathing. "What did you do to her?" Sanders spat through clenched teeth.

"She's fine, unconscious is all," said the sentry.

While Sanders tended to her, Owens asked, "How many men guard this facility?"

No response.

Owens shot him in the left forearm.

"Fuck!" Blood spewed through the fingers he pressed against the wound.

Owens leveled the Heckler & Koch at his chest. "This is the last time I'll ask. How many?"

Before the man could answer, a sniper on the roof put a bullet in his head.

Mazlow had Owens covered and fired. The sniper was struck in the chest and tumbled to the ground without managing to squeeze off another shot.

"Thanks, Burton. I owe you."

More rifle fire. A dull thud and puff of sand near his Nikes alerted Owens to another sniper.

"Preston, get Jackie behind those fallen trees," Owens ordered.

Sanders wasted no time, lifting her like she was a rag doll.

On the roof, the shooter rose up and aimed at them, revealing his hiding place behind an air-conditioning unit. Owens fired, nailing him between the eyes.

Mazlow's finger remained on the trigger while Owens joined his friends behind the pile of trees.

Jackie stirred, smiled at Sanders and was about to say something when her hand shot up to her forehead. "Shit, that bastard hit me with his rifle. Where is he? Did you get him?"

"He won't be hurting anyone ever again," Sanders said.

"Good."

"Jackie, did you see Sophia while you were inside?" Owens asked.

Her face wrinkled as she tried to think. "No, but I heard Trachmann talking on his phone. Lukker gave him orders to kill us both. If Sophia's alive, she won't be for long."

"I'm surprised their cell phones are working."

"They aren't. They're using transceivers instead."

"Any idea how many mercenaries are guarding this place?"

"No, but I've seen at least a couple dozen."

While considering what to do next, Owens's eyes settled on the transceiver hooked on the belt of a dead sentry. "If only we knew the frequency they were using."

Jackie proved useful. "Trachmann used the PA system to order everyone inside to tune in to 460.671 MHz."

"That makes sense. UHF frequencies perform best inside steel or concrete structures, although they're vulnerable to eavesdropping. Lukker probably authorized a 'voice scramble' for protection." He set down his rifle and unzipped the front of his wetsuit. It was becoming unbearably warm. "Burton, cover me."

He dashed for the transceiver, plucked it from the dead man's belt, raced back to cover. A bullet struck a chunk of palm tree less than a foot from his head.

Mazlow released several rounds, but someone on the roof continued firing at them.

Owens pulled his cell from a watertight pocket in his wetsuit. Cell service might be down on the island, but *Sotto Voce* technology was capable of the impossible. He punched a number, sighed with relief when Casper answered.

"Nike! What do you need now? More croc lullabies?"

"This time I need something to attract mercenaries. Have you been plugged in to where we are and why?"

"Yes. What do you need?"

Owens filled him in on what he had in mind and gave the frequency provided by Jackie.

"I think I can help, mate," Casper said. "NSA has positioned its Echelon satellite over the region to photograph *Marlene* and alert those in her path to get the 'ell out of the way. I can adjust the electro-optic modulators to carry an old-fashioned UHF signal. But I'm receiving photos that show the eye is about to move away from Bimini. When that happens, *Marlene* will get testy again. No transmission will be able to break through until she moves off."

"Then we'd better hurry. A murder is about to take place."

"Copy, Nike. I'm making the adjustments. Good luck."

He pocketed his cell and stared at the transceiver, holding his breath and willing it to work. A crawling dread crept down his spine when the device remained mute. Had Casper encountered an impenetrable "voice scramble?" Had Trachmann ordered a change of frequency? He was already searching for another solution when the black box crackled and came to life, in concert with nearby transceivers strapped to dead sentries:

Attention everyone on Sequene Cay. This warning will not be repeated. Bimini's local government has alerted the Central Government in Nassau to recent activities in violation of Bahamian and International law. The Governor General has requested assistance from the U.S. Navy to arrest American citizen Everett Lukker and his associates for crimes against humanity.

To avoid charges for crimes you might have unwittingly participated in, proceed to the front entrance and surrender your weapons. Sequene Cay is surrounded, escape impossible. You have ten minutes to comply. Those failing to do so will suffer severe consequences.

All lies, but Casper spoke them convincingly, his British accent lending credibility to the ruse.

One by one, mercenaries poked their heads out of the front door, their gaze bouncing between their comrades lying dead in the sand and three men in wetsuits aiming automatic rifles at them.

"Everyone in a circle, face down in the sand," Owens ordered.

The pile of discarded weapons grew as several dozen men surrendered. Absent from them were Everett Lukker and Arnold Trachmann.

CHAPTER FIFTY-NINE

Sunday: 3:34 p.m.

Lukker pressed his damp palms against the jacket of his suit as he scurried toward Station #1, in his pocket a Ruger semi-automatic. Outside, the wind was starting to build, rattling the metal shutters shielding the windows. He passed Stations #8-4, where partially autopsied chimpanzees lay on tables, their bodies decomposing quickly in the tropical heat. The stench made his eyes water.

He plucked a white silk handkerchief from his breast pocket, pressed it over his mouth and nose, and hurried along. The building was withstanding the hurricane admirably, but the power supply had taken a hit. No electricity, except backup for computers and emergency lighting, no refrigeration or air-conditioning.

A large rhesus monkey had managed to escape its cage. This one eyed him curiously, refused to scurry out of his path. He pulled the semi-automatic from his pocket, blasted it and proceeded on his way.

His steps quickened, leather soles echoing on the concrete floor. Trachmann had failed to confirm that he'd completed his task. Lukker, on his way to see if his orders had been carried out, brought the gun in case he needed to do the job himself.

The reporter was a nuisance. And he didn't need the other woman any longer; his researchers had extracted from her all the data they could, along with an analysis of blood and tissue samples. Future tests would be conducted with information stored in offsite computers.

Lukker had been holding one of the transceivers when Bahamian authorities broadcast their warning, but it was unlikely an attack could be launched until *Marlene* blew herself out. Still, if their security *had* been breached, it would be foolish to leave the girl, or that pesky reporter, to testify against him. Along with the weapon, he'd pocketed the girl's locket, another piece of evidence to throw into the acid bath.

Without air-conditioning, his wire rims fogged over and red emergency lighting glistened on his damp forehead. He loosened the knot on his tie as he proceeded through the maze of corridors on the top floor.

He reached Station #1, but something in the room was odd. The girl was visible, but she wasn't alone. After swiping at the condensation on his glasses, Lukker squinted through the dim red lighting and saw the monkeys surrounding her bed, more than he could count. He shook his head: monkeys were supposed to be confined to the research floor below.

Unconscious, Sophia moaned, her arms held by restraints. Several of the primates had climbed up onto the bed and were gently poking her, hugging themselves and rocking back and forth while observing her with big solemn eyes.

The researchers in charge of the primates had been gone for several days. These monkeys had to be hungry, if not starving, but if he thought they'd kill and eat her, save him from the cumbersome task of throwing her into the acid vat, he was wrong.

A sizable monkey, scabby patches of skin visible through missing fur, watched him aim the gun at her head. Springing from its location beside the girl, it sank its fangs into his wrist.

He howled. The gun dropped from his hand, clattered on the concrete floor. The monkey refused to let go. Lukker dragged himself to a nearby workstation, reached for a microscope and struck the creature with it repeatedly until it released its grip on his wrist.

One of his veins had been punctured and he bled profusely. Tossing the microscope aside, he wrapped the handkerchief tightly around his wrist to staunch the flow. He hadn't noticed the monkeys climbing down from the bed or others swarming into the room, surrounding him, their eyes dark with uncontrollable rage, lips pulled back to expose razor-sharp teeth.

He panted heavily, a dark stain seeping through the handkerchief, droplets of blood falling to the floor where they were sniffed and lapped up.

"You'll all end up in the acid vat!" Lukker shrieked, panic settling in.

Some of them tilted their heads as if they could understand him. Most simply licked their lips.

"The secret to immortality is waiting for me. I refuse to be thwarted by a few goddamned monkeys. Get out of my way!" He kicked a few aside but stopped when one clawed up his pant leg and chomped into his thigh.

"Trachmann!" he howled. "Where the hell are you?"

The only response came from the growing wind outside as *Marlene* began moving away.

He screamed one more time.

And then they were on him.

Chapter Sixty

Squinting like *Dirty Harry*, Owens pointed his rifle at the crotch of one of the prisoners and said, "I'm only going to ask once; where's the girl?"

"Don't shoot! She's in Station #1 on the top floor."

He left Mazlow in charge of the mercenaries and wasted no time entering the building, even though Trachmann and Lukker were probably holed up inside. He assumed the elevators weren't working and dashed up the stairs, taking three at a time. On the top floor, heat and red lighting made it seem he'd entered a massive microwave.

Station #1 was where he was told it would be, but not even the welcome sight of Sophia could shut out the gruesome scene before him. A partially consumed carcass was barely visible beneath a writhing tangle of fur and tails. Sophia's bed was in the center of a sea of frenzied monkeys.

From the doorway he noticed the blood-free sheet beneath her. It didn't look like the monkeys had attacked her, but her eyes were closed, and he couldn't be certain she was alive. Until she moaned.

Nudging monkeys aside, he inched into the room, hoping they were too preoccupied with their meal to pay him much attention. He hadn't gotten far when he heard a crunch beneath his foot, saw the glimmer of mangled wire rims protruding from under his shoe, along with a partially chewed photograph of Lukker's long-dead sister.

The monkeys responded by releasing a cacophony of chatter and howls, painfully loud in the confined space. They jumped up and down, showed blood-soaked teeth and eyed him in a way that made sweat trickle down his armpits. He continued, a slow-motion progression toward Sophia, the monkeys parting slowly, scratching at his neoprene pant legs if he proceeded too quickly.

Reaching the bed, he glanced at the bag hanging from a nearby IV stand, empty, a tube still connected to a needle inserted into a vein near her right wrist. The bruised flesh and puncture marks on her arms—evidence of slow IV push. *What drugs has Lukker poisoned her with?* he wondered.

He stroked her hair and softly reassured her. "It's okay. You're safe."

She was wearing a white hospital gown, much too big for her. Her ever-present locket was missing. Had she been naked she couldn't have looked more vulnerable.

Electrodes connected to machines monitored her vital statistics, but the machines weren't operational. He wiped sweat from his brow, pressed two fingers against her carotid artery and felt a pulse, extremely weak. After slinging the rifle over his shoulder, he undid the restraints and carefully removed the electrodes and IV, lifting her from the bed as the emergency lights began flickering. A nearby monkey watched with interest but its teeth failed to pierce the neoprene when it nipped his forearm.

Owens turned toward the door, saw a large silhouette backlit by the blinking light in the hall. Trachmann, rifle in hand, blocked his exit. "Prince Charming rescuing his Sleeping Beauty. Well, not this time."

Trachmann inched closer, squinted and leered. "I haven't seen you since you broke into the Lukker Pharmaceutical facility in Costa Rica. Lukker and I watched you fumble around. Such an accomplished little spy, breaking into a poorly guarded building and retrieving drug samples left for you to find—a pathetic marionette with Lukker pulling the strings. Your being here shows you have admirable skills and I applaud your initiative, but you should stick with dog grooming."

With Sophia in his arms, he wasn't able to reach over his shoulder for the rifle. He tilted his chin at the chewed photo and mangled wire rims lying in a smear of monkey dung. "Lukker won't be pulling any more strings."

"True, but neither will you."

The flickering light winked off. Owens shifted Sophia to his shoulder and reached into his waistband for the pistol Pomeroy had given him. Mazlow had called it a peashooter, but when light returned it was enough to wipe the smirk off Trachmann's face.

When the light conked out again, Owens dropped to the floor behind the bed and shielded Sophia with his arms. Monkeys scrambled to get out of his way, shrieked when Trachmann fired blindly at the location where he'd stood seconds before.

Owens returned fire, the sound of his plastic pistol surprisingly loud. Trachmann cried out, and Owens aimed at the sound, fired again. The light returned, and this time remained on. Trachmann was gone, fresh blood trailing out of the room.

With Sophia in his arms he proceeded toward the door, disrupting the monkeys as little as possible. As he inched along he felt something else beneath his foot. Another glimmer of gold. A fragment from Lukker's wire rims? No. It was her locket. Careful not to drop her, he squatted down and reached for it.

*   *   *

Outside, *Marlene* was revving up for her finale. Fresh air never smelled or felt so good. Owens inhaled deeply, squinted at the brilliant sunshine being gobbled up by the far side of *Marlene's* eye wall as she continued toward Miami. He set Sophia down on the sand.

Mazlow, ever handy, had thought to bring plasticuffs. He and Sanders were binding hands while Jackie, semi-automatic in hand, provided cover. Thanks to Mazlow's *Amelia*, removing Sophia from the island wouldn't pose much of a problem, but repairing the emotional damage she'd endured wouldn't be so easy.

It felt like years since Owens had first looked into her eyes and seen that curious shade of cerulean laced with silver. He was terrified she might never again open her eyes.

But she chose that moment to do so.

He squeezed her hand, swallowed hard and tried to ignore the clamping feeling in his chest. He didn't recognize what he saw in her eyes.

CHAPTER SIXTY-ONE

Tuesday: 9:20 a.m.

CDC PROGERIA BULLETIN #74

Current number of documented infections:

16,001

The President's eyes skimmed the damage assessment Cotton had placed on her desk.

Miami had fared better than expected, spared the brunt of *Marlene's* force when the hurricane weakened and altered course at the last minute, blowing herself out in the open Atlantic. No deaths, but a considerable amount of damage between Miami and Cape Hatteras. *Marlene* had been downgraded to a tropical storm.

She smiled, something she hadn't done much of lately. "This is good news."

"Air Force One leaves in an hour. Local authorities have arranged for you to tour the damage zone."

"Is that necessary, Ralph? I can't help but think it's a nuisance for victims to have to endure these presidential visits, after all they've gone through."

"Madame President, you don't want your absence to be misconstrued as indifference. You know how important Florida will be in the next election."

"Assuming I decide to run for a second term."

Cotton's jaw dropped. "Why wouldn't you? This Lukker business didn't blow up in our faces. Progeria symptoms in infected children are dissipating. CDC had thought the serum they'd created would need to be taken for life by these kids, but now it appears they can be weaned off the serum in a few years. You read the report I put on your desk yesterday concerning the bonus Lukker unwittingly provided?"

"Yes. Everett didn't find his Fountain of Youth, but his search wasn't futile. He may have been diverted by self-interests, but he inadvertently hit upon the very thing we'd entrusted him to find—a drug that shows promise as an immunization against Alzheimer's disease. At least some good came from all this."

"So, there's no reason you shouldn't run again."

She didn't look convinced. "I should have seen Lukker for what he was, unprincipled, self-serving. I put him in a position to do great harm. Don't you think the American people deserve a president with better judgment?"

"I think the American people are lucky you're sitting behind this desk. Presidents aren't robots, they have feelings, flaws, but nobody loves this country more than you. Besides, I've known you for years; you seldom make mistakes and never repeat one."

She rubbed the back of her neck. "You're a good chief of staff and a better friend, even though your connection with Dr. Pomeroy shouldn't have been kept from me, but I can't shake the notion it would be best if I returned to Oregon. I think Arthur would be happier back home in his vineyard."

"Have you asked him?"

"Not in so many words."

"I think his answer might surprise you."

She changed the subject. "How is Miss Briggs doing?"

"She's improving, slowly. Physically, anyway. Still hasn't spoken since her rescue, but she's walking, starting to eat solids. Mr. Owens and Dr. Sanders want to take her home to Sarasota in a few days. They believe she'll recover there more quickly."

"A temporary solution. She's like that fellow in the story *The Man Without a Country*. She, too, has lived much of her life at sea, without home or country to call her own. Eventually, a more permanent situation for her will need to be arranged. It's hardly proper to release her to a couple of bachelors."

"Of course you're right, but this is a unique situation, and I believe Miss Briggs is in the best of hands."

CHAPTER SIXTY-TWO

Thursday: 2:10 p.m.

Sophia hadn't spoken since waking up in a Miami hospital, remained silent in the backseat while Sanders drove them across Florida back to Sarasota. The sky overhead was gray with remnants of _Marlene._ The back of Owens's shirt was damp even though they were driving with the windows down.

Jackie tried repeatedly to engage her in conversation from the front passenger seat, without success. What troubled Owens more than Sophia's silence—she'd never been a chatterbox—was the vacant look in her eyes.

He pulled her locket from his pocket and dangled it in front of her face. It glinted in the afternoon light as he swung it back and forth like a hypnotist's watch. "Sophia, do you remember this?"

No response.

He dug a fingernail into the clasp and opened it. Yellowed photographs of a stern-faced couple. "Do you know them?"

She looked at the photographs without interest.

Frustrated, Owens pressed on. "Do you know your name? Do you remember working on cruise ships? _Convento de Santa Isabel_? The explosion at Gospel of the Redeemer Church?"

He slipped the chain over her head; the locket dangled over her heart.

Her memory had always been a road filled with potholes, but now she'd left the road altogether.

* * *

When they reached Sarasota, Owens left Sophia with Sanders and Jackie; hopefully, they could coax life back into her. _Sotto Voce_ operatives had investigated the Bimini complex after their departure, and he hurried to Tuscaloosa to learn what they'd uncovered.

Chapter Sixty-Three

Friday: 4:15 p.m.
CDC Progeria Bulletin #108

Current number of documented infections:

243

"So that's the end of Lukker," Owens said, replenishing his glass from Pomeroy's new bottle of Glen Garioch. "Was anything left of him to bury?"

Pomeroy swirled the amber liquid in his glass. "Not much. Those starving monkeys did quite a number on him; consumed everything but bone, although his skull prevented them from getting at most of his brain. It seems that until recently, Lukker was living on borrowed time."

"Borrowed time?" Owens asked.

"Yes. While examining his brain, we discovered malignant tumors, quite a few of them. Despite his assertions to the contrary before Congressional Committees, it's likely he'd been injecting himself with HGH for years. Human growth hormones are notorious for causing brain tumors, and his all showed slow growth patterns. But something extraordinary happened. Biopsies showed most of the cancerous tumors were in the process of being replaced with healthy tissue. We believe the new tissue was only a few weeks old."

"What prompted this conclusion?"

Setting his glass down, Pomeroy said, "Traces of lipofuscin found in Lukker's brain."

"You're talking about the 'aging pigment.' "

"Yes, an appropriate nickname."

"Professor, this isn't my field of expertise, but I've never heard of lipofuscin being found in the brain."

"Before now it hasn't been observed there. In Lukker's brain we can follow the growth traces of this pigment and extrapolate on how long it's been in his body. In this case, not very long. Had Lukker lived, he could have ended up cancer-free."

"You think this unknown lipofuscin resulted from drugs derived from Sophia's blood and tissue samples?"

"It's a reasonable assumption, although it's hard to imagine how her samples could have had such a quick effect." Pomeroy sighed and changed the subject. "Interesting that a woman named after the Greek word for wisdom would be found by a man whose code name is *Nike*, Greek for victory. In addition to thanking Lukker, the world is indebted to you and her."

Owens brushed it off. "Did we recover his hidden files?"

Pomeroy's eyes narrowed. "Not yet, but few things remain lost forever."

"Assuming they exist."

"I have confidence they exist. Lukker was too savvy to risk losing everything he'd worked so hard for. The computers on Bimini were destroyed; he or someone at his direction poured acid into those hard drives making them worthless, but I'm convinced there were backup files."

"Where do you suppose he's hidden them?"

"I don't know, but you can bet *Sotto Voce* won't be the only organization dedicated to retrieving that information," Pomeroy said, taking a sip of scotch. "What we are currently learning from Lukker's brain tumors is only a promising start, one that will keep scientists busy for years. But the real cure for cancer is undoubtedly in those files."

Owens scowled at the notion that Lukker wouldn't be vanquished completely until those files were recovered. "Trachmann must know where the files are hidden? I know I hit him. I saw a blood trail, but it's possible he's still alive."

"Doubtful. Along with Lukker, several unidentified bodies were found on the island, but those starving monkeys didn't leave much to identify, not that we have a sample of Trachmann's DNA for comparison. He probably passed out after being shot, and the monkeys made good use of him."

"I hope you're right," Owens said.

They shared a quiet moment before Pomeroy said, "President Burbridge is close to getting her Alzheimer's immunization, and in a few months when we hand over our research on Lukker's tumors her administration will be credited with backing a breakthrough in cancer treatment. She should be able to parlay these two accomplishments into bipartisan support for her healthcare reforms. She's about to become the most popular president since Teddy Roosevelt."

Pomeroy continued. "By the way, the President is extremely grateful for all you've done. Would like to thank you personally."

"Thanks aren't necessary."

"Think carefully. The President is in a position to grant favors."

"Well..."

"I do have a stack of speeding tickets."

Pomeroy stroked his goatee and laughed. "How about Sophia? Is she recovering from her ordeal? Is she talking again?"

"Not yet."

"You're returning home tonight?"

"Yes. I have my show to get back to."

"Great. I'll be tuned in." Pomeroy finished his drink, and frowned. "I think I'm losing my taste for scotch."

"Have you tried Mountain Dew?"

Chapter Sixty-Four

—————

Saturday: 12:00 p.m.

Owens returned to Sarasota.

Before heading to Preston's bungalow, he detoured to his Airstream, showered, shaved, and retrieved Sophia's satchel. He hadn't been gone long, and it was unlikely Sophia had returned to normal, but as he rode to the bungalow he found himself on the verge of doing something he hadn't done since he was a kid—praying. He still felt it ridiculous to beseech an all-powerful deity to intercede on Sophia's behalf, especially if everything was part of His divine plan, but he was desperate to be reunited with the woman he remembered.

At the bungalow, she sat in a corner and greeted him with silence, her blank eyes looking through him like he was the one not there. He set the satchel on the coffee table, reached inside and placed the faceless doll on her lap, hoping it might comfort her.

At first, she blinked at it without interest, but when Owens reached for the doll she surprised him by wrapping her arms around it, slowly rocking back and forth, reminding him of the tortured monkeys back in that lab.

*   *   *

Jackie had gone to Bimini hoping for a scoop of a lifetime, but for Sophia's sake she'd edited out the meat of the story—the inexplicable circumstances of Sophia's past, her age, and her involvement in the creation of a fountain of youth drug. Had Jackie revealed all she knew, crackpots, including many of the weirdos who regularly tuned in to his program, would have come out of the woodwork trying to catch glimpses of Sophia.

When she came to the bungalow for an extended stay, she admitted, "I couldn't contribute to turning the woman into a freak."

Owens bunked on the couch in the living room for a few days, eventually returning to his trailer and radio show, leaving the couple to watch over Sophia.

*   *   *

Torpid summer days faded into fall; thunderclouds crackled overhead on their way north. On a lazy Saturday afternoon in September, Jackie took Sophia to the mall to buy clothes, something that always brought a sparkle to Jackie's eyes. Sanders spent the day making repairs to *Isabella*.

Sophia tagged along behind Jackie and politely tried on everything she suggested, but in the days that followed Sophia showed no interest in new clothes, continued wearing the jeans, sweatshirt, and sneakers Owens picked up at a Miami Walmart near the hospital.

One night in late October he swung by the bungalow after his broadcast and saw lights in the living room. He killed the bike's engine and coasted up the driveway. He hadn't seen Jackie in a while, but she and Sanders were engaged in an animated conversation. The front door was ajar and through the screen door he could hear her talking.

"It's been two and a half months without any change. Besides, if she wakes up one day and isn't a zombie anymore, what do you intend to do?"

Sanders didn't answer.

Owens felt guilty eavesdropping on them and noisily pushed through the screen door. They were curled up on the couch. The empty Dos Equis bottles on the coffee table indicated the conversation had been going on for some time. "Hey, guys. Warm night."

"Mountain Dews in the fridge." Sanders sounded glad for the interruption.

Owens returned with a cold one. "How'd it go today?"

"Fine," Sanders said. "Sophia did the dishes tonight without being told."

"That's progress, I suppose."

Jackie disengaged from Sanders, stood and yawned. "Time for me to hit the sheets. But before I go, we've got exciting news to share."

He had a hunch what it was.

"We've set a date for our wedding," Sanders said, beaming.

He clapped his best friend on the shoulder, gave Jackie a hug and peck on the cheek. "So, when's the special day? Not too soon, I hope. Peggy's been fattening me up and I need time to squeeze into a tux."

"You'll have plenty of time, ten months. We've chosen next year on September 11," Sanders said.

He nearly spit out his Mountain Dew. "September 11?" His glance bounced between them.

"Preston picked the date, and I also thought it was a strange choice, at first," Jackie said. She gave Sanders a hug and a light kiss on the lips. "Don't stay up too late, Preston. Goodnight, Anderson."

When she'd retired, Owens asked, "Why did you choose to tie the knot on the anniversary of the disaster that took your parents, a date that's haunted you for over twenty years."

Sanders rose from the couch and began gathering empty beer bottles. "I've been haunted by that date long enough. The 9/11 incident and loss of my parents altered my perspective, colored my thoughts with years of depression and self-loathing over the part I played on that day. It's time for me to let them rest in peace by forgiving myself."

He left with the bottles, dumped them in the recycle container under the sink and returned with another beer. "This might come as a surprise, but not long ago I was thinking about breaking up with Jackie."

He *was* surprised.

"I convinced myself that the fault rested with our jobs, different interests, but I was wrong. *I* was the problem, not our jobs." He leaned forward on the couch. "I was beginning to believe I was too plagued by my past, too damaged to be a good husband. But I've changed my mind."

"What prompted this Road to Damascus moment?"

"Sophia."

"Sophia? I don't see how..."

"I know you like solving mysteries, Anderson, but here's one you or I may never solve. How Sophia, without saying a word, made clear what you've been telling me for years; I'm not to blame for my parents' deaths. I can't explain it, but she's provided me with the strength to make a fresh start, one without ghosts."

A ruby slipper moment. "Don't you think the ability to do this was already inside you?"

"Probably, but people often don't see what's directly in front of them. Sometimes it takes a miracle."

There was that word again. Owens downed a slug of Mountain Dew and tried to drown the sensation that life was pulling his best friend away from him. He remembered words his mother had said to him after the church explosion: *Miracles are for those smart enough to believe in them.*

He'd always prided himself on his ability to ferret out the truth, but other than discovering who Sophia was and where she'd been for the last hundred and fifty years, they were still left with unanswered questions. How did she survive when the rest of *Mary Celeste's* crew didn't? Why was she aging so slowly and what was the secret of her longevity?

Sanders yawned. "I think I'll call it a night. As always, feel free to sleep on the couch."

He shook his head. "You and Jackie have too little privacy as it is. Will you be going to the dock tomorrow to work on *Isabella*?"

"Yes."

"Maybe I'll see you there."

Before leaving he went to the sunroom at the back of the bungalow and stepped through the French doors into the night air. Earlier, the moon had risen like a blood orange but was now in hiding behind a cloud. Without a breeze, the sea grasses sprouting on the banks of the canal were motionless, as was Sanders's 25-foot Sea Ray tied to the launch.

Returning to his bike, he coasted down the driveway and to the corner, revving the engine when too far away to disturb anyone.

He picked up speed, faster and faster, roaring around the curving coastal road in the direction of his Airstream. The turn leading to home passed by in a blur. Nesting pelicans and gulls were roused into flight as he charged through the darkness, the wheels of his motor-cycle trying to free themselves of the pavement. He couldn't decide what he was running from, or toward.

He wanted and needed to believe again. Wanted lazy summer days awash with endless possibilities. Wanted his childhood friend before 9/11 ruined everything. He wanted to convince himself that he wasn't jealous of what Sanders had.

Such were his thoughts when red and white lights lit up his rearview mirror.

Chapter Sixty-Five

Sunday: 2:45 a.m.

The flashing lights were a hundred yards behind Owens. He could easily have outrun them. Instead, he pulled to the side of the road and killed the engine while the cop pulled up behind him. As he ran Owens's plates a backup appeared.

After what seemed a long time, both cops approached him. One asked, "Do you have any idea just how fast you were going?"

"Sorry. Wasn't paying much attention."

The other smelled Owens's breath. "Have you been drinking tonight, sir?"

"Yes. Three or four Mountain Dews."

The confronting officer remained grim-faced. "License and registration, please. Also, since you're driving without a helmet we need proof of insurance. And give me the keys."

Owens plucked the keys from the ignition and handed them over, along with the info he dug out of his wallet.

"You were traveling in excess of a hundred miles an hour."

The other cop added, "With quite a few unpaid speeding tickets, Mr. Owe—wait a minute—I recognize you. You're that guy fingered on TV for breaking into that pharmaceutical building. There's a warrant out for your arrest." The cop pulled out his gun.

A phone call to *Sotto Voce* was all it would have taken to prompt the President of the United States to shock the shit out of this traffic cop by calling and demanding the dismissal of all charges against him, but he chose not to. Besides, the tickets were his responsibility, and it was time to face the music.

Ten minutes later he was cuffed and leaning against one of the patrol cars, watching a tow truck with a flatbed arrive and screech to a halt. The fat driver in dirty overalls picked up his Moto Guzzi. "Nice bike," he said, running a dirty hand over the chrome, a cigarette dangling from his rubbery lips. "Eye-talian?"

"Yeah. Be good to her," he said as one of the cops nudged him into the backseat of the patrol car.

The tow truck drove off to deliver the bike to the impound yard, and Owens was delivered to the Sarasota jail.

* * *

Sanders and Jackie were still sleeping when he called. The phone rang a long time.

Finally, "Yeah?"

"Preston, Anderson here."

"What do you want?" he rasped.

"I'm in jail."

"Can't think of a better place for you. Goodbye."

"Seriously, I need you to bail me out."

"What time is it?"

"Nine thirty." Owens could hear Jackie lightly snoring in the background.

"I had too many Dos Equis last night and I'm not in the mood for jokes, so tell me you're kidding."

"Not this time."

The silence stretched so long that Owens thought he'd fallen back asleep.

"Preston?"

"Why didn't you call that secret organization of yours to bail you out?"

"I did."

After sitting in jail all night, he'd finally called *Sotto Voce*. "The President was contacted and she responded by ordering the Attorney General of the United States to rescind the warrant for my arrest."

"So why are you still in jail," Sanders grumbled.

"Another warrant, for unpaid parking tickets."

"Why the hell are you calling *me*? You have a credit card, so use it."

"They'll only take cash."

"How much do they want?"
"If I tell you, you won't come."
"Crap!"

* * *

He didn't relish the notion of languishing in jail for the rest of the weekend. With Sanders's help, he could opt for a standard bond schedule that allowed him to "bond out" without waiting until Monday to see a judge.

When Sanders arrived, he was low on cash and Owens directed him to the ATM across the street. "It's next to Krispy Kreme. Two glazed old-fashioned and a cup of coffee would be nice," he said, grinning.

If looks could kill, Owens would have been a dead man.

* * *

Having spent hours in the urine-smelling clink, he was anxious for fresh air and found a bench where they could attack the coffee and donuts.

"I hope you grabbed me an old-fashioned."

"I got fritters. If you don't like them, too bad," Sanders snarled.

"I guess you have the right to be grumpy."

"What's that blue on your fingers?" Sanders asked.

"They fingerprinted me. I'll need to have *Sotto Voce* purge my prints from the system." He tore into the bag and saw that they were decorated like jack-o'-lanterns. "Pumpkin fritters?" he asked, wrinkling his nose at the gooey orange frosting.

"They're apple. Decorated for Halloween."

Halloween? Of course. With so much on his mind the date had gotten away from him. He could expect to get an earful this evening; his Halloween-loving callers always sounded off on their favorite holiday. A worm of thought wiggled in his brain.

He stopped chewing when he remembered looking up the birth-date of a missing two-year-old several months ago. October 31. To-day was Sophia's birthday.

They ate the fritters, sipped the coffee and discussed how to celebrate Sophia's special day. Peggy had suggested Chuck E. Cheese, and he was willing to do anything if it would bring a smile to Sophia's face and get her talking again. He was beginning to forget what her voice sounded like.

Sanders answered when his cell chirped. "What? You're kidding. She is?"

Owens licked orange frosting from his fingers. "What's up?" he asked.

A look of disbelief spread over Sanders's face. "It's Jackie. Professor Pomeroy and his assistant just left. They came for Sophia, but..."

He didn't want to believe it. He grabbed the phone. "Jackie, what did these men look like? Uh-huh, uh-huh. Yeah, that's Pomeroy and Franklin all right. I don't suppose they gave a reason for wanting her. What's that? You've got to be kidding—protective custody?"

His voice was filled with rage when he handed back the phone. "Pomeroy has gone too far," he spat when Sanders hung up the phone. "Sophia would be better off with us."

"Are you sure?" Sanders asked. "She's been severely traumatized. Maybe Pomeroy can connect her with mental health experts capable of bringing her back to us."

"I don't care. She belongs with us."

"Well, it doesn't really matter," Sanders said. "What matters is that Pomeroy was too late. According to Jackie, Sophia had already made her bed, grabbed her satchel and was gone before they arrived. Jackie had more news for us."

"She didn't want Pomeroy to know about this, but right before they arrived, she was awakened by a call from the Sarasota harbormaster. Someone just sailed *Isabella* out of the harbor."

* * *

A deputy from Harbor Patrol Division was waiting, his twin engine patrol boat churning water beside the dock. He spat a mouthful of chewing tobacco over the side and said, "Your vessel departed forty minutes ago, but there isn't much breeze to speak of. We should be able to catch up with her in no time."

Owens and Sanders climbed into the patrol boat and sped off toward the horizon, cutting across the wakes of numerous pleasure craft enjoying the sunny Sunday morning.

Land soon disappeared. The pleasure craft thinned out, and before long they were alone on the wide and open sea.

"There she is," Sanders shouted, long before anyone else spotted her. He pointed to a place near the horizon. "She's sailing with limited sails at less than three knots. Won't take long to reach her."

Bright light danced on the waves and Owens squinted into the glare. What he saw made his mouth drop open and reduced his breathing to shallow gulps of salty air. *I'm getting lightheaded. Need to take deep breaths.*

He'd said it often enough, spinning out the words like so much cotton candy:

> Welcome to the Anderson Owens Show, where our Holy Trinity consists of extraterrestrial events, supernatural occurrences, and conspiracy theories....

True, he'd sometimes glean useful information to pass on to *Sotto Voce*, but too often he'd used the words like a sideshow huckster to reel in an audience and pander to their delusions. Well, who was delusional now?

They were a nautical mile away. He couldn't deny the vision before him, an apparition pulling him out of time and space, transporting him to a place reached only by imagination, to a destination he hadn't visited since he'd outgrown his dreams.

"You alright?" Sanders asked, eying him curiously.

Owens managed a slight nod and Sanders's attention returned to the chase.

With difficulty, he turned his head to study his best friend since childhood, wondering why his expression didn't include astonishment. *He doesn't see what I see. Neither does the deputy piloting this boat. Impossible. I refuse to believe.* Owens rubbed his eyes like a toddler waking from a nap and considered the possibility that he was going insane. Maybe Lukker wasn't the only one with brain tumors. He saw a ship, an old sailing ship, but not *Isabella*, not even a schooner. *How is it that Preston doesn't realize we're chasing the wrong ship?*

"She's magnificent, isn't she?" Sanders exclaimed, rapture in his voice. "Just look at her lines, the way she slices into the wind."

Hadn't they labored in the sun restoring *Isabella*, sanded every inch of her until their hands oozed with blisters? Hadn't they caressed her with spar varnish until she gleamed like a floating Stradivarius? His vision was 20/20, but they were still too far away to read the name painted on the ship's stern. It didn't matter; Owens didn't need to. He'd done his research, recognized the shape, the size, the rigging.

She was *Mary Celeste*.

The air had been still, but now a breeze kicked up and the patrol boat bounced over the waves. A pod of porpoises broke the surface forward of their starboard beam, gleamed in the sunlight before disappearing. The patrol boat was closing in, near enough to see gulls circling the old rigging, diving toward the deck like Kamikazes, hoping for a handout.

"What the hell?" The deputy's first words since leaving the dock.

For a moment, Owens thought someone else was finally seeing what he was seeing. But that notion flew out of his head when he spun around and saw a jet boat racing toward them. He recognized it as one of the boats in the flotilla near the mouth of the bay.

They'd all been too preoccupied looking for *Isabella* to notice the pleasure craft trailing them. Now it was close enough for him to recognize the malicious face behind the wheel, a ragged scar on the right cheek. Owens also recognized the weapon on Trachmann's shoulder, an FIM-92 Stinger surface-to-air missile launcher.

He didn't even have his plastic peashooter. "Give me your weapon!" He shouted at the deputy.

When the deputy hesitated, Owens snatched the pistol from his holster. *Whooosh.* A missile tore through the sky, a faint trail of smoke marring the pristine blue sky.

He stopped breathing, as if his heart was being squeezed by icy fingers. The missile soared overhead, missing the patrol boat. Trachmann hadn't aimed at them. Owens followed the missile's trajectory, toward a ship that no longer resembled *Mary Celeste*. Owens now saw only *Isabella*, and Trachmann had fired on her.

There was a chance the missile might miss its target, unless it was a "heat-seeker." From what he could see, *Isabella's* engines weren't currently in use, but infrared homing could pick up Sophia's body heat along with whatever pent-up heat had accumulated below deck. Trachmann had fired on *Isabella* first so they'd be forced to watch her destruction.

He felt like he'd been hit in the stomach with a shovel as the missile headed directly toward *Isabella*. He couldn't look and turned his head.

Trachmann stopped laughing when he saw that the missile inexplicably veered off course, missing its target.

The patrol boat picked up speed and bounded over the waves harder than before. The explosion of the errant missile heated the air in front of them, the distinctive stench of nitro wafting in their direction. The deputy ignored the explosion and stayed on course. Owens locked his eyes on Trachmann, who'd picked up speed and was closing in on them while struggling to reload the missile launcher.

It was a difficult shot, especially with a revolver. Owens fired, striking Trachmann in the chest, propelling him backward as he leveled the reloaded missile launcher at them.

Trachmann was unable to prevent his finger from squeezing the trigger. The missile shot out of the launcher and struck the canister containing the missiles. Most detonated on the deck of the vessel, with one taking flight and heading in the direction of *Isabella*, the heat of the explosions carrying over to the patrol boat, scorching the hands and faces of everyone aboard.

When a fireball engulfed Trachmann, Owens's grasp on the pistol loosened. It dropped to the bottom of the patrol boat. Afraid to look up, he stared at the gun for what seemed a lifetime. Finally, when he couldn't stand it any longer, he lifted his head and looked in the direction of *Isabella*. What he saw shattered his belief in a rational universe, crumbled the cornerstone upon which he'd built his life. His hands reached out to embrace it, to share an experience connecting him to the dawn of awareness, a gesture that transmuted his years of doubt into a childhood prayer of salvation.

He realized it had been a mistake asking Sophia if she knew *WHO* she was. The answer was obvious; she had no answers explaining the great mystery engulfing her. A better question would have been: "Do you know *WHAT* you are?" A demon? An angel? A saint?

Mama's favorite Bible stories were filled with miracles, but they always served to bring home the notion that God was in control, guiding mortals toward a salvation unachievable on our own.

What guided Sophia's actions? Did goodness exist independently in the universe, or did it need to be sanctified by divine command?

Owen's head hurt. He'd always diminished religion by comparing it to a hamster's wheel, going round and round without getting anywhere, something to engage the mind by providing answers made up by Iron Age people who didn't know where the sun went at night, a tool to keep most from going insane contemplating the unknowable, and to provide authority for those in power.

He understood that spinning on a wheel of dogma and ritual was easy, even if it reduced one to the status of a hamster; still, more comforting than stepping away from the wheel and pondering the possibility that we are insignificant creatures made of dust lost in a vast and infinite void.

Mama had her answers, and she was content with them. His love for her prevented him from attacking beliefs that brought her spiritual clarity, comfort, and joy. Only a monster would consider stripping that away from her.

Would living a life like a hamster (without questions or answers) have been preferable, even if it meant running in endless circles going nowhere? He knew it was a question he'd struggle to answer for the rest of his life.

Chapter Sixty-Six

Tuesday: 9:10 a.m.

CDC Progeria Bulletin #116

Current number of documented infections:

92

On a Tuesday morning three weeks later, Sanders received a phone call from a buddy down at the harbor where *Isabella* had been moored. "There's something here you need to see," he was told.

Owens's driving privilege had been restored, and he'd recently retrieved his bike from the impound yard. He was turning into Sanders's driveway when Owens saw him climbing into the Land Cruiser.

"Get in," he ordered.

"What's up?" Owens asked, dismounting and pulling off his helmet.

"I'm not sure. Another mystery," was all he'd say.

"I would have thought you'd be avoiding mysteries for the time being," Owens commented, sliding into the front passenger seat and buckling up.

Sanders didn't answer.

When they rounded a bend and drove down the road leading to the dock, they were speechless. Moored in *Isabella's* place was another schooner, nearly a replica of *Isabella*. She needed work but was still a beauty.

They parked and walked up to the ship, admiring the clean lines and craftsmanship.

"What do you think?" came a voice from behind them. It was Captain Kornievsky from the USS *Wilcox*. "She's a bit rough around the edges, but she sails like a dream."

Sanders had told him about meeting Kornievsky at Norfolk when he'd retrieved *Isabella* from the Navy. "She's a fine ship," Sanders said. "You should be proud of her."

Kornievsky grinned. "Why should I be? She belongs to you, not me."

"You can't be serious."

"I am."

Sanders's mouth opened, but no sound emerged.

"The order to hand her over to you came from the Secretary of the Navy."

"It must be a mistake. You'd better double-check."

Kornievsky shrugged. "I take orders, I don't question them. And my orders are to turn this ship over to you unless, of course, you don't want her."

"But where did this ship come from?" When Kornievsky didn't answer, Sanders turned and looked at his best friend. "What do you know about this?"

"It's a mystery."

"A *Sotto Voce* mystery?"

"If I tell, I'll have to kill you."

"I hate it when you say that."

*   *   *

Sanders was captaining his new ship, recently christened *Sophia*. Content to be first mate, Owens helped with the sails and watched the regatta of clouds racing above them. He'd decided not to grow back his dreads, but his hair was long enough to be ruffled by the stiff breeze at their backs.

Owens struggled with the dull, endless ache of losing Sophia. Sanders also missed her, but he had faced tragedy before and hid the pain better. Yet on several occasions while hanging out at the bungalow, he'd seen him gazing pensively in the direction of Sophia's bedroom. He, too, often gazed in that direction, seeing a ghost with large blue eyes and a wistful smile.

He stared at a pelican hovering overhead and thought about those he loved and admired: his family, Sanders and Jackie, Miles Burbridge, but mostly Sophia. Before leaving on *Isabella* that morning, she'd scribbled a note thanking him for all he'd done for her and explaining that time had finally run out. She left the note pinned on the faceless doll from her satchel.

"Something troubles me," Owens said.

"You want to know how Jackie knew to go to Bimini."

Owens nodded.

"I asked her that very question. Her answer was curious."

"What did she say?"

"She said it was time for us to join a church."

Chapter Sixty-Seven

<hr>

A Few Weeks Later

Sanders had a new ship to restore, and he and Jackie had the distraction of a wedding to plan, but Sanders was well aware of the light fading in his best friend. Miles Burbridge had questioned the appropriateness of a doll as a gift for a guy, yet Owens now spent hours sitting in his Airstream, unable to sleep with Sophia's faceless doll on his lap.

A weight had settled on him, like being covered by a lead X-ray bib in a dental office. Sophia continued to loom large in his mind, and he spent hours reliving their brief time together.

Peggy was worried about him and frequently knocked on his door with platters of baked goodies in hand and a yellow boa wrapped around an arm. He appreciated the treats even though his appetite had abandoned him.

Whenever he tried to eat, Trachmann's first missile came to mind, the one that had missed *Isabella*. Why had it inexplicably veered off course? Was Sophia responsible for that? If so, why did she allow the second missile to reach her moments later, a missile that seemed to launch itself in her direction? Was her departure deliberate? Did it have to do with something she'd said earlier, about her time almost being up?

*   *   *

When he returned to the airwaves, Owens's enthusiasm for his radio show was waning. Night after night he listened to callers' absurd notions and conspiracy theories, but he was no longer protected by the armor of certainty that had always been a hallmark of his show.

Vicki, his producer, had noticed the change in him and was taking on a bigger role filling in for him when he couldn't face his microphone. Even though it was woven tightly into his self-image, maybe it was time to axe *The Anderson Owens Show*. Had *that* Anderson Owens disappeared along with Sophia Briggs? Only time would tell.

Swirling in the stew of his thoughts was Old Scipio. From a protective glass display case, the dead fire horse had stared at the world with glass eyes and nothing but sawdust in his head. Owens was beginning to envy Old Scipio, who was incapable of thoughts or feelings. Old Scipio had been composed of pieces of other horses and Owens felt like he, too, was an assemblage of random fragments masquerading as a whole person.

Sanders arrived at the Airstream one evening. He reached for the plate of chocolate chip cookies Peggy had left days earlier. "These are stale," he grumbled after taking a bite. Several drinks later he repeated a question that Owens refused to answer. "I could tell you saw something I missed when that missile struck *Isabella*. What did you see?"

Owens wanted to answer, but the words wouldn't come.

"Okay, how 'bout another question: Do you really think Sophia was capable of miracles?"

Owens considered his answer for a long time. "I'm trying desperately to rule it out, but there's just too much evidence to the contrary."

"What are we to make of those things she did?" Sanders asked. "Were there rules governing what she could do?"

"I've looked for a pattern, rules governing her supernatural activities."

"...And?"

"Well, I think there *was* a pattern."

"Go on."

"Most of her so-called miracles had to do with protecting innocent human life. That first encounter on the rock near the water—she said she'd been waiting for me, but I don't think she was controlling the Land Cruiser to save herself."

Sanders knew the answer to his next question, but he asked it anyway. "Who do you think she was saving?"

"I think she was there to save *me*."

Sanders was in no position to challenge his best friend's answer. "What about the others?" he asked.

"Agent Fulton reported that while locked in the trunk of that car he heard Sophia refusing to let Trachmann shoot him, right before the gun jammed. Then there's the Paxton church explosion where she saved all of those innocent lives. It also seems that she was responsible for, if not saving Miles Burbridge, easing his passing by materializing at the White House with a gift to ease his passing."

"You mean the doll without a face?"

Owens nodded. "And I'm sure she had something to do with Trachmann's first missile inexplicably veering off course."

"Okay, but what about Lukker?"

"Sophia was unconscious when he met his end, not that he was an innocent life, but something else confuses me."

"What?"

"The animals. What explanation is there for her encounter with that poisonous water moccasin? Why didn't those starving monkeys have a feeding frenzy with her the way they did with Lukker?"

Sanders ran a hand through his hair and considered the question. "As a marine biologist I've witnessed animals doing unpredictable things: dolphins saving baby seals from sharks, orcas surrounding humans to keep predators away. And it isn't just in the ocean. There are countless instances of all types of animals being protective with certain humans."

"As a scientist, how do you explain these occurrences?"

"I can't. No doubt there are explanations for such actions, but extensive research is needed to understand most animal behaviors. Sometimes, animals can sense if an encounter is benign or a danger, and I suspect Sophia radiated compassion to animals as well as humans."

Owens tried to satisfy himself with the knowledge that, like most everything else concerning Sophia, this was another mystery to be solved.

CHAPTER SIXTY-EIGHT

The Present

With the mahogany wheel of newly christened *Sophia* firmly in his grip, Sanders repeated the question: "Are you going to tell me what you saw?" He sensed that the answer to this question held the secret to what troubled his best friend.

Owens wanted to tell, had decided to tell. But how? All his life he'd wanted to feel part of something larger than himself. As a lonely kid, he'd listen as Mama told stories from the Bible, her eyes dancing with rapture at a world where morality was laid out in black and white. But like an old pair of Nikes, he'd outgrown religion. Life had hardened his imagination, made it brittle as ancient bone, unable to bend or accept the illogical, improbable.

"What did you see?" his best friend pressed.

His head filled with a thousand conversations, and he experienced a tsunami of regret, callers on his program beseeching him to believe, reassure them they weren't crazy, or worse—alone. Night after night, his callers were full of theories that previously would have sparked his interest, but now his mind was elsewhere.

"What did *I* see?" He often repeated the question aloud when no one was around.

He'd been so glib, using his wit to entertain his audience, often at the caller's expense. Now he was the one on the other end of the phone, pleading with himself, trying to believe he wasn't crazy, or alone.

Insecurity had prompted him to hide behind his radio persona, claim it was his job as well as his nature to be skeptical. But that's when Sophia gave him something special, the realization and conviction to spread the news: We're not crazy, or alone.

A stiff breeze brushed over him as he stared out to sea. His arms remained at his side but in his mind they were stretched out like wings capable of spanning the immeasurable distance between fantasy and reality.

"I think you'll feel better when you tell me what you saw," Sanders said.

He remembered the tall tale of Sra. Correia's grandfather, the story of a little mermaid transformed into a baby girl, a child who could walk upon the water. Playing through his mind were words his mother spoke often: miracles are only for those smart enough to believe in them. He knew he'd share what he saw, but until then he rehearsed it in his head.

This is what I saw:

I turned my head and saw that time had finally run out for Sophia. Or so I thought when Isabella exploded into a billion splinters, the orange fireball fanning over the water, expanding into a blue/silver sky the color of Sophia's eyes. Through the smoke and haze, I saw a slender figure on a rope ladder, someone eternally young climbing down the side—Sophia. The air cleared and I saw her grow smaller and younger as she neared the water. She wore the lace and pearl dress she'd bequeathed to Sr. Oliveira for his museum. She looked like a tiny bride.

I saw her place a foot on the ocean and release her hand from the ladder. She hovered a moment, fingered the locket hanging over her heart. She stepped away from the ship, tentatively at first, then with building confidence. Pausing, she looked back in my direction. I was too far away to see her clearly, but I felt the warmth of her smile, a gift for me alone. Then she continued on her way, her shape diminishing with each stride until she disappeared into a fogbank I hadn't noticed approaching. That's what I saw.

He'd tell. He had no doubt.

Someday.

The End

Acknowledgments

Thanks to Sue, my wife, and soulmate, whose limitless support made this book possible.

Paul Begg, for his insightful book: Mary Celeste: The Greatest Mystery of the Sea.

Clara Moskowitz, LiveScience staff writer, for her article: Submersible Robot Runs on Sea's Heat.

Captain Dave Williams, author of a 1997 theory: Evidence Indicating That The Crew Of The Mary Celeste Were Victims Of An Earthquake At Sea.

Colin Hayes for his mechanical and electronics expertise. The errors in this book would have been far more numerous without his help.

Jo Barney, for her expertise and friendship.

José Reis for his help with Portuguese.

Author's Note

Before sailing into legend to become one of the greatest mysteries of the sea, *Mary Celeste* was a modest commercial ship as real as any other. Since her fateful voyage a hundred and fifty-three years ago, a tidal wave of conjecture has taken place, washing away the factual details of her story and drowning *Mary Celeste* beneath inaccuracies of outlandish proportion. Sir Arthur Conan Doyle was among the first to speculate on the mystery that engulfed the ship and her star-crossed crew, and similar speculation has continued to this very day.

I feel it important to remember that *Mary Celeste*'s passengers and crew were victims of a great tragedy, and I've no desire to dishonor them for the sake of fiction, although this has certainly been done often enough. As a writer, I admit to taking certain liberties, but I've tried to depict these individuals respectfully, and in as accurate a manner as possible. They deserve no less. Where I've strayed, I ask their forgiveness.

S.H.

Independent publisher.
Uncompromising standards.

www.ingramcontent.com/pod-product-compliance
Lightning Source LLC
Chambersburg PA
CBHW021336150726

47989CB00005B/2009